SPLIT SECOND SOLUTION

BOOK 1

SPLIT SECOND SOLUTION

BOOK ONE

A NOVEL BY

DENNY TAYLOR

GARN PRESS
NEW YORK, NY

Published by Garn Press, LLC
New York, NY
www.garnpress.com

Book and cover design by Benjamin J. Taylor
Cover image by Susan DuFresne

Library of Congress Control Number: 2016911721

Publisher's Cataloging-in-Publication Data

Names: Taylor, Denny, 1947-
Title: Split second solution / Denny Taylor.
Description: New York : Garn Press, 2016
Identifiers: New York : Garn Press, 2016. | Series: Split second solution, bk. 1.
Identifiers: LCCN 2016911721 | ISBN 978-1-942146-45-2 (pbk.) | ISBN 978-1-942146-46-9 (hardcover) | ISBN 978-1-942146-44-5 (Kindle)
Subjects: LCSH: Fantasy fiction, American. | Time travel--Fiction. | Dystopias--Fiction. | Voyages, imaginary--Fiction. | Extraterrestrial beings--Fiction. | New York (N.Y.) --Fiction. | BISAC: FICTION / Fantasy/ Dark Fantasy. | FICTION / Fantasy/ Romantic. | FICTION / Science Fiction / Time Travel. | FICTION / Science Fiction / Apocalyptic & Post-Apocalyptic. | FICTION / Visionary & Metaphysical. | GSAFD: Dystopias. | Fantasy fiction.
Classification: LCC PS3620.A9416 S65 2016 (print) | LCC PS3620.A9416 (ebook) | DDC 813/.6--dc23.

For

C.L.

E.K.

A.S.

S.R.

H.H.

M.G.

M.M.

&

R.B.

All Young People of Infinite Possibility

Who Rules the World?

So imagine that you're an extraterrestrial observer who is trying to take a neutral stance and figure out what's happening here …

You'd see something quite remarkable …

For the first time in the history of the species, we have clearly developed the capacity to destroy ourselves …

So the danger has always been a lot worse than we thought it was …

The question is: What are people doing about it?

It's not that there are no alternatives. The alternatives just aren't being taken. That's dangerous. So if you ask what the world is going to look like, it's not a pretty picture. Unless people do something about it. We always can.

Noam Chomsky, 2016

Dear Readers,

I'm writing in haste. Cat's in a hurry and she's said she'll drop this book off at the Mysterious Bookshop in New York City in 2016. She says 6 years should be enough for you to change the future. I can't tell you what will happen in 2022 if you do not. Cat says you'll figure it out when you read Split. *I hope she's right.*

It's inconceivable to most of us what the future will bring. It's always difficult for people to think about what's not yet happened. Life is full of surprises, some good, some bad, and some terrifying. Rushing – sorry.

I asked Et (you'll meet her soon) if a book could be a thought experiment that can change the nature of reality? She said yes. I told her I think Split Second Solution *could change the future, and she said she thought so too, but she can no longer see the future so it's difficult for her to tell.*

In Split *science and myth unite to foretell what happens to our species – you and me. It's only a novel but it's not science fiction. This stuff's happening. We're all under surveillance. Honest. NSA. GCHQ. CitizenFour. Paranoia. Not. Check it out. We all live in the panopticon. Right? They've been watching and hunting me all my life, but in my darkest moments when all hope is gone I hold onto the thought that by reading* Split, *you – brave readers – will stop the cataclysm that's about to happen.*

The borders between science and myth are porous after all and it's true that "myths nourish science, and science nourishes myth," as Carlo Rovelli the great Italian physicist tells us. We do have the capacity to unite our external world (the universe) and our internal world (our consciousness) by reading a book. Please trust me on this, for I'm absolutely certain the split between the universe and ourselves is ultimately spurious – for as Rovelli reminds us, "we are made of the same stardust of which all things are made."

We've been led to believe that this is not so – but we've been misled. The false dichotomy between our external and internal worlds distorts our understanding of just about everything. Especially time. *Did you know that time's flow appears nowhere in current theories of physics? And yet, humans are obsessed by time. We are mythologically* time bound, *with a before and after, a past, present, and future, which have no counterpart in science.*

Split challenges our erroneous understandings of "the flow" of time in "this strange, multicolored, and astonishing world," as Rovelli writes, "where space is granular, time does not exist, and things are nowhere" – that's where Et exists.

Cat is yowling and looking maniacal. Bad sign. Gotta go. Remember Cat's your friend. Don't be put off when you find out who she really is – forget all you have been told. Also be careful, the Lunatic Eight are vile and ruthless. And watch out for the Sick-Reapers. They have privileged access to all your secrets and they're vicious. Don't let them hack your consciousness. And, and, *there are so many ands! And* try *not to get stuck in the split second!*

Gotta go! Cat's going ballistic. We'll meet up at the end – hopefully not the end – of the book. In the beginning …

Good luck!

Word, The Last Truth Keeper

One

Dead to the world an Old Crone sat hunched on a wooden chair cradling a bowl of soup that was her supper. The Fire crackled in the hearth and the flames made flickering shadows that danced about the room and disappeared into the Four Corners that were empty of light and filled with old thoughts and feelings that could both terrify and delight. They were on guard at all times ready to protect and even kill if anyone tried to hurt the Old Crone. Only Death – who the Four Corners loved – visited regularly in need of a friend to listen to her and help her overcome her neurotic tendencies about the dead and the dying piling up.

The Old Crone liked suppertime – it was her favorite fantasy. The soup bubbled in the pot that hung over the Fire and newly baked bread lay cooling on the three-legged stool that stood beside her chair. When she dipped her bread into the soup she tried not to fret about the fast approaching – *fast approaching?* What? Not her own death – for that she would have to be alive. No not her own demise. It was not being able to see the future that she feared. She felt she was standing on the edge of a precipice about to fall into the abyss – where there was nothing. *Nothing.* Nothing at all.

"Not even in air that once was breath," the Old Crone said to herself. "When old names are gone and there will be no new names to take their place. No bodies. No souls. Just emptiness."

The Old Crone knew that Death felt it too. She'd been more neurotic of late – her costumes more garish – including frequent appearances as an enormous bat wearing glittering red strappy high-heeled shoes.

"Make time," Death kept telling her, "till time ends and there are no bodies or souls left."

"Time's up," the Old Crone muttered to herself. "There's no future for Eternity." She looked around expecting to see Death nagging her to *make* time but she did not appear. She was alone.

The Old Crone drew comfort from her solitude. Only the Fire lit the room and soon when the Fire was just embers the flickering shadows would grow dim. Outside it was already dark and night was closing in. But she did not need light to see and she sighed worriedly as she stretched out the claw that was once her right hand and pierced some crumbs of bread with nails as hard and sharp as a hawk's beak. The grey gnarly bones of her fingers were visible through her ancient skin as she raised them to her dried-up lips that split open to a gaping maw. Then with surprising delicacy she used her broken and cracked teeth to slide the crumbs from her claw onto her shriveled tongue that was more purple than pink.

The crumbs tasted good and she used the sharp pointed nail on her twisted right forefinger to cut through the bread. There was something incongruous about the way she slashed the loaf, and then delicately with her thumb and forefinger dipped a piece of the crust into the soup, and bending even further forward she sucked it into her mouth before it could fall apart and drop sodden, splashing her with soup.

But this once blissful moment, as ancient as the Old Crone was old, ended abruptly – as she'd foretold – when she heard the unfamiliar sound of someone or something landing with a thump on the stone step outside her great iron clad oak door.

"It's just the wind," she whispered, in denial that the long wait was over. Her eyes closed and disappeared in the deep wrinkles of her face. She knew the end was fast approaching and she wanted fiercely to hold on to the very last moments of her solitary existence as an Old Crone.

"Yes," she said, her eyes now open, "the wind."

But someone or something was scraping their fingernails on the great oak door.

"A branch of a tree must have broken off," the Old Crone said, nodding, still in denial that the end had come. "Yes. A tree branch, that's it." But she knew it was not. She sat very still, holding her breath. She waited, clinging to her last moments of tranquility, refusing to accept that it was over and avoiding thinking about what she could not see.

Then came a new sound, as silent as dust falling or a last breath gently passing. The Old Crone found it difficult to con-centrate on the sound. For five hundred years she had seen in her mind's eye the end of the future when the last Truth Keeper was attacked by the Sick-Reapers and died. She could see no future for anyone after that. It terrified her. Gnawed at her. Twisted her fingers and her insides – except at suppertime when she remembered the past and the moments of blissful contentment in her once peaceful life.

She could still see the past – millions of years back – but her ability to see the future abruptly stopped in 2022, when the last Truth Keeper – escaping from the Sick-Reapers – chose to take her own life and drown in the Hudson River near the 79th Street Boat Basin in New York City. After that? The future? There wasn't one. She saw *nothing, nothing at all* – just empty space, sort of grey, not light, not dark, *just empty*. And people? None. No place at all. *She couldn't see any.*

"Was it a trick?" the Old Crone asked, devastated by her inability to see the future. "Had the Sick-Reapers – officially the Super-Recognizers – charged by the Lunatic Eight with finding and killing the last Truth Keeper also been ordered to find and kill her?"

"Not possible," she reasoned. "Paranoia." She'd lived alone too long with Death her only companion. Even the last Truth Keeper did not know of her existence. Her house sat high in some meadows, hidden by trees and surrounded by mountains. There was only one dirt road with deep ruts that circled the mountains that surrounded her house. The dirt road was snow blocked in winter and flooded in spring. And the paths over the mountains that led from the dirt road through the woods to her house were overgrown with brambles that had razor sharp thorns. It had been many years since anyone had found the Old Crone's house and those who once knew where the house was located were long since dead.

She had lived alone for almost five hundred years and even though her nightmares consumed her she had enjoyed the fantasy of a simple existence, eating her supper every night without interruption – except when Death visited – until this moment when, after centuries of silence, someone or some*thing* was lying outside on the stone step.

There it was again, another sound, fingernails scratching and then – making her jump – a knock, hard and sharp, upon her great oak door. She felt it – as if she had been hit. She knew the effort it must have taken to make such a loud and decisive noise. She could feel the urgency and the desperation in the sound that circled around her room making the Fire crackle and sparks fly as the Four Corners moved closer in trepidation of the moment when the Old Crone opened the door.

Still she hesitated. Was it a trap? The Old Crone shook her head, angry with herself for being so fearful. Unable to move she closed her eyes tight again and then slowly opened them as the Walls buckled and the Four Corners moved closer so the room was no bigger than a coffin.

Could it be a Sick-Reaper? No, no, not yet. She stretched out her fingers on her right hand and looked at them for reassurance as they became young and slender. "No, not yet," she said, as her fingers became bent and twisted again and her hand a claw once more.

She hoped that whoever or whatever had fallen outside her door would quickly crawl away. But the knocking came again, softer and more muffled, more troubled, more urgent and insistent than before, and she knew the noise she heard was not knuckles on wood, sharp and quick, but the beating of a dying heart sounding its own death knell.

"Are you deaf?" Death asked arriving abruptly with screams and cries and a fetid smell of rotting matter filling the room.

"Why are you here?" the Old Crone asked, knowing the answer before she asked the question. "Go away."

"When *someone knocks* you're supposed to *open the door!"* Death said, coughing as though she had swallowed a lot of water.

"What are you doing here?" the Old Crone asked again "and why are you amorphous? Show yourself! I don't like it when you look like nothing at all."

"Open the door!" Death rasped, appearing as a drowned cat coughing up minnows and river detritus. "Our future depends upon it!"

"Our future?" the Old Crone said, not at all impressed by Death's theatric performance.

"Yes. *Our* future!" Death said. "You know that!" And then in a whisper, "There is no death without life, and all life will end if this one dies."

"You're the bane of my existence," the Old Crone said shaking her head. "It's dangerous. *Think* of the consequences – they could be cataclysmic."

"Think?" Death said, her fur drying. "You've been *thinking* for *five hundred years* and I'm the one who jumped in the Hudson

River and saved her."

"What do you mean you saved her?" the Old Crone asked standing up, speaking quickly, fearing the worst. "She didn't drown in the river? *She's still alive?* And you brought her here? She's outside?" The Old Crone sat down on her chair. "I should have known," she said, with a small shake of her head. "How I *hate* not seeing the future!"

"She had one second left," Death said. "So I split it." She looked defiantly at the Old Crone. "She's still in it – the split second," Death said. "Whadyathink? Can you save her?"

Two

The Old Crone stared at the lifeless body on the stone step. Small, shapeless, covered in mud and blood, it could be a child, but the Old Crone knew that it was not.

"Well? Can you save her?" Death asked, re-appearing this time with psychedelic make-up and theatrical garb looking very much like a rock star – of similar ilk to David Bowie, Lady Gaga, or one of the rock band Kiss. She looked pixelated but she was not a digital image.

"No," the Old Crone said, ignoring Death's theatrics, "but she can save herself." The Old Crone looked at Death whose mascara was running in multi-colored rivers with purple, red, and yellow tributaries down her face. "Why are you dressed like that?"

"This is the sixth age of extinction," Death said. "Whole species are dying out! In the day, in the night, in I glide, but I'm never welcome! No one knows how much I suffer. I'm delicate!"

"What am I supposed to say to that?" the Old Crone asked, but Death knew it was not a question. "I like you best when you're a cat."

Death responded by shedding her garish outfit and taking

the shape of a six-foot bat, but still wearing her glittering red strappy high-heeled shoes.

"I said *Cat* not Bat!" the Old Crone said.

"I know I'm losing it," Bat said, spreading her massive bat wings. Her head drooped. "The living don't want me and the dead don't care what happens to me."

"I care," the Old Crone said, looking at Bat with kindness in her eyes. "I'll do what I can for the girl if you promise to get some rest. Promise?"

"I promise," Bat said, shrinking a bit, taking off her glittery red shoes, and wondering if the Old Crone would mind if she hung upside down from the mantle.

"No more nonsense!" the Old Crone said, anticipating Death's next move. "Go now!" she said, and Bat disappeared.

Death's sudden arrival had drained the Old Crone's strength, and she'd left the girl still clinging to life on the stone step. It bothered her that her sight had failed her – that she had not seen Death scoop the girl out of the Hudson River. She secretly admired Death for splitting the last second of the girl's life, but it did create problems now she could no longer see the future. The Old Crone shook her head and made her way back into her house not knowing what would happen next.

By the time she'd lowered her ancient bones onto her chair, the young woman was lying minus her wet clothes on the rug in front of the Fire. There was a pillow under her head and a blanket covering her body. Her breathing was erratic – quick shallow breaths and then no breath at all, followed by quick shallow breaths and no breath at all.

Each time her breathing stopped the Four Corners moved closer, oozing anxiety that spilled on the great flagstones in putrid puddles that evaporated quickly when the girl gasped – still alive – and repeated the motif of quick shallow breaths.

The ash grey embers of the Fire glowed, determined to be of more use than the Four Corners, and flames flickered warming the girl – but still her breathing was shallow and she did not stir when the flames shot up the chimney lighting the room that alternated between cavernous and small.

The girl's rapid breathing with long breaks continued for what seemed like hours. The Old Crone sat quietly, her hands in her lap, watching the girl. She had black hair, and even though she had not opened them the Old Crone knew she had green eyes. But it was the girl's skin that held the Old Crone's attention. Her face was scratched and bruised and her bottom lip was badly swollen, but now that the blood and mud had been removed she could see the girl was ink stained – her entire body was covered with tattoos. Her skin reminded the Old Crone of a piece of vellum on which a great scribe had written words with a quill pen and then discarded because the ink had blotched and run – but the blotches were blue, purple, and black bruises where she had been hit, punched, and kicked.

"Can you save her?" the Four Corners asked in chorus, puddles of anxiety oozing from the baseboard as they spoke.

"You heard Death ask that question," the Old Crone said, her voice, no more than a hoarse whisper. "What was my answer?"

"She can save herself."

"Yes she can," the Old Crone said, sharply. "She is the only one who can decide whether or not she lives or dies."

"But you'll help her decide?" the Four Corners persisted in chorus.

"Of course," the Old Crone said, as she closed her eyes.

The Four Corners watched her intently. Was she sleeping? The Old Crone stopped breathing, then gasped and breathed rapidly in time with the girl's shallow breaths. The Four Corners couldn't help themselves – they breathed in unison with the girl and the Old Crone.

The quick-quick-stop of the girl's breathing continued for what seemed like many hours, and the Four Corners were just about to go to sleep when the girl's eyes opened then closed again.

The Old Crone's eyes opened at the very same moment but did not close, for Death had reappeared in her feline form.

"She was a split second from dying," Death said, disheveled and overwrought. "She was dead to the world and yet she refuses to die. Tell me! Tell me. Have you made up your mind? Is she going live?"

"It's not *my mind* that has to be made up," the Old Crone said,

"Just save her!" Death wailed.

"There'll be deadly consequences", the Old Crone said, looking at Death and thinking to herself that she'd never seen her so distraught.

"You don't know that!" Death wailed, hysterically. "If you hadn't hidden yourself away in these mountains for the past five hundred years –" she said, sobbing, "– you might have got your sight back!"

"No," the Old Crone said. "This awful moment would've come anyway – five hundred years and no solution – if we save the girl many others might die. *Will die.* You know that."

"They're *dying already*," Death said, her voice more of a whimper. "It's the *only* chance we've got to change the future."

"Either way we're stuck in this split second," the Old Crone said. "We're boxed in and I'm not sure we'll be able to get out."

"Perhaps the split second *is* the solution," Death said, for a moment feeling hopeful.

"Perhaps," the Old Crone said, her attention suddenly taken by the girl.

The girl's breathing had changed. Her breaths became short and quick – *quick – quick – stop, quick – quick – stop.* The Old Crone watched her intently – *quick – quick – stop, quick – quick – stop.* Then the girl's green eyes opened wide and closed quickly. And in that moment – between the girl's eyes opening and closing – there was a thud and a groan as another body landed on the stone step heaving and choking in a putrid puddle of anxiety oozing from the Four Corners that had seeped under the great oak door.

"Who's that?" the Old Crone whispered, looking at Death in alarm.

"Don't know," Death said, her feline body growing a little smaller.

"This is *not* a funeral parlor," the Old Crone whispered, pointing a twisted finger at Death and singeing her fur. "Do *not* bring any more of your dead or dying here!"

"I only brought the girl," Death whispered with considerable urgency before adopting her Bat persona minus her glittery red strappy shoes and hanging upside-down from the mantelpiece – coughing slightly after inhaling the smoke from her smoldering fur.

"This one's not yours?" the Old Crone asked incredulously, getting up and opening the great oak door and pointing at the choking heap that was tangled up in so much debris it was hard to tell either age or gender.

"I've brought no other!" Death said, emphatically back as a cat.

The Old Crone turned and looked down at the girl who was still hovering uncertainly between life and death. "Why does she equivocate?" the Old Crone asked. "She is *so close* to death she should have taken her last breath *and yet* she lingers." She pointed a wizened finger at the body on the stone step. "Do you know who that is?" she asked Death.

"The girl's boyfriend, I think," Death said. "He jumped in the Hudson River to save her. He must have got caught up in the split second when I brought the girl to you."

"*She* must have brought him," the Old Crone said, looking at the girl. "She equivocates for him."

"She looks peaceful," Death said, resisting her desire to purr.

The girl's eyes were closed but her breathing had changed again. There were no more quick breaths. No long breaks between breaths either.

"She knows the boy is safe," the Old Crone said. "She will live." And with that she closed the great oak door leaving the boy clinging to life on the stone step.

Three

The Old Crone sat back down by the Fire, while the Four Corners adjusted their right angles.

"You're leaving him outside?" Death asked sitting on the rug next to the girl and tucking her front paws under her feline body preparing for the vigil.

"He's not going to die," the Old Crone said looking at the girl. "She won't let him, although I doubt she knows she has that power." She sighed, looking at her hands so gnarled and twisted as she unfurled them. Her wizened fingers grew long and slender and her skin was no longer ancient and grey but iridescent and pale blue.

Death looked at her face and the Old Crone seemed to have fewer wrinkles than before. Death took this to be a hopeful sign.

"Not yet," the Old Crone said, her hands claws once more and the gnarly grey bones of her fingers visible through her ancient skin. "The girl has faced many dangers. Since they were children the boy has been at her side," the Old Crone told Death. "But nothing has prepared them for what is about to happen."

"Happen – because I split a second?" Death said.

"No, I've been thinking your split second might provide us with a solution," the Old Crone said. She looked at Death who gave her a guilty lopsided Cheshire Cat grin. She watched as the cat's fur stood on end, rippling before rearranging itself close to her body.

"Have you split seconds before?" the Old Crone asked suspiciously.

"How else d'you think I cope with all the dying?" Death said mewing miserably. "It's a permanent pandemic. Total crappiness! I can't keep up."

"Shhh. We can talk about it later," the Old Crone said kindly. "I'm going to put the girl somewhere safe and then we'll interrogate the boy."

"Interrogate?" Death said.

"Yes," the Old Crone said. "What if he's not who we think he is? What if he's a Sick-Reaper sent to make sure the girl's dead? Or if –"

"Or, if he's a Sick-Reaper sent to kill you instead," Death said. "That could be the reason you can't see the future!"

The Four Corners had relaxed but immediately went on high alert signaling to the Fire that the Old Crone was in imminent danger. The room grew hot and the Walls, familiar with the Inquisition, covered themselves with a wallpaper of torturous devices including the rack and thumbscrews in full working order that could be used in the interrogation.

"Very funny," the Old Crone said to the Walls that rippled good humoredly. Then she turned to Death and said more sarcastically, "How on Earth would he kill *me* –" it was not a question.

"Oh, I don't know," Death said, again with her signature lopsided Cheshire Cat grin. "A stake through the heart – if you had one."

"Enough! Go now and *don't* come back," the Old Crone said, not serious. "Unless you sit by my Fire and become *my Cat!*"

"I've no time for that," Death answered. "Too many living about to expire – although it would be nice to stay here with you and cuddle by your Fire."

"You're right," the Old Crone said, sighing. "It would be nice."

"She will die if you turn him away," Death said, this time with no artifice or guise. "And if she dies he will die and that will be the end of –"

"I know, I know," the Old Crone said, putting her hand up to stop Death from continuing. "I will bring him in and question him but not with the girl here."

The Old Crone looked intently at the girl while Death padded around her as she had done several times before and with her teeth she tugged at the blanket drawing it back so she could see the bruises on her body.

"No deep wounds," Death said. "Did they rape her?"

"No," the Old Crone said. "They were going to but she got away just in time. I can see them kicking and punching her but somehow she escaped and jumped in the river. Nothing after that."

"Nothing at all?" Death asked anxiously, knowing what that meant.

"Nothing," the Old Crone said, shaking her head.

"Have you seen the tattoo on the inside of the girl's left wrist?" Death asked changing the subject because there was *nothing* either of them could say about that.

"It's not a tattoo," the Old Crone said. "She was born with it – it's the sign for the powers of the human soul."

"Her mother too," Death said. "And her mother before that – stretching back – I knew them. They were all very special."

"Let's not get sentimental," the Old Crone said. "The girl must rest. It's time to bring in the boy. For the moment she is dead to the world, her future uncertain, perhaps that will be her fate." And with that she pointed a claw like finger at the girl who promptly disappeared at the exact moment there came a feeble knock at the great oak door.

"Mind if I stay?" Death asked.

"Oh, all right," the Crone said. "Don't mention the girl. No funny stuff."

Another knock. This time it was more hesitant, a dull and hopeless sound. Feeling fearless and frightened by this ending of her peaceful life, the Old Crone pushed back the bolts, top and bottom, lifted the latch, and flung open the door.

On the stone steps there stood a very wet boy, a youth, more than eighteen but not much more than twenty, bent over coughing, as he tried to catch his breath. The heat from inside the house was intense and he staggered back thinking it must be on fire.

"Cool it," Death whispered making herself small on the rug by the Fire. "And get rid of that wallpaper!"

"A boy!" the Old Crone exclaimed as if she had no idea who he was. "Just a boy!" she croaked. "A very large wet noisy boy!"

"I fell," the boy said, explaining without apologizing.

"Fell from the sky?" the Old Crone asked looking up wanting to know if he knew he had indeed dropped from above.

"Of course not," the boy responded, but for a second the irrational thought entered his head that he might have – no, the old hag was not serious. "I didn't see the step," he said. "You need a light out here."

The Old Crone stared at him through squinting eyes as he stood up straight but she knew it was a struggle. She could see the fear in his eyes and she knew terrible things had happened to him. The boy – really a very thin young man – tried to look tough. He pressed his lips together and stuck out his chin, but his shoulders could not hold the position and he put his arm out so his right hand was flat against the old stone of the house. Neither of them spoke. For a few endless seconds they stared at each other. Then the Old Crone peered into the darkness behind him.

"What d'you want?" she asked, not as sharply as she might, but without disguising her irritation at what he thought must be his unexpected intrusion.

"My dog," the boy said lying, "I've lost my dog."

"There are no dogs here," the Old Crone spoke sharply, disappointed that he lied. "Go back from where you came."

"I can't," the boy said, looking at her suspiciously wondering if she was a spy.

The Old Crone stared at the boy in silence wondering if she had made a mistake and that he was not the girl's boyfriend. His body was bent over again, and his head hanging. He was no longer looking at her, not looking at anything. He had gone some place deep inside himself, and in the darkness he was still looking for – not his dog, that's for sure.

"How did you get here?" the Old Crone asked again, more gently this time.

"I walked," the boy replied, raising his head and looking at the Old Crone as if challenging her to say he hadn't.

"Walked? Walked?" the Old Crone almost squawked, as if not to disappoint him. "Where from?" she demanded. "This place is a long way from anywhere. No one comes here."

The boy tried to stand up straight. "I got on a bus," he told her staring at her again wondering if there were Sick-Reapers hiding behind the open door. Again the doubt, she could be a spy he thought, dropping his eyes and looking at his feet.

"I couldn't find my dog," he said. "People were being put on buses. Someone told me to get on." His voice trembled. He looked up for a moment at the Old Crone. "I thought my Mom and Dad might be on the bus," he said, "so I got on."

"Did you know where the bus was going?" the Old Crone asked, realizing that while the boy was lying about how he got to her house, the story he was telling was true – perhaps when he was a small child?

"They wouldn't tell us," the boy said, a tear running down his cheek, which he brushed off as he took his hand off the wall and tried to straighten up. "All they kept saying was, 'Get on! Get on!'" He shrugged. "I started walking when I got off the bus."

"And you have been walking ever since," the Old Crone said quietly.

"Something like that," the boy said, with a fleeting smile. "I've been walking for a long time."

The Old Crone moved closer and looked at the boy. She raised her claw hand and put a twisted finger under his chin and peered deep into his eyes. The boy did not stop her. He looked back at her and did not blink. He was exhausted and frightened, but he held her gaze. Suddenly the Old Crone drew in her breath and stepped back as if she had been surprised by what she'd seen in his eyes.

"Is anyone with you?" she asked, gaining her composure and nervously peering into the darkness behind him.

"No," the boy said, unable to make out what it was she'd seen when she'd looked so intently into his eyes.

"How long were you on the bus?" the Old Crone asked, her voice no longer croaking, sounded strong and authoritative.

"Days," the boy replied, on alert now, because he was sure he was right. She *was* a spy.

"How many?" the Old Crone asked not caring what he was thinking.

"Four? Five?" he said, making it up. "Not sure."

"How long have you been walking?" she asked, sounding less irritated.

"Three days, maybe four," the boy replied, too tired to figure out why the Old Crone was asking him so many questions.

"What's your name?" the Old Crone asked, speaking quickly.

"Max," the boy said, just as quick.

"What's your dog's name?"

"Ma –"

"Max!" the Old Crone almost crowed. "You're story is a lie!"

"It's not a lie!" the boy replied, furiously, taking a step toward the Old Crone as she moved back before he could touch her. "It's just not the truth you want." He stared at her, surprised at how quickly she had moved away from him. Again they stood staring at each other.

"I might be lying – but you're a spy!" the boy suddenly said bent over and swaying as if he might fall.

The Old Crone sighed. "You'd better come in," she said. She stepped back and pushed the door open wide. The boy hesitated for a moment and then took a step but his legs buckled and he collapsed just inside the Old Crone's front door.

Four

"Tell me I'm dreaming," the boy said, sitting on a wooden chair opposite the Old Crone's chair. He felt a little less lightheaded now he was sitting down.

"A figment of your imagination?" the Old Crone laughed. "Is that what you think I am?"

"I don't know," the boy said, not wanting to be rude but thinking the Old Crone was shriveled enough to be his great grandmother's great grandmother. He was on guard and decided he would throw her in the fire if she were a spy.

Hearing his thoughts Fire turned ash grey and cooled her embers, agreeing with the Four Corners that they should oust the boy. Working in unison they started redrawing the boundaries of the room so that the boy would find himself outside – banished to the stone step. It was a complicated process and the Four Corners were not very well coordinated so the boy saw the Walls wobble and the ceiling sag and the Four Corners renegotiate their angles but he was still in the room.

"I think I'm delirious!" the boy said. "Maybe I have a fever."

"Possibly," the Old Crone said smiling as one of the Four

Corners affectionately pulled her Walls around her.

"Drink some soup," the Old Crone said handing the boy a bowl through the narrow gap left by the Four Corners and the wobbly Walls so she could see him. "Then you must exit – you don't seem to be the person we were expecting."

"X-it!" The boy said lifting the bowl with both hands and drinking some soup. "How did you know that's my name?"

"Exit?" the Old Crone asked, "E-x-i-t?"

"No!" the boy said, taking another gulp before spelling his name for her. "X-hyphen-i-t!"

"Well X-it," the Old Crone said taking the empty bowl from him, "It's time for you to exit."

"There," Death said, exchanging her feline form for a psychedelic David Bowie. "I told you. He's not dying so he is not one of mine."

"He will be if you don't leave," the Old Crone said in a mock threat that the boy thought was for real. "You know as well as I do that he's not supposed to see you."

"A rock star impersonator?" Death retorted, going out the door rather than just evaporating. "They're ten a penny," she shouted from far off, "I bet he's seen many!"

The boy stood up, planning his escape.

"Sit," the Old Crone said, as the boy looked around the empty room. There was nothing in it except for the two chairs and a stool. There were no windows and the only door was the one he had come through. The room had Four Corners, one of which he was sure he'd seen move. The Walls had no pictures on them. No shelves. It was difficult in the dim light of the Fire to tell if they were green or blue. They looked like a cloudy night sky. He looked for a light switch. There was none.

"That's because there's no light," the boy thought to himself, grinning as if he finally got it. He was no longer wet. His clothes were dry and his arms and legs were clean. "A lucid dream," he said out loud. "The old hag's not real!"

The Old Crone ignored his comment as she bent over the iron pot hanging over the Fire. Gripping the ladle she gave the soup a good stir before filling a second wooden bowl, which had suddenly appeared.

Taking this delusional act as confirmation of his lucid dream theory the boy thanked the Old Crone when she gave the bowl to him and he wrapped his hands around it feeling the warmth spread through his fingers. It felt so good he wanted to cry but he closed his eyes and kept them shut to hold back his tears.

The Old Crone broke off some bread. "Eat!" she scolded, holding out the bread. She could see from his face that something terrible had happened to the boy. "Eat! Eat!" she told him, her voice hard and abrasive, as if offended at being called an old hag but not actually caring what he called her. She was much more concerned that he would start crying. She hated it when people cried.

The boy took the bread and resting the bowl on his knees he dipped it in the soup. When he put the bread in his mouth the warmth spread up his arms, through his body, and down his legs. He couldn't help himself, and despite all his efforts not to, he started to cry.

The Old Crone sat down on her chair and watched him as he ate. She knew he was crying even though she could only see the top of his head as he bent low over the bowl of soup that he had balanced precariously on his knees. Finally, when all the soup was gone, he took the last piece of bread and wiped it around the inside of the bowl and ate it. By this time he had stopped crying and the Old Crone was visibly relieved.

"Thanks," he said, looking up and nodding at her.

"Your friends might call you X-it," the Old Crone said, "but that is not your given name." She smiled. "X-it. What kind of name is that?"

The boy shrugged.

"It's an outsider's name," the Old Crone said, "a rebel's name, a name that hides the person but reveals the truth." She was looking at him intently. She bent forward and picked up a stick from the woodpile by the Fire and she drew a large "X" in the ashes, followed by a hyphen, and then "it".

"X-it", she said pondering the many meanings of the word. "I'm sure when you've rested you'll tell me how you got the name and what it means."

"I will," the boy said, not knowing why. "I'll tell you the truth."

"And I," the Old Crone replied with a faint smile "will tell you about being a spy."

Five

X-it slept for a long time. The Old Crone had given him a pillow and a blanket that she'd taken from one of the Four Corners. "Sleep now," she'd said, "I have things to do". Too tired to argue X-it had placed the pillow on the rug in front of the Fire where the girl had lain and covered himself up with the blanket.

The Old Crone had watched. "If a cat comes and lies with you, ignore her," she'd said. "Whatever you do don't follow her if she tries to get you to go with her."

"How would she do that?" X-it had asked, looking up at her wondering if the old hag was senile. He shouldn't have thought that. She'd stood looking down at him, her eyes like the night sky penetrating his and he'd suddenly felt sick as if the world had tipped.

The odd thing was that now he was awake he could remember what happened, but in that moment he'd *known* nothing. Without language he'd been nothing. Not who he was. Not who she was. Names escaped him. He could not name the things he could see. Without language he had no memory. Without memory he had no past. He felt nothing, not fear, not love.

When he woke for a moment, he could hear sounds but he

could not comprehend them. And then he remembered that the Old Crone had spoken to him without moving her lips. "Watch your thoughts or you will have none," he'd heard her say.

"I have things to do," the Old Crone had said out loud as she'd walked into one of the Four Corners and disappeared. In his head X-it heard her say, "Don't mess with Cat!"

When X-it finally woke, he was flat on his back with a black cat sitting on his abdomen kneading his chest, rhythmically alternating paws, and as Cat pushed, out came her claws. Cat's eyes were open wide, yellow rings with black holes at the center. Later X-it would say he was sure the black holes were electromagnetic filled with hot dark matter pulling him in. Not his body he would say, but his mind, everything he knew and felt, all his experiences were being hacked by Cat.

Cat held his gaze even when he tried to look away but couldn't. Cat started purring, still kneading rhythmically but without exposing her claws. Deep in his mind she played with him, rubbed up against his fears to comfort him but with the opposite effect, making connections between thoughts and ideas that he had never made.

And then she stopped, curled up on his belly and went to sleep – or at least X-it thought she was sleeping. He lay still, not a muscle moving. Terrified he remembered what the Old Crone had said about not following Cat.

"Did she say that?" he heard a velvet voice say, not sure if it was out loud or in his head. "She knows you can't follow me unless you are dead." Cat pushed with a paw and exposed a red claw, which she dug into X-it's chest until he cried out. "And you are *not* dead," the voice said, ending with a purr.

Knowing he was under surveillance X-it tried to control what he was thinking. His thoughts were racing and muddled up when, without thinking, he started stroking the back of the sleeping Cat. Instantly he was asleep again, dreaming.

In his dream Cat turned into Bat and was hanging from the mantle over the Fireplace, and he was sitting in the Old Crone's chair telling Bat what had happened to him, blurting it all out, as the Four Corners moved closer to hear his tale.

Bat said, "All the devils are here and they are listening to you" and he saw their vile faces in the Fire and their arms reached out and tried to grab him.

"Stop them!" he yelled. "They've got Word!"

It was at that moment that the Old Crone came back and found X-it with his arms wrapped tightly around Cat crying out in his sleep, "Assholes! They've killed Word!"

The Old Crone caught hold of Cat by the scruff of the neck and X-it woke up with a start but powerless to move. The Old Crone held Cat at arm's length as the Four Corners drew back. X-it watched transfixed. Cat went limp, hanging in mid-air, forlorn and pitiful, and the Old Crone, tired from her journey and filled with despair, lowered herself slowly into her chair.

"I know the whole story," Cat said, sitting on the Old Crone's lap.

"I know it too," the Old Crone said.

"Of course you do," Cat said, jumping off the Old Crone's lap and appearing once more in her psychedelic garb with her face painted white with black jagged lines around one eye, her tongue red and lapping, and with small black horns.

"Like it?" Death asked the Old Crone. "The Kiss of Death!"

"You'll be the death of me!" the Old Crone said, smiling.

"No," Death said, feigning sadness. "You will never be my cadaver."

"Fool!" the Old Crone said, as Death returned to her feline self and jumped back on the Old Crone's lap.

X-it's muscles twitched but he lay still and with a quick look from the Old Crone his mind fogged and he went back to sleep.

"So what are we going to do?" Cat asked tucking her front paws underneath her body.

"Break all the rules," the Old Crone said. "Start by telling the boy why he was hacked by a Cat."

Six

When X-it finally woke his first thought was to wonder why he didn't have an erection, and his second thought was to wonder why he didn't need a pee. Then he wondered if all his bodily functions had stopped, and was it possible he was dead?

He looked across at the Old Crone who was asleep with Cat on her lap. Cat was staring into the Fire and turned and looked at him. "You're body parts are all functioning," Cat said, in X-it's head. "Just not right now."

X-it's next thought was how could he get Cat out of his head?

"For many reasons I wouldn't even think about getting rid of me," Cat said. "I've mooched around. Fired a few synapses. You're very intelligent but not very smart. Did you know you're under surveillance by some other entity as well as by me?"

Cat purred.

"Let me revise that," she said. "I'm not actually trying to keep tabs on you, so strictly speaking you are not under surveillance by me, but you are by the other entity – a bio-hacker or artificial intelligence."

"I am theoretically not a stupid person," X-it said to Cat, smarting at not being considered smart. "So has it occurred to you that if I am under surveillance this conversation is being monitored?"

"Silly boy!" Cat responded purring. "A-I is not capable of monitoring the thought communications of cats! Or, communications of animals across species. Not yet anyway. All the entity is picking up is you listening to a cat yowling and having a psychotic monolingual moment talking back to the cat as if it was human and understood what you are saying."

"Fucking stupid Cat!" X-it said.

"Purrfect!" Cat said. "Keep saying that, and we will get rid of the entity very quickly. Would you mind saying it again?"

"*You are* a fucking stupid Cat!" X-it said, totally incensed that his pejorative was not only acceptable but expressly requested by Cat.

"Somewhere," Cat continued, "A biological or artificial life form is monitoring this conversation, at least your utterances, and grumbling about having to analyze what you said. The A-I will be perturbed because it can hear you but not me. All it will pick up is a cat purring. If you concentrate harder you should be able to pick up what the hacker is thinking. Only you would have to train yourself not to react and that's a lot harder. People have died talking back to that entity."

Cat was silent for a second and X-it tried to concentrate but heard nothing. Then Cat started yowling and upped the volume as she coughed up a fur ball that was mostly maggots. X-it started retching.

The maggots had turned into bloody severed fingers that were beckoning to him. X-it's stomach was heaving.

"I'm going to be sick!" Retch! Retch! "Revolting! Fuck Cat! Fuck Cat!"

The fingers turned back into maggots and the maggots waved goodbye and disappeared.

"Did you hear him?" Cat asked X-it. "The entity?" she added, clarifying.

X-it shook his head miserably.

"He just said, 'I'm not listening to this shit!'" Cat said. "'The kid's being sick!' but he's continuing to listen because earlier A-I picked up your 'hacked by a Cat' – all kinds of alarms must have gone off. A-I interpreted 'hacked by a Cat' to mean hacked by them. They think you know you're being monitored."

"So tell me, why have I been hacked by a cat?" X-it asked without speaking, getting the hang of communicating with Cat.

Now the maggots and severed fingers had gone he no longer felt sick. He got up and went over to the Fire. He put his forefinger on his left hand to his lips, while he repeated over and over in his head, "Stupid fucking Cat!"

He picked up a stick with his right hand and wrote in the ashes in the hearth "chipped" and then he dropped his head and with his left hand he felt the back of his neck searching for the chip.

"When I was in kindergarten all the little kids were –"

"– chipped," Death said in her role as Cat, caterwauling her response. "I understand," she said, knowing that neither an A-I nor a bio-hacker would be able to decipher what she said. "The chip is similar to an old GPS tracking device. More sophisticated. But basically to make sure they can find you. We could remove it," Cat said, "but if we do the A-I and bio-hackers will know and so will the Super-Recognizers."

"You figure it out," X-it said sarcastically to Cat. "You're smarter than me."

Cat nodded in agreement ignoring the sarcasm. "Getting the entity out of your head is much more complicated," Cat said. "I don't think we can."

"But you could change his designation," the Old Crone said, "from EDM – Extremely Dangerous Male, to EDP – Extremely Dangerous Psychotic."

"And how are we going to do that?" Death asked, excited by the possibilities and appearing like Kiss but keeping her tail and swishing it.

The Old Crone beckoned to her and Death bent over and the Old Crone whispered in her ear. Death nodded and immediately returned to being a Cat, and in that form she grew larger, her eyes became cadmium yellow slits, and she unsheathed her claws that were red and glittery.

Cat looked at X-it and she gave him an unexpected Cheshire Cat smile and a wink before arching her back and with another swish of her tale she attacked him. Her claws dug deep in his face and he yelled out as the blood flow in his brain registered his excruciating pain. One of Cat's claws caught the lid of his left eye and blood from the deep scratch blinded him.

For one terrifying moment X-it thought he'd lost his sight and he screamed, "Fucking Cat!" Hysterical, he shouted, "Fuck Cat!" over and over. The hackers studying every galvanic response and every articulation documented what he felt and what he said. It was better than waterboarding. Any second now he would tell them what they wanted to hear. X-it was hysterical, insane with pain. His heart pumping, blood pressure off the scale, and sweating from every pore.

"Fuck Cat!" he screamed in a total panic. "Fuck the fucking Cat!"

He stood up and started walking around. The Four Corners drew back while the Old Crone sat with her hands in her lap and Cat, still slit eyed, waited on the rug pushing her front paws out to expose her claws, which she inspected in case she had damaged them.

"Fucking Cat!" X-it yelled, his voice shrill as he screamed obscenities.

"Apologies," Cat said unperturbed and even dismissive inside his head. "Excuse me while I mooch."

Gradually X-it calmed down. Not shouting now, he used his sleeve to wipe away the blood on his face and he covered his right eye to make sure he could still see out of his left. He could see blurry images through the blood and tears and he was so relieved he wrapped his arms around his legs and dropped his head so it was resting on his knees.

"They killed her," he sobbed. "Word's dead. They killed her. Now she's dead and I've got a Cat in my head. Fucking Cat. I can't live like this. I'd be better off dead."

Cat yowled as the A-I hacker recommended "delete" and the entity signed off, making a note before he did, "Girl dead. Boy psychotic. Surveillance low priority. Recommend terminating."

"Apologies for the scratches," Cat said, in his head. "They would have known if you faked it. You were in pain and you disclosed the information they wanted to hear – that the girl is dead – so they're no longer interested in you." Cat did not tell X-it the recommendation was to terminate him.

"Do you know what happened to her?" X-it asked, his anxiety clearly written on his face. "I tried to save her but the current was so strong and the water was so full of shit I lost sight of her."

The Old Crone sat quietly her hands still in her lap staring at X-it. Then she looked at Death who had resumed her Kiss persona and was standing in front of the Fire.

"Perhaps we should wait for the truth telling in case the hacker smells a rat and comes back," Death said. "You've been recategorized and reassigned but we don't want to tempt fate."

"Smells a Cat you mean." X-it couldn't help himself. He started laughing. "I'm God knows where talking to an old woman who looks as if she was born before the year dot, *talking* to the Kiss of Death who keeps turning into a Cat that likes to *mooch* in my head, and you talk of *tempting fate!*" X-it shook his head. "God help me!"

"She's trying to," Death said.

Seven

They sat in silence. X-it on the rug by the Fire. Death who needed comforting was once again Cat sitting on the Old Crone's lap in her favorite position with her front paws tucked under staring into the Fire. And the Old Crone with one claw hand on Cat's back appeared to be sleeping.

"I saw devils in the Fire," X-it said, in a monotone.

"You imagined them," the Old Crone said, opening her eyes and staring at him.

"Did I imagine being hacked by Cat?" X-it asked sarcastically. "Tell me I imagined that!"

"No," Cat said, turning and speaking out loud, "*that* was real."

"I'm lost," X-it said. Angrily, anxiously, he whispered his grieving and his loss. "We've endured infinite misery and reached the point of our final doom and all I want is to know what happened to –"

"*No!*" The Old Crone said authoritatively. "Don't think about her. Not until you have learned to detect the A-I or bio-hacker monitoring your thoughts."

"And how would I do that?" X-it asked, the desperation in his voice indicating that he was close to breaking.

"I'll teach you," Cat said, turning her head to look at him. "We know you are very intelligent just not very smart. I will teach you to be smart."

"Okay," X-it said, staring back at Cat, "but just tell me is –" he hesitated "– my friend okay?"

"Your friend is in a deep sleep," the Old Crone said. "It is best she stay that way until we can find a way to save her."

"Is she here?" X-it asked, trying to contain his thoughts by remembering the maggots and severed fingers.

"You're smarter than I think!" Cat said.

"Don't distract me!" X-it said. "It's difficult to think one thing and say another!"

"Yes," the Old Crone said. "She's here in a room above us."

"Can I see her?" X-it asked, his heart beating faster.

"Careful," Cat said.

"Maggots!" X-it said out loud. "Maggots!"

"Keep thinking maggots," the Old Crone said. "No. You cannot see her. It would endanger her life and yours. We don't know yet if her mind has also been infiltrated."

X-it shook his head. "Not possible. She's encrypted – I hate maggots! – No one knows –"

"Stop!" the Old Crone said, fiercely. "Reveal nothing. It's her only hope of survival."

"I'll have a mooch," Cat said, purring as she opened her eyes wide and looked directly into X-it's eyes. "Just keep thinking about bloody little fingers."

X-it made up his mind to cooperate and began thinking about maggots and severed fingers. He tried to think of something just as gross and Cat said in his head "worms in feces?" and he couldn't help himself, he started laughing. But he quickly stopped when he heard what sounded like a bird chirping.

Even though he had lost his concentration X-it was sure he felt a ripple in his consciousness and Cat leaving his head. He also felt an urgency, which he didn't understand, almost like panic. He knew something was happening that had nothing to do with Cat having a mooch – but what?

The Walls of the room were rippling, the Four Corners bending, and the Old Crone was gone.

"Where'd she go?" X-it asked Cat, who was now covered in mange sitting beside him on the rug swishing her tail. "What's happening?"

The chirping became shrill, the bird's song sounding like a pulsing high-pitched siren and then it suddenly stopped.

"Don't know," Cat said. "I think I'm having an anxiety attack.

Can I sit on your lap?" Cat gave X-it a screwed up Cheshire Cat smile and he picked her up even though she was now covered with sores that were foul smelling and oozing.

"Thank you," Cat said. "You're a kind boy. I won't forget your kindness," she said as she curled up on his lap her teeth chattering. "I hope she doesn't die," she mewed. "Please God, don't let her die!"

"Let's concentrate on mooching," X-it said, thinking to himself that he couldn't believe he was cuddling a mangy Cat that sometimes looked like Kiss and had a soft spot for David Bowie.

"You're right, the entity and A-I *can* pass through matter without interacting with it so –" Cat did not finish the sentence.

In the room above the girl opened her eyes, ready to fight and possibly die, if she was not already dead. She reached for the knife that she kept strapped to her leg but the sheaf was empty and so she clenched her fists instead. But the effort to be conscious was too much and she began to drift, light headed, and unable to think of anything except her determination to survive.

"This is the moment," Cat said, her eyes dilated and her claws out digging into X-it's leg. "Oh god! Oh god!" the scabrous Cat started yowling. "I know she's dying and I don't know what to do! I don't want to let her down! Or you! We've got to get this right."

"We will!" X-it said, having no idea how they were going to do that.

"There are no cowards," Cat said, yowling a lament. "People

are dying so beautifully, with great courage, but it's wrong, and we've got to stop it!"

X-it thought it peculiar that it was Death who was agonizing about people dying, and he had no idea how Cat thought they were going to stop what was happening. But for the first time he was convinced he could trust her and he would continue the struggle alongside her. At a loss to know what to say next to comfort Cat, X-it just blathered.

"It's just a momentary ripple in the pond of spacetime," he said.

"That's profound," Cat said, her distress diminishing with the introduction of this new and interesting thought.

Eight

When the girl opened her eyes the second time the Old Crone was there looking down at her. "You're safe," she said, soothing her. "Shhh. We love you. Shhh. Don't try to talk."

The girl looked up at the Old Crone and saw her mother smiling, loving and reassuring, looking down at her. She pushed her glasses up onto her head so the girl could see her eyes that were filled with morning light.

The girl's mother looked just the way she remembered her, dark brown hair pulled back in a clip, white t-shirt and blue cardigan, jeans, and sneakers. She remembered the way her mother pushed her glasses up on her head before … before … the girl's eyes filled with pain.

"You're safe my darling," her mother said. "Make sure you block incomings."

The girl nodded, a small movement of her head, looking at her mother with worried eyes.

"Do you still have it?" her mother asked. "Is it safe?"

Once again the girl nodded. With her hand she pulled off

the soft blanket that was covering her and then caught hold of the hem of her t-shirt, lifting it to show her abdomen. Letting go her shirt she traced her fingers over the tiny lines of writing that were tattooed on her skin.

"I am vellum," she whispered, the pain in her eyes bringing tears to her mother's eyes. Then with a look that was sharp and unsullied by emotion the girl said, "If I live we have a back-up."

"Everything is going to be okay," her mother said, as the girl pulled her t-shirt down and the blanket up. "You can trust Cat and Et," she said, holding her hand. "Now, my darling girl, I want you to close your eyes and sleep a little longer."

Drifting, the girl imagined holding her mother's fingers and turning her hand over so she could see the birthmark on the inside of her wrist.

"*In the beginning …*" the girl whispered. Smiling, she closed her eyes. By the time her eyelashes touched her cheeks her mother was gone and there in her place was the Old Crone, wanting to hold her hand, looking down at her.

"*…. was the word,*" the Old Crone said, looking at the ancient sign for the human soul, handed down through time from the very first Truth Keeper. The Old Crone knew she must protect the girl. She was an old soul and must endure.

"Sleep," the Old Crone said. "We'll watch over you."

The Walls rippled once more and then straightened, the Four Corners bent and adjusted their right angles and the Walls sighed, satisfied that they were doing a good job watching over the girl.

"Yes," the little bird chirped, flying about the room, and landing on the pillow close to the sleeping girl. "We will watch over you."

"Call if you need me," the Old Crone said to the bird and then turning in a circle she thanked the Four Corners and the Walls.

When X-it looked up the Old Crone was back in her chair.

"I've been telling Cat about gravitational waves and black hole mergers," X-it told her, without commenting on her swift return.

"X-it knows a lot about astrophysics," Death said, back to her psychedelic self, looking more like Bowie than Kiss in a red body suit, a black eye patch, and a yellow scarf with black polka dots tied around her neck.

"Gravitational waves and black hole mergers?" the Old Crone asked raising her eyebrows.

"He thinks that consciousness and space are analogous," Death said.

"*If* consciousness is like deep space," X-it hypothesized. "Mind mergers could create the equivalent of gravitational waves that are imperceptible to people – don't you think? Theoretically, this would make it possible for hackers to enter our consciousness and pass through our minds without us knowing they are there. But while gravitational waves could pass through the mind and be *un*detectable, *theoretically* they should be *de*tectable in the brain, because they would distort synaptic connections in the mind-brain continuum."

X-it looked at the Old Crone and then at Death. "Roughly," he said. "Sort of. You get the idea."

Death was beside herself with glee at this banality and for a moment there were two psychedelic creatures in the room in red body suits and with black eye patches. They circled each other and then merged sending pseudo-psychedelic gravitational rings ricocheting around the room.

"Enough!" the Old Crone said, speaking sharply to Death. "X-it has formulated a way of thinking about the task we have set him. His analogy is a stretch, but if it helps him detect the entity or A-I that has infiltrated his consciousness that's all that matters."

"So what's your plan?" Death asked X-it looking skeptical.

"Well," X-it began. "You said you could teach me how to detect mind-hackers but the problem is I have to be thinking about something while you are teaching me to detect the hackers."

"Okay," Death said. "What are you going to think about so no alarms go off in Hackerland?"

"I thought about that," X-it said. "If I was really psychotic a psychiatrist would be asking me about my childhood."

"Dream on," Death said. "The hackers would send a few electrical charges to zap you." She clasped her hands together. "And then you would be mine!"

"Not funny," X-it said.

"No," Death said. "A bit insensitive of me but the truth nevertheless."

"I think it's a good plan," the Old Crone said. "If Einstein could theorize about ripples in the spacetime continuum of the Universe there is no reason why X-it can't theorize about ripples in the spacetime continuum of consciousness. If it works we might be able to –" the Old Crone shrugged her shoulders and raised her eyebrows in an anything-is-possible-but-unlikely moment.

"Exactly," Death said. "Let's get started."

Nine

"Do you think we're weird?" Death asked, no longer a mangy or glossy coated Cat or a psychedelic rock star, but a bat-like creature with black shiny wings hanging upside-down from the mantle.

"Not as weird as the world in which I live," X-it replied. He was sitting on the chair opposite the Old Crone, who once again had her hands in her lap, head down, and eyes closed. She appeared to be sleeping, although X-it was sure she was not.

"In my world," X-it said, "just to survive," his voice tremoring, "you go from the most heinous, vicious people to the most courageous, brave, and caring people every single day."

"Are you ready to tell us about your world?" the Old Crone asked opening her eyes.

"After I've had a mooch," Death said as she flew as Bat from the mantle and landed as Cat on X-it's lap.

X-it smiled. He opened his eyes wide.

"You don't have to do that," Cat said.

"Thought I did," X-it said, feeling just a little bit foolish.

"But I do like it when you stroke my back," said Cat, giving him her signature lopsided Cheshire Cat smile to make up for making him feel foolish.

X-it laughed and stroked her as she went inside. The embers of the Fire glowed and the Four Corners drew closer. X-it thought he could feel Cat fur brushing up against his thoughts.

"You have an overactive imagination," he heard Cat say. "It's an important lesson. You are stroking my fur and imagining it as a mindful experience. Your biggest challenge is to distinguish between what you physically feel on the outside and what you think you feel on the inside."

"Got-it," X-it said, imagining being in some superhuman state, while he sat quietly stroking her.

"No visions of grandeur," Cat said. "That's not very smart. Could cost you your life in a tight spot. It's important that you distinguish between what's real and what's not. It's the only way you will be able to tell if the hackers are garnering your thoughts."

"Okay," X-it said. "I haven't got it. But I am smart!"

"You will be if you pay attention," Cat said. "Like now!" she said, swishing her tail. "In an emergency if you see me swish my tail you will know I'm inside. A simple signal that might be useful in the near future."

"You swish your tail all the time," X-it said, without speaking. "Are you going to stop?"

"No," Cat said. "Tail swishing is part of my emotional repertoire, but I can control it if I want and if there is an emergency you'll need a signal –"

"Why not just speak to me when you're in my head?" he asked.

X-it felt Cat shudder, but because he was stroking her he wasn't sure if he felt it on the inside or the outside. He thought it could have been his own empathetic feelings for Cat who seemed to have become a fur ball of anxiety.

"Are you okay?" he asked.

Cat yowled a huge Caterwaul of a lament.

"Shit!" X-it said. "Try not to do that when you're mooching! Felt like I was electrocuted."

"Apologies," Cat said, sounding techy. "Which question do you want me to answer first? – 'Am I okay?' – *No!* – 'Why not just speak to you when I am in your head?' – Because there might be a time when something dreadful is happening and speaking could be dangerous," Cat said, tail swishing in agitation.

"What Cat is trying to communicate," the Old Crone said, one eye open, "is there might be a moment when the situation is so dire that she enters your mind because you're the conduit to the entity and A-I and she might learn something from their occupation of your mind that will save your friend."

"Save all of us! And it's going to happen soon! *Very* soon," Cat said, jumping down off X-it's lap and leaping onto the lap of the Old Crone. "All clear," she said. "No hackers in his head." She nuzzled the Old Crone under the chin. "I'm so frightened," she said.

"Shhh," the Old Crone said. "Now that I am back it will be okay. I apologize for staying away for so long."

"You were really mean to me when I first arrived with the girl," Cat said.

"You're right, I was," the Old Crone agreed. "You understand why," she said, giving Cat a matter-of-fact pat to end the conversation as she looked across the room at X-it who had just learned that it was Cat who had brought – the Old Crone stopped him mid-thought.

"Brought your friend to me," the Old Crone said. "Be careful," she said sharply, cautioning him. "Remember, try not to think of her and do not say her name." And then calmly and more kindly with a smile, "Would you like to tell us about Max?"

"Max?" X-it repeated jarred by the sudden switching of topics and wondering how the Old Crone knew about Max.

"When you first arrived you said your name was Max and then you said your dog was called Max, do you remember? Something about a bus?" the Old Crone said. "Where would you like to start?"

"Max is a big old black lab," X-it said. "Max is not my name. I think my family started calling me X-it when I was about six – that's a whole other story – so much has happened I've forgotten my birth name."

"Are we playing psychiatrists now?" Cat asked. "Shall I become Hack Cat?"

"Perhaps you'll remember if you tell us what happened to Max," the Old Crone said, frowning at Cat. "How did you lose him?"

"The thunder frightened him," X-it said.

The Old Crone could see the pain in his eyes. She waited.

X-it was quiet.

Cat jumped off the Old Crone's lap and jumped back up on X-it's lap and he started stroking her. It was becoming part of their routine.

"My dad used to say you can't do anything during a hurricane except wait for it to be gone," X-it said, looking into the Fire. "But Mr. Zuki came and said a tree had fallen on his house and Mrs. Zuki was hurt. My dad went to help and Max ran out. My dad came back with Mr. and Mrs. Zuki but Max was gone. Dad wouldn't let me go after him." X-it paused.

The Old Crone listened, knowing that it was a much younger boy who was telling the tale.

X-it stroked Cat, who was sharing thoughts with the Old Crone. "How old were you?" Cat asked.

"Maybe seven or eight?" X-it said.

"Young," the Old Crone said. "Life was different then."

"We knew the hurricane was coming and we'd got everything ready," X-it said, as he glanced up at the Old Crone, "but we didn't think it was going to be so bad – it was – it stretched from Texas City to Mobile."

He continued in no more than a whisper. "Mrs. Zuki was crying, and Mr. Zuki and my mom were trying to take care of her. She had a cut on her head. A scratch. Nothing at all really. Then trees started falling down around our house."

The Fire crackled frightening Cat who hissed and the Old Crone tutted at the Fire and Cat.

"One tree smashed the glass in the patio door and the water was flowing in." X-it said, taking no notice of the interruption.

"You could hear the wind gust and then a sound almost like a locomotive coming and we'd know it was a tornado," X-it said, his voice changing, and a young boy speaking. "We'd get down in a safe part of the house and everybody would huddle together."

The Four Corners inched in.

"In a couple of minutes it would pass," X-it said, once again eight. "You'd notice the rain was sideways and then it would fall straight. Then you'd hear it again, and other trees would come down and you'd hear them crashing all around the house."

"My dad and mom had prepared for the storm," X-it said, once again grown. He looked intently at the Old Crone as if it was important to him that she knew his dad and mom were good people. "We thought we'd be okay but there'd never been a storm like this one."

"I'm sure they did everything they could," the Old Crone said, fascinated by the way he'd switched back and forth, younger, then older. She wanted to ask what happened to his mom and dad, but decided to wait.

The room had grown so small as the Four Corners had drawn closer to listen to X-it that it was no larger than a closet. The Old Crone raised her arms and spread her fingers as if pushing outward with her hands and the Four Corners moved out, making adjustments to their angles.

"It was quiet for a while," X-it said, in a moment of peacefulness, which was quickly replaced by a wild look in his eyes. "Then we heard the wind again, like a locomotive. We got down on the floor and held on to each other, but the noise got louder and louder and we knew that the tornado was very close. The noise was so loud it hurt my ears. It was hard to breathe."

"You must have been very frightened," the Old Crone said when X-it looked at her as if for reassurance, "but very brave."

"Trees were falling so fast the noise was deafening and bits of the roof of our house were flying about," X-it said, his arms around Cat who was trembling at his near death experience.

"Then like a freight train leaving the station the tornado was gone and everything went quiet, except for Mrs. Zuki who was still crying. Most of the roof was gone and the rain was pouring in. My dad said we had to leave and get to a safe place. Then Mrs.

Zuki started screaming that we were going to die, and my mother told her everything would be okay, and we left the house to go to my Aunt Cecilia's.

"When we got outside I heard Max barking and my dad told me that I had to stay with him, but Max sounded as if he had been hurt so I ran off to look for him." He wanted the Old Crone to understand. "I could hear my father shouting my name but Max was hurt and I had to find him."

The Old Crone nodded.

"Then the wind changed again and the rain lashed my face as another tornado touched down," X-it looked terrified, as if he was reliving what had happened to him. "The noise was deafening. I threw myself on the ground by the old stone wall and the trees, more and more trees, started to fall. They were all falling in the same direction and one landed on the stone wall above me and I thought it was going to crush me." His words bumped into each other as he spoke. "I couldn't hear anything except the sound of the locomotive. It was difficult to breathe. I lay on the ground with my face in my baseball cap and covered my head with my hands."

X-it began to cry.

"When it finally passed I was gasping for breath, the trunk of the tree was almost touching my back. I'm not sure how the old stone wall had stayed put but I'm thankful that it did. I crawled out and I tried to shout for my dad, but got no answer. Then I shouted for Max but he didn't bark. I heard nothing, not even a whimper."

"This is quite a story," the Old Crone said. "I think we should stop for a while and you can tell us what happened next after you rest?"

"Sure," X-it said, suddenly very sleepy. He looked down at Cat. "Did you hack?"

"Got caught up in the story," Cat said. "Forgot!"

"Good," X-it said laughing, "because I didn't feel a thing!"

"I'm going to go and spend a little time with your friend," the Old Crone said, trying not to be exasperated with Cat.

"Can I come?" X-it asked.

"After you sleep," the Old Crone said, "and you tell us what happened when you got on the bus."

"That's where I met her," X-it said, looking troubled.

"Time to hack," Cat said. "Hopefully no intruders, otherwise it might come to combat!"

Ten

X-it woke, wondering again why none of his bodily functions worked.

"You'll figure it out," Death said, this time looking more like Lady Gaga than Kiss. "Your kidneys are working fine, just not at the moment, and you don't have erectile dysfunction, you'll have many boners, biggies, and hard-ons in your life time – that's *if* you live."

"You were in my head!" X-it protested.

"A quick mooch," the voluptuous psychedelic apparition said in a low seductive voice.

"Not without asking!" X-it complained, thinking he would rather discuss his dysfunctional body parts with Cat.

"We discussed before you went to sleep!" Cat said, her feline form replacing the psychedelic apparition. "How will you ever detect an intruder if I don't intrude?" She gave X-it a knowing wink.

"Why were you dressed up like that?" X-it asked, annoyed with her.

"Would you be more comfortable if I appeared like most humans imagine me?" Cat asked, momentarily the voluptuous lady again before an evil looking skull replaced her beautiful face. Her low cut extravagant dress becoming a ragged black cloak stained with blood that reached from shoulder to floor of the huge wraith-like *man*ifestation of death that took her place. The bones of the wraith's fingers were wrapped around a gigantic scythe with a blade blackened from millennia of use.

"Death will punish the wicked even if everyone in creation dies!" the apparition shouted raising his blade in a battle cry before disappearing.

"Is that the way you think of me?" the psychedelic apparition said, returning, her voluptuous voice as smooth as milk chocolate. "It's a sick male image," she said, the chocolate in her voice turning bitter. "I prefer to imagine myself female."

"Not that I am either," Death said, discarding her voluptuous femininity and becoming Cat. "I have no form except the one I give myself or you give to me." Cat gave a lamenting yowl, "Sadly, I am nothing. Nothing at all."

"But you exist?" X-it asked. "You must otherwise we wouldn't be having this conversation."

"That's the spirit," Cat said, cheering up.

"I like it when you're Cat," X-it said.

"Me too," said Death, enjoying her feline form, and with her tongue she began to groom the fur on her stretched out left front paw.

"Tell us what happened when you got on the bus," the Old Crone said, reappearing with her hands in her lap sitting on her chair.

"All the houses in my neighborhood were destroyed," X-it said, staring into space. "No buildings were left standing in Louisiana, Mississippi and Texas, and even Illinois was devastated by the storm. All along the Gulf Coast towns, entire cities were gone. So many kids lost their parents." He looked at the Old Crone with an intense look on his face.

"What we know now that we didn't know then is that it was more than a Category 5 hurricane with winds of more than 185 miles per hour that devastated the region," X-it said. "Violent storms were increasing because of the extreme weather changes taking place but this was also a man-made event."

"Mooch time," said Cat. "Watch my tail. One swish for 'you're being hacked,' twice for 'severe risk of termination,' and three times for 'you're about to be terminated.'"

"What do I do then?" X-it asked, his voice climbing an octave.

"Nothing," Cat said. "If that happens you'll be like me, nothing at all."

"Stop-it!" the Old Crone said staring at Cat in exasperation. "You play with X-it as if he was a ball of yarn for your Cat persona to unravel. Let's get on with the story." She looked across at X-it.

"You are not going to be terminated. I won't let them."

X-it didn't find that very reassuring.

"The hurricane was used as a cover-up for targeted attacks," he said. "Most people still don't know what happened and most of those who did have been killed."

He paused, glancing down at Cat's tail that was uncharacteristically still and when he started speaking again his voice had changed. He'd become the young boy again searching for his mom and dad and for Max.

"I kept shouting 'Mom! Dad! Max! I'm over here!'" he said. "I even called for Mr. Zuki and Mrs. Zuki but I never found any of them and they didn't find me."

Cat drew in her claw and stroked X-it's leg and he responded by stroking her back while keeping his eyes on her tail.

"I searched for them for three days. I managed to get through the narrow spaces between huge piles of debris, watched people digging in the rubble of buildings trying to find members of their families. The Mississippi River flooded the land for hundreds of miles, and the waters of the Gulf invaded the wetlands at such a fast pace people were taken by surprise and few survived."

X-it had become the boy he was and he was reliving moment by moment what had happened to him.

"Swollen bodies were floating in the water in the steamy heat," he said. "I waded through water that was filled with shit and other foul smelling stuff trying to get to some place where people were gathering in the hope of being rescued," he said. "A body in the water had got caught in an eddy and was turning in circles and then it broke free and bumped into me."

X-it stopped stroking Cat and gasped for air. He started crying. "I pushed it away but it came back rolling over." He tried to catch his breath. "I can see the man's face, the look of terror, his eyes were wide open, his stomach swollen –"

"Then what happened?" the Old Crone asked, moving X-it along.

"When I finally got to a place on high ground where people were gathering there were lots of soldiers waiting in full battle gear with submachine guns," X-it said, his voice no longer that of the young boy he once was. "I thought they were there to help us. They were assisting people, giving them water and packs of food, but they were also searching for someone.

"I thought at first they were looking for someone important who had been lost, but they were asking for identification and treating the people they questioned as if they were looking for someone who had escaped from prison –

"– that's what I thought at the time," X-it said, his eyes dark and wary. "And that's what they were doing, only not quite –"

"Go on," the Old Crone said.

"I knew my dad was an astrophysicist working on gravitational waves – Einstein's ripples in spacetime – but he had never talked about his work and I used to tell people he was a school teacher." X-it smiled, "And so when they asked me my name and what my parents did I said my parents were both school teachers – which was a half-truth because my mom actually was a teacher. I named her school and my dad did some work there too.

"Another soldier checked a data base and as my dad sometimes taught a class at the school both their names were on the list and they let me get in line for the next bus," X-it's eyes softened. He looked at Cat's tail that had not moved since he had begun his story.

"All clear," Cat said. "I think we're being overly cautious, but better safe than sorry."

"Don't say any names," the Old Crone reminded him.

"I should have said, we were actually lined-up alongside the bus and there were soldiers monitoring the line," X-it said. "But there was a lot going on and once I was in the line no one took any notice of me. I stood looking down making myself as insignificant I could, and a small hand came out from under the bus and untied the shoelace of my right sneaker. Then the hand disappeared."

"Go on!" Cat said, fur standing on end but tail still.

"I bent down to tie my shoelace and saw a very small girl under the bus," X-it looked worried. "I've never told anyone this story. Are you sure it is safe?"

He looked around and saw that the Four Corners had drawn close and the embers of the Fire were glowing in strange hues that he found strangely comforting.

"When you arrived the A-I was already in your head," the Old Crone said. "You brought the hackers with you. It's unlikely they would have been able to find you here on their own. Imagine this place as a ripple in the spacetime continuum. Imagine it as a bubble floating close to Earth. It's highly unlikely your location is still showing up in their database or that they could monitor the conversation even if it did. But there's no telling how far technology has taken them so we are super vigilant and quite capable of responding – even if the signal for trouble is transmitted via Cat's tail!"

X-it smiled. It all made sense to him. Actually nothing made sense, but he had put his trust in the Old Crone and he was simpatico with Cat – in a nonsensical world it was as straightforward as that.

"I looked back at my shoe and pretended I was having trouble tying the lace," X-it said. "The girl pushed her back-pack towards me. 'Take it!' she whispered looking fierce. I hesitated. 'Please!' she whispered, this time the desperation in her voice matched by the terror in her eyes.

"I finished tying the one lace and as I switched legs to retie the other lace I pulled the backpack out from under the bus hoping no one was looking," X-it said, with more than a little pride in his voice at the action he had taken. "I couldn't take the bag and leave the girl and so I grabbed her hand and pulled her out from under the bus. She didn't try to stop me because that would have brought the soldiers.

"'Is she the girl they're looking for?' the woman behind me asked in a low voice.

"'No,' I said, not looking back. 'She's my sister,' I said, making it up. 'We got separated and if I get out of the line and tell them she's here we'll lose our place in the line to get on the bus.'

"'Stick to your story,' the woman said. 'If they find out and she's the girl they're looking for they'll kill her and you too most likely. Don't worry, I saw nothing and I'll say nothing.'

"'Here,' the woman said. 'I have some pralines,' and she gave me two. 'One each,' she said. 'You both look as if you need feeding.'"

"What was in the backpack?" Cat asked.

"I think," X-it hesitated. "My *friend* should tell you."

"I agree," said the Old Crone, lifting herself carefully off her chair and walking slowly into the North Corner of the room. "I think it's time."

Eleven

X-it looked at Death who was now Bat wearing her red glittery strappy shoes. "Very exciting!" she said, spreading her huge black bat wings.

"Better get back to being Cat," X-it said, without elaborating.

"You think so?" Bat asked. "I'm more majestic as a bat."

"You're much more empathetic when you're Cat," X-it said.

"I can't believe you're having this conversation," the girl said smiling at X-it as she walked out of one of the Four Corners with the Old Crone.

X-it was on his feet, arms out almost falling over as he rushed towards her.

The girl put her hand up and smiling at him she shook her head, and instead of embracing her he took her hand and kissed it.

"Forgive me," she said to X-it. "I'm so overwhelmed right now if you put your arms around me I would drown in my own tears." She was almost as tall as him and she reached up and kissed him on the forehead. Then as their eyes met she said, "And as I've just been rescued from drowning I don't intend to need rescuing again." Word smiled at X-it. "Besides I want to know what's been going on while I was in a comatose state."

Cat walked over to greet the girl with her tail up and curled. She rubbed against her legs and said with a polite mew, "I am so relieved that you are able to join us."

"You must be Death," the girl said, as if she had spent her whole life talking to cats. "Et told me you saved me so I am grateful and count myself in your debt."

"Et?" X-it asked. "Who's Et?"

"I am," the Old Crone said solemnly. "My friends call me Et."

"And you can call me Word," the girl said to Et. "It is a bit peculiar but that is actually my given name."

"I've been telling Cat and the old – and *Et* how we met," X-it said. "And I stopped at the point when the woman standing behind us in line for the bus gave us pralines with pecans."

"First food in three days!" Word said, laughing and rubbing the flat of her hand on her stomach. "It was a good moment." Her laughter was short lived and she looked troubled. "It was a terrible time. X-it lost his mother and father *and* his dog. If X-it had been with them he would have died as well."

"Your mom died too," X-it said quietly He pointed at the chair inviting her to sit where he had been sitting but she shook her head.

Word nodded. "I'd like to sit by the Fire," she said, sitting on the rug.

"Should I mooch?" Cat asked padding over to the rug, and tucking her front paws under she settled next to Word.

Et shook her head.

"You're welcome to mooch as you call it," Word said. "My thoughts are encrypted and I would be surprised if you could decipher them, but there could be an A-I or bio-hacker, or some Super-Recognizer trying to break my encryption."

Word looked up at X-it who had sat back down on the chair he'd been occupying. "Do you remember what the woman said about us posing as brother and sister?" she asked him.

"She said we should tell them we have different fathers to explain our different skin colors."

"She said to you 'remember your mommy's black and your daddy's white," Word said, "and then to me, 'same black mommy, not sure about your daddy. Pick a country you know something about.'"

"I remember," X-it said. "What was funny is that we both knew the histories of our families but they would have carted us off and killed us if they'd had found out."

"And I remember you said, making it up, 'Our daddies were born in New Orleans and were just different colors of creole – French, Spanish, and African descent.'"

"'Good thinking,' the woman said. 'Stick to that.'"

"Tell us what was in your backpack," Cat said, to the point and without asking roundabout.

Word looked at X-it and shook her head.

"There are other parts of the story you need to hear first," X-it said. "For instance how Word ended up under the bus."

"My mother was a world renowned linguist who studied ancient texts," Word said, finding her own beginning. "She grew up in New York City. Her mother was French, her father Italian. My father was from North Africa. He was an archeologist. He was killed before I was born. That's all I know." She looked at Et and then down at Cat stroking her back. "It's the reason I was hiding under the bus."

"Okay," Cat said. "Mooch time. I'm going in."

"I'll watch your tail," X-it said, and in response got a Cheshire grin.

Word put her index finger to her mouth and for a moment everyone was quiet. "There you are," she said looking at Cat. "You were easier to detect than I expected." Then she laughed. "Having trouble with my encryption?"

"Very peculiar," Cat said. "It's as if you are in rem sleep experiencing a vivid dream or, or, or –"

"Having orgasm?" Word asked.

"Yes!" Cat said, looking at her, "but you are very definitely not!"

"The pseudo dream state has saved me several times from intruders," she said, matter of fact. "When A-I report that I am orgasmic, operatives tune in. Sometimes I hcar them ejaculating. It's a bit disconcerting, but I'm never hacked."

"T-M-I," X-it said, looking mortified. "I don't want to know!"

"I thought you knew?" Word said.

"No," X-it replied. "Not that. I didn't know."

"It doesn't happen often," Word said. "Bit tedious really but it does say a lot for my encryption – using pseudo sexual activity as a deterrent. It distracts the intruders and alters their mental state while I remain impenetrable."

"When we –" X-it began.

"You're the only one," Word said, looking lovingly at him. "You're the only one who has *ever* been inside me."

"Ancient texts," Et said, getting everyone to refocus. "You were telling us about your mother studying ancient texts."

Twelve

"My mother said I was born reading," Word said. "Not true of course. I was two when I read Homer. Always a favorite."

"The epic poet," Cat said with her Cheshire grin. "*Iliad* and *Odyssey.* You've read Herodotus?"

"The father of history," Word said, nodding as she spoke. "I read them all in Greek. I know every word. Once I've read a text I remember it forever," she said, and then pulling a face and looking contrite, "Not so keen on some of the English versions. I'm not very tolerant. I hate a bad translation. Can't stand the modern versions."

Cat nodded but not listening. "I liked Herodotus," she said, remembering him. "He was convinced the purpose of writing is to prevent the traces of human events from being erased by time."

"Doesn't matter now," Word said, looking at Et and shaking her head. "There are no books. Only digital propaganda, indoctrinating people to believe in the Empire that has obliterated human history to protect the lies of the political masters and the Lunatic Eight who are vicious." Word's voice trailed off as she said, "Sometimes I think I'm the only one who remembers them," and then as if a pleasant thought had replaced an unpleasant one, she smiled and said, "books I mean," her eyes lighting up as repeated, "books!"

Word lifted her sweatshirt revealing the writing tattooed on her body – tiny texts in minuscule fonts, squarely Roman, rounded from the Enlightenment, in the Roman alphabet, in Greek, Latin, hieroglyphs, and signs more ancient, oracle bones, logographic, Sinitic, arranged in blocks of text with other signs in between.

"I am the book," Word said. "An illuminated manuscript. Vellum. That's why our political masters and the Lunatic Eight are trying to kill me."

"Actually," Cat said. "As far as they're concerned you're already dead."

"They'll keep looking," Word said. "They'll want my body. They'll know if the Truth Protectors find it they will make copies of my tattoos and preserve all the writing."

"Do you know if there are any books still in existence?" Et asked.

Word shook her head, smiling at Et and then without dropping her eyes from Et's gaze, "You already know the answer. You're asking to find out if *I* know," she said. "I *know* who you are and I'm not intimidated."

"I would be disappointed if you were," Et said, returning the smile.

"Who is she?" X-it asked Word in what was supposed to be a whisper but with the sound of his voice filling the room.

Cat gave a swish of her tail and glared at X-it and the Four Corners drew back no longer at right angles but ready to move in any direction necessary depending on what next occurred.

"To you, X-it", Et said, saying his name in a voice he had not heard before, "I am the Old Crone!"

"But I can't call you that!" X-it said, as the room became cavernous. And the Fire hunkered down, no longer glowing, becoming just a few grey ash embers.

"*If* you *speak* my name," she said, "*which* you *should not*, you can call me Et –"

"Thank you," X-it said, as if he had been bestowed a great honor.

"*But,*" Et continued, holding up her hand to silence him, "when you *think* of me, think of me as the Old Crone."

X-it looked at Cat who stared back at him. Her body was still feline but the fur on her face looked as if it had been painted by Kiss. She had jagged white lines around her eyes and her whiskers were bright red.

"Can you mooch?" X-it said. "Please" he added. "I need you."

"Of course," said Cat with tears glittering in her yellow eyes.

"I'm touched," X-it heard Cat say in his mind. "It's a rare thing for me to be needed", and with that she started to cry. "Excuse me," she mewed, "I'm feeling a little emotional right now."

"When you've learned to detect intruders in your conscious-ness in that viaduct you call a mind," Et said to X-it, wanting to smack Cat, "I'll tell you who I am."

"Let's get back to the story shall we?" Cat said, speaking out loud, smoothing over the ripples she felt were coming her way if she did not stop crying.

"Yes," X-it said, relieved that the moment had passed. He looked at Word. "Tell us how you came to be under the bus."

Thirteen

"It wasn't the great storm of 2008 that killed my mother," Word said, without emotion, matter-of-fact, this is the way it was, this is the way it is, this is the way it *will be*. "Our –" she said, her voice changing as she spoke bitterly – "*Our* political masters and the Lunatic Eight killed her and ever since they have been trying to kill me."

"I was eight years old," Word continued quietly, looking at Et, then at Cat, and finally at X-it. Smiling at him, speaking softly, she said, "X-it and I have been together day and night ever since."

"In another world, in another time, we might have had a different life," Word continued, without a trace of the child she once was finding her way back to life. "We might all have. But here in this world, on this planet, it's the way it is, and the way it will be if we don't stop our political masters and the Lunatic Eight."

"I know the world's fucked-up," X-it said, "but being with you –"

His voice cracked as he tried to finish the sentence. "I can't imagine –"

Word reached up from where she was sitting on the rug

by the Fire and grasped his hand, and Cat covered up that she was close to an emotional meltdown by stretching one paw after another, left-right, front-back, before padding over to X-it and jumping up on his lap. She licked his other hand, the one that Word was not holding, with her rough tongue before turning several times in precarious circles, balancing on X-it's bony knees, and making herself comfortable.

"Are you here to mooch?" X-it asked her, glad of the distraction.

"That too," Cat said, "more like a smooch."

Word laughed letting go of X-it's hand and settling back on the rug.

Et smiled too and then when the moment was past she looked at Word. "Go on," she said, matter of fact. "Why did the political masters and the Lunatic Eight kill your mother? And, how did an eight year old girl manage to stay alive for another twelve years when they were – are – also trying to kill you?"

Cat made an excruciating screech similar to the sound she would make if one of the Lunatic Eight had stomped on her tail.

"Do you have to be so tactless?" she asked, narrowing her yellow eyes to slits and scowling at Et.

"Quiet!" Et commanded making the Walls wobble.

"We were inland, closer to Baton Rouge than New Orleans," Word said, ignoring the interchange. "There was a –" she hesitated "secret research facility there and my mother had flown from

New York – she always took me with her – a few days before the storm to attend an urgent meeting, that was held in the closely guarded facility. There were scientists, philosophers, and linguists from around the world. They were all renowned and venerable scholars who studied the nature of the Universe, but they were like aunts and uncles to me. I'd known them since I was a baby and I loved them. They were kind and generous and made up for my not having a dad."

Again Word paused, but her voice did not waiver. "The meeting had been hastily arranged and they knew they were in great danger – not from the storm – but from the code breakers who worked for the – Lunatic Eight."

"They were the Truth Keepers," Et said, "guarding ancient texts from corruption. They were – special – they shared a gift – every one of them could trace their ancestry back to the time of the first sign in the Universe – when the first signs were made so that others could read them."

"You knew them?" Word asked.

"Not as well as the Truth Keepers who went before them," Et said, looking sad. "The world can make you weary and I have not been so vigilant in recent years. I knew they were meeting. I should have been there to protect them."

"Could you have saved them?" Word asked.

"I am an observer," Et said, "I am not supposed to interfere. But I regret not –" she hesitated. "It was a mistake."

"A dilemma," Word said, looking at Et intently. "My being here, X-it being here – you *are* interfering now."

"I know," Et said. "It's why I was angry with Death when she brought you here. And X-it. You know just by being here you've – *we've* – changed the future."

"You've kept me alive," Word said, nodding. "I'm grateful."

"How did your mother die?" Et asked again, and this time Cat jumped down off X-it's lap and jumped up on Et who stroked her with her claw-like hand, and as she began to imagine the turn the world would take when she listened to Word's story, her fingers began to straighten.

Fourteen

"Truth Keepers were metaphor makers but also metaphor *breakers*," Word said. "If you seek the truth you destroy the metaphors used by the political masters and the Lunatic Eight to imprison people's minds and make them fearful."

"For example, man's metaphor for Death," X-it said, looking affectionately at Cat. "I never thought about it before but the idea that Death is a vicious ghoul coming to get us is not true."

"Grotesque!" Cat said sounding deeply offended. "Frightens everyone. There's nothing to fear. I've never hurt a living thing!"

"Shhh," Et said, stroking Cat's hat with a beautiful hand that seemed to be translucent and blue.

X-it could not take his eyes off her. He still thought of Et as an Old Crone, which she no longer was and he realized now had never been.

"The lives of the Truth Keepers have always been complicated," Word said, aware that Et's face was less wrinkled and turning sky blue.

"Once the first sign was made the Truth Keepers had to protect it." Et said, "and they did so for millions of years before the ones who became the political masters even found out there were signs in the Universe."

"My mother told me it was always difficult for them," Word said. "They were scholars, learned men and women, including my mother, seeking the truth and finding ways to record it, and guarding ancient texts and passing them from one generation to another."

"And the truth they recorded in ancient texts does not fit with the official texts of the illusion mongers who are now our political masters – who lied to gain power and now lie to keep it," X-it said, joining in the conversation.

Again Word took his hand. "Without X-it," she said. "The Lunatic Eight who control the political masters would have killed me long ago. When I was younger I used to joke that X-it gets-it." She laughed. "Now I'm more respectful of his gifts."

"My parents used to call me X-it when I was very young because I would draw something and then cross it out," he said. "Somehow they turned this negative act into something positive. They'd say something like, 'Such a great picture! Are you going to put an X on it?' And the negative became a positive – get it?"

"They get it," Word said, squeezing his hand. She was sure Et knew the whole story and was really interested in what she knew. X-it too.

"What happened to your mother?" Et asked again, returning to the story that was so difficult for Word to tell.

"We arrived two days before the storm and stayed at the compound – the research facility," she said. "The Truth Keepers were arriving constantly and there were many hand wringing conversations whispered in the stacks of the great library that filled the entire ground floor of the compound.

"An ancient sign had surfaced after thousands of years of being hidden and the political masters and the Lunatic Eight were searching for it.

"The Truth Keepers were used to being watched and if caught interrogated, and in the past, tortured and killed. How any of them stayed alive is beyond me."

"No it isn't," X-it said smiling. "They stayed alive the way you stay alive because they were vigilant and had people protecting them in the same way that you are vigilant and I protect you."

Word nodded.

"I remember the sound of water flowing," she said, "and the sound of crickets chirping and every insect imaginable making such a din I couldn't sleep. I just wanted to listen to them and wait for the every so often croak of the frogs.

"My mother thought I was sleeping," Word continued. "There was a knock at the door and my mother opened it. I could hear urgent whispering – something like 'Is it hidden? Is it safe?'

"I sat up and watched as she took a package from the wall safe and put it in the old tin in my knapsack where I kept precious things – some stones, a dead flower, the exoskeleton of a beetle, and don't laugh, some of my baby teeth. The package – wrapped in oiled paper and tied up with an old piece of string – fit right in and looked like a child's precious thing.

"'What's happening?' I asked.

"'We have to leave quickly,' she said. 'Hurry. Put your sneakers on. Turn off the light.'

"I was wearing shorts and a t-shirt and hadn't undressed so I quickly put on my sneakers and we climbed out the window so quickly I didn't have time to think about my bear that I'd left behind. Alarms were going off. People were running. Shouting. There were cries of pain. Someone screaming. My mother ran with me tree-to-tree to the high fence that surrounded the compound and told me to climb over.

"'Up you go,' she whispered. 'Quick!'

"Terrified. I climbed. The fence was usually electrified but the generator must have been destroyed. I could hear trucks approaching with searchlights and the deafening sound of guns being fired, Sick-Reapers shouting orders, people crying.

"'Come on!' I whispered anxiously to my mother when I reached the top of the fence and before I climbed down the other side.

"'I can't go with you!' she whispered, anxious and afraid. 'I have to stay and help the others,' she said. 'Jump!' she whispered fiercely, and then gentle and pleading. 'Please hurry! You have what they are looking for! Keep it safe!' I jumped and heard her say 'I love you' as I landed on the other side of the fence. 'I love you!' she said again and I knew she was saying goodbye. 'Remember you're a Truth Keeper – the only one left. You must survive.'"

Word stopped. No one spoke.

Cat's front paws were covering her head and she was making gurgling sounds, moaning and crying.

"She blew me a kiss before turning and running back into the shadows away from where I was standing on the other side of the fence.

"She never looked back at me so they wouldn't know where she'd been. When she reached the building she opened and slammed the door and made it look as if she had just come out of the building. A military truck came around the side of the compound and shone a spotlight on her. She put her arms up to cover her eyes. Then I heard gunfire and she fell. I watched one of the men with a gun go over and kick her to see if she was dead. I wanted to cry out, scream at them for killing my mother, but I did what she wanted me to do. I ran."

Fifteen

"After I saw them kill my mother I started running and I heard a huge explosion," Word continued. "I looked back and saw they'd blown-up the library, which was filled with the irreplaceable ancient texts that my mother loved so much. Pages of very old books were falling from the sky. A few pages landed near me and small pieces of vellum fell like confetti and I picked them up quickly and ran on. When I stopped to catch my breath I slipped them singed and crumbling into a notebook in my backpack."

"Do you still have them?" Cat asked, stretching out on the rug by the Fire as if the question did not have any consequences.

"Hush!" Et said, "just for once don't interrupt".

"Well, do you?" Cat asked, ignoring Et and taking on her Bat persona.

"I still have them," Word said. She hesitated, "and the package."

"Here?" Bat asked, nonchalantly hanging upside-down swinging from the mantle.

"No," she said, looking worried. "Not here."

"What happened next?" Et asked, looking furiously at Death.

"What's with the bat?" Word asked.

"I was getting too comfortable," Death said. "All that fur."

"Shall we get back to what happened on the bus?" Et said, not used to interruptions.

"Besides," Death said, "Et has turned blue."

"Why?" X-it asked.

"Because we may be running out of time," Word said, looking at Et who now looked more like a painter's rendition of the sky in the early morning light.

"We're *out* of time," Et said, smiling sadly.

"What do you mean," X-it asked, nervous about the possibilities. "Are you saying we have somehow left the galaxy? Universe? And that the spacetime continuum no longer applies? *Or –*" X-it looked at Word and then at Et. "Or that we've reached *the end* of time?"

"Smart!" said Death giving up Bat and returning to being Cat. She padded over to where X-it was sitting and rubbed against his legs.

"Are we *out* of time?" Word asked quietly looking intently at Et who seemed to be less blue. "Or have we reached *the end* of time?"

"Both," Et said, her claw hands returning, "but we might be able to *suspend* time a little longer, and if we are very clever, when the moment comes, we might be able to *alter* time."

"Can we delay?" Word asked. "I'm not ready."

"Me neither," X-it said, then he added, "Ready for what?"

"You must have worked out by now that we are stuck in a split second," Et said back in her Old Crone form, looking first at Word and then at X-it. "The longer we stay in this moment in time the more likely it is some Super Recognizer – some advanced A-I programed to sweep human consciousness – will find us."

"When we leave this split second," X-it asked, his heart beating faster and starting to sweat, totally getting it. "Will we be back in the water?"

"No," Et said. "Not quite."

"I'm not ready!" X-it said, standing and whisking Cat up and cuddling her.

Flames from the Fire shot up the chimney and the Four Corners prepared for whatever happened next.

"Can we delay?" Word asked.

"We will stand a better chance if we go back undetected," Et said, "rather than being forced back because we're under attack."

"Agreed," Word said. "But we'll stand a better chance if we're ready. It would help, I think, if we could tell you what happened to us and how I ended up in the Hudson."

"You never know," X-it said, "there might be some part of the story – of what happened to Word and me – because I jumped in the river to save her – that'll clue us in to – to what to do when this bubble bursts – if you see what I mean."

"I do indeed," Et said, smiling at X-it. "Let's get back to the story."

"I heard three more large explosions but I didn't look back," Word said, picking up the thread, relieved to be staying in the split second. "I also heard automatic weapons being fired and there were military vehicles speeding along the road I was following. The headlights of the vehicles actually made it possible for me to see the road as they flashed by. I kept in the shadows – it was really helpful when the road was lit up because I could see the places where there was deep water and avoid them.

"It took three days for X-it to reach the buses where he waited in the line for hours," Word said.

"I saw the buses just by chance in the parking lot of Walmart that had been totally destroyed by the storm. So many of the people standing in line for buses seemed to be in a confused state, as if they were not sure what was happening. It was easy to crawl underneath the nearest bus, which was parked close to some trees where the lower branches were scraping the windows.

"I knew I couldn't come out from under the bus without the woman standing behind X-it seeing me," Word said, "but she was brown-skinned and wearing Mardi Gras beads."

"When we were on the bus," X-it said, "she told us the beads meant a lot to her because of the good times she'd had with her kids at Mardi Gras, so she put them on as the water was rising in the Lower Ninth Ward of New Orleans, flooding her home."

"More military were arriving," Word said. "High-ups – giving orders to search for a girl they thought might try to get on a bus. They had a photo of me and I thought I was going to die like my mother. But I remembered what she'd said. I was the last Truth Keeper and I had to keep whatever was in that package safe."

"By then I had been cleared to board the bus we were lining up next to," X-it said. "Soldiers were walking towards us and the woman whispered to call her Grann and with her back to the soldiers she pulled an old yellow 'Happy Mardi Gras' t-shirt out of the plastic garbage bag she was carrying and gave it to Word."

"I put it on over my clothes and it came almost to my knees," Word said. "I remember it had a cartoon face with a Mardi Gras mask and a harlequin hat on it and I liked that."

"The driver of the bus arrived," X-it said. "And a soldier came up and gave him a list to check people getting on the bus."

"'Git!' the woman said, giving us a push and putting some strands of beads over my head," Word said. "Then she started crying and wringing her hands calling on God to help her because she'd been left with her grandchildren to look after."

"It was brave of her," X-it said. "So cool."

"She whispered, 'Remember I'm your Grann'," Word said.

"'You've got the same mother but different fathers.'"

"We climbed on the bus and she started yelling and swearing that she needed help to get on," X-it said, "and the bus driver gave her a hand. Then the soldier started swearing at the driver but by that time Grann was on the bus and moving down the aisle behind us."

"Grann kept scolding us and telling us to keep moving," Word said, "and when we were a couple of rows from the back of the bus she told us to sit down."

"She dropped some plastic bags and a duffle bag on the seat behind us," X-it said, "and she dumped the garbage sack on my lap. 'Put this under your sister's seat for Grann,' she said, loud enough for those around us to hear."

Word picked up the story her eyes wide open as if it was just happening. "'Wait!' Grann said. 'I'm going to be cold' and she opened the garbage sack on X-it's lap and started pulling out damp smelly clothes until she found the t-shirt she wanted, and then she reached across and took my backpack and shoved it to the bottom of the garbage bag and started putting all the clothes back in the sack.

"People were trying to get by and one man cursed at her and she cursed back and bending over further she shoved the garbage bag under the seat in front of me and standing up she looked around at the people now sitting around us and said, 'Don't like the smell of my washin'? Maybe you should git off the bus!' And with that she sat down occupying two seats and making sure that nobody made a fuss."

"Then," X-it laughed, still impressed by what Grann did next, "she started swearing big time and bending forward she pulled a piece of paper off the bottom of her shoe. It was the list the soldier had given to the bus driver. She smoothed it out and swore again as – apparently by accident – she tore the list just where my name was written. Then she spat on her fingers and rubbed the paper as if trying to use spittle to glue it together. Then she got up and squeezing by the other people on the bus, upsetting many of them, she made her way to the front of the bus and gave the bus driver the almost unrecognizable list."

"The bus driver thanked her!" Word said, laughing. "He hadn't reported that he'd lost it. He was too frightened."

"Grann told us later," X-it said, "she knew he'd be grateful to her for giving him the list back – even if it was dirty, torn, and some names incomprehensible."

"She also said that many of the people on the bus knew she was hiding us," Word said. "Many of them knew her and she was revered by many in her community."

"The people on the bus helped her protect us," X-it said, agreeing with Word.

"We got stopped several times," Word said, smiling, "and it was always a collaborative act of deception to save our lives."

Sixteen

"Erectile dysfunction!" X-it yelled. "Cat's tail! Wank! Wank! Wank!"

"Hacked!" Cat said, springing up on X-it's lap. "Going in!" But she landed on his empty chair. X-it was no longer there.

"Where'd he go?" Word said, the surprise in her voice rapidly changing to fear. She scrambled to her feet, aware the Four Corners were moving, the Walls were rippling, and somewhere the bird was screeching, as she stood staring at X-it's empty chair.

Cat was shattered. She looked like an alley cat again covered in mange and weeping sores. "My fault," she said in a hoarse whisper, "I should have been on the prowl and I wasn't."

"Where'd he go?" Word asked again. Ignoring the lamenting Cat she turned to look at Et but her chair was also empty.

"Where's Et?" she asked, her voice rising.

"Should have known!" Cat exclaimed, her fur less mangy. "Et's got X-it," she said. "He'll be all right," she added, but Word caught the doubt in Cat's voice and felt her scabs oozing as she rubbed against her legs.

No energy left, Word sat on X-it's chair and Cat padded back to the rug and started licking a sore on her stretched out right front paw.

"Erectile dysfunction?" Word said. "Cat's tail? Wank? Wank? Wank?" She looked at Cat. "What's with that?"

Cat stopped licking. She gave Word a Cheshire Cat lopsided grin. "Short story," she said. "X-it had been hacked when I brought him to Et. There was an intruder in his consciousness. I attacked him –"

"The hacker?" Word asked.

"No X-it," Cat said. "I clawed his face. He screamed 'fuck Cat' and a whole lot of other crazy stuff and it was enough to get him reassigned from an EDM – Extremely Dangerous Male, to EDP – Extremely Dangerous Psychotic."

"Okay, I got it," Word said. "You made it so they thought he was crazy, but what's with the erectile dysfunction?"

"Crazy talk," Cat said. "X-it was – *is* – smart. He had to do two things at once. First communicate with me that he had been hacked. Second communicate that he was psychotic to the hacker."

"He's something else," Word said, appreciatively. "He confirmed his EDP biometric profile and alerted you that he was being hacked. I'm impressed. And wank?"

"I'd told him when I was mooching in his consciousness to watch my tail," Cat said, her Cheshire smile less lopsided. "One swish for the presence of an intruder in his consciousness, two for danger, three for him about to be terminated."

"The wank went with" – Word smiled – "the condition he was describing."

"He'd never detected his consciousness being attacked before," Cat said. "It must have been a deadly hack of his mind-brain continuum."

"I have to ask," Word said looking intently at Cat, "is there any chance they killed him?"

"Do *not* forget," Cat said, "who I am," finishing the sentence in her persona as the Grim Reaper.

"Could he die without you?" Word asked.

"Nobody dies without me," Death said. "I am always there – it's why this split second is so – I'm trying to find the word – I know terrible things are happening but to be stuck – as it were – in this split second with you and with X-it is such a – a – a wonderful thing for me."

"And Et?" Word asked.

"I've known her forever," Death said, once again Cat. "She's taking care of X-it. She got him away quick. He's probably in the same room where Et kept you safe."

"I heard the bird screech," Word said, remembering the bird that had watched over her.

"The bird knew the moment I knew, so did the Four Corners, every animate and inanimate –" Cat was stuck for a word "– *thing* – in this split second went on high alert the moment X-it signaled what was happening."

"And Et?" Word asked.

"Yes," Cat said looking at Word. "She knew. You must know by now that her part in all this is – is – is complicated."

"If the hacker was still in X-it's consciousness when Et took him –?"

"It will not have survived," Cat said decisively. "Fortunately I do not have to be present at the death of an A-I, nor when their motherboards die."

"Is that significant?" Word asked.

"Et will have traced the hacker back to its source," Cat said. "It'll be lights-out for many Super-Recognizers in their surveillance installations and it's even possible that millions of people will get their consciousness back."

Seventeen

Word sat in X-it's chair thinking about the moment when he was there and then not there. It was tough keeping up her own safeguards against being hacked and also living constantly with the threat of invisible enemies existing undetected in X-it's consciousness. The thought that if hackers were collecting data on everything he did, they were also collecting data on what she did, was always on her mind. Suddenly it was all too much.

"I'm grateful for this split second too," Word said to Cat. "X-it is safe with Et and I have a moment to *just exist* without being overwhelmed by the nightmare of living."

"Exactly," Death said, appearing for a liberating moment as her psychedelic Bowie self before returning to the more comforting persona of Cat. "But what's the alternative?" she asked, adding a hasty, "don't go there."

"Sometimes I wonder if being a Truth Keeper in this day and age makes any sense at all?" Word said, as much to herself as Cat.

"Of course it makes sense," Cat said. "It's the *only* thing that makes sense – you don't seem to realize that because you are a Truth Keeper you might save the people who still live in this world."

"Protecting ancient works and finding lost scribal copies has occupied scholars for millennia," Word said, looking pensive. "My mother would get so excited about the discovery of an early philological construction. Now digital texts have subverted the truths of ancient works and there is an all-out assault on the people – the Truth Keepers – who know something about these books of ancient truths."

"Kill them all!" Cat said turning into the Ginger Tom, the most malevolent of the Lunatic Eight, but keeping her whiskers, as well as her tail, which turned orange. Then turning back into Cat again.

"Don't do that!" Word laughed. "It's not funny!"

"Gotta laugh," Cat said, changing from black to marmalade. "What do you think of my yellow hair?"

"Stop it!" Word said, trying not to laugh. "You're making me nervous. I met that one in Manhattan once, in Central Park, near what's left of Columbus Circle –"

"The Ginger Tom?" Cat asked.

"Yes!" Word said, her skin creeping. "Terrifying."

"Someone shouted, 'It's the Ginger Tom!' and people started cheering and clapping. A crowd surrounded him and his bodyguards, and his personal militia looked nervous but less threatening than they usually did when they kept the people back.

"In the crowd people shouted, 'We're with you Ginger Tom!'" Word said, shaking her head. "I've no idea why he liked the people calling him that, but he smiled and waved, and taking a baby from her mother's arms he held her up and the crowd clapped and someone said, 'Isn't he great!' as he gave the baby to one of the militia and said something to him. In full riot gear the militia man took the baby back to her mother who was holding her arms out but instead of giving the baby back to her mother he grabbed her arm and pulled her out of the crowd and took her off."

"I remember," Cat said, sores appearing.

"But still the crowd didn't get it," Word said, trying to move on and not think about what must have happened to the mother and her baby. "The Ginger Tom was a wild man with enormous power and people flocked to him.

"'I'm bursting for joy when I hear him!' a woman cried.

"'He speaks his mind!' a man said.

"'I believe in him!' a woman said.

"What was taking place was an insurgence," Word said. "A natural phenomenon. He was giving people emotional satisfaction, exploiting the simmering tensions in society.

"The other side of the Ginger Tom is that he is a shark gobbling up everything he encounters and people don't see it. They followed him blindly. They *adored him*.

"Other members of the Lunatic Eight were operating in other megacities around the world and young people knew less about them. But the opulent and immensely rich Ginger Tom lived in New York City. He controlled all of the commerce there.

The Freaky Geek – the richest man in the world – worked on A-I until A-I worked on him. The Posh Boy from Eton who was also called the 'Elitist Twit' endowed the rich and ravaged the poor – he brought back feudalism. And Tricky Dickey, the Media Mogul –"

"What happened next?" Cat asked, glancing at Et.

"A Sick-Reaper was in the crowd and he went up and said something to the Ginger Tom," Word said. "And the Ginger Tom looked straight at me and I was sure he knew I was the book he was looking for.

"The Ginger Tom pointed at me and said something to one of his bodyguards who was standing next to him in riot gear. I was terrified, but a man in the crowd started yelling 'books!' He shouted, 'Only ignorant fanatics would destroy the wisdom in books! Truth is power! Your click bait's not working!'"

"Brave of him," Cat said, unsheathing her front claws to inspect them.

"He *was* brave," Word said. "The Sick-Reapers had dogs but they lost interest in me. They looked at the Ginger Tom and he nodded, and then he turned and walked with his bodyguards – thug protectors – to a helicopter that was landing in Sheep's Meadow. The man who was shouting 'really bad people are destroying all the books' was in his twenties, couldn't have been more than thirty, muscular and strong. He fought back when four of the Ginger Tom's thugs attacked him, but they beat him to the ground. Then they decapitated him right there in front of everybody in Central Park."

"He was protecting you," Cat said, standing by the Fire leaning on the mantle in her Bowie-Gaga psychedelic garb.

"You think?" Word asked, not taking any notice of Death's insistence on self-expression to overcome her fear of herself – in other words her fear of dying.

"I do," Death said, shrouded in a black gossamer cape of mourning. "He was a Truth Protector. His mission was to protect the last Truth Keeper – you – at all cost. He gave his life for you. I was there when he was decapitated."

"So many people have died," Word said. "I'm not sure any of us are going to survive."

"Our political masters and the Lunatic Eight are omnipresent," Death said. "The Ginger Tom, the Freaky Geek, the Posh Boy, and the others – wicked evil men. The A-I and Sick-Reapers – the Super-Recognizers – in their militias hack in and exploit human weaknesses to pacify people. Ultimately the goal is to return those who're still alive to feudalism," Death said, fixing the folds in her gossamer cape. "You're the last great threat to them."

"I keep thinking about what happened by the river," Word said, shivering even though the room was warm and the embers of the Fire were radiating heat. "I had to make a decision and the choice was to face the men who'd caught me or jump in the river."

"You survived," Death said, appearing again as Cat. "They were vicious. If they'd –"

"– Don't go there."

"You've always known really bad people are following you," Death said, softening what she was going to say. "But did you know I've been following you too?"

"Why?" Word asked, not getting it.

"Simple," Cat said. "If I keep you alive many others won't die."

"Only if we are in time," Word said.

Eighteen

"Split seconds are detectable," Et said, reappearing in her Old Crone state and talking as if she'd been participating in the conversation. "It will not be long now before they have our coordinates."

"Is X-it okay?" Word asked jumping up to give Et a hug.

"Yes," Et said, with her claw hand up. "You cannot touch me!"

Word stopped short. "I can touch Cat," she said, "why can't I touch you?"

"It would be the end of everything if you did," Et said.

"Let me explain –" Cat said.

"No time for that," Et said, decisively. She looked at Word. "You asked about X-it. He's sleeping. There are no intruders in his consciousness. I've done a sweep. Several installations, their A-I and Super-Recognizers have all been rendered inoperable, but others will quickly pick up the slack. Some will malfunction. All are on high alert. They know contact has been made, that you are still alive, and a global search has begun. No A-I or human Super-Recognizer can penetrate the room that you were in and in which X-it is now sleeping. But he cannot come out of the room until we are ready to return to the second in time when Death saved you."

"Can I go and see him?" Word asked.

"No," Et said. "You must have realized by now that he's not actually in a 'room' – it's just a useful metaphor – there is no way in because in your world it does not exist. But you've been there so you know he's okay."

"Understood," Word said. "What happens next?"

"I want you to tell me the whole story," Et said, and then, looking at Cat, "I want you to tell *us* what happened – starting from when you got off the bus. You were eight years old – How did you survive? How did you live?"

"But *you know*," Word said, following it with, "Don't you?" But it was not a question.

"After I tell you will you tell me who you are and what your purpose is?" Word asked. "My mother told me about you but it was a long time ago and if what she said is true –" she hesitated "– I'd like you to tell me."

"I'll tell you what you need to know," Et said. "No more."

"Understood," Word said, sitting down on X-it's chair. "Thank you."

"Okay," Cat said, jumping back up on Word's lap "Let's get back on – no *off* – the bus."

"The storm knocked out all the sub-stations in the Gulf

States *and* many of the backup generators," Word said. "I heard someone on the bus say there were also program malfunctions and software errors, so the A-I's were of no use and the Super-Recognizers were told to stop trying to fix their computers and go look for any Truth Keepers who might have survived the purge."

"But their primary mission," Cat said, "was to find the little girl with the backpack who had escaped from the compound."

"Exactly," Word responded.

Et pointed a crooked finger at Cat, "One more comment from you and I'll make you sit in a corner!" The Four Corners readied themselves, becoming cavernous.

"We'd been travelling for a few hours," Word continued, as Cat ignored Et and tucked her front paws. "When the bus was stopped at a checkpoint with steel barriers, police or military in riot gear as if they were responding to a national security disaster and two Sick-Reapers got on the bus." Word looked at Et and she had difficulty getting through the next sentence. "One was carry-ing my teddy bear that I'd left in the room when my mother told me to get my shoes on quick."

Word stopped. Her eyes filled with tears and her breathing quickened. The embers of the Fire turned grey in sympathy and for a moment the Walls and Four Corners tied themselves up with black ribbons. Word sat stroking Cat until her breathing slowed and she got her voice back.

"In my mind I was putting on my shoes, running with my mother. I heard the gun, I saw her fall, and the library explode in flames," Word said, almost in a whisper. Then her voice got louder. "One woman near the front of the bus started telling them she'd seen a young girl standing on her own in a line for one of the other buses, and a man sitting a few seats back said he'd seen her too. Then someone else said they'd seen a girl in another line with a backpack and that she must be the one they were looking for. I was so terrified I started retching and X-it quickly jumped up and Grann immediately started yelling that her granddaughter was sick.

"'Git out the way!' Grann shouted at X-it, leaning over and hauling me out of my seat as I retched again and started crying. 'Bring that garbage bag!' she told X-it as she took my hand and walked in front of me pulling me down the aisle of the bus retching. Just as we got to the row of seats where one of the Sick-Reapers was standing questioning a woman passenger, I vomited not only on myself but also down his leg.

"He cursed and Grann cursed him back, '*Beck moi tchew!*' – *Kiss my ass!* – as she pulled me along, commiserating, 'It's okay baby, Grann's got another t-shirt you can put on.'

"X-it followed with the garbage sack of clothes and Grann's other plastic bags saying something like, 'I don't know which bag Grann needs.' When the other Sick-Reaper stopped him and opened the big garbage sack X-it said he held his breath – partly because the clothes inside smelled so bad but mostly because my backpack was at the bottom hidden under the moldy clothes. The Sick-Reaper looked inside the plastic sack and I heard him swear 'Jesus Christ!' at the stench and he told X-it to get the garbage sack off the bus.

"The people on the bus must have vouched for us being Grann's grandkids," Word said, "and the military and riot police at the checkpoint must've presumed we'd been cleared, because they left Grann alone as she took take care of me. Then we started walking."

"Was X-it also sick?" Cat asked, untucking her front paws and stretching them out so she could inspect her claws.

"He didn't throw up but he had a really bad stomach ache for a couple of days," Word said.

"Clever," Cat said. "It was the pralines."

"The one's Grann gave us?" Word asked.

"She knew at some point she'd need to get you off the bus and what better way for a quick exit than a sick kid," Cat said, this time turning her head to look at Word and giving her the best of her lopsided Cheshire smiles. "You cooperated by getting sick at the precise moment when the Sick-Reapers got on the bus!"

"Grann never told us she was a Truth Protector but she must have been," Word said, looking at Et, whose skin now had a hint of blue.

Et nodded. "She was very special," she said.

"You'd better fast forward," Cat said, not wanting to dwell on what had happened to Grann. "There's only so long Et can stretch a split second."

Nineteen

"The journey from Baton Rouge to New York City was really fun," Word said. "I know that must sound awful, but there was no time for me to think about what'd happened to my mother. She'd given me a mission – to keep the package in my backpack safe – and she'd told me I was the last Truth Keeper. I wanted to do my best to protect the package and I began to think of myself as a Truth Keeper."

"A huge responsibility," Et said.

"Millions of people were moving north away from the three hurricane states that had been devastated, not only by the storm, but also by catastrophic 'accidents' – the carefully orchestrated man-made destruction set in motion by the powerful global corporations that were morphing into our political masters."

"More people lost their lives in those catastrophic 'accidents' than lost their lives in the storm," Death said, trying to maintain her Cat persona, "It was very distressing. Exhausting really. I was overcome with grief but –"

"Yes, we know you suffered," Et said, in a matter-of-fact, let's-get-on-with-it-shall-we? voice. She looked at Word who, returning her gaze, was struck by how blue Et had become.

"We hid in full view of the Sick-Reapers who *didn't* recognize us," Word said, "Grann was questioned many times but we'd become a make-shift family and we behaved as if we had been together forever. Also, Grann had put my pukey t-shirt at the top of the plastic garbage bag," she said smiling at Et, "and every time we were stopped by a militia or the police and Grann was told to open the sack they gagged, and calling her names that I won't repeat they told her to close it up.

"Grann called them names and told us they were racist," Word said. "She said she was Creole, that she could trace her ancestors back hundreds of years to the West Coast of Africa, that they were brought in chains to New Orleans and sold as slaves, and that their blood became mixed with the slave owners who raped her great, great grandmothers and her great grandmothers. She also said that one of her great grandfathers was French and that she had indigenous blood from the native tribes who inhabited the Delta.

"'I am the Earth,' she'd say to X-it and me. 'My heart is the Delta and my arteries the great rivers that flow into the Delta and my veins the tributaries that flow through the wetlands and into the sea. But to those dumb Super-Recognizers I am just a stupid old woman.' Then her eyes would become slits and her skin would get darker and she would look at X-it and at me and cussing she'd say, 'They should be careful because even when she's asleep this old black woman can out think them, and I am strong enough to wrestle ten of them to the ground'. Then she'd say, 'Dead they'll be if they mess with me.'"

"Better fast forward," Cat said. "What happened when you got to New York City?" – adding – "Et's in a hurry."

"I know we don't have much time but I want to tell you how incredible the people were who helped Grann get X-it and me to New York City," Word said, looking at Et, who was totally blue.

"Stay in your feline form," Et said pointing a long slim finger at Death, "or you will have no form at all."

"First responders from across the country were establishing emergency shelters for evacuees who were moving north because of the total devastation of the southern states," Word said, hurrying on. "But we avoided all shelters and food kitchens. Grann said we'd find another way to get to New York. So we stayed with families Grann knew and travelled in cars with northern license plates, keeping off the highways that were jammed with trucks travelling south carrying huge drainage pipes, electrical generators, and heavy duty building materials.

"There was one stretch of highway that we couldn't avoid, and so we travelled north as the trucks travelled south in a jam that stretched for hundreds of miles.

"Grann pointed out that the company names on these trucks were the global corporations owned by our political masters. She had us keep a tally and X-it and I counted the trucks and played a game to see who could spot the most corporate logos – but there were only five. It's important because it was the first time X-it and I made the connections between the hunting down of the Truth Keepers and the Lunatic Eight – the rich and powerful men who took over the world just a few years later.

"When we stopped at a diner," Word said, moving on, "Grann would order pancakes, coffee and milkshakes for X-it and me, and she'd talk loudly about the family reunion we'd just come from in North Carolina. She'd get out her digital camera and show photographs of a family gathering that had taken place the previous summer, explaining she didn't have any photos this year because of the 'storm and all.'

"She'd say, 'There's Dee-Dee' – which was the name she gave me – 'Dee-Dee is that you? No, *there* you are!'" Word smiled. "There were so many children in the photos it was impossible to tell one from the other. They were all much of a muchness as far as skin tone and there were several little girls that could've been me.

"We learned when we reached Baltimore that someone on one of the other buses at the Walmart checkpoint and transportation hub near Baton Rouge had reported seeing me, and the driver of our bus had been interrogated and he confessed he'd known I was on the bus. We were told they'd killed him on the spot and a hunt was on for the other people on the bus. But Grann told us they were her people and they would never find them because once we were off the bus they left too. One by one they doubled back into the Louisiana bayous to help with the clean up as if they had been volunteering all along and never been on any bus.

"When we reached New Jersey we stayed in Newark for several nights in an abandoned three story house that had been boarded up because it was unsafe. The families who lived there only went in and out at night through a window in the back of the house.

"There were meetings and heated arguments about my insistence on returning to Manhattan," Word said. "I argued there were a hundred thousand homeless kids in the city, most of them brown or black, light skinned as well as dark, and that X-it and I'd fit right in."

"Kind of different," Cat said. "Don't you think?" Cat said. "You were eight years old but you could already speak, read, and write in multiple languages and in multiple sign systems, ancient as well as modern. You might've looked like them but you were not one of them."

"Do you think I don't know that?" Word responded, irritated with Cat.

"Just sayin'," Cat responded.

"Try not to," Et said.

"And from the age of eight I lived with them," Word said, not willing to let it go, "and X-it did too."

"I have to leave," Et said to Word. "When I come back I want you to tell me what happened when you returned to New York City. In the meantime make peace with that irritating Cat. As strange as it seems she has always tried to protect you."

Twenty

"Why do you keep asking me what's in the package my mother gave me if you already know?" Word asked Cat. She was sitting in X-it's chair with Cat on her lap waiting for Et to come back.

"I keep asking you because I *don't* know," Cat said, sniffing, miffed. "Et does, but she won't tell me."

"How does she know and you don't?" Word asked, surprised by Cat's response.

"She knows because she was there at the beginning of time," Cat said, matter of fact. "She's the consciousness of the galaxy. She gave birth to the Universe, and she was there when the first life-forms on Earth gained consciousness.

"You're making it up!" Word said.

"Of course I'm making it up," Cat said, not very convincingly.

"You're *not* making it up," Word said, sensing Cat was playing with her.

"No, I'm not making it up," Cat said, with a quizzical look

and her usual Cheshire Cat grin.

"That's a lot to take in," Word said.

"Not really," Cat said, looking solemnly at her. "When you look up at the sky and the vastness of space what you're contemplating is the vast consciousness of the spacetime continuum. You can't hold it or contain it – it's not an inert object, it's a living thing. *It's Et.* When you contemplate your own consciousness you can't hold it or contain it. It's not an inert object, it's a living thing – *it's you*, Word."

"Heavy," Word said, trying to get her head around the implications of what Cat was telling her, "Especially if you are the one who has to cope with the death of this unimaginably vast living thing."

"And the end is fast approaching," Cat said, instantly mangy and covered in weeping sores. "Et knows the end is coming," Cat said. "She can go back –"

"And forward?" Word said.

"That's the problem," Cat said. "There is no forward. For the first time in billions of years she cannot travel into the future. Spacetime ends with you."

Word turned her wrist over to show Cat the sign. "My mother said it's an ancient sign for the powers of the human soul. Doesn't matter what language people speak when they see it they all say, "In the beginning was the word."

"And when the end comes there will be no word," Cat said.

She looked up at Word. "There is no future without you."

"You make it sound as if I'm the world's consciousness," Word said.

"I think the first word ever written is in the package that you have protected since your mother gave it to you," Cat said, "and the last words are written on your body."

"Go on," Word said.

"If you had not jumped in the river those men would've done terrible things to you," Cat said, "and then they would have flayed you alive to get what's written on your body and you would have died."

"I embody them as they embody me," Word said.

"Et says the words mean nothing without you," Cat said.

"The words are all chosen so carefully," Word said. "I've always known they are wrapped up with my destiny."

"Your destiny is to save what people think of as time – even though it does not exist – actually to save Et," Cat said. "If you do not save her there will be no one to make time or save time. There will be no ripples or wrinkles in time. A great consciousness will die, and all living things on Earth will die with her."

"I've no idea what you just said," Word said. "So is this the reason you're so neurotic?" she asked. "Don't you think you're exaggerating? Being just a bit too dramatic?"

"I love her you know," Cat said. "We've been together for-ever – well – not quite *forever*. I didn't arrive on the scene until the first conscious soul was dying and Et goes back before that to the very beginning of the spacetime continuum."

"The two of you *must have* been together for a long time – you've got bickering down to a fine art," Word said, still trying to get her head around what Cat was telling her. "Where's Et now?" she asked. "I presumed she was with X-it but –"

"She's on reconnaissance," Cat said. "Checking things out, seeing for herself how close to the end we are, and hopefully figur-ing out what we can do to avert a cataclysmic disaster."

"I keep thinking of Rumi," Word said, surprising Cat with what seemed like a non-segue. "He wrote '*What you seek is seek-ing you.*'"

"And?" Cat asked, irritated by the interruption to her melo-drama.

"I think Et is right when she says we have to go back to the moment I jumped in the Hudson River," Word said. "But I think we have to go back a few minutes before that. Those men had been *seeking* me for a long time. I have to go back and face them to find out what it means to be a *Truth Keeper* – if we're going to find a way to save the future and the spacetime continuum."

Cat looked up at Word, her sores starting to dry up. "Rumi also wrote," she said, "'*And you? When will you begin the long journey into yourself?*'"

"My journey into myself – my own consciousness – began the day they killed my mother," Word said. "Now it's a journey into the deep and meaningful consciousness I share with you and with Et and with X-it."

"Let's celebrate that!" Cat said, springing off Word's lap and appearing as Lady Gaga in a midnight blue, low cut, floor length, taffeta gown. "Isn't life extraordinary!" she said. "Let's hold on to it for as long as we can dear sweet Word. I am so grateful to you. I know Et is too."

"Not sure about the 'dear' and 'sweet' or why you would be grateful," Word laughed. "I didn't ask to be a superhero but it seems that's what I am about to become." She looked seriously at Lady Gaga. "You look very beautiful," she said. "But I hope you won't mind my saying, I like you best when you are a Cat."

"Is this better," Cat said, jumping back on her lap.

"Much," Word said, reflecting on what Cat had told her. "My mother told me she'd been absolutely terrified every moment of her life. But she also said she'd never let anyone keep her from doing a single thing she wanted to do."

"What she wanted to do was read books," Cat said, matter of factly, "and that's the truth."

"True," Word said. "She created her own world but it wasn't a selfish act. She was driven by the knowledge – more than just a belief – that the only way to save the future was hidden in ancient texts."

"I think she was also driven by what happened to your father."

"I believe she also knew what was going to happen to me."

"I agree."

"I wasn't quite truthful when I said I didn't know anything about my dad."

"I know," Cat said. "It's a painful story and you didn't want to repeat it."

"Something like that," Word said, stroking Cat whose coat was now silky. "But if I talk to you about my dad I will also have to talk about my mother and even after all these years it's still hard."

"Understood," Cat said, kneading Word's left leg.

"I'd like to tell you," Word said. "Shall I wait until Et gets back?"

"The Four Corners will tell her," Cat said. "They are in constant communication."

"Really?"

Cat's eyes were closing.

"You're falling asleep!"

"No," Cat said, her eyes opening wide. "I'm enjoying a rare moment of contentment."

Twenty-One

"When I was a little girl I imagined my mother working as an archeologist in North Africa," Word said. "She had ancient texts from Mesopotamia – the cradle of civilization, which no longer exists – and that's where I imagined her working."

"Go on," Cat said.

"Her work *was* very secret, very dangerous," Word said. "I *didn't* imagine that. She told me she'd made a discovery that could change the future of the world. What *I imagined* was that before I was born she was working with the man who would become my father and that together they excavated the site where the discovery was made."

"You were a very precocious little girl," Cat said. "I have to remember you were reading Greek and Latin when you were two years old."

"Hieroglyphs and Sanskrit too," Word said, "just to be accurate. Hieroglyphs are really fun when you are two years old."

"I'll take your word for it," Cat said, laughing at her own joke. "Get it – *word* for it?"

"My mother studied Sumerian, which was an ancient language women as well as men learned to read in Mesopotamia," Word said, dismissing Cat's joke and revealing her enormous capacity for learning. "Many scholars believe Mesopotamians invented writing, making it possible for them to find a new way of looking at the world. My mother was convinced writing was invented many millennia before that."

"Back to your father," Cat said, impatient with Word's history lesson.

"My mother did tell me he was gentle, kind, and very brave," Word said. "In my imaginary account of what happened to my father there was a raid at the archeological site where they were working. There was a spy –"

"They're all louts," Cat said.

"But in my version of their story," Word said, leaning forward and kissing Cat's head, "there was a secret chamber at the dig and my father placed the small oilskin package in my mother's hands, and telling her to keep it safe, he persuaded her to climb down into the chamber. I used to imagine my father in flowing desert robes *embracing* my mother – a hug seemed too ordinary – and telling her it was her only chance of survival. I could almost hear him saying, 'I'll love you till the end of time.' And then guns firing, killing him."

"You have a very vivid imagination," Cat said.

"Wait," Word said, "there's more."

"Go on," Cat said, pretending that the story was too long.

"I used to imagine my mother in the chamber for almost a week," Word said. "My father, being a good man –"

"Are there any?" Cat asked.

"Yes there are," Word said. "You're too cynical. X-it is a good man. Back to the story. I imagined my father had prepared for the attack at the archeological site and my mother had water and food and even clothes – a hijab – money and a passport. I imagined that to the men who killed my father, the entrance to the chamber looked like just a crack between the stones. It was very narrow and a large man could not have got through. My mother made sure that if they shone a light through there were no signs that anyone was in what seemed like a small indent at the entrance. It was not possible for the killers to see at an angle that there was an underground room and that it was cavernous."

"We can take any shape, anywhere, at any time," the Four Corners said in unison, making Word jump. "Apologies for interrupting," they said.

"Let's get back to the story shall we?" Cat said irritated, and sounding very much like Et when she was scolding her.

"I imagined my mother put on the hijab," Word said, not fazed a bit by the talking right angles, "and made her way to Cairo to the hotel where she had a room. Then she became western again and used the passport to travel to Milan and from there to New York where I was born."

"There's no sex in your story," Cat said.

"I was a little girl!" Word said. "I didn't imagine my mother having sex with my father." For a moment Word did not speak. Cat closed her eyes and waited.

"The *real* story was very steamy," Word said, quietly, in a voice that gave away that she was going to tell Cat what really happened when her mother met her father.

"At the beginning of 2000 my mother flew from Milan to Cairo to research some ancient documents that were in the Egyptian National Library and Archives.

"She'd joined the faculty at the University of Milano-Bicocca in 1999 a year after the university was founded and she'd moved from Paris to Milan," Word said. "It was, of course, a cover so she could continue her research on ancient texts that she was convinced would change the future of the world."

The Walls shuddered.

"She stayed at a hotel near the National Library and Archives and received a telephone call from a researcher who said he was on the faculty of Alexandria University and he had some documents he thought she would want to see."

"Did she check his credentials?" Cat asked.

"I don't know," Word said. "Wait. She said she'd met him once before at a conference so she must have known who he was."

"Go on," Cat said.

"She told me they had dinner," Word said.

"And?" Cat asked.

"I don't know what they talked about at dinner but my mother said she was mesmerized by him," Word said.

"Yes?" Cat asked. "Did they?"

"Yes," Word said. "My mother said she wanted me to know I was not an accident. She said she was sure they both knew they were making me. My father went back to her room and it was the most magical night of her life. Her face would flush and her back would arch when she told me about it – as if just the thought of being with him was enough for her to become orgasmic. Now, I imagine that night the way I used to imagine the archeological dig, only it's my mother holding my father's hand as she takes him into her room and they undress together and she runs her tongue over his body and he kisses her breasts and she lies back on the bed and he parts her legs and –"

"Is it like that for you?" Cat asked.

"That's not a question you should ask," Word said, slapping Cat.

"Bad of me," Cat said. "Apologies."

"Do you think it's possible for a memory to be created at the moment of conception – when egg meets sperm?" Word asked. "Do you think in deep memory in my own spacetime continuum there is a trace of the very second when I was conceived? Could that be? Is it possible that traces of my mother's orgasm and my father's ejaculation – the beginning of time and space for me – are still rippling through my body and could be somewhere way back in my consciousness?"

"In the beginning was the word," Cat said. "The beginning was Word."

"I like to think I was there," Word said. "It was the only time they were together. My mother told me they made love all night and my father left at 5:00 a.m. saying he would meet her again at the library," Word said. "My mother packed her overnight bag and checked out of the hotel and arrived at the library at ten o'clock. She said there were officials – high-ups in the government – and police everywhere. The streets around the library were cordoned off but before she knew what had happened they let her through the barricades and escorted her to the library.

"She was told that one of the library's research associates from Alexandria University had been murdered. They'd found him on the steps of the library with his throat cut. The police questioned my mother but she didn't tell them that she had spent the night with the man who had been murdered, so they had no reason to suspect that she was involved in the killing."

"It's a terribly sad story," Cat said, "but for you to have been conceived on such a night of love – and perhaps to even have a memory of the moment you were made – that is very special."

"There's a bit more to the story," Word said. "My mother had booked a flight back to Milan late in the afternoon and the police saw no reason for her to remain in Cairo so she left. When she returned to her apartment in Milan she unpacked her overnight bag and wrapped in her nightdress she found a package – oiled paper tied up with old string – the same one she gave to me. She said that she also found a scrap of paper in her brief case on which my father had written, 'In the beginning was the word. Keep it safe. I love you.'"

"So what was in the package?" Cat asked.

"I don't know," Word said. "My mother never opened it and neither have I."

Twenty-Two

"What happened when you left Newark?" Et asked, appearing as the Old Crone and sitting in her chair as if she'd always been there.

"You're back!" Word said. "Is X-it okay? Can I see him?"

"Yes, he's okay. No you cannot see him," Et said. "The people's camp in the Field at 74th and Riverside Drive that borders the Westside Highway is gone. Destroyed. They sent in the military – more accurately the militia, the Ginger Tom's armed thugs – with tear gas and heavy machinery –"

"The Field where I was living?" Word asked, incredulous that Et had been there. "Everyone called it 'The Jungle' after the camp in Calais that was destroyed in 2016. The young people in the Field were just as vulnerable."

"There was no warning. The people living there – mostly young women, many with children – didn't have time to gather their possessions," Et said. "The ones that protested were beaten and gassed. Some were shot – killing children is now acceptable. Heinous."

"They were looking for me," Word said, in tears.

"Yes," Et said, "but the Field is also too close to the river and what's left of the West Side Highway. The Ginger Tom wanted them out but the hacking of X-it's consciousness may have alerted them to the possibility that you're still alive. They've surrounded the Field with razor sharp barbed wire. It sparkles in the sunlight but would cut people to shreds if they tried to go back to search for their possessions –"

"And the package?" Death asked, taking on her Bat persona and hanging from the mantle.

"It's not there," Word said, shaking her head. She gave Et a worried look. "But it's close by."

Death did a sort of somersault and landed in the hearth on her feet in her glittery red strappy shoes. She spread her bat wings. "I think I'll go and have a look –"

"No!" Et said. "We're too close to the end –"

"Could the end be a new beginning?" Word asked, thinking of a story she'd read in which this question is asked.

"Possibly," Et said. "If Death doesn't have a meltdown at an inopportune moment."

"I love you too," Death said to Et, still caught up with Word's love story.

"I know," Et said. "And if love was an emotion I experienced I would do my best to love you, even though you are a neurotic after-life apparition who feels too much."

"Could we fast forward and not worry about what happened after Newark?" Word asked, still thinking about the destruction of the camp in the Field.

"No," Et said decisively. "X-it was right. We can't change the ending unless we know the whole story. When we leave this split second there will be no turning back. There can be no 'I forgot to tell you' or 'I thought you knew.'"

"Or, 'Where did you hide that package?'" Bat said, spreading her wings, which were sparkling with silver glitter that accentuated the glitter on her red strappy shoes.

"She'll tell you where it is when you need to know," Et said, sharply. "We have to become a thought-collective inhabiting each other's minds –"

"Your mind?" Word said, distracted by Bat. "Is that possible? And if it is possible, do you think X-it could –"

"The Four Corners will come with us," Et said. "We'll need them anyway and they'll only reveal the part of me that is – hypothetically – a metaphor for human consciousness," Et explained, as if that made sense. "For a short time it will seem as if I have a human mind – which I do not," she added, being careful not to sound disparaging. "X-it will be fine. We'll communicate telepathically and have to be vigilant that no A-I penetrates our collective. Death can you handle that?"

"I'm hurt," Bat said, losing her sparkle. "Hurt. You've wounded me."

"Nonsense," Et said. "I'm putting you in charge of repelling hackers."

"Oh, got it," Bat said, jumping up on Et and landing in her feline form on her lap.

"Newark. A quick update." Et said, stroking Cat. "Just the headlines. What happened between 2008 and 2022?"

"What didn't?" Word said. "I'll stick to what happened to X-it and me but you should get him to tell you about his analysis of existential risk before we leave here. It's easy to forget his father was an astrophysicist who for the last ten years of his life studied the possibilities of a cataclysmic or combination of cataclysmic disasters annihilating our species."

"Your species," Cat said. "It's the reason I'm so nervous."

"We'll have that conversation," Et said, "just before we leave the split second."

"Thank you," Word said, "X-it is super intelligent, he's just *not* always super smart."

"The headlines," Et said.

"A car picked us up in Newark and we traveled north on local roads avoiding the New Jersey Turnpike," Word said. "Grann came with us. In Nyack we went into a fast food place –"

"Headlines," Et said.

"I know, but it was delicious," Word said, "and I'm getting

back into the story. There were other kids in the place and we sat down with them. Grann bought huge tubs of fried chicken and lemonade and we all ate together. Grann told the kids we were their cousins from Massachusetts. She told them a convoluted story involving cousins they knew and by the time she finished we were family.

"We all left together," Word said. "Greasy and loaded with sugar, we climbed into a minivan with Massachusetts' plates that was waiting in the parking lot. All the kids had backpacks and they were piled at the back. Mine included. There were also some balloons and a box with the remains of a birthday cake."

Et smiled at Word.

"I know, skip the details," Word said, "but getting back into the city was carefully planned. All traffic on the Tappan Zee Bridge was at a standstill and the police were checking every vehicle with kids.

"Grann did an encore of her Louisiana bus routine," Word said, laughing. "She fussed and swore and the kids whose blood sugar was so high from all that lemonade could have flown across the river. We were waved on and once safely across the river we headed into the Bronx and Grann took us all in a convenience store where the kids bought lots of candy and sodas and got back in the minivan and drove off while we walked down the Grand Concourse with Grann eating Twizzlers."

Twenty-Three

"My mother's obituary was published in *The New York Times*," Word said. "There was a photograph included of her holding me in her arms when I was two or three years old – more baby than little girl. Certainly not recognizable. The obituary stated we had both been killed in the hurricane. My name was given as Parola – the Italian for Word. There was a lot about her scholarship and her university work in Milan. It stated we had no living relatives."

"Questa è la Parola," Cat said.

"I've always had a sense that people I didn't know were watching over me and that they were watching over X-it too," Word said, stroking Cat and smiling, glad she'd given up her appearance as a glittery bat.

"You think?" Cat said, looking across the room at Et.

"Just being here with you –" Word said "– I'm so grateful."

"Any black cats cross your path?" Et asked.

"Better not go there," Cat said, for once advising Et. "Go on," she said to Word, quietly, already knowing what had happened next.

"We lived for the next three years in the Bronx with Grann right out in the open," Word said, remembering black cats. "There were still a few dilapidated houses along the Grand Concourse, which was more like a highway than a city street, and we lived in one of them. Grann knew everyone in the house and nobody came in or went out without her knowing.

"We didn't go to school," Word said. "Grann used to laugh and say if we ever stepped into a school the teachers would know something was up. Somehow she managed to keep us in books. At first she gave us children's books with lots of wonderful pictures and great stories. I'd never had any before and loved them. I'd read one then recite it cover-to-cover, over-and-over.

"'Give me that book,' Grann said one day, taking a book from me not really thinking I was reciting. 'Go on,' she said, opening the book to the title page, 'I'm listening.' And I recited the story word for word and included detailed descriptions of the illustrations on each page. 'Well I'm damned,' Grann said.

"Shortly after that, on a sunny afternoon, a truck arrived with some huge crates filled with what I can only describe as an ancient library. Some of books I recognized as texts my mother studied and they might even have been her books, but Grann said it was best I didn't know where they had come from. X-it found some old books on mathematics and astrology in one of the crates so he was as happy as I was with this unexpected –"

"We're running out of time," Et said.

"We left the Bronx when Grann was killed," Word said, as if it wouldn't hurt so much if she said it quickly, but also signaling to Et not to rush her so much.

"We were walking along the Grand Concourse with Grann," Word said quietly. "About two blocks farther down the street we saw the man who lived in the third floor apartment in Grann's house. I was just about to wave to him when he lit a cigarette. He didn't smoke. It was a signal that there was a security breach."

"Spies," Cat said, repeating her earlier comment. "They're all louts."

"Super-Recognizers," Word said. "Sick-Reapers."

"We watched as two men dodging traffic crossed the Grand Concourse and walked quickly towards him," Word said. "My arm stopped in mid-air. I couldn't put it up or down.

"'Don't look,' Grann said, the fear in her voice audible, as she took hold of my hand and brought my arm down. But it was too late. One of the men had a long steel blade that caught the sunlight then turned red as he stabbed the man who was one of our protectors.

"'*Git!*' Grann said before the knife entered his heart for the second time. 'Not home. *Stay together*. Hide. *Keep it safe.*'

"We'd practiced. We knew we had to get away," Word said. "The light was green. Traffic was moving fast when Grann stepped off the curb and walked out onto the Grand Concourse. X-it had hold of me stopping me from running after her to pull her back and the screeching of brakes drowned my scream. A truck hit Grann and ended up sideways across the road. There was another screeching of brakes as two cars crashed into the side of the truck. Then more screeching brakes as other cars tried to avoid the collision. People were screaming. Running towards the crash and running away from the crash, hiding their eyes and crying. The drivers in the first two cars were badly injured, and there were drivers and passengers in the cars behind them in the pile-up who were also hurt.

"The driver of the truck had got out of the cab and was walking around in a daze. I couldn't see Grann. There couldn't have been much left of her and what was left must have been under the truck. I stood there unable to move. X-it's arms were still around me. When he let go he caught hold of my hand just as Grann had done a few minutes ago. 'Come on,' he said. 'Grann told us to 'Git!'

"The man who lived upstairs was lying on the pavement and the two men were running towards us," Word said. "X-it pulled me into the crowd and we went around the cars that had crashed and crossed Grand Concourse. All the traffic traveling in the opposite direction had stopped and people were getting out of their cars, some running towards the crash to do what they could for the drivers of the two badly smashed cars and the other people who were injured.

"'Don't look back,' X-it said. 'For Grann's sake we have got to get away. Otherwise she died for nothing.'

"'She might not be dead,' I said.

"'She was hit head-on by a truck,' X-it said. 'She's dead.'"

Twenty-Four

"Nothing was the same after Grann died," Word said. "We constantly felt our lives were in danger and there were risks everywhere. There wasn't a moment when we were not vigilant. So many people had died to keep me safe and I wasn't safe. Neither was X-it."

"What about the package?" Cat asked. "Was the package safe?"

"Actually it was *in* a safe," Word said, picking up the thread of the story with an amused smile, and feeling a little less overwhelmed by this retelling of her story.

"Grann and I agreed we needed to find a place that was unlikely to be discovered," Word explained. "Grann had told us many times that we had to be careful because there were Sick-Reapers everywhere. We knew that if we were discovered the backpack had to be someplace else. We knew we'd have to leave the Bronx fast," Word said. "So we worked out an exit strategy. But first we'd have to get the key."

"The key?" Cat asked her interest piqued.

"To the safe," Word said. "We knew what to do. Grann had

said the password must be 'kid friendly' and so we'd settled on 'Twizzlers.'

"Might sound callous but in my mind 'get the key' replaced 'Grann is dead.' I'd done this before when my mother died. I had to 'keep it safe' and 'stay alive.' I would always be Grann's kid but – and I know this sounds silly – I kept saying to myself 'I'm the last Truth Keeper. The future of the world depends on me.'

"We slipped through the crowd – I was in front and X-it about ten feet behind me – and we turned left onto a cross street to the Grand Concourse. Then we turned right and walked together a few blocks along on a street running parallel to the Concourse before doubling back to the Concourse right by the convenience store where we had bought Twizzlers when we first arrived in the Bronx.

"There were customers in the store when we walked inside together. The owner of the store had always called me Dee-Dee but not that day.

"'Jacqueline!' the owner said. 'And Marco! Your grand-mother said you've been a good girl Jacqueline and to give you some Twizzlers! You can have some too Marco.'

"He gave X-it a bag of Twizzlers from the counter display and then he opened a drawer and gave me a bag of Twizzlers that to customers would have appeared the same as X-it's.

"'Don't eat them all at once,' he said. 'The key is to wait a while. The Twizzlers will last longer if you do.'

"'Thank you,' I said. 'I'll eat them later.'

"'Good girl,' he said. 'I know your grandmother would be proud of you.' I nodded. He smiled at me but his eyes were filled with sadness and I was sure he knew Grann was dead."

"What happened next?" Cat asked, with an eye on Et in case she tried to banish her into one of the Corners. "Where did you go?"

"We walked along the street eating X-it's Twizzlers. We headed towards the George Washington Bridge and the path along the Hudson River.

"I should have mentioned," Word said, "while I spent most of my time at Grann's studying the ancient books she'd got for me, I also studied maps and books about New York City. Grann repeated often that if we left the Bronx we should make our way to the Upper West Side.

"We took the path along the river," Word said, "and late in the afternoon we sat on bench overlooking the Hudson and New Jersey on the other side of the river and we opened the Twizzlers I'd been given.

"The key was painted black and wrapped in plastic and taped to one of the sticks of liquorice." Word said. "The teeth of the key were unlike any I'd seen before. X-it said it would have been difficult to make a copy. He was not sure of the metal. Titanium possibly. I wore it on a piece of string around my neck."

"How did you live?" Cat asked, so caught up in the story she didn't care if Et was cross with her.

"'Trust no one,' Grann used to say. 'The world is overcome with treachery but there are good people living in New York City and you'll always find someone willing to help you.'

"Grann was right," Word said. "We had to be constantly vigilant but we met so many wonderful people on the Upper West Side. Everyone looked shabby. Not like the snobby Upper East Side where I lived for the first eight years of my life. We were never hungry. Bought or begged. Fairways, Citerella, Zabar's all fed the community. But all that changed when –"

"Tell us about getting the package back," Et said, keeping Word from jumping ahead.

"We found the jewelry store on Amsterdam and 72nd Street where the safe was supposed to be without any difficulty," Word said, not minding Et. "It was totally unremarkable, the size of a New York shoe repair shop, squeezed in between an ice cream parlor and a diner – it was possible to walk right by and not notice it.

"For X-it and me – so intent on getting the package – it was the perfect spot. Multiple roads meeting – Amsterdam, Broadway, 71st, 72nd, 73rd, two blocks from Riverside Drive and the West Side Highway, Riverside Park and the Hudson River, and in the other direction, Columbus, Central Park West, and then Central Park.

"Grann knew the owner of the jewelry store but she didn't tell him what she wanted to hide in the special safe in his store," Word said. "We'd sit on the benches by the entrance to the 72nd

subway and from there we could watch the store. We knew Grann trusted the owner, but we were still not entirely convinced that he was legit. After agonizing for weeks X-it and I agreed we should retrieve the package.

"We went into the store together. I told the owner, who was tall and bent with an unhealthy pallor and a face of many wrinkles, that I had come to pick up my mother's bracelet." Word said. "He asked me to describe it. I said it was a charm bracelet and that there were four charms on it, each a letter of the alphabet. I said the letters were W-O-R-D. He said, 'In the beginning was the word' and I held out my left arm and turned my hand over so he could read the ancient birthmark on my wrist – *In the beginning was the word.* He lifted a flap in the counter and gestured for us to go through and join him.

"'Come with me,' he said.

"We climbed the narrow stairs and he unlocked a door to the room above the store. There was a table with some mugs and a coffee maker and two chairs, a battered old refrigerator, and two safes. 'Your mother's bracelet is in this safe,' he said, indicating with his right hand the one that I had the key to open.

"'Please –' I said, hesitating and trying to sound deferential, 'I'd like the key to lock the door.' I think it was such a straight-forward request he was taken by surprise. He shrugged and gave me the key. He stood there for a moment and I realized he hadn't understood that I expected him to leave. 'Please wait downstairs,' I said, and reluctantly with another shrug he left and I watched him go down the stairs before I closed the door and locked it.

"X-it immediately started looking for an exit. There was none. The windows had bars on the outside. The only window without bars was in a bathroom at the back of the room with the two safes. The shower was decrepit and used to store stuff. The toilet was filthy and smelled foul.

"'I wouldn't put my arse over that hole!' X-it said, making me laugh, because I was frightened silly. He undid the catch and pushed the tiny window open. Standing on the toilet he looked down.

"'Child's play,' he said, grinning at me. 'Get the backpack,' he said. 'We can do this.' He lifted his sweatshirt and began unwinding the rope that he'd wound around his body. He looped the rope around the toilet bowl turning his head away as he wrapped it around the base of the cistern and tied it. Then he tossed the other end out of the window.

"The jeweler called from downstairs, 'Do you have it?'

"'No,' I shouted, 'Had to pee. Won't be a minute.'

"X-it flushed the toilet.

"I took the key and unlocked the safe," Word said, speaking rapidly as if being chased. "Inside was a smaller safe with a rotary combination lock. Of course I knew the numbers by heart. I pulled open the door and took out my backpack, adjusted the straps, and put it on. I ran into the bathroom and climbed up on the toilet seat. X-it gave me a boost and after a nerve-wracking moment when I got stuck because of the backpack I was through the window and slithering down the rope. We were only one floor up so it wasn't much of a drop. X-it was right behind me. We heard gunshots as we negotiated our way past the trash cans from the surrounding buildings. Once out of sight and the line of fire X-it stuffed his sweatshirt into one of the cans. I took off the backpack, stuffed it in a black canvas bag, and then covered it with the red t-shirt I'd been wearing with a black one underneath. Then we walked out into the crowds of people crossing roads in so many directions – including to and from the subway which is located on two islands one each side of 72nd street where Broadway and Amsterdam meet.

"The gunfire sent people running in all directions and so the usual chaos had become total mayhem," Word said. "It was almost a repeat performance of the Grand Concourse. We walked slowly. X-it asked me if I'd like a hot dog and we crossed 72nd street and went into Gray's Papaya.

"While we were standing getting our hot dogs I said I had to go home to study for a test and we talked about school that day – making it up in case people working there were questioned. 'Two kids were in here but they were on their way home from school – the girl was talking about the test she'd gotta take tomorrow. Seemed worried about it. Didn't look very smart.'

"We could hear police and ambulance sirens and we got our hot dogs and left. We stopped and looked across the street with everyone else before slipping away unnoticed. Within minutes the entire area was cordoned off but by then we were on our way to Riverside Park and the path along the Hudson River.

"We realized later that the jeweler had called up to us with a gun pointed at his head," Word said. "One of the Sick-Reapers had killed him when they ran upstairs and found out we'd escaped through the bathroom window. They were never caught –" Word shrugged, then without looking up she said bitterly, "but *they* caugh*t me* the night I jumped into the Hudson River."

Twenty-Five

"Not much time left," Et said. "How d'you want to proceed?"

"There's *no* time to tell you all that's happened to us," Word said. "We lived small. Practiced being invisible. We always seemed to have a roof over our heads. We stayed in one basement apartment in a brownstone for almost a year while the owner was in Paris. But we were always ready to run, hide, and fight if necessary. Bits of the story are important, some not, but X-it needs to be here –"

"Agreed," Et said. "But when X-it returns he might not be –" she hesitated "– the same, and we cannot risk –" again she hesitated "– our time together in this split second will run out soon."

"Understood," Word said.

"Wait," Cat said.

"Enough!" Et said. "No more questions."

"But she hasn't told us what happened to all those pieces of parchment –" Cat said, not at all phased by Et's sharp tone "– the bits of the old books Word picked up after the library at the compound was blown up."

"I thought you'd have figured that out by now," Et said.

"They're tattooed on my body," Word said pushing Cat off her lap and standing up. She lifted the front of her t-shirt and then turned around and lifted the back. "Each tattoo is an exact replica of all those pieces of parchment and vellum that I saved. I still have the originals but they're very fragile and some are disintegrating. It's very sad but as long as I'm alive the texts will survive. I'm vellum."

It was a heavy moment. They all felt it. Word pulled her t-shirt down and sat back on the chair. Unable to cope with the tension Cat jumped up on Word's lap and used her nose to get her head under Word's t-shirt.

"They're not *all* ancient texts," Cat said with her nose almost in Word's navel, sticking out her rough tongue and giving her a quick lick.

"That tickles!" Word said, laughing, "Don't do that!" She extricated Cat and pulled her t-shirt down. "I've added quotes from other ancient texts, Lucretius of course – I used Montaigne's edition of Lucretius – but also quotes from Marlow and Shakespeare, and Montaigne himself, and more recently Italo Calvino. They're on my body because they are part of my ancestry as a Truth Keeper. There are also lines from writers who are deep in my heart – Langston Hughes, and James Baldwin. Similarly, there are not many women in the ancient texts, so I've added some lines from Jane Austen, Emily Dickenson, Toni Morrison, others too, Maya Angelou, Isabel Allende."

"Why?" Cat asked. "I understand why you would have your

body tattooed with the ancient texts that fell from the sky but why all the others? Just pick up a book and read."

"By the time I was eighteen there were no books," Word said. "From eleven till sixteen I could always find books to read, and once read they remained in my head.

"In the city I could go to libraries, universities, book stores, *and* scavenge for them the way we scavenged for food," Word said. "There were always books in the trash – often bags of book were left out for recycle. Also, there were really great second hand books sold on tables on the sidewalk on Broadway near the 72nd subway.

"Friends gave you books – you gave books to friends – more friends gave you more books," she said. "That's how it was. We had a huge underground book exchange and books were always available.

"In 2016 that all changed. Books started disappearing and friends became reluctant to share them. There were book disposal centers where people could get 5 cents a book the way people used to get 5 cents for collecting plastic bottles and soda cans.

"X-it and I started hoarding books. We had an immense library that we kept in an old subway maintenance depot under Riverside Park just north of the 79th street entrance to the West Side Highway. There were great iron gates but X-it found a way in and we stored our books there in boxes covered with tarps.

"By 2017 the Ginger Tom, the Freaky Geek, and the Posh Boy were blatantly confiscating books. People were fearful and so were the political masters around the world. They knew what was going on but nobody was talking about it," Word said. "Reading books became a crime against our political masters. It was regarded as seditious –"

Word stopped. She looked into the Fire that glowed as if sending warm thoughts to let her know that the embers cared for her.

"The closer we get to leaving the more I want to stay," Word said.

The Four Corners sighed circling the room.

"Me too," Et said.

"This split second is the longest time X-it and I have been apart since we were eight," Word said, she paused, and picked up where she'd left off.

"Cat-*astrophe*," Cat mewed, shakily. "I love Word and I love you, Et. I cannot imagine *being* without you." She jumped off Word's lap and coughed up a fur ball. "What if X-it is hacked and I don't stop it?" Death was dissolving, no longer Cat, no longer Bat, Kiss for a moment, then Lady Gaga, followed by Bowie for several seconds before reappearing as a mangiest of mangy cats.

"It's not good," Cat said, her sores weeping. "When we leave the split second everything will take place in less time than it just took me to go from Cat to Bat and back again." She coughed up another fur ball. "Et," she said. "Forty five million centuries and all we'll have left is a split second? If just *one* of us makes a mistake – *me* for instance or X-it – it will be like a giant asteroid hitting the planet. We'll all be annihilated."

"Instantaneously," Et said, factually. "But it'll be so quick you won't know anything about it."

"Oh that makes me feel a whole lot better!" Cat hissed, the mew gone. "I'm going to stay in my feline form even though I've almost no fur left." She jumped up on Et's lap.

"I might get a whole lot bigger," Cat said, turning and looking up at Et. Black panther? Saber-tooth tiger? Whadyathink?

Et stroked Cat and her fur came back.

"I'll be with you," Et said, still stroking Cat. "This is the first time in forty five million centuries that I've been stuck in a split second, so it's new for me too."

Et gave Cat a quizzical look.

"Better move on quickly to 2022 then X-it will come back," Cat said, avoiding Et's gaze.

"In 2018 there were book purges," Word said, missing the significance of the quizzical look. "Organized militias, mutants with the Ginger Tom's insignia, in full riot gear with balaclavas and face shields, went street-by-street, building-by-building, and apartment-by-apartment, confiscating books and hauling them off to landfills. If anyone protested they were taken away. Rumor had it some people were shot.

"'The wrecking madness in the mind of man,'" Word said, "that's what H.G. Wells called it."

"I'm going to remember that," Cat said.

"Great libraries of precious books were burned," Word said, speaking quickly. "There were big bonfires in Central Park of the rare and irreplaceable books from the Metropolitan Museum of Art. It took almost a week to burn all the books in the New York Public Library at 42nd Street and Bryant Park. It took another week to burn the immense holdings of the Morgan Library, which ranged from Egyptian art to Renaissance paintings, illuminated, literary, and historical manuscripts, early printed books, and old master drawings and prints."

"The Morgan also contained some of the earliest evidence of writing on the planet," Et said. "Ancient seals, tablets, and papyrus fragments from Egypt and the Near East."

"Like the ones tattooed on your body?" Cat asked.

"Yes," Word said. "Some of the earliest evidence of writing still in existence was in the Morgan Library, but I think the very earliest evidence of a sign in the Universe is in the package my mother gave to me."

"Is it safe?" Cat asked.

"Yes," Word said. "It's safe."

"Where?" Cat asked. "What if someone has found it? *And,* if we only have a moment, how are we going to get it back?"

"Shhh!" Et said.

"People were hauled off if they kept books after the purge,"

Word continued, not admitting she was also wondering how she was going to get the package when they left the split second. "The purge was not just the books it was really *the stories* books contained – *the knowledge inside them.* It was our collective memory, the fabulous human mind that was being exterminated – who we were, who we *are,* who we will be, *everything* we believe in. The dark side of *men's* imagination was expunging it all.

"The Ginger Tom wanted people to be burned with their books because he's a monster, while the Freaky Geek was a Truth Slayer. He wanted books eliminated because he's obsessed with transcending biology by using neuro-technology to merge humans with the advanced computers he's building.

"But then the unexpected happened," Word said. "Young people stopped being spectators. Betrayed by their elders, who did nothing to stop the political masters and the Ginger Tom and the Freaky Geek, they began to organize, hold meetings, plan protests, and fight back. They used social media to spread the word – psychic contagion – literally at the speed of light.

"It was an extraordinary moment. Within twenty four hours young people covered nearly every building in New York City with graffiti – identical copies of the pages of book – words and illustrations.

"It *was* a well-organized effort," Word said her eyes sparkling. "The *entire* works of Shakespeare were written on the apartment buildings along West End Avenue. There were almost two million young people in the five boroughs and I would say over a million of them participated in making New York City a giant pop-up book."

"Where'd they get the books?" Cat asked.

"X-it and I gave them the books we'd been hoarding," Word said. "The location made it possible. Just above 79th Street there are so many routes – paths, roads, and river walks – to, in, *and* through Riverside Park. It made it easy for young people to come and get books.

"Many of them knew us you see. Since the time we arrived on the Upper West Side we'd been supporting book clubs, reading novels, participating in poetry slams. We met with many young people who shared their own writing. It was the way they rebelled.

"The reaction of the Ginger Tom and the Freaky Geek was swift and deadly. They shut down all the substations and Manhattan was paralyzed without electricity. Supermarket shelves were empty within days. Supply chains were disrupted. But the biggest problem and what transformed the lives of young people – *all* the people in New York City – was the very *deliberate* shutting down of the Internet and social media – that's a whole other story that would take many split seconds to tell you. The city had become a bleak and dangerous place for young people, for everyone, *especially kids.*

"What's important here is that young people knew what it was like to have books taken away, because their books had been taken away in schools," Word said. "When there were schools for them to go to they did test prep hooked up to galvanic devices that monitored their emotions as they sat at the Freaky Geek's computers being programmed all day," Word said. "That's *another* whole other story there isn't time to tell – and yet it's such an important part of what happened to us.

"We could sit here for hours while I tell you about the young people who we met on the Upper West Side who had come from all over the city," Word said. "The word got out – excuse the pun – that a new civilization with books at the center was being created by young people who were rejecting the brutality of the political masters, the Ginger Tom and the Freaky Geek. The confiscation and elimination of books was years in the making and young people knew that life was being forced out of them. It was as if we were using books to conjure a new world into being that was magical and, and *kind* and filled *with love*," Word said. She looked at Et.

"You'd better tell us what happened next when X-it's back," Et said, "so he can fill in the gaps."

"Wait!" Cat said, doing her jump-off act, landing on the floor from Et's lap.

"No!" Et said, evaporating slightly. Then reappearing and turning puce knowing what question Cat was going to ask. "This is *not* the time."

"Does he know?" Cat asked, ignoring Et.

"Know what?" Word responded.

"That you're pregnant," Cat said. "Is it his?"

Word slapped Cat. "Of course it's his."

"Now," Cat said. "I'll answer your question."

"What question?"

"Do you think it's possible for a memory to be created at the moment of conception?" Cat said. "The answer is yes."

"How do you know?" Word asked, guessing the answer.

"I had a little mooch when I was under your shirt," Cat said with the most lopsided of all Cheshire Cat grins.

"That's a problem," Et said, no longer angry at Cat.

"Why?" Cat asked. "I was very respectful."

Word understood and Cat, instantly mangy, jumped off Word's lap and went and curled up on the rug.

"Better we know now than when we leave the split second," Et said. "I should have been paying more attention."

"If Death can detect the consciousness of your baby without you knowing," Et said, "then so can A-I hackers and Super Recognizers."

"Sick-Reapers," Cat said.

"What happens," Word asked, "when we leave the split second?"

"Death will have to remain in her Cat persona so she can mooch," Et said. "We will be in constant communication."

"Mooch?" Cat said, looking at Et, and her mange disappearing now Et was on it. "Be careful you're being enculturated!"

"Indoctrinated!" Et said, in an attempt to joke.

"X-it doesn't know," Word said, but was drowned out by the mooch interchange between Cat and Et.

"X-it doesn't know," Word said again.

"You haven't told him?" Cat asked.

"No," Word said. "We thought A-I was hacking X-it's consciousness before I was pregnant. Things happened and it was the only explanation. I knew I couldn't talk with him about it because they would have known. The last months were harrowing. Totally. We were being hunted and I had to stop sharing everything with X-it and I couldn't tell him why. Imagine how much worse it would've been if the Ginger Tom or the Freaky Geek knew I was *not* the last Truth Keeper."

"We *can't* tell him," Cat said.

"If he *knows* there is a new living being in this potentially existential life ending scenario," Et said, "he can help us take defensive action." She hesitated, "But even if we fail, which we could – remember I can no longer see the future – X-it *should know* he's going to be a father and that together you've made a child."

"We *have to* tell him," Et said, before she disappeared.

Twenty-Six

"What if the baby is hacked?" Cat asked, her voice sounding as if she was on a rotary phone with a bad connection. "Would the A-I *hack a baby?*"

"If Et was here she would tell you off for asking me that," Word said. "If they detect the baby –"

"Okay, let's not go there," Cat said, her voice breaking up. "Let's talk about death and dying. Whadyathink?"

"Let's *not*," Word said, annoyed with Cat. "You're being incredibly irritating. *Why* are you talking like this?"

"I'm nervous," Cat said, "When Et gets back with X-it our time in the split second will end and I'm not happy about that." Turning her head around as far as it would go she tugged out a tuft of fur from her back. "See," she said, this time her voice muffled. "I'm losing my fur again."

"Stop that!" Word said. "You're *not* losing your fur. But you *are* losing your mind."

"I don't have a mind," Cat said.

"You're just being neurotic," Word said as she tried to help Cat get the fur out of her mouth.

"Can you be neurotic without a mind?" Cat asked.

Cat spat and a clump of fur landed on Word's lap.

"Did you know Michel de Montaigne had a Cat?" Word asked ignoring the flying fur and trying to distract her.

"Yes," Cat said, with an apologetic smile. "Me."

"Me what?" Word asked, picking the wet fur off her lap.

"I was Montaigne's Cat."

"Really?" Word asked, surprised that this very silly conversation had suddenly taken an interesting turn. "Do you want to tell me about that?"

"You sound like a therapist," Cat said, with her usual Cheshire Cat grin, but looking relieved that they had found something to talk about while they waited for Et to bring back X-it.

"'*Qui sçait si elle passe son temps de moy plus que je ne fay d'elle?*'"Word said, quoting from the original writings of Montaigne that she had read and remembered. "The literal translation is '*who knows if she*' –" Word stopped to explain, "– '*she*' is Montaigne's Cat –" and then she began again, "– the literal translation is '*who knows if she passes her time more with me than I do with her?*'"

"He could be asking that question about us – you and me –

don'tyathink?" Cat said. "Now we'd say – '*When I am playing with my Cat, how do I know she's not playing with me?*'"

"Were you serious about being his Cat?" Word asked, suddenly doubtful. It sounded far-fetched.

"Cross my heart and hope to die," Cat said. "I was Montaigne's Cat. '*Hope to die*' – Death dying – that's pretty funny."

"How did you manage?" Word said. "Wars, the plague, a lot of people died," Word said.

"There are between seven and eight *billion* people on the planet," Cat said. "There were less than five hundred *million* in Montaigne's time. I had a much easier time. Being with him actually helped me cope – I've always been highly strung you see. Playing with Michel –" Cat paused "– well, he was very special."

"Late in his life Montaigne wrote that he knew Cat was playing with him," Word said, smiling at Cat. "How did you come to know the sixteenth century Gascon nobleman?"

"His baby daughter died when she was two months old," Cat said, "so naturally I was there. He also lost his younger brother who was killed by a blow from a tennis ball. A tragic death. A bit weird. On top of that his friend Etienne de La Boétie died of plague, *and* his father had a prolonged and agonizing death from a kidney stone. *Also* there was a religious war spreading across France with massacres and murders and –"

"Got it," Word said. "*Danse macabre*, you helped Montaigne survive all the deaths in his life – the way you're helping me –"

"Sort of," Cat said. "Did you know Montaigne was a Truth Keeper?"

"I figured that," Word said. "My mother had some of his original manuscripts and copies of others. She spent years studying them."

"I liked playing with him," Cat said. "He was often very melancholy but he found the truth in simple pleasures and I was one of them. He was skeptical about everything and would mutter to himself 'what do I know?' – *'Que sais-je?'* –"

"Did he know?" Word asked.

"What? That I'm Death?" Cat asked. "No. No. You're the only one I've ever told."

"I'm honored," Word said, still picking Cat's hair off her pants.

"When I met him he was quite young – it was just before he gave up his public life and retired to his ancestral château to brood on the death of the people he loved and to wait for his own death," Cat said.

"Wait for *Death?*" Word said. "Sometimes –"

"He didn't have to wait long," Cat said, Cheshire smiling at her own joke. "I became his Cat and he wrote about me."

"Do you think you changed his mind about dying?" Word asked more seriously, totally caught up with this unexpected story that connected Montaigne and Cat with her mother's scholarship.

"I can't take credit," Cat said, "but he spent a lot of time playing with me. He turned away from his meditations on death – '*to philosophize is to learn to die*' became transformed into '*living happily, not … dying happily, that is the source of human happiness.*'"

"My understanding is that Montaigne thought that human arrogance is ignorance," Word said, "and that animals live *with* nature and humans live in opposition to nature."

"Yes," Cat said. "And Montaigne thought meditating on animal communication would help humans step outside themselves and lead to a new conception of what it means to be human. I like to think I contributed to that."

"Just by being with you," Word said, patting Cat. "I've had to reimagine being human. *My life.* I've had to step outside myself. That's what this split second is about isn't it? Shaking things up. Making me see myself differently. You've also challenged my understandings of the ways my species thinks about Death *and* Eternity. I haven't worked it all out but I am thinking differently."

"Do you *feel* different?" Cat asked.

"Yes, I do," Word said, "and it's a good thing, don't you think?"

"There's more to it, you know," Cat said, her voice dropping, as if what she was about to say was a secret. She stared at Word, her yellow eyes reduced to black slits.

"Et?" Word said, guessing. "Was she there?"

Cat nodded.

"She knew Montaigne too?" Word asked, lowering her voice, but not sure why. "Is it okay that I know?"

Cat nodded again.

Word frowned. "What is it I know?" she whispered.

Cat looked around at the room. The Fire sent out sparks and glowed red. The Walls rippled and the Four Corners moved closer.

"Should we be talking about this?" Word asked, feeling nervous, not wanting to upset the Fire or the Four Corners.

"We *have* to talk about it," Cat said. "The Fire, Walls, and Four Corners all agree." The Fire sent flames up the chimney and the Walls stood tall with the Four Corners at exactly 90 degrees.

"Et stayed with Montaigne for many years, walking with him in his gardens, learning from him as he learned from her," Cat said. "She was like his adopted daughter."

"Marie de Gournay?" Word asked. "I've read about her. She lived with Montaigne and his family for the last five years of his life."

"He was only sixty when he died," Cat said, her eyes closing and her head drooping.

"Marie was arguably the first feminist writer of literary criticism," Word said, hurrying on before Cat started losing her fur again. "She gathered Montaigne's last writings together after his death and left over one thousand pages of her own writing. My mother studied them. Marie wrote, '*Happy are you, reader, if you do not belong to this sex to which all good is forbidden!'"*

"Doesn't that sound like something Et would write?" Cat said. "It was particularly nice for me that she was there with Montaigne because I got to sit on her lap – a lot!"

"I remember reading," Word said, caught up in Cat's revelations, "that Flaubert told a depressed friend, 'If you want to get in touch with life read Montaigne. You will love him, you'll see.'"

"Exactly," Cat said, "that was my experience, *and* Et's, but –"

"What happened?" Word asked.

The Walls shuddered, the Four Corners became acute, and the Fire for all pretense and purposes went out.

"Tell me!" she said, shivering suddenly and feeling cold.

"Descartes happened," Cat said. "I met him first when he was a small child and his mother died so it was very easy to feel sorry for him."

"Descartes is thought to have ushered in the modern world," Word said. "'*Cogito ergo sum*' – I think, therefore I am,"

"Exactly," Cat said, whispering again. "He was Montaigne's opposite. Rather than define and divide things – Montaigne wanted to bring them together in the quest for commonality rather than difference. Descartes wanted to mathematically divide everything up. Slice and dice. Chop. Chop."

"My mother said Montaigne considered human relations

the primal scene of knowledge and that through human relationships trust is restored and truth follows," Word said. "We often discussed the dynamic relationships between knowledge, human relationships, trust, *and* truth."

"Exactly," Cat said, "but Descartes thought differently. He was a bitter man, reclusive, cantankerous, and a loner, living in a small room without real friendships, and with a war going on. His quest for certainty led to his severing of mind and body *and* his severing of humans from their animal counterparts – chop, chop." Cat looked at Word. "Doesn't matter what people feel, only what powerful men think – that's how we've ended up the A-I, minds without bodies."

"So what happened?" Word asked, wanting to know more about Et and Montaigne.

"All of a sudden Et couldn't see the future," Cat said. "Normally she could see forty five million centuries into the past and even more millions of centuries into the future – and all of a sudden she couldn't see forward – *the future disappeared.*"

"But that was five hundred years ago?" Word said, not getting it.

"Well, Et could see *that* far," Cat said, "but in the grand scheme of things, when she had always been able to see backward *and* forward hundreds of millions of years, it was a big deal. And, Et *knew* that it was the philosophy of Descartes that was taking humans along the wrong path – metaphorically *and* literally."

"Makes sense to me," Word said. "Every aspect of modern

life is based on his Cartesian ways of thinking – science, the economy, education – the paranoiac test, test, prove-it, quest for certainty. The twisted, *I-think-therefore-I-am-important,* bad, daft, minds of powerful men can be traced back to Descartes."

"Exactly," Cat said, impressed by Word's articulation of the problem and wanting to show her own prowess. "The quest has been for the unlimited power of male domination – omnipotence – creating existential risks that could wipe out humanity within this century."

"So Et cut out?" Word said.

"You could put it that way," Cat said. "Although I don't think she actually did that."

"What I don't understand is, if she could see the last five hundred or so years," Word said, "she must have known that X-it and I would arrive on her doorstep, don't you think?"

"I *do* think," Cat said, "and I also think for the past five hundred years she's been trying to figure out what to do to save humans from becoming extinct. True, I've been splitting seconds when people die – just because there are so many of them and only one of me – but Et is the only one who can come up with a split second solution."

Twenty-Seven

"Where's Et?" X-it asked, standing in front of the Fire with his elbow on the mantle, smiling at Word.

The embers glowed and the Walls wrinkled in what looked like smiley faces, while the Four Corners drew closer and relaxed their right angles.

"You're back!" Word said, quickly getting up and giving him a hug. "We thought Et was with you."

"I thought she was with you," X-it said, hugging her back and showing no signs of letting her go.

Word gently pushed him away and turned and looked quizzically at Cat whose persona changed suddenly to her quirky and distinctly original Kiss-Bowie self.

"It's close to show time," Death said. "Et's back out on reconnaissance. She's worried about what happens when we return to Riverside Park and the scene by the Hudson River."

"I was thinking about that," X-it said.

Death stretched out her right arm with the flat of her hand

less than an inch from X-it's face. "Don't think," she said. "Not till Et gets back." She turned her hand so X-it was looking at her long black fingernails. "Do you like them?" she said.

X-it looked at Word and then at Death. He nodded. "Yes," he said. "You need sparkles on them."

"You're right," Death said, without moving her hand away from his face. "Something like this?"

"Beautiful," X-it said, mesmerized by the stars in the night sky that had appeared in front of him. He nodded, knowing that Cat was not playing with him. "I had two dreams while I had a nap," he said, making sure that they knew *he* was making sure he did not think about what had happened in Riverside Park or about going back.

Word sat back down on the chair. "Tell us," she said cautiously, knowing that with X-it in the room without Et there could be a security breach that would put an end to Et's split second solution.

Death resumed her Cat persona and jumped up on Word's lap. She padded around in a circle before sitting so that her eyes were fixed on X-it.

"Well," X-it said, nodding at Cat and then blowing a kiss to Word. He chose his words carefully. "The first dream took place in a room very much like this one. I was sleeping on a rug in front of the Fire and I pulled the blanket up to my chin, and lay on my side watching the flames as they leapt up the chimney and licked the pot of soup that was bubbling, sending savory smells into the room."

Word smiled at X-it and Cat gave him her widest and most lop-sided of Cheshire grins.

"It was such a lucid dream," X-it said. "Far away I could hear the clattering of pans and the stirring of spoons, but I lay still enjoying the last moments of the night. Then like a nightmare I remembered a great storm, and for a moment I couldn't breathe and the noise of the freight train filled my head."

Word rested her hand on Cat's back. Both were alert and worried, realizing that X-it was not making the dream up.

"I thought of my mother and father," X-it said. "Where were they? Were they looking for me? Had they found Max? I tried not to think about Max. I concentrated on the new smells in the air, which joined the smell of the soup, still bubbling in the pot that hung over the Fire."

Word felt Cat relax.

"In my dream I realized I was in my grandmother's house," X-it said, caught up with storytelling. "And I decided I would get up and follow the mouthwatering smells, and I made my way through the rooms of the old house to the kitchen."

Cat tucked her front paws under her and Word stroked her.

"The room was filled with the smell of freshly baked cookies and flakey buttermilk biscuits," X-it said, "sweet jams and jellies, pungent cheeses, mixed together with smoked meats, strings of onions and bunches of dried herbs hung on hooks from the wooden beams of the ceiling. They filled the room. Coppery pots bubbled on an old iron range and a shiny kettle whistled hoarsely as it waited to scald and brew my grandmother's tea."

Imagining all these smells drew Cat in and Word tapped her to remind her to stay alert when she started purring.

"I stood in the doorway mesmerized by the clattering, sweet smelling room," X-it said. "And then a voice greeted me from somewhere in the muddle. 'Good morning!' my grandmother sang, her voice lilting. She was wrapped in layers of flannel night-gowns, all tied up by the strings of her apron that gathered her in the middle and kept her gowns from dragging on the floor. In the morning light she seemed smaller, older and more wrinkled than I remembered her. She had wispy hair and a scrawny neck, but her sharp black eyes gave her strength and made her look both fierce and wise.

"'I'm making bread,' she said, and I asked her if I could try. My grandmother waved her hand towards the dough and I dug my fingers deep in the dough and moved them around trying to do as she had done but all I made was a sticky mess.

"'Let me show you,' my grandmother said, giving me a push out of the way. 'Twist and push.' This time I watched more care-fully. Then I tried again, keeping my fingers out of the dough as I kneaded it into a respectable shape. 'Twist and push,' I said. 'How's this?'

"'That's it!' my grandmother said. 'That's how you knead dough!' Then she began to laugh. 'Now you can make bread.'

"'Breakfast,' my grandmother said, as she put some sausages in a pan to fry. 'The biscuits are still warm and there's a jug of milk on the table.'

"'You cooked a lot of food,' I said.

"'I enjoy cooking,' she said, 'and I don't get many opportunities to cook. I eat like a bird, just nibble, nibble, nibble, except for soup. I have soup every night for supper. Help yourself!'

"I took a plate and a cup from a shelf and ate biscuits, thick with butter, and drank glasses of milk in record time. Then my grandmother put some sausages on my plate and I took more biscuits, poured another glass of milk, and began eating all over again.

"My grandmother washed the dishes in an old stone sink, and then lowered herself into the sagging cushions of her favorite kitchen chair and watched me eat.

"'You have a good appetite,' she said, pleased that her cooking was so appreciated.

"'I'm so hungry!' I said.

"My grandmother smiled. 'Eat up,' she said. 'When you've finished I'll help you find your way through the woods. You must leave this morning.'

"'Please let me stay,' I said to her, in a small flat voice. 'I'm so tired. I'll leave early tomorrow morning.'

"'No!' my grandmother said sharply. 'No one stays here!'

"'The storm destroyed my home!' I said, trying not to cry. 'I can't find my mother and father,' I sobbed, no longer able to hold back the tears, 'and I've lost my dog!' I shouted.

"'No,' my grandmother said, muttering 'You can*not* stay here.'

"'Please,' I pleaded, refusing to give up. 'Just one day?'

"'No!' my grandmother shouted, angry with me for putting her in such an impossible position. She was silent for a moment and then spoke quietly, 'You can't stay here,' she said.

"'I'll keep out of your way,' I said, beginning to cry again. 'Please! Let me stay!'

"'One day!' my grandmother said. 'One day!' she said, as she walked out of the kitchen. 'But tomorrow morning you go!'"

X-it looked at Word and Cat. The telling of his dream visibly shook him.

"I'm the boy in the storm looking for my mother and father and lost dog," X-it said. "I feel safe and I'm enjoying being taken care of by my grandmother –"

"Et," Word and Cat said together.

"Et," X-it repeated nodding his head "– wanting to stay in the room that had become a sanctuary, knowing I couldn't stay, knowing I must leave –"

"You were *reliving* your traumatic memories of losing your

mother and father and your dog Max, *and* Word and your fear of dying," Cat said.

"– and *avoiding*," Word said, "what you fear is going to happen next."

"You said you had two dreams," Cat said, wishing Et would return and worried that if they dwelled too long on the meaning of X-it's first dream he might think thoughts that might alert the A-I and the Sick-Reapers.

"Yes," said Word said, smiling at X-it. "Tell us about your other dream."

"This dream kind of picks up where the other one left off," X-it said, glad to be storytelling again, even though neither of his stories had happy endings.

"I was in the kitchen drinking a glass of milk and eating cookies and my grandmother walked back into the room," he said. "She'd put on a long blue cotton dress over her layers of night flannel and in her hand she carried a stout stick. She was smiling and she spoke to me as if there had been no argument.

"'The pots are cooking nicely and the dishes are all clean,' she said, 'Come on. Now that the work is done we can go for a walk.'

"I got up from the table and followed her out of the kitchen door and down the stone steps that led into the meadow," X-it said. "She took me on a tour of her gardens, pointing things out to me as with her stick.

"'Now over there,' she said, 'are butternut trees, and just

beyond the barn is an orchard. There are lots of apples this year. Bears like to come out of the woods and shake the trees. They eat the apples that drop. Some they leave for the raccoons.'

"She talked on and on, and I trotted along besides her listening to her as she tried to fit five hundred years of history into a single sentence.

"'Just beyond those rocks is a fresh water spring,' my grandmother said. 'Five gallons of water a minute – more than enough for a thousand years. Even if we had no rain at all that spring would never run dry. Later on I'll show you the beaver pond. It's one hundred and fifty years old, same beaver family, one generation follows another.' Suddenly she stopped walking and frowned at me. 'You should have gone today,' she said. 'I should not have let you stay.'

"'What do beavers do in the winter?' I asked, taking a few steps, walking ahead of her, hoping she would answer my question and forget that she had told me I had to go.

"'Don't change the subject,' she snapped.

"I stopped abruptly and looked back at her. She was breathless from hurrying to catch up with me. 'There's a world out there and you don't know anything about it!' I shouted at her.

"'*Know?* Of course I know!' my grandmother shouted. 'But I'm too old to argue with a bothersome boy,' she said.

"'And I'm too young to argue with you,' I shouted back.

"My grandmother laughed and sat down on a rock. 'Anger

eats you up and makes you frail,' she said.

"I lay down on the grass beside the rock where my grand-mother sat," X-it said, "and there we stayed. Not speaking very much. Just glad to sit quietly and think about our lives and the strange events that had brought us together, a tiny old woman and a big strong boy, past and present, hoping for a future but knowing there might not be one."

"If we can't go forward we might have to go back," Et said, sitting on her chair with her hands in her lap.

"How far can you see now?" Word asked, glad that Et had returned and hoping that she'd fixed everything and once again could see the future.

"Nothing beyond this split second," Et said. "But I can still see back. X-it's second dream reminded me of Montaigne's ancestral home. There were bears in the region and beavers in the nearby river, and of course there were apple orchards."

"In some ways it was a hopeful dream," Word said. "It was about life, living, the pots cooking nicely, always having food, the spring that would never run dry, always having water, arguing and then being peaceful, at one with nature, not in opposition to it –"

"Like Montaigne," said Cat.

"Strange," Et said. "I keep thinking of Antoinette de Louppes de Villanueva – she was – Michou's mother. She outlived her son and her family had survived the Spanish Inquisition, authoritar-ian religious intolerance, and racism. In some ways the sixteenth century was like the twenty first century but without the threat of extinction."

No one spoke.

"It might not be the end," Word said, noticing that Cat had lost nearly all her fur and was completely covered in sores that were oozing.

"I'd like to think so," Et said, hunched over on her chair. Her Old Crone hands more twisted and claw-like than they had been before. "Like X-it, I don't want to leave the split second, but time's up and we still don't have a plan for what to do next. We must find a solution."

Twenty-Eight

"I went back to New York City," Et said, glancing at X-it, and her eyes resting on Word, who was sitting with Cat on her lap. "It was eerily quiet and there were candles everywhere – Bryant Park, Union Square."

"I thought everyone would be stuck in the split second with us," Word said.

"They are – but a split second is just that," Et said, smiling. "For us – inside this room – it might seem like a very long time, but it's not – it's just a momentary ripple in the spacetime continuum. No more than an imperceptible hesitation in striking a match to light a candle."

"Do they know what happened to me?" Word asked.

Et shook her head. "They don't know the Sick-Reapers caught you or that you almost drowned in the Hudson trying to get away," she said. "The clampdown on dissidents is the reason there are no people on the streets. They come out with a lighted candle and a forbidden poem or drawing and place it with all the other poems and drawings and then quickly disappear."

"That's how we were living when the Sick-Reapers caught

me," Word said. "People are in mourning for their loved ones and the lives they've lost. So sad. I keep thinking about the Field where families lived and read books that is now surrounded by barbed wire. And the buildings that became books now with most of the writing washed off."

"Cities implode," Et said. "Petra did."

"Did you see anyone at all?" X-it asked, trying to remember what he knew about Petra – Pliny the Elder, the Roman naturalist, wrote about it and the caravan trade in the first century AD.

"It's exactly as it was when you left," Et said with a nod, her eyes giving away that she had read his thoughts. "The city is on high alert and there's a curfew. Kennedy, LaGuardia and Newark airports are all closed. There are no subways running. No buses or taxis either. No cars. Not one person on a bicycle. Militias are patrolling, but it wasn't possible to tell who's in charge of them – *if* anyone is in charge."

"Do any of them have the Ginger Tom's insignia?" Word asked.

"No insignias at all," Et said. "What must be really frightening for people is that the Sick-Reapers are everywhere looking for anomalous situations and committing appalling acts. Doing *anything* out of the ordinary is a death sentence," Et said, shaking her head. "That's why there are no people on the streets. I think the candles are –"

"Is it possible it's because of the split second?" X-it asked, interrupting. "Could it be that life goes on when we split time and separate the past from the present *and* the future –” X-it looked at Et.

“You’re very clever X-it,” Et said. “Splitting time is a phenomenon that can have lethal consequences. And the *risks* to people – *all* humanity – are very great –”

“My fault,” Cat said, shedding and oozing. “I dropped Word on Et’s doorstep. *Still* don’t know how X-it got here.”

Cat gave Word a piercing look, and Word gave X-it a look that was totally incomprehensible. X-it shrugged. “Don’t ask me,” he said, shaking his head.

“It’s *nobody’s* fault,” Word said, looking at Et. “Doesn’t matter how we got here,” she said to Cat and X-it. “Whatever has happened in New York City is not our fault. There is *no* split second effect in New York City. If there were it would be a cause-effect Cartesian phenomenon and we reject that possibility. Also it would also be a case of gaslighting – when something goes wrong people are blamed and then they blame themselves and *we reject that* as well.”

“You’re right,” X-it said. “I just thought –”

“You know enough about gaslighting not to ask Et that question,” Word said.

“Gaslighting?” Cat asked, a little more furry, her curiosity getting the better of her. “What’s gaslighting?”

“Gaslighting is mind manipulation,” Word said visualizing the definition she’d read. “It’s when information is twisted or spun, or selectively omitted, or false information is presented, making people doubt their own memories, perception, and sanity."

"How'd you do that?" X-it said, not really asking, but smiling at Word. "You're a walking dictionary."

"Could apply," Et said, "except a fundamental part of gaslighting is the intent to do harm, which applies to the political masters and the Lunatic Eight but not to Death or to you so it's not the case here."

"D'you think it might help if X-it shared his research on existential risk and the Lunatic Eight?" Word asked, feeling bad that she criticized him.

"X-istential," Cat said, her sores gone. "Get it X-it?"

"Of course he gets it," Word said laughing. "That why he kept his childhood name!"

"X-it," Et said, "It's time to speak up. Tell us what you know. Maybe it will help."

"Better mooch," X-it said, smiling at Cat.

"Thanks," Cat said. "It's been a while. I'll try to stay awake this time."

"You won't want to sleep when you hear what I have to say," X-it said.

"Going in," Cat said, entering X-it's consciousness. "Wow!" she said, echoing in his head. "They sure messed things up in here!"

X-it put his hands each side of this head and groaning, dropped to his knees on the rug in front of the Fire as flames shot up the chimney.

"Just kidding," Cat said, watching from her comfortable seat on Word's lap.

"Me too," X-it said, laughing.

"Enough!" Et said. "The Fire thought you were serious."

"My fault," Cat said. "But I actually was making sure X-it hasn't been hacked. No A-I's."

"I started studying existential risks round about 2014," X-it said. "Since the big storm in '08 I'd been obsessed by the 'what-if's' – What if the Sick-Reapers are around the corner? – What if we get stopped? – What if they catch Word?" X-it looked at Word and the pain etched on his face brought tears to Word's eyes.

"You kept me safe since I was eight," she said quietly "for *fourteen years* as the political masters and the Lunatic Eight became more and more maniacal."

"That's for sure," X-it said with a small smile, grateful that Word did not blame him for what happened to her. "But they should never have caught you."

"Gaslighting," Word said, "Start there."

"Gaslighting is a form of abuse," X-it said, "used by the

political masters and the Lunatic Eight worldwide to convince the people that all the problems stem from them and all the actions taken by the political masters and Lunatic Eight are benevolent and for the good of the people."

"It's pervasive," Word said. "The truth is twisted. False information is given to people that's why X-it and I made such a good team."

"*Made?*" X-it said. "We're *still* a team. I've always been interested in the *what ifs of risk* and Word has always been interested in *finding the truth*."

"There are *other* reasons," Word said, smiling.

"Political bosses have always twisted or spun information, or omitted or falsified information," X-it said. "Which is exactly what they did with existential – end of humans – risks. Climate change for example was covered up – denied, falsified, twisted, spun – so at least two of the Lunatic Eight could keep amassing vast wealth and gaining political power."

"Others too," Word said. "Big oil companies, frackers for gas, and shale oil strippers."

"False information was sugared with hope and fed to the people," X-it said, "benefitting the rich and penalizing the poor. It's always gone on, but there came a tipping point – when the ways humans communicate changed because of advances in technology."

Cat stretched her front paws out in front of her. "People

didn't look up from their cell phones and computers long enough to realize that the machines they were using were also using them," she said.

"Concentrate on mooching," Word said, giving Cat a tap.

"All clear," Cat said. "I'm embedded in X-it's consciousness. Any A-I who hacks him will hear a series of yowls followed by two alley cats fighting."

"Thanks for warning me," X-it said with a grin. Then looking serious he continued giving his take on existential risks.

"We've been studying four billion years of evolution and we're *still* mystified by life," X-it said. "We *know* we have the same number of genes as a worm and we *don't know* why – but we can now *make* worms *and* engineer humans."

"Genetic engineering," Et said. "It's dangerous. I've been wondering if it's part of the reason I can no longer see the future."

"When you say you can't see the future," Word said, "are you talking about the *future of the planet* or the *future of human beings* – life as X-it and I know it?"

Cat looked at Et and gave her a quizzical smile wondering if Et would evade the question.

"Humans," Et said, raising her eyebrows as she looked at Word. "People," she said, shaking her head and closing her eyes. "*People.* The planet will go on for billions of years." She opened her eyes and looked at X-it. "Please continue," she said.

"Even the political masters were overwhelmed by what was happening," X-it said.

"They were really stupid," Word said. "Full of their own importance."

"Power, privilege, and ignorance are a fatal combination," Et said.

"The Lunatic Eight were different," X-it said. "I'm not sure what's worse – people feeling powerless because their leaders are ignorant and stupid. Or feeling powerless because the Lunatic Eight – who seized power when the political masters lost control – hadn't worked out what would happen when their A-I started thinking for themselves –"

"And started the cyber wars," Word said. "Machines with thoughts and feelings – most of them vicious."

"*Or* what would happen," X-it continued, "when the Lunatic Eight's enthusiasm for genetic engineering led to hostile life forms capable of committing acts of violence both in the real world *and* the virtual world."

"What was inexplicable to most of us," Word said, "was that while some people felt powerless and filled with fear and anxiety and were shocked by the brutality, *some* people *applauded* the brutality of the A-I and hostile bioengineered life forms and actually joined in."

"Nobody knows what a terrible time I've had," Cat said, her voice once again resembling the sound of broken vocal chords heard when there is a bad phone connection "So many people dying," she cried. "Torture. Murder. Total insanity. Digital suicide. Malfunctioning programs. Software errors. *Ha! Ha!* – Oops! Unintended consequences. Autonomous systems – acting *independently*. Robots. Artificial Intelligence hostile to biological intelligence – running amok all over the world. Hacking essential systems and causing catastrophic accidents. *Accidents*? *Ha! Ha!* Not likely! Humans down! Women down! Children down! Deliberately exterminated. Mass fratricide. No one's in charge! Where's Dr. Strangelove? A-I – acting autonomously – commandeering unmanned weapons. *BOOM!*"

"Cat!" Et said.

"Shhh. You'll have no fur left." Word said, trying to sooth Cat. "It's okay."

"No! It's *not* okay!" Cat said, totally breaking up. "*My nerves*! They're also creating living things. *Ha! Ha!* Boogeymen coming to get us! They can make them! Adding genes from other organisms. Frankenstein's alive! He's growing living organisms in fermenters. Neural mapping – implications beyond people's grasp. They don't know Sick-Reapers are genetically modified! *Or do they*? Wicked! Evil!"

"Cat!" Et said. "Calm down!"

"The Ginger Tom was ignorant," Cat shouted. "A buffoon. He was building an empire, branding people, making them in incubators, exploiting human behavior, and amassing a fortune from their sick tendencies and unfortunate vulnerabilities. It was an outrage, *outrage*. Rage, *rage*, against the *dying* of the light."

Cat looked as if she'd been electrocuted and she spoke quietly as if sharing a terrible secret. "Freaky Geek, Posh Boy, *all* the Lunatic Eight collaborated with the political masters. They privatized war for their own profit – until the A-I and the Sick-Reapers decapitated the Ginger Tom and *all* the rich loonies." Cat started yowling. "Now there are no rules! Mutants and machines will decide our existence! *And* our demise! –" The frazzled feline was turning in circles chasing her own tail when she suddenly stopped and looked at Word and X-it.

"You know more about existential risk than I do!" X-it said to Cat. "I didn't know the Sick-Reapers are genetically modified."

"I can't take it anymore," Cat wailed. "People keep dying. Humans are so-so-so – temporary!"

"Cat," Word said. "How about a mooch?"

"Yes, yes, mooch, mooch," Cat said, "I know you're trying to distract me but when we leave the split second we're going to have to face them sickerty Sick-Reapers and I'll die if you die and X-it dies." She gave out a yowl that shook the room and made the Walls and Four Corners wobble so badly Word almost fell off her chair and X-it had to hold on to the mantle.

"The problem is that the implications are beyond our grasp," Et said, unaffected by the wobble. "This little blue dot of a planet will go on, and while it might heat up a bit making it conducive to some other life forms, it will not be fatally impacted –"

"Unless the A-I destroy it," X-it said. "Or some bioengineered organism does something we cannot imagine."

"It's not out of the question," Et said, seriously considering this possibility. "The A-I and other mutant life forms that humans have created are taking Earth into uncharted territory. It's entirely possible all biological life forms will die."

"Mooching," Cat said. "Apologies. It's a real problem when you're Death and you can't stand people dying."

"Understood," Et said.

"Can I ask a question?" X-it asked.

Et nodded.

"For a short time you were a beautiful blue," X-it said. "But most of the time you just look like a very old woman. Why's that?"

"Simple," Et said. "We're here in this room, not a palace or a temple, not a cloud. I'd like you to be comfortable. Besides, I like being an old woman."

"So why did you turn blue?" X-it asked, wanting a more definitive answer.

"So you get the experience of seeing me in a form you might not expect," Et said. "Might distract you at a moment when you might die if you lose your concentration."

"Got it," X-it said, "heavy," his heart beating rapidly, then slowing. "Can I say one more thing?"

Et nodded.

"I apologize for my – my – *whatever* – behavior – just before you took me to the room with the bird," X-it said, looking embarrassed.

"No worries," Cat said, forgetting *her* worries. "No erection detection needed. Penal implant not required."

"Cat!" Word said.

"Well he has to know," Cat said. "Et said so."

"Know what?" X-it said.

"I'm pregnant," Word said.

"What?" X-it said.

"A baby," Cat said. "Word's having a baby!"

"Then we can't go back!" X-it said, alarmed at the idea of Word facing her attackers again.

"We can't stay in the split second," Word said. "We *have* to go back."

"No!" X-it said, looking first at Word and then at Cat. "How close to death – to dying – in the river – was Word when you arrived?"

"A split second," Cat said.

Twenty-Nine

"We can't go," X-it said. "If they find out Word's pregnant they will abort the baby. You must know there are no more *totally* human babies – they're all genetically engineered. Their DNA is mixed with the DNA of other life forms."

X-it started walking back and forth on the rug in front of the Fire, which seemed to get longer and shorter as he turned.

"*And* there are *no* natural births," X-it said, one hand on his head and the other gesticulating. He looked at Et. "Babies are grown in fermenters. What *chance* will our baby have if we go back?"

"We have to go," Word said, getting up and putting her arms around him. "*I* have to go. You forget I'm a Truth Keeper. I think my mother knew this moment would come. I think Grann did too. I have to go back and get the package and keep it safe – though I still don't know what's inside it."

"I just don't understand *how* what's in it can be *that* important," Ex-it said his face so close to Word's that their foreheads were together. They stayed like that, arms around each other, not talking, while Cat jumped up on Et's lap and Et comforted her.

"I *know* you're right," X-it said, holding on to her. "We have to go back, but I'd stay in this room with you and with Et and Cat forever to keep *you* safe."

"Me too," said Cat, who was looking much thinner than before. "Could we do that Et?"

"Possibly," Et said, "if we were in a room, but we're not."

"So *where are* we?" X-it asked.

"Before I tell you where we are let's talk about what happens when we return to – to –" Et said, not finishing the sentence. She backed up. "I actually don't know what will happen – this is the first time humans have –" She stopped. "Remember, I can no longer see the future. For five hundred years I haven't been able to see anything after Word jumped in the Hudson River to get away from the Sick-Reapers."

"So why can't we just skip that bit?" X-it said. "Can't we go on as if it never happened? Et, you could drop Word and me off and we'll go light candles or something. Live with the people who are left in the city?"

"Even if Et could, I can't live like that anymore," Word said. "It's been so nice to be here and not be hunted. I don't want – I'd rather be –"

"Dead," Cat said, yowling. "Et, I can't take this anymore."

"You don't have to," Et said. "What we do next will change the future."

"And how will we do that?" Cat asked.

"When we undo the string on the package," Word said, "we'll find the answer to your question."

"Are you sure?" Cat said. "Definitely sure? Or are you guessing?"

Word looked at X-it.

"Don't you think this *has* to be the moment when the package is unwrapped –" Word said, looking at Et – "and we save the world?"

"Almost," Et said. "I'm convinced there's a message written on the inside of the oiled paper but –" Et hesitated "– I'm not sure how to tell you but there's a little more to it than that –"

"Tell us!" Cat said, yowling. "I'm done for. The suspense is killing me!"

"Just by the shape of package there has to be an oblong box inside the wrapper," Word said, "and whatever is in the box is a relic that goes back forty-five million centuries – or as far back as the first sign in the Universe? Is *that* really what's in the box?"

"I'm dying!" Cat said, going limp on Et's lap. "*Dying!*"

"You can't die," Et said, exasperated. "You're *Death*."

"And you're making it hard to concentrate," Word said, poking Cat. Then to Et, "Tell us, the first sign in the Universe, is it in the box?"

"Sort of," Et said. "If you can think of me as a sign."

"You've lost me," X-it said.

"You're in the box?" Word asked, laughing. "If you're in the box *we're* in the box and that doesn't make sense."

"Sense or not," Et said. "We're *all* in the box."

"Right now?" Word asked, eyes wide, trying to grasp this new twist..

"Seriously?" Cat said, suddenly up on her paws with her tail in the air staring at Et with a look that can only be described as maniacal. "We're in the package tied up with a bit of old string? You're making it up!"

"I don't get it," Word said.

"Four Corners, Walls, but no windows," Et said, quietly. "We're *in* the box – look around. There are no windows. Just Four Corners when we need them. For those in the box the room can be big or small."

"But you took me upstairs –" X-it said.

"Look around. There are no stairs," Et said. "I took you to a space in the box that is impenetrable so Sick-Reapers couldn't hack your consciousness and find the package."

"Why did you keep asking me about the package?" Word asked Cat.

"Weren't you listening? I didn't know! Et *didn't tell me* she was living in a box!" Cat said. "When I pulled Word out of the Hudson I homed in – if you like – on Et. I had no idea where she was. I just knew that Word's life would be lost if I didn't find Et –"

"Don't," X-it said. "It's too much –"

"I'm still not sure how *you* got here." Cat said, looking at X-it, her eyes narrowed to black slits. "It's a mystery." She looked at Word. "Do you know?"

Word shook her head, surprised at Cat's question. She was uncomfortably aware that Et and Cat were both looking at her intently as if they'd like to hack her consciousness but knew that she'd know if they did.

"It's not important," Cat said, making light of it with a lopsided Cheshire Cat grin and her narrowed eyes now opened wide – more a brash orange than yellow – as she said to Et, "Never thought you'd be living in a cardboard box!"

"It's not *cardboard*," Et said, laughing, "but now you mention it – it could be cardboard – sometimes the Walls are corrugated."

"Ha! Ha!" Cat said, a little too forced. "*I'm* the funny one! You're the serious one! You never told me –"

"Cat," X-it said quietly, still trying to take in what Et had just said.

"Wait!" Word said, eyes wide. "Does that mean we're – at this moment – in the *exact* spot where I hid the package?"

"Yes," Et said, smiling.

"You've gotta be kidding," X-it said, both hands holding his head.

"Where's that?" Cat said. "I thought we were off the planet. We're not?"

"Far from it," Word said.

"*Am I the only one who doesn't know where we are*?" Cat said, yowling. "Why didn't you tell me?"

"Because we didn't know!" X-it said.

"Et did!" Cat said.

"But Cat dropped me on your front door step," X-it said, still not getting that Cat did not bring him. It seemed a trivial matter even though it was not.

"It was an illusion," Et explained. "You were dropped *inside* the box. The stone step, the door, like the Fire were – *are* – all illusions. The mountains, rivers, meadows are all –"

"In the box?" X-it said, incredulously.

"Like Whoville?" Word asked, "in *Horton Hears a Who* – a micro world?"

"Sort of. It's a good analogy," Et said.

"I still don't get it," X-it said.

"Believe me when I say I cannot see the future after Word escaped from the Sick-Reapers by jumping in the Hudson River," Et said. "You've only got to think of your own exploration of existential risks to know that it's entirely possible –"

"That a cataclysmic event is going to happen," X-it said. "But it's unlikely that it would take place at the exact moment that Word jumped in the river."

"I need to get this," Word said to Et. "You used to be able to see the future but now you can't – right?"

Et nodded.

"You can still see the past?" Word asked.

Again, Et nodded.

No one spoke.

"Can you see any people in the future?" X-it asked.

Et shook her head.

"What about the planet?" X-it asked, his voice rising.

Et shook her head.

Silence.

"I have a question," Cat said, her vocal chords stretched thin.

Et, Word, and X-it looked at Cat, and so did the Walls and Four Corners.

"I've forgotten," Cat said, frazzled. "This is all so complicated. Wait!" she said, her fur looking as if she'd had a frizzy perm. "Here's my question – what was the point of the big old door and stone step if we were already in the box?"

"Good question," X-it said. "I was wondering that too."

"My answer's not logical but it is truthful," Et said. "For the first time in forty five million centuries I'm scared – it's a human emotion I've never felt before. It's a terrible moment. And yet – what's happening might still be averted. I just didn't know how."

"I'm not sure how a door and a step have anything to do with what you've just said," X-it responded. "It can't be that complicated."

"I needed a barrier," Et said. "Something between me and whoever, whatever, accessed the box – my room – something between me and some man-made machine or advanced A-I that hacked into the box."

"Highly unlikely," X-it said.

"Man is now creating new life forms," Et said. "How likely or unlikely was that? Cyber wars are taking place. You heard Cat. Artificial Intelligence hostile to biological intelligence, running amok all over the world."

"Human induced alterations to the biosphere," X-it said, "creating a post human era."

"So the huge iron and wood door," Cat said her fur straightening, "was like an archaic portcullis to protect you from the dangers of the new anarchistic technological world?"

"Precisely," Et said. "It gave me a sense of protection from hostile interlopers."

"I get it," X-it said. "Actually the stone step and the door are humorous, if you think about it –" he looked at Et, unsure if she would find it funny. "If you don't mind my saying – like a sign 'Keep Out Sick-Reapers!'"

"Impenetrable that's for sure," Et said. "What's really funny is that Death has the power to split a second, but it's taken me five hundred years to figure out what happens next and I still don't get it."

"We've just got to think longer and harder," Word said. "And that's exactly what we'll do."

"You know," Et said. "You live in a solar system that is one planetary system among billions. One galaxy among billions."

"I'm cool with that," X-it said.

"Every atom in your bodies can be traced back to before the solar system was formed." Et looked intently at Word and then at X-it. "I keep thinking the clue to the future is somehow hidden in that fact."

"Go on," Word said.

"Every person on the planet has inside them atoms from hundreds of different stars," Et said, "which lived and died in different parts of the Milky Way galaxy more than five billion years ago." She smiled. "So you're all intimately linked to the stars – and this is the wonderful way in which we realize the unity of the cosmos."

"And you?" X-it asked.

"Like you, I am also the stuff of stars." Et said, without elaborating.

"Isti mirant stellae!" Word said. "We are the ones who look in wonder at the stars – and we are made of them."

"I'm not made of dead stars," Cat said. "I don't have atoms. I'm just a specter."

"How does knowing our atoms can be traced back to dead stars help us?" X-it asked, ignoring Cat.

"It interrupts the clockwork of our mechanistic world," Word said. "And changes the way we think about the Universe."

"Imagining ourselves," X-it said, "as being midway between atoms and stars changes the ways in which we think about the complex relationships between people and the planet."

"We have to imagine the spacetime continuum differently," Word said. "Et, when you see the past or the future do you see it as X-it or I would see it – like movies?"

"No," Et laughed. "Hard to explain but you could say I see it in the form of energy –"

"Like atoms?" X-it asked, beyond impressed.

"Something like that," Et said.

"Can you distinguish X-it from me?" Word asked.

"I can," Et said. "I can see you up to the moment you took a dip in the Hudson."

"But if we're made up of atoms of dead stars shouldn't you be able to see those atoms in the future?" Word asked.

"Exactly," Et said, glad that Word understood. "It's not just that *you* disappear, it's that your atoms disappear."

"So whatever the A-I are doing they have reached a point at which they can destroy life forms at the atomic level?" X-it said.

"If you look back can you see us?" Word asked again looking intensely at Et. "Not just people – X-it and me?"

"*Yes!*" Et said wrinkles fading. "I can see you –"

"You remember the ending of Italo Calvino's *Daughters of the Moon?*" Word asked, rushing on. "'We were seized by a frenzy' – remember?"

"I don't remember Calvino," X-it said, "Let alone the ending of *Daughters of the Moon.*"

"'We began to gallop across the continent, through the savannahs and forests that had covered over the Earth again and buried cities and roads, obliterating all trace of everything that had been,'" Word said, quoting Calvino.

"Oh, I do remember," X-it said. "You used to read it to us in the Field and the kids would pretend to be woolly mammoths and use their arms for tusks or trunks."

"'And we trumpeted,'" Word continued quoting, smiling and nodding at X-it, "'lifting up to the sky our trunks and our long thin tusks, shaking the long hair of our croups with the violent anguish that lays hold of all us young mammoths, when we realize that now is when life begins –'"

"Are you suggesting we go back to the time of woolly mammoths?" X-it asked sounding worried.

"No," Word said. "But if we've interrupted the spacetime continuum by remaining in the split second, perhaps our *future* is now sometime in the *past*?"

"But when and where?" Et said, not actually asking.

"Tell us what you see," Word said.

"Hard to explain," Et said. "I can't see you in a way that you'd understand, but what I can see is the sign on your wrist."

"*And* my tattoos? My quotes from books?" Word asked.

"No. Just the ancient sign. That's all," Et said. "There could be a disturbance in the spacetime continuum caused by the Cat's split second."

"It's not *my* split second," Cat grumbled.

"Perhaps when we untie the string on the package we'll find

instructions," Word said.

"I still don't know where the box is!" Cat said.

"You will," Et said. "Word, tell Cat."

Thirty

"So we just pick up where we left off?" Word asked. "The Sick-Reapers have caught me and I've jumped in the Hudson and X-it has jumped in to save me?"

"Not quite," Et said. "Listen carefully. Cat! Are you listening? Remember, once we leave this room – box – X-it will be hacked immediately and the Sick-Reapers will know where he is – and therefore where Word is."

"We'd better stay together," X-it said to Cat. "Do whatever you can to stop them entering my consciousness. Trash me if you have to."

"Gotcha," Cat said. "You know the signal – two alley cats fighting – if that fails I'll clang some lids of garbage cans."

"Be serious!" X-it asked.

"Seriously," Cat said.

"Wait," Word said. "Back up. Everything will happen so quickly it's important that we all know what we're supposed to do."

"Gotcha," Cat said again, wearing night goggles.

"Cat!" Et said. "Take them off. How can you hack like that?"

"Oops," Cat said, and the goggles disappeared. "I've thought of something. When we get out of the box, Et you stick close to Word. X-it and I will untie the string. X-it will read what's written on the paper wrapper and then we'll – we'll – what will we do then?"

"Good thinking Cat," Word said. "We have to hope there are instructions –"

"A clue," Et said. "Not instructions. The most we can hope for is a clue that would have been written long ago."

"Problem!" X-it said. "I can't read 'long ago' – English, some Spanish, a little French, math and physics notations, advanced computer programming – no Greek, Latin, Sanskrit, or hieroglyphs –"

"Stop," Word said. "You've been hanging out with Cat too much. She's messed with your head."

"Have not," Cat said. "You're joking, right?"

"Yes, I'm joking," Word said. "We're all nervous so we're being silly."

"Let's be serious," Et said. "There's too much at stake for any more silliness."

"Apologies," Word said. "X-it, Cat, if you can't read what's written on the wrapper you'll have to give it to me or to Et."

"Not to Et," Cat said, immediately shedding.

"Once out of the box I cannot touch anything and no one can touch me," Et said.

"Why not?" Word asked. "What will happen if one of us touches you?"

"There are some things humans are not supposed to know," Et said, "or understand."

"Is this to do with dark matter?" X-it asked.

"No," Et said. "Dark matter particles pass through you more often than you might think. Electromagnetic interactions are much more common and exchange much more energy."

"Et," Cat said. "Enough with the physics lesson. What Word and X-it need to know is that *if* anything touches you or you touch anything it will have the same effect as galaxies colliding – total annihilation of the Earth and the galaxy –"

"What Death – Cat – is telling you," Et said, "*without* per-mission, I might add, is close to the truth – think massive colli-sion – a giant asteroid hitting the planet with cascading effects on the galaxy."

"Okay," X-it said. "Got it," he said, voice rising, speeding up.

"So, we're inside a box that I used a bicycle chain to attach to the rusty iron mesh in the darkest spot on one of the five stone arches that provides access and ventilation to the railway tracks that run under Riverside Park. *Not only* are Word and me – along with *Et*, a creature from another galaxy, possible the creator of the Universe, *and Death,* who likes to appear as Cat, Bat, Kiss, Gaga, and Bowie – *in a box,* which is wrapped up in old parchment or vellum and tied up with old string, but *our very survival* depends on us getting *out of the box, reading a clue,* which is written on the wrapper, and confronting the Sick-Reapers *before* they capture Word!"

X-it looked at Et, then Word, then Cat. "And *our baby!*" he said, holding his head. "And, if we can do all that," he shouted, "*We'll save the world!*" He looked at Word and then at Et. "Is that it? Did I leave anything out? It's totally nuts!"

"You forgot – no one touches Et," Cat said. "Her real name, which I don't think she's told you, is Eternity."

"You also missed out," Et said, "that whatever happens, Word must not jump in the Hudson River." Et looked at Word, "This time you would not survive."

"What if they –?" Word began.

"We'll stop them," Et said.

"How?" Word asked.

"Don't know yet," Et said, smiling. "It's a mystery."

"Have we forgotten anything?" Word asked.

"I think X-it covered just about everything," Cat said, with a lopsided Cheshire smile. "Just in case things go wrong I just want you to know –"

"Don't," Word said. "Your fur will fall out."

"I have to say it," Cat said, the last few clumps of fur dropping. "I love you all."

"We love you too," Et said.

"I have a question," X-it said, resisting an urge to say something sentimental. "How come Cat can sit on your lap?"

"Because I'm a specter of course," Cat said, her fur back.

"Death does not have a form," Et said, "and so she appears as apparitions of her own choosing."

"But we touched her," X-it said.

"That's because you have fabulous imaginations and you're inside the box," Et said. "Ready?"

Thirty-One

Out of the box, X-it fumbled in the dark with the combination lock on the bicycle chain.

"Hurry," Et said. She looked more ancient and frail than she did inside the box. Her long blue coat dragged in the dirt a few feet from the railway tracks under Riverside Park on which trains traveling out of the city used to run. Under her coat, hidden in the folds, Et's feet hovered a few inches above the ground.

"Word!" a young woman shouted from across the tracks.

"Hey Aisha!" Word called back. "How's it going? Sorry – in a hurry!"

The young woman was wearing work-boots and baggy jeans and a man's vest, which was too big for her, dipping low at the front and the back revealing tattoos of quill pens, splashes of ink, and inkwells with ribbons of poetry coming out of them. A string of tattooed letters like the keys of an old Remington typewriter made a necklace and followed the curve of each breast and read, "I am myself the matter of my book."

"Come see!" Aisha shouted again, "We're painting a mural!"

"We didn't plan for this!" Cat whispered.

"Sorry, gotta go!" Word called back, and then she whispered back to Cat, "Last time I was walking by the Hudson when they caught me. Not here! We've changed what happened!"

"Sick-Reapers?" Aisha asked, stepping over the tracks and walking over to where Word was standing with Et and X-it. Aisha didn't notice Cat. "We'll make sure they don't get you," she said, waving to the five mural painters who were watching from the other side of the tracks.

"See what we've written?" Aisha asked, pointing at the mural. "'*We are such stuff, as dreams are made on, and our little life is rounded with a sleep*'. Shakespeare! *The Tempest! –*"

Word was chilled by the parallels between what was happening to them and the quote the young people from the Field had chosen.

"You know 'sleep' is code for –" she said, not finishing the sentence.

"Death," Aisha said. "I know. Everybody knows. Hope is gone, but we'll resist till our last breath."

"The quote you've chosen is beautiful," Et said. She looked at Aisha and then at the mural, and Word could see the sadness in her eyes, but then with a look of authority, Et said to Aisha, "Please excuse us we're in a great hurry."

"One, five, eight, five," X-it said. His hands were shaking. "Can't open it!"

"Wrong number?" one of the muralists asked, stepping over

the tracks and joining them.

"No!" X-it said, irritated. "Quiet. I'm concentrating. One! Five! Eight! Five!" he said, his hands shaking badly.

"Try again," Word said. "I think the eight slipped to a nine."

"It won't open," X-it said, sounding desperate.

"What are the numbers?" Aisha asked taking the lock from X-it.

"One, five, eight, five," X-it said, putting his hands up to his head and grimacing.

"Mooch time," Cat said telepathically, her yellow eyes becoming black slits. "Going in."

"One, five, eight, five," Aisha repeated, and this time the lock opened and she quickly untangled the chain from the package.

"Careful!" Et said sharply. "Give the package to Word."

"Hey Aisha," one of the young men who'd continued working on the mural called out as he crossed the tracks to join them. "What you doin' with that bicycle chain? Can I have it?"

"They're my friends from the Field," Word whispered to Et. "Hey everyone, what's happ'nin' is life an' death. Don't get in the way. An' don't touch my grandmother. She's got psoriasis. Hurts. Okay?"

"Hurry!" Et said to Word as she tried to untie the knots in

the string.

"Cut it," the young muralist said who'd wanted the bicycle chain. Producing a knife in one hand, he reached out with the other to grab the package from Word, just as X-it shouted "Hacked!" and staggered towards the young muralist, who dropped the knife and caught him as Word stepped back and held onto the package.

"Hacked!" X-it cried. "No …! Yes …! Coming to get us!"

"Sounds like a cat fight in X-it's head," the muralists said, as ferocious snarls, growls, yowls, and fiendish screams echoed through the railway tunnel.

Word had undone one of the knots and was trying to untie the other knots as the yowls and caterwauling grew louder and louder followed by a sound like trashcan lids clashing. Then silence.

"All clear," Cat said, appearing at X-it's feet and gasping for breath. "Not much time," she panted. "They'll be here soon."

"Whatever's in that package it must be important," Aisha said, staring at Word, who had ignored what was happening to X-it and was still working on untying the knots. "Tell us what's going on and we'll help you," Aisha said.

It was at that moment that they heard dogs barking a ways a way in the dark tunnel. The two muralists who were still working on the other side of the tracks dropped their paint cans and ran across the tracks.

"They're coming from both directions," one of them said,

just as the white light of floodlights blinded them and they all closed their eyes and covered their faces with their forearms to shield themselves from the light.

"Sick-Reapers!" Aisha said. "Come on!" And she opened the iron mesh door that led to the footpaths, one with steps, the other with a steep slope running north and south up to Riverside Park. But at right angles to this path was another path that led to the tunnel under the six lanes of the West Side Highway to the River Walk and the Hudson River.

"We've gotta go!" Aisha said, whispering now, urgently, and desperately. "Or die."

But Word stood still ignoring the advancing Sick-Reapers. She'd untied the last knot in the string and she carefully took off the wrapper. X-it stood beside her, and next to him Et hovered never touching anything, and all the while Cat rubbed against Word's legs as the last Truth Keeper held the old piece of paper up to the light from the Sick-Reapers spotlights.

"'*Qui sçait si elle passe son temps de moy plus que je ne fay d'elle?*'" she read.

"What does that mean?" X-it asked. "Tell me!"

"We've gotta go!" Aisha whispered fiercely, not understanding why Word and X-it weren't running. "*Now!*" she suddenly shouted, looking down the tunnel at the Sick-Reapers who were close enough they no longer needed a spotlight.

"Good luck!" one of the young muralists said to Aisha as he

quickly ran out of the steel mesh door between the great stone arches. Three more followed whispering "Peace!" "In solidarity!" "Stay safe!" as they ran up the path to Riverside Park and scattered, running in different directions at the top towards the Warsaw Memorial and Grant's Tomb.

"Go now!" Word said to Aisha, seeing no point in continuing to whisper. "You can't help us."

"I'm not going without you," Aisha said to Word. "You've always been there for us when we needed you."

"Get as far away from here as you can," Word said, pleading with Aisha just as a few moments ago Aisha had pleaded with her. "You don't want to die because of us."

"Can you think of a better reason?" Aisha asked. She glanced down the train tracks at the Sick-Reapers who were rapidly approaching.

"Where Aisha goes I go," the muralist with the bicycle chain said.

"Come on!" Aisha shouted. "We've gotta go!" She held the steel mesh door open and the muralist ran out, followed by Word, X-it, and Et. In the distance up above in Riverside Park close to the Warsaw Memorial they heard rapid gunfire and cries from one or perhaps two of the young muralists.

"Cat!" Word shouted, when she didn't follow them out.

"Coming! You go on! I'll catch up!" Cat called, as she disappeared and a depraved wraith took her place. Now twelve feet tall, with an evil looking skull, a maw of a mouth, and a vicious scythe dripping with blood, Death advanced on the Sick-Reapers who were coming from the south. She let out a blood-curdling cry that echoed the length of the tunnel, terrifying their ferocious genetically engineered dogs that turned tail and ran.

The robots with the Sick-Reapers fired their unmanned weapons and the bullets went right through the wraith and ricocheted off the Walls of the tunnel, finding their targets in the army of Sick-Reapers coming from the north. Infuriated by the stupidity of the Sick-Reapers' robots moving north, the Sick-Reapers' robots moving south fired back.

"Oops!" Death thought, impressed by how many bullets had passed through her. "I knew it! Unintended consequences! Autonomous systems – acting *independently. Ha! Ha!* Artificial Intelligence hostile to biological intelligence – running amok in a railway tunnel. *Ha! Ha!* Sick-Reapers down! Deliberately annihilated! *Ha! Ha!* Crawling attack robots with sea slug parts made on 3-D printers! Sea slugs down! *Yowl!*"

"Cat!" Word called, frantically running back, "Cat!"

"All set," Cat said, joining Word. "I've always wanted to do that," she said, as they caught up with the others. "I've delayed them but more of them will be coming from the train tunnel *and* the paths from Riverside Park in less than no time."

"By now every Sick-Reaper in Manhattan and Northern New Jersey is homing in on the 79th Street Boat Basin," X-it said as he edged his way with Word along the wall through the tunnel under the West Side Highway to the Hudson River.

"What happens next?" Cat whispered.

"Is that cat *talking* to you?" Aisha whispered to Word.

"No time for questions," Word said, suddenly feeling responsible for Aisha and her boyfriend. "When we get through the tunnel just watch me for – for –signals."

"Okay," Aisha whispered inching her way along the wall. "But I'm tellin' you that cat can talk and your grandmother's feet are floating three or four inches from the ground."

"Better be quick," X-it whispered. "The Sick-Reapers are behind us and closing in on the river walk –"

"From both directions," Cat said. "From the George Washington Bridge *and* the Boat Basin."

"Jamaal," Aisha's friend with the bicycle chain whispered, putting his hand on his heart as he addressed Cat. "My name is Jamaal."

"How about that!" Cat mewed. "Death," she whispered. "My name is Death. No one has introduced themselves to me before."

"Of course it is," Jamaal whispered, with a little chuckle. "Cool name for a cat."

"No," X-it whispered. "That's who she is – Death."

"No time left," Word whispered, putting her hand on his arm before he could finish explaining. They were midway along the tunnel flat against the wall.

"Et," Word said. *"Qui sçait si elle passe son temps de moy plus que je ne fay d'elle?"*

Et smiled at Word.

"The clue," Word whispered with a sparkle in her eyes. "You know who wrote it?"

"I do," Et whispered.

"It was written in the sixteenth century and I know the handwriting," Word whispered, her excitement far exceeding her fear of the Sick-Reapers. "It's Montaigne's."

"Qui sçait si elle passe son temps de moy plus que je ne fay d'elle?" Cat whispered. "Literal translation, 'Who knows if she passes her time more with me than I do with her?'"

"'When I am playing with my cat, how do I know she's not playing with me?'" Word said, whispering the twenty first Century version.

"The Sick-Reapers are going to kill you – *us* – and you're *translating* something written on some wrapping paper in the sixteenth century?" Aisha whispered. "You've lost me."

"It's a clue – all we have to do is figure it out," Word whispered looking at Aisha.

"Do you know what it means?" Aisha asked.

"I know what it says but not what it means," Word said, adding hastily, "but I think Et does." She turned and for the first time she saw the thick mob of militia and robots with heavy artillery standing along the railings to the Hudson River. Then a dozen or so Sick-Reapers with their guns pointing at them moved into the entrance to the tunnel. Behind them the Sick-Reapers were blocking the other end of the tunnel under the West Side Highway.

"Just thought," Cat said, trying not to lose her fur, "if a bullet hits Et –"

"Cat," Et said. "It won't. Concentrate." Et continued telepathically. "If we succeed it will be because of you."

X-it reached out and clasped Word's hand, carefully taking the box she was holding from her and bending down to tie his shoe lace. He stuck the box, which the Four Corners and the Walls had made very tiny, into his sock. Slowly he stood up as the spotlight shone on him, and he opened his hands to show the Sick-Reapers he was holding nothing.

"Here we go," X-it said, grasping Word's hand again and slowly taking a step forward. "No sudden moves."

"We want the Truth Keeper," one of the Sick-Reapers called. "The one they call Word."

"I'm here," Word said, letting go X-it's hand. "Don't hurt my friends and I'll come with you."

"Let's see who your friends are," a Sick-Reaper shouted. "All of you – *out!*"

"Hands where we can see them," another commanded.

"Put 'em up," Jamaal whispered mocking the Sick-Reapers.

"Do you know Montaigne?" Cat whispered to Aisha.

"Word read to us from his essays," Aisha whispered as they slowly moved towards the Sick-Reapers. "He believed the mind's eye is able to visualize what it has read and transform it –"

"Impressive," Cat said. "I'm anticipating but don't know for sure that Et is going to tell us to visualize Montaigne playing with his cat – that's me." Cat paused listening to Et. "Yes, that's *exactly* what she's going to do," Cat whispered. "She told me telepathically," Cat confided. And then, telepathically Cat said, "Jamaal, have you got that?"

"Got it," Jamaal whispered with a grin. "I can contemplate that – if the Sick-Reapers don't kill me."

"Aisha," Cat said, inside her head. "Got that?"

"Sure thing," Aisha said, without speaking.

"Wait!" X-it whispered in a panic. "Et! What year?"

"The combination," Et whispered, disappearing.

"What were the numbers of that lock?" Aisha whispered. "One, five, eight, seven?"

"No! One, five, eight, five," X-it whispered. "Think of Montaigne playing with his cat in 1585!" He looked at Word, eyebrows raised, and she nodded.

"Got-it!" Aisha whispered. "Here they come!"

"Let's see those tattoos!" a Sick-Reaper shouted, walking the last ten feet into the tunnel and grabbing Word. Another Sick-Reaper grabbed X-it and Jamaal put his hands up knowing that when the killing started he was likely to be first. Another Sick-Reaper took Aisha by the arm and dragged her out of the tunnel towards the river. One of the Sick-Reapers tried to kick Cat and seemed to miss, although what actually happened is that the Sick-Reaper's boot went right through her.

But Et, where was Et? X-it looked around trying to find her in the chaos but he could not. She had disappeared. Suddenly he felt a gun against his temple.

"Stay calm," Cat said, inside his head.

"Where's Et?" X-it asked Cat without speaking.

"She's here," Cat said. "Or will be."

"Now's not the time for her to leave!" X-it said.

"Concentrate," Cat said.

"So *you're* the Truth Keeper," the Sick-Reaper who was holding Word said, as he grabbed her t-shirt.

X-it lunged at the Sick-Reaper, but Jamaal and Aisha caught hold of him and held him back as the militia standing against the railing along the Hudson trained their guns on him.

"You're friends just saved your life," one of the Sick-Reapers snarled at X-it.

"Stupid!" Cat said in X-it's head. "That Sick-Reaper is right."

Word closed her eyes as the Sick-Reaper pulled her t-shirt over her head.

"You are very brave," Et said telepathically to Word. "I won't let him hurt you."

Word tried to cover her breasts but the Sick-Reaper grabbed her arms, and she could smell his fetid breath as he bent forward so his face was inches from her body.

"What language is this?" the Sick-Reaper asked. "The writing's too small for me to read." Still holding one of her arms he undid his belt. "Don't be shy," he said, turning around and looking at the Sick-Reapers who had formed a circle around Word, X-it, Aisha, and Jamaal. "*We're* not are we?"

"They want her alive," a Sick-Reaper who was watching said. "Don't mess with her." He looked at Aisha. "'Ave the other one. I like her tattoos better."

"This one first," the Sick-Reaper said, unzipping Word's jeans.

"I'd like to be first," a mesmerizing voice said from behind the Sick-Reaper who already had his belt undone. "*If* you think you're up for it."

The Sick-Reaper turned to find Et – Eternity – in the middle of the circle of Sick-Reapers, who had moved away from her although they were not sure why.

Et was towering above them, the color of the early morning sky. Naked except for her long coppery red hair, she'd arrived from nowhere as beautiful and ethereal as Botticelli's Venus. The Sick-Reapers stood transfixed, staring at her, thinking she must be some genetic mutation, part human and part machine. Man's gift to themselves, a beautiful bioengineered Barbie doll just made for them – but only if they were men enough to take her.

The Sick-Reaper let go of Word's arm and she quickly zipped up her jeans and picked her t-shirt up off the ground and put it back on. The Sick-Reapers had lost interest in her. Word smiled at X-it, who had tears streaming down his face, and she held out her hand as he walked over to where she was standing and put his arms around her. Then he took her hand and kissed it. Word nodded to Aisha and Jamaal who moved slowly between the Sick-Reapers until they were standing with Word and X-it.

Holding hands they watched the Sick-Reapers, who were transfixed by the vision of Venus. Eternity was enticing them with Shakespeare. "*All hail, great masters!*" Et cried. "*Grave sirs, hail! I come to answer thy best pleasures.*"

The Sick-Reapers started arguing about who was to be first. The Sick-Reaper who'd been about to rape Word said he was going to be first.

"Where's Cat?" Word whispered.

"I'm here," Cat said. "I'll meet you there."

"Where?" Aisha whispered.

"Montaigne's garden of course," Cat said.

Instantly, Et's eyes flashed and Cat's fur suddenly looked as if she'd had an electric shock. "Library!" Cat said out loud, and then telepathically, her voice jittery, and her fur frizzy, "*Library! Montaigne's Library* 1585!" Cat added, "Et says, 'Get the year right or we'll never meet again!'"

"Alright," the Sick-Reaper said taking a step closer to Et. "I don't care what color you are, or what kind of genetic mutant you are, let's get on with it."

"It all has to happen in a split second," Cat whispered. "Hold hands. Don't let go –"

"Wait!" Aisha whispered. "What about you Cat?" Letting go of Word and Jamaal's hands and bending down to pick Cat up.

"No!" Word whispered, fiercely. "Don't let go!" She grabbed Aisha's hand and looked to make sure Jamaal had done the same.

"Thank you for thinking of me," Cat said. "Not easy this. Wait – Wait – Not yet –"

"Here you are blue girl," the Sick-Reaper said. His pants were undone and he was holding his erect penis in one hand while he stroked it with the other. "Here's what I've got for you –"

"Wait –" the Cat said. "Remember Montaigne's Cat, 1585."

"*Library!*" Word said. "Montaigne's Library, 1585!"

"Yes – yes!" Cat stuttered. "Li -library!"

"Look," another Sick-Reaper shouted. "She's floating. Her feet are off the ground."

Et lovingly looked at Cat, then Word, and smiled.

"Wait – Wait –" Cat whispered loudly.

Et looked down at the Sick-Reaper. No longer soft and loving, her eyes were cold and menacing, but still she smiled. Her body became more iridescent, mesmerizing the Sick-Reapers, the militias, and the robot killing machines. She stood like Botticelli's Venus as she moved her hand away, exposing that part of her body that admirers of the painting had so often imagined and the Sick-Reapers wanted to see.

"*Wait –*" Cat whispered again, as Et reached out her hand and her long beautiful fingers –

"*Wait –*" Cat whispered, in a small tight voice.

The Sick-Reaper with his penis in his hand took a step towards her –

"For the ones who look in wonder at the stars!" Et said, looking up at the sky and then giving the Sick-Reaper an enticing smile.

"**NOW!**" Cat shouted.

"*Montaigne's Library! 1585!*" Word, X-it, Aisha, and Jamaal shouted in unison.

"*Isti mirant stellae!*" Et cried, as the tip of her forefinger touched the tip of the Sick-Reaper's penis, and in that split second what people knew was going to happen did happen, but they would never know it.

Except for the Truth Keepers – because in that very instant when the world ended, four humans survived. Word, X-it, Aisha, and Jamaal from 2022 were transported back to Michel Montaigne's library in 1585. In the split second between being and not being, between something and nothing, they were the only ones to survive.

Epilogue

1585

In 1585 when Word, X-it, Aisha, and Jamaal landed in a heap on the floor of the great library in the round tower of the castle – Château de Montaigne, Guyenne, France – Montaigne was not there. He was instead sitting in his garden. Eternity was standing next to him with her feet just a few inches off the ground looking like Botticelli's Venus in a beautifully embroidered blue silk gown. At Montaigne's feet was his Cat, looking a little worse for wear, but playing with the buckles on his shoes.

Disentangling themselves from each other, the four time-travellers found sanctuary in Montaigne's magnificent library. Each in their own way tried to block thoughts of the Sick-Reapers from their minds. For Word, just being surrounded by leather bound hand written books brought comfort. There was nowhere she would rather be than in Montaigne's library of lost scribal manuscripts and ancient texts, knowing that most would be lost in a great fire in the eighteen century. For X-it, Aisha, and Jamaal – they were just thankful to be alive and in a place of such tranquility where no Sick-Reapers could hack their consciousness.

The four time-travellers scrambled to their feet and looked

around.

"I read there are forty-eight oak joists and two supporting beams," Word said, deliberately steering the conversation away from what had happened in Riverside Park by the Hudson River.

X-it started counting the joists, in tacit agreement with Word not to talk about the last split second they'd spent in the 21st Century – not yet. He already knew that for the rest of their lives they would struggle to turn the world and set it on a new path to the future but they needed time – time to recover.

"And forty-six of the joists are painted with Greek and Latin citations," Word said, "that Montaigne likes to read and think about when he is working on his essays,"

"Forty-eight," X-it said. "There *are* forty eight joists." He smiled, "and forty- six of them are tattooed like you." He looked lovingly at Word. "Are you alright?" he asked gently. "I should have stopped him."

"They'd have killed you," Word said. "Let's not talk about it."

"Do you think Montaigne will let us read some of his books?" Jamaal asked Word, breaking the tension, and steering the conversation back to the library.

"I expect so," Word said, her eyes looking around at Montaigne's vast literary collection.

"Nietzsche wanted to hang out with Montaigne," Jamaal said. "He wrote that he 'truly augmented the joy of living on earth' and that he could make himself 'at home in the world with him'. We might have to – if he'll let us."

"We *are* asylum seekers," X-it said, looking pensive.

Jamaal nodded as his eyes settled on the murals painted on the Walls of the little room off the library that was Montaigne's study. "I wonder if he would let me copy some of his murals."

"We can ask him," Word said, still reading the citations on the joists. "There are sixty-seven sayings taken from classic authors written on these joists. It's a cosmic mind map," Word said, refusing to allow the Sick-Reaper who had pulled her t-shirt off to enter her consciousness.

"Look!" she said pointing. "Quotes from the writings of Horace, Menander, and Sophocles! I have some quotes from them on my body!"

"Here's a Lucretius quote from the poem he wrote more than two thousand years ago on *The Nature of Universe*!" Word said. "Montaigne's Essays contain almost a hundred quotes from *De Rerum Natura*."

"You know too much!" X-it said, the relief in his voice audible as he suddenly realized that Word had not only survived, she was still a Truth Keeper.

"And here is the very same quote on me!" Word said, and without hesitating she lifted her t-shirt and showed them the Lucretius quote tattooed on her left breast. Aisha looked at her questioningly and Word shrugged. "Just taking back my body," she said.

                    Denny Taylor

"I second that," Aisha said, and in solidarity she turned and undid her pants and bent over to show them the quotes on her rear and they all laughed.

"Many of these quotes are in Montaigne's *Essays*, either verbatim, in translation, or in paraphrase," Word said, smiling at Aisha as the moment passed. "Montaigne reads them when he is writing in this library. I read that they influenced the structure of some of his essays," she said.

"They say that?" the sixteenth century Gascony nobleman asked, speaking in the Middle French of the Renaissance, gravely bowing to Word as he entered the library.

"Seigneur de Montaigne," Word said, bowing her head and speaking in Montaigne's Middle French. "They do. And much more."

The man was dressed in opulently embroidered 16th century robes of red and blue silks and he had a fine linen ruff edged with lace around his neck. Bowing a second time he introduced himself as Michel de Montaigne.

Word bowed, thinking she should have curtsied, introduced her friends and then herself, before translating the interchange for X-it, Aisha, and Jamaal, who had all made low bows to Montaigne. And so it went, a conversation between Word and Montaigne and Word translating for her young friends.

"Eternity has told me about you," Montaigne said. "She says you are called Word and that you are the last Truth Keeper." He reached out and took her hand in his and turned it over so he could read the sign on her wrist. "*In the beginning was the word –*"

He nodded and gave a little smile. "You are welcome to stay here in the Château," he said to Word, and looking at X-it, Aisha, and Jamaal, "You are welcome too, for you are the only humans to survive the twenty first century."

Montaigne continued, speaking formally, "Eternite has also told me that you were exceedingly brave and that with the help of my Cat you saved the life of the last Truth Keeper – and for that Eternite has named you all Truth Keepers."

X-it, Aisha, and Jamaal bowed again as Word translated what he had said. They bowed again and thanked Montaigne, asking Word to tell him they were grateful for his hospitality.

"Merci" Aisha said, this time curtsying in her men's vest and jeans.

Montaigne bowed to Aisha, and raising his eyebrows he looked at the letters on the tattooed typewriter keys that were like a necklace dipping low on her breasts.

"I am myself the matter of my book," Aisha said to Montaigne, and then they both looked at Word, anticipating her translation.

"Je suis moy-mesmes la matiere de mon livre," Word said, adding in Middle French to Montaigne, "I know you have much to say on reading and being."

Montaigne said something that Word did not translate. She just nodded and smiled, and then to Aisha she said, "We are to have clothes and we must make sure our tattoos are covered up. Some of the texts haven't been written yet."

Turning towards the entrance of the library, Montaigne bowed again and with a flourish of his arm he said "Eternite," as if introducing her to them for the first time. "Botticelli's Venus," he said. "She is and always will be –"

"Michou," Et said, smiling, "such an exaggeration."

"And I am just Montaigne's Cat," Cat said telepathically, "but for almost five hundred years people will read and wonder about me. After that? Well, who knows? We'll see."

Et smiled at Montaigne, shook her head at Cat, and then looked at Word, X-it, Aisha, and Jamaal, nodding, not speaking, just taking them in, and it was as if the Universe sighed as she looked at them and saw for herself that they were still mortal and alive.

"X-it," Et asked, "do you still have my box?"

"Hope so!" X-it said, not sure if it was still in his sock. He bent down quickly and felt around, first right and then left.

"Left," Word said, looking for even the smallest of lumps in X-it's sock.

"Here it is!" X-it said, holding the box – which was smaller than a bracelet charm – between his thumb and forefinger.

"Thank you," Et said. "Michou has kindly said we can put it near the lake so we can see the Château when Cat and I step outside."

"Even when the whole earth, rocked by the terrifying tumult of war, shudderingly quaked and came to an end," Montaigne said solemnly, looking at Et and then Cat and the four time travellers, "nothing at all had the power to affect you."

"Lucretius," Word said, translating for her friends, "an interpretation, perhaps not quite what he meant."

"We are grateful," Word said to Montaigne in Middle French. "I have learned from ancient texts and from my own experience that human beings are not the center of the Universe, But we are here to find a way, as Lucretius foresaw, to swerve the ancient atoms and change the future for all living things on the planet."

"Well that should keep you busy," Cat said, telepathically. "Glad I'm here to take part in this adventure."

"We *cannot* let everyone die," Word said. "We have to stop the Sick-Reapers, the genetic mutants, and the A-I"

"You are truly the last Truth Keeper," Et said smiling at Word. "How are you going to undertake this great task?"

"We must change the mind of René Descartes," Word said without hesitation. "Help him *feel* as well as think. Reconnect his mind and his body."

"It is the misinterpretation of Descartes' *Meditations* by powerful men," Et said, "that led them along the path to the end of the world."

"And yet," Word said, "it was Descartes who wrote, 'If you would be a real seeker after truth, it is necessary that at least once in your life you doubt, as far as possible, all things.'"

Aisha smiled and giving a knowing look to Word pointed at her behind.

"I know that," Cat said telepathically, "Aisha's got that quote from Descartes tattooed on her –!"

"And so the conversation begins," Montaigne said. "I understand from Eternite that Descartes will be born four years after I die – this gives us time for many conversations before your next adventure begins."

Dear Readers,

This is Word. X-it, Aisha, and Jamaal are psyched that you've reached the end of Split *and participated with us in this dangerous thought experiment. Together we've explored some of the connections between the Universe and our consciousness. We've named our nightmares and traumatic memories, and if our thought experiment has worked we've changed – if only for a split second – the nature of our reality.*

Now that we're in 1585, and the A-I and Sick-Reapers are not after us, we're trying to figure out how to change the course of human history. Sounds irrational? Doesn't even come close to the evil irrationality of the rich and powerful men of the 21st century. While our story might seem far-fetched it is grounded in science. X-it has written about the underlying science, which you can read below. The technological 'breakthroughs' that are incorporated into the story may also seem futuristic but they are all dangerously authentic – like making new life forms using biogenetic technology to manipulate letters in DNA to create chemical machines that can be assembled from parts. It's happening – constituting potential end-of-the-world-as-we-know-it existential risks.

The political backstory is also fiction based on fact – the corruption of governments, the activities of our political masters, and the totally insane self-aggrandizement of the richest men in human societies who equate their wealth with sovereignty that bestows on them the inalienable right to determine our fate. They are represented by the Fanatical Eight – the Ginger Tom, the Freaky Geek, and the Posh Boy, composites of wicked men. We all know them.

X-it is going to write to you now, but before I sign off I'm sure you'll want to know if – given that our circumstances have changed – Et can now see the future after 2022. She cannot. But she says she hasn't given up hope, *which she calls the best of all human characteristics, perhaps even greater that love. What I hope is that X-it, Aisha, Jamaal and I will find a way to change the future by changing events in the past, but what we all hope is that you will find ways to change events in the year in which you read* Split. *Go back and read the quote at the front of the book from* Who Rules the World? *by Noam Chomsky. I met him once before the fall of New York City. Eating chocolate cake in Café Luxembourg, Noam said, "It's not that there are no alternatives. The alternatives just aren't being taken. And that's dangerous. So if you ask what the world is going to look like, it's not a pretty picture. Unless people do something about it. We always can." This is our message to you – we always can. It's up to you.*

This is X-it. Word didn't tell you she's okay and our baby is safe inside her. Aisha and Jamaal are also well. And the bird is here with Et. We're all getting used to 16th century garb, which is made up of many pieces that fit together like a jigsaw puzzle. We see Michel Montaigne once or twice every day, Et not that often, and Cat has abandoned us for her Michou, who she follows around playing with the buckles on his shoes or sitting on his lap purring. She says she has taken care of all the dying and dead for the next 500 years, so now she wants to rest and get ready for what happens next.

None of us are quite sure what's going to happen now we are in the 16th century. We do have access to Michou's library, and when he is not there we climb the stone steps and sit on the floor, surrounded by his books, reading the quotes on the joists, trying to *figure out how we get back to the 21st century and what to do when we get there.*

We wish you could help us. The one decision we've all made is to include in this letter some references to the science that underlies Split. Don't laugh. What we've done is copy some of the quotes tattooed on Word from a book we hope you can get. It was – or rather will be (isn't that weird?) published in English in 2016. It's called, Seven Brief Lessons on Physics by Carlo Rovelli. It was originally published in Italian under the title Sette bevi lezioni in 2014.

Don't be put off because it's physics. Many of us were schooled to reject the idea that we can be scientists. I never felt that way because of my Dad, who you might remember was an astrophysicist, but also because after I was eight I didn't go to school. I learned what I know for myself. You can too. Here's a cool trick. You can read Carlo Rovelli as if I am him or he is me. Seriously. Turns out Einstein's equation was/will be correct. Here's me being Rovelli on Einstein:

> *In short, the theory describes a colorful and amazing world where universes explode, space collapses into bottomless holes, time sags and slows near a planet, and the unbounded extensions of interstellar space ripple and sway like the surface of the sea … And all of this, which emerged gradually from my mice-gnawed book, was not a tale told by an idiot in a fit of lunacy or a hallucination caused by Calabria's burning Mediterranean sun and its dazzling sea. It was reality.*

Rovelli's 'mice-gnawed book' fits with our story, don't you think? And, more importantly, our story fits with Einstein's theory.

What's really wild is that Split *also reflects theories of quantum mechanics and the 'hot box' calculated by the German physicist Max Planck. Once again, here's me as Rovelli:*

> Quantum mechanics and experiments with particles
> have taught us that the world is a continuous, restless
> swarming of things, a continuous coming to light and
> disappearance of ephemeral entities. A set of vibrations,
> as in the switched-on hippie world of the 1960s. A world
> of happenings, not of things.

Don't you love the 'continuous coming to light and disappearance of ephemeral entities'? Doesn't it remind you of Et – the Old Crone becoming Botticelli's Venus, larger than life, beautiful, with extraterrestrial powers, and blue? Also, the switched-on hippy world of the 1960's is reminiscent of Death as David Bowie and his 1969 Space Oddity *single and his 2015* Black Star, *recorded at the Magic Shop and Human Worldwide Studios in New York City, which by 2022 will surely be gone.*

Again, this is me as Rovelli, for when he asks, 'And what then are our values, our dreams, our emotions, our individual knowledge? What are we, in this boundless and glowing world?', these are my questions too. And my response would be the same as his:

> We belong to a short-lived genus of species. All of our
> cousins are already extinct. What's more, we do damage.
> The brutal climate and environmental changes that we
> have triggered are unlikely to spare us. For Earth they
> may turn out to be a small irrelevant blip, but I do not
> think that we will outlast them unscathed—especially
> since public and political opinion prefers to ignore the

dangers that we are running, hiding our heads in the sand. We are perhaps the only species on Earth to be conscious of the inevitability of our individual mortality. I fear that soon we shall also have to become the only species that will knowingly watch the coming of its own collective demise, or at least the demise of its civilization.

It is in this dangerous space that the Split Second Solution takes place. However, unreal the fictional story may seem, the underlying scientific and political circumstances are real. Rovelli writes:

We are born and die as stars are born and die, both individually and collectively. This is our reality …

This strange, multicolored, and astonishing world that we explore—where space is granular, time does not exist, and things are nowhere—is not something that estranges us from our true selves, for this is only what our natural curiosity reveals to us about the place of our dwelling. About the stuff of which we ourselves are made. We are made of the same stardust of which all things are made, and when we are immersed in suffering or when we are experiencing intense joy, we are being nothing other than what we can't help but be: a part of our world.

Our thought experiment will have worked if you think about the frontiers of human learning differently. It will have worked if you begin to see yourself as woven into the fabric of space, connected to the origins of the cosmos, reimagining the nature of time and the ways we think.

We leave you now. Aisha and Jamaal will write the letters to *you in the next book. They send their love and will have much to tell. Will we change the future? Possibly. It will be up to you – what you do – when you read the* Split Second Solution.

With love from Word and X-it

Library of Michel Montaigne, 1585

ACKNOWLEDGEMENTS

Thank you (in order of appearance) to Mike McPhail, John G. Hemry, Steve White, Bud Sparhawk, Keith R.A. DeCandido, Jody Lynn Nye, Jack McDevitt, Michael Z. Williamson, Peter Prellwitz, Brenda Cooper, David Sherman, Charles E. Gannon, and Paul Levinson for their thoughtful introductions to each story, and to Bethlynne Prellwitz for her proofreading prowess.

Building Blocks originally published in *Barbarians at the Jumpgate*, edited by Bruce Gehweiler and published by Padwolf Publishing.

Carbon Copy originally published in *Space Pirates*, edited by David Lee Summers and published by Flying Pen Press.

Zinn Mensch originally published in *Trails of Indiscretion Magazine* and later republished in Tales of the Talisman Magazine.

Oracle was originally published in NthDegree Magazine.

Travellin' Show originally published in *Space Tramps*, edited by Jennifer Brozek and published by Flying Pen Press.

Devil You Don't originally published in *The Stories In Between*, edited by Greg Schauer, et al and published by Fantasist Enterprises.

By Any Means originally published in *New Blood*, edited by Patrick Thomas and Diane Raetz and published by Padwolf Publishing.

In the Dying Light originally published in *Breach the Hull*, edited by Mike McPhail and published first by Marietta Publishing, then subsequently by Dark Quest Books.

True Colors originally published in *By Other Means*, edited by Mike McPhail and published by Dark Quest Books.

Last Man Standing originally published in *Space Horrors*, edited by David Lee Summers and published by Flying Pen Press.

Ghosts on the Battlefield originally published in *No Man's Land*, edited by Mike McPhail and published by Dark Quest Books.

First Line originally published in *So It Begins*, edited by Mike McPhail and published by Dark Quest Books.

CONTENTS

FOREWORD

As a fellow author and editor, I've often described Danielle as a "natural-born writer," someone who is as comfortable smithing the written word as most of us are speaking it. And yet when asked how she does it she is often at a loss to explain. Her style is truly organic, more instinct and intuition, than textbook structure. I feel this is one of the primary reasons why her stories are populated by such rich and lively characters. But that is just the beginning of what distinguishes her fiction.

Being an engineer, I'm obsessive about getting the details, or at least the anatomy or illusion of form-to-function, correct. Time and time again Danielle has impressed me with her wisdom when it comes to this. She'll sit down and do the research—or confer with someone familiar with the topic—but where she shines is when she extrapolates the possibilities and comes up with answers and concepts on her own, often finding new insights. Then she takes the results and expands upon them, raising the whole to a new pinnacle.

For those of us who know her, we would all agree Danielle is a true "literary force of nature." She has proven herself blessed with an unbounded imagination and a unique vision when it comes to melding kernels of knowledge—be they scientific fact, military protocol, or mythological details—with creative inspiration to give life to characters, worlds, and situations that draw the reader in and grip them long after the last word has been read. Nowhere is this more evident than in her science fiction. Being the editor of the *Defending the Future* anthology series, I am in a unique position to know, having gladly accepted several of her stories for publication.

As you turn the pages of *A Legacy of Stars* you will discover the diversity of concept that is characteristic of Danielle's work. From hard-core science fiction to the distinctly surreal and everything in between. I hope you enjoy the journey as much as the rest of us have.

Mike McPhail, uc51

BUILDING BLOCKS

Gone! Gone! Gone!

The cry went out, an uncontrollable shiver, growing in intensity until it encompassed the planet.

Gone.... those of The Unity whispered in stunned disbelief. *So many.... Billions...gone.* They drew their remaining loved ones close, grasping for what comfort there was to be had in the moments following devastation.

The world would never be the same again.

*　　　*　　　*

The five veteran members of the ship's crew were absolutely silent, waiting for a signal from their captain as they had many times before. But then....

"Captain," the crewman at the monitoring station spoke, drawing Kyle Dunjen away from the bittersweet satisfaction that came with each successful set-down on an untouched world. "Landing protocol is complete. Shall I deploy the Remote Specimen Extractors?"

The atmosphere on the deck seemed to tighten in a sympathetic cringe the crew was too disciplined to indulge. Dunjen turned to catch the eye of the kid that had interrupted his ritual. He knew the crew had filled Sanders in, and yet the first thing the crewman does is off the *Cortez's* basic rhythm. The captain mentally shrugged away his annoyance and drew a centering breath.

"Crewman Sanders," Dunjen responded in a still, reverent voice, "you and this planet both just lost your virginity; that's a moment to be honored, respected...not promptly dismissed in favor of procedure."

He turned away. He didn't like invading these celestial Edens. It felt somehow wrong to bring humanity to somewhere unspoiled, knowing by the time they left that would be the last word anyone would use to describe the place. Still, if it had to be done, he felt it best done respectfully. Showing respect was a prelude to mourning the planet's ultimate fate. That was why he was here.

It was bad enough when corporations were involved; even worse when the military went mercenary. Something like this shouldn't be about the bottom line. He loved the exploration, but he hated what came after: Command would plant a colony or two on the largest continents, strip the place of everything useful, and then head for the next coordinates on the charts. Mankind was a plague, leaving behind nothing but dead or dying planets in its wake.

Dunjen shut down his dark thoughts and eased back into his ritual.

The first ten minutes post-planetfall were his; he would not allow a wet-behind-the-ears green recruit to rush him. No matter what the kid had learned by rote—from training manuals Dunjen himself had written practically single-handed—this was important. It kept him balanced, and that translated to the crew and the mission.

Reaching deep inside, he tried to reclaim what his men, inspired by his precise positioning and intense contemplation, called his *zen shui*. It eluded him. Tension dominated instead, strung along the rod-straight length of his back and up his neck, ending in a band looped tight around his temples. Regardless, he stood at the view port, staring at the planet's surface the full six hundred seconds he always allotted himself.

It was a matter of principle.

Snapping around as the last second passed, Dunjen noted the carefully neutral expressions on every face but Sanders'. The kid merely looked confused. Dunjen felt the tension hardening his features, but made no effort to soften them. Planetfall had started off bad. It was important Sanders realized that. Either the lesson would stick, or he would lose his prized assignment on the *Cortez*.

Dunjen moved forward in measured steps. He stopped with a mere inch between him and Sanders and held the crewman's gaze. Displeasure wrapped around them like a smothering cloud. Dunjen let it.

He could tell the exact moment realization kicked in with cold, hard clarity. Sanders paled and dropped his gaze, a slight tremor rippling down his throat. He might not understand the nature of his transgression, but he would never forget it—or repeat it.

"I'm sorry, sir."

The captain did not acknowledge the apology. To do so would blunt the rebuke and erode his position of command. Instead, he redirected the crew back to protocol.

"Callaghan," he called out to his XO, not taking his eyes from Sanders' face. "Deploy the RSEs."

*   *   *

What has caused this? they questioned one another. *How did this happen?*

There were no answers, only effects. Harmony broke. Confusion reigned. Those struck down left an inconceivable wound none knew how to heal. Repeated jags of pain traveled through the survivors' awareness like a low-voltage electric shock. Suffering left them disoriented. Stunned.

Why?
Why?
Why?

The question rippled out through the masses until it reached those closest to the raw lesion.

A rumble. A roar. Vibrations disrupted the air. Ran through The Unity. Brought with it a new level of agony. The rumple continued, drawing closer.

What? they cried, who had never known pain. Never known death. Never known intrusion.

The only answer from those on the edge: silence. Another billion souls lost to the encroaching Void.

*   *   *

"Captain?"

Dunjen sighed and electronically tagged his place in the geological scans he was monitoring. This is why he had turned off the comm to all but emergency hails. It was the only way he could get anything done with only minimal interruption. He might be captain, but everyone on board the *Cortez* served in multiple capacities. When it came to maximizing efficiency, less crew meant less cost. They all, to some extent, could carry out the various duties required to fly and maintain the ship, but each had one skill vital to the mission that they excelled at above the others. Command could send a smaller vessel, eat up less of their budget on crew necessities like rations and accommodations, and redirect it toward maintenance and development.

As captain, he of all the crew had the hardest time balancing his duties. Something always trumped research. This current intrusion couldn't have come at a worse time. At this moment his mindset was firmly entrenched in the science of the scans. The implications of the data were amazing; it could totally transform their concepts of planetary development. Yet he had no choice but to set it all aside; by necessity, he was captain first and a scientist second. He hated when the two conflicted. He loved the science; the rest just made what he did possible.

He straightened, and then arched his back. His neck popped when he cast a disgruntled glance toward the hatch. Crewman Sanders waited there at attention. The man stood rock-steady, his face unnaturally pale. His eyes betrayed the slightest flicker of tension. From under the edges of Sanders' shipsuit the acrid scent of stress began to tinge the surrounding air. Sanders' primary duty was Master Technician.

Dunjen had a bad feeling.

Immediately Kyle Dunjen, Ph.D, sank beneath the surface, and like preset emergency protocols, the Captain fully reinstated. With a couple powerful strides he moved across the room, addressing the crewman. "Sanders, report."

"Sorry to disturb you, sir, but we were unable to raise you on the comm," Sanders responded, his throat bobbing. "The RSEs have experienced an undetermined malfunction. Diagnostics indicate the radio signal is being received and that the units' systems should be operational, but they have lost maneuverability. The nearest one is ten meters out from our perimeter. I have had no success getting them to reengage."

"Send another one."

The response took a beat too long in coming.

"They've all been sent."

Dunjen worked his jaw, silently considering the scenario, trying to focus on the immediate problem without allowing himself to be influenced by his annoyance with Sanders. It took more effort than it should. Eight Remote Specimen Extractors and every one of them malfunctioned. Even given the...*quality* of military issue, that rate of failure stretched the probability.

The captain moved past Sanders and through the hatch. He headed for the bridge, not waiting to see if the crewman followed. "Do sensors indicate an obstruction?"

A slight laboring of breath betrayed Sanders' effort to keep pace. "Sensors are experiencing interference and we have not been able to gain clear visual."

"Right." Planetfall hadn't just started bad, it persisted that way exponentially. Dunjen ignored the crewman the rest of the trip to the bridge. Instead, he spent the short walk mentally tallying the possible sources of the problem, matched with potential fixes. Ducking through the final hatch, he headed for the monitoring station. "Callaghan, report."

"Preliminary scans confirmed non-corrosive atmosphere, primarily oxygen/hydrogen/nitrogen mix, high humidity, breathable, but not comfortably and not for long. Temperature readings are at 24 degrees Celsius. Gravity registers at .8 Earth-norm and sensors detect no complex life forms. RSEs were deployed per protocol, two units to a sector. All units were deployed before reduced functionality began to register. The fourth RSE group deployed at roughly 0300 ship-time. The final unit processed the first two quadrants out from the ship's perimeter, transmitting a steady stream of data. By the time it entered the third, sensors registered a progressive decrease in mobility. Now the unit is fully stationary. Diagnostics indicate no identifiable malfunction. We attempted to retrieve it using the docking grapple, but the unit is too far out."

The data didn't give Dunjen much to go on. Initiating the external sensors, he frowned at the screen. "What is this distortion?"

"We have been unable to determine, sir," Callaghan answered. "The theory is condensation from the extreme humidity in the atmosphere, but we won't know for sure without physical inspection."

A grimace twisted Dunjen's mouth. This expedition held no satisfaction, only one complication after another. And how was he to salvage the situation? It was a hard call. If he sent a skip out after the unit, the jet craft could be affected by whatever knocked out the RSEs; but his only other option was to send an EVA team without knowing the cause of these malfunctions, without more time to observe their surroundings. Normally, he looked forward to this moment, but not when they were unprepared. More than one tragedy had stemmed from the decision to EVA too soon after Planetfall.

Jet craft were expensive...feed-a-small-colony-for-a-year expensive. And people...well, Dunjen didn't like his choices one bit.

✳   ✳   ✳

More and more the foreignness intruded. Each new surface they encountered sizzled with current. The composition was tight, slick. Solid mass blocked eternally open pathways, cutting them off from aspects of the whole. Isolation was introduced to The Unity. Impurities intruded like a poison. The world was dying.

Those doomed by proximity came out of their stunned stupor. They murmured among themselves, bent logic against the senselessness that eroded The Unity. Observed and probed. Some went forward to plumb the nature of the threat to all they knew. They took some of that nature unto themselves.

Hard, one offered, before fading away. *Cold,* another observed.
Impermeable.
Alien.
Unnatural.
Pain.

And, in a quiet, final voice, all those remaining murmured in agitation as they drew back from the new concept forced upon them: *Death.*

No!

With instantaneous resolve, they embraced the only hope left.

Love took on a bittersweet tang. The doomed brushed a fleeting caress across those to be protected. The Unity suffered sorrow as divisiveness was introduced. Those scarred by the edges of Intrusion turned away, let the hardening encompass them completely, detached from The Unity in the only move they could make to preserve it. They cleaved to the Intrusion, encased it...blocked its path to their beloved.

The Unity learned sacrifice.

✳   ✳   ✳

"We have no choice, sir." Callaghan spoke softly, his tone even and his expression neutral.

"And you're sure the secondary units can't be repaired?"

At Callaghan's affirmative, Dunjen's jaw clenched. Flexed. His fingers curled until his hands were in fists on his desk. Not only had they been unable to remotely activate any of the RSEs, but they were steadily losing functionality in the external sensors, and atmospherics were exhibiting a marked decline in efficiency. Not one thing had gone smoothly this tour, and he suspected an EVA wouldn't either. He leveled a glare at his XO.

"I don't like it."

"I didn't expect you would, sir."

Dunjen couldn't help his grim almost-smile at Callaghan's dry, matter-of-fact tone. The man was more than an XO; he was a friend. At odd moments glimmers of that crept into command situations. "It will have to be Sanders."

"Yes, sir. I'm afraid so, sir."

"Damn!" The captain wanted to smash something. Sanders might be their equipment expert, but he was also the least-prepared member of the crew. "Damn!"

Ignoring the determination creeping into Callaghan's eye, Dunjen made an executive decision. "Sanders," he sent over the comm.

"Aye, Captain," Sanders voice responded from the comm speaker mounted in the desktop.

"Report to the equipment locker. Suit up for EVA."

"A-acknowledged, sir. I'll-I'll make it right." Something about the crewman's response unsettled Dunjen, but there wasn't time to figure out why. The captain cut the connection and turned to his XO.

"Callaghan...." Dunjen paused, not really liking his options, but knowing there was only one choice he could make. He stood and moved in front of Callaghan.

"I'll take care of him, sir." Callaghan spoke into the gap.

But Dunjen continued as if the man hadn't said a word. "XO, report to the bridge and assume the con. Run full diagnostics. I want this bird ready to lift off for the southern continent as soon as Sanders and I have retrieved the closest Rover."

"Hell no!"

The emotions that played across Sean Callaghan's face were to be expected. After all, he was the closest thing Dunjen had to a brother; he could teach a dog lessons about loyalty. No, the fact that Callaghan had lost control enough to show them...*that* was remarkable. The XO was the king of dead-pan.

"Kyle, you can't!"

"I have to."

"Bullshit!"

"XO Callaghan, as captain I am responsible for the security and well-being of each member of this crew, would you agree?"

Callaghan growled in frustration. "Yes, sir."

"Very good. And would you concur that of the two of us, your secondary duties of Astrogation are more vital than my geological skills?" Dunjen kept his own voice neutral, calm. He watched as his question burrowed past Callaghan's objections. The XO's facial muscles tensed until his clenched teeth were bare.

"Yes, sir." Callaghan's voice had lost all expression, and his eyes were as dark and brittle as slate.

"Would you also agree that of the entire crew, I have the most EVA hours logged, and the most rescue training?" This time Callaghan glowered and only nodded in agreement.

Dunjen turned away to head for the equipment locker.

"Captain?"

"Yes?"

Callaghan swallowed hard and snapped a regulation salute. His eyes were shadowed and just above his left eye pulsed an uncharacteristic tic, but he'd once again composed his expression. Dunjen knew how he felt anyway. He returned the salute and headed for the equipment locker, his long strides decimating the distance. His heart held the same apprehension as his XO's, but without at least one RSE they'd have to scrub the three-year mission before it barely began.

✳   ✳   ✳

The muscles along Dunjen's shoulders and back coiled with each step he took toward the airlock. Normally comforting, like age lines on a long-time lover, the conduits and pipes running the length of the corridor barely registered with him today. For the first time in his service he did not look forward to an EVA on an untouched planet. He drew a deep breath and his throat gave an odd hitch. Sniffing, he once more caught a persistent whiff of an out-of-place odor. The air was noticeably more meaty than it should be, unusually thick with the scents of close habitation. The muscles of his face twitched as Dunjen silently cursed the faceless button-pusher that had assigned them this sector. He'd never served on or commanded a mission this problematic. If one more thing went wrong, he was pulling them from the planet all together. Diverting his path to the nearest comm unit, he jabbed in the code for the bridge.

"Thompson, respond," Dunjen barked into the mic.

"Thompson reporting, Captain." The crewman's voice filtered through the speaker. A tell-tale electric hum sounded, the only indiction of the open connection as the crewman awaited orders.

"Run full diagnostics of the Environmental systems, priority one," Dunjen ordered. "I'm in the port aft compartment and something is seriously off in the mix down here."

"Aye, Captain," the crewman responded. "Thompson, over and out." The comm clicked quietly as it disengaged.

Dunjen continued on his way to the airlock, his steps tapping a bit more quickly on the deck plates. Maybe he was just being twitchy, but the more aft he went, the harder he found it to breathe. A deep, barking cough did little to clear the thick feeling clogging his airways. Restricting himself to shallow breaths, he entered the lock.

"Oh, hell!"

The first thing he noted when he crossed the hatch was Sanders' empty suit bay; the second was the man's absence. His thoughts went back to Sanders' earlier response: *I'll make it right*, the kid had said, like he had to redeem himself. Salvaging the mission—and his place on the crew—was likely the only thing more important to him than procedure. *Hell!*

With a smack, Dunjen activated the external scanners from the console next to the hatch. They came on, but the image resembled the pre-cable television of a hundred years earlier: grainy and full of interference. Some areas of the transmission looked like they were outright filtered through ice. Even so, he could make out the lumbering form of Sanders heading toward the RSE.

Growling a few more choice curses, Dunjen fought the urge to ignore protocol and suit up without going through the safety checklist. He resisted the impulse, moved with controlled steps toward his environment suit, and completed his inspection in record time. Other than some fine, ash-grey dust coating the outer skin, all was in order. He kept his eye on the monitor as he slid into the suit. Sanders was going to get someone killed one day if he didn't learn some sense.

✳   ✳   ✳

Loved ones hovered nearby, contemplating the Intrusion, trying to understand, to recognize those they had lost in the hard, crystalline edges of the Barrier; all that stood between the fractured Unity and Chaos. They whispered a vow to the young ones they drew close one final time, a vow that while more would be lost before the end, Unity would be restored to their world.

Determination hardened their features as they set the young aside, passing them to the embrace of others. Hope must be preserved. No more waiting. No more reacting. The Intrusion must be stopped; it must be buried until it smothered, compressed until nothing was left. They propelled themselves away from The Unity, as cut off as their brethren that formed the Barrier.

Hard. The Dis-Unity growled. *Strong.*

Fast.

Seek.

END!

The Unity came to grips with the grim necessity of the offensive.

✳   ✳   ✳

Something was in the air. Something more than just trouble.

Dunjen felt like he slogged through a greasy fog...the kind that clung and pulled at a man's limbs until he expected to hear a sucking sound with each step forward. It unsettled him further when his suit began to crackle. It was, at first, a soft sound, kind of like crumpling cellophane. By the time Sanders came into sight, it had grown sharper, like thin ice shattering.

He didn't like this. Not one bit. It became harder and harder to move, and whatever formed on the outside of the suit started to interfer with his visibility as well.

"You stupid shit," Dunjen murmured as he swiped at his faceplate once more, not sure if he spoke to himself or the crewman marching awkwardly ahead. It amounted to the same; the comm circuit was closed.

Activating a toggle in the index finger of his right gauntlet, he remotely triggered a subtle alert pattern that played across the interior peripheral of Sanders' helmet. A precurser tone accompanied the lightshow to warn the EVA crew there was an incoming message. Dunjen was glad of the feature. It wouldn't do to startle the kid. If Sanders' already jerky motions were any indication, he was barely holding it together. Anything unexpected would likely trigger a violent reaction, and that led to ruptured seals, or worse. As it was, the crewman's head jerked sharp enough to make Dunjen wince. He stopped moving forward, uneasy with putting too much distance between him and the ship. Now that he had the man's attention he activated the comm.

The sound of Sanders' breath came across the circuit: deep inhales paired with rapid exhales. If he didn't get that under control he would empty his tanks long before they hit the airlock.

"What the *hell* do you think you are doing?" Dunjen didn't wait for an answer before continuing. "Crewman, tell me: what does the manual say about unaccompanied extravehicular activities?"

Sanders turned and Dunjen gasped himself. The man's faceplate was nearly obscured and his suit glittered as if encased in ice. Dunjen looked down to find his own nearly as coated. What the hell was it? It couldn't be ice, the ambient temperature was way too warm for that, and minerals took years to form to the extent he saw. Gripped by deep foreboding he barely heard Sanders' response.

"Sir, no[inhale]crewmember[inhale]will perform[inhale]EVA without...."

The captain cut him off before he finished. "Glad to see you read it, now get your ass back to the ship before I bust you down to civilian and dump you at the next station!"

"But...." Sanders replied, turning awkwardly, as if his articulated joints were locked. "The RSE...."

"Just go!" Dunjen barked, any patience he had left long worn away by the tension wrapped like a hot sheath around each nerve. "Just get back to the ship and get ready for lift-off." He reached out to grab Sanders' arm and whatever encased his elbow joint shattered like glass, tearing through the specially engineered microfiber skin.

Shit! Dunjen actually felt the blood drain clear down to his toes. *Shit! Forget the other continent; we're getting off this cursed planet.* The material of the suit was designed to withstand even a tungsten carbide-edged blade. Nothing should have gone through it. Surprisingly, no trail of blood ran into his glove.

"Go! GO!" he yelled, as he propelled Sanders forward. "We're getting out of here! Just go!" As he ran, he toggled the comm to connect to the ship.

"Callaghan, report!"

"We had some trouble, sir, but systems are ready for lift-off."

"Start the sequence...now! We're coming in."

Dunjen had no idea if Callaghan answered. He couldn't afford to be distracted right now. He closed the comm link and kept his eyes locked on the airlock hatch. The alien substance had begun encasing the ship as well. No wonder they'd had so many malfunctions. They would be lucky to achieve launch. If they made it off planet, whoever approved this place for exploration would get a visit from him. Dunjen shut down those thoughts. Moving forward became a battle as whatever clung to him grew thicker and faster each time he broke its hold. He caught himself gasping for breath as bad as Sanders had earlier. He regulated his intake more rigidly and pushed harder.

They were almost there. Sanders reached the hatch; fell through it, actually. He turned to look back, but Dunjen knew there was no point. He was too far away. He'd never make it. Whatever leeched upon them had slipped in through the tear in his sleeve. It flowed across his skin, wrapped hard and tight around his torso and limbs until it bound his body as tightly as it did the suit and the ship. His steps slowed, and then stopped. It was like being encased in diamond. He could do nothing but watch as Sanders tried to come back for him.

He was so close! But he couldn't put his crew at risk. Even as he watched the ship looked more and more like an ancient artifact found in a glacier than a space vessel. Would they even be able to launch?

"Damnit! Sanders," Dunjen yelled across the reactivated comm link. "Get back in there! Callaghan, lock her down and lift that bird, now!"

"I'm afraid I can't do that, sir." Callaghan's voice came across the link devoid of emotion, but his very disobedience spoke volumes.

"XO, I issued you an order!"

"I must respectfully decline, sir. All options have not been exhausted."

"What the hell are you talking about?! Just go!"

Dunjen roared that last part with all his failing breath, the surface covering him cracked where it remained thin. "Just go! Just go! Just go!"

He fell silent, confused. The order he issued tingled along his skin. It pulsed through him completely independent of any heartbeat. It pounded against his skull:

Just Go! Just Go! Just Go!

It felt so odd. So alien. Like someone else's voice crying out of him. His own words echoed back, only growing louder in his thoughts, not fading. He felt compelled, though he had no hope of complying, any more than an ice-sculpted swan had any hope of taking flight. He watched as the engines at the tail end of the *Cortez* began their first-stage burn.

All Dunjen could think was: Callaghan had seen reason! Whatever echoed his order drowned out everything else. *Just Go! Just Go! Just Go...NOW!*

If only you knew how much I'd love to, he thought, wondering if he'd finally spaced his mind. Pushing the persistent echo from his thoughts, Dunjen tried to run through the lift-off procedure in his head, estimating the time left before second burn. Only something wasn't right. The next stage was external vent closure. Instead, the port side docking hatch opened.

"Callaghan, what the hell are you doing?"

"Getting you back to your ship, sir...and, sir? Brace for impact!"

Right on the heels of Callaghan's warning, the docking grapple rocketed out from its bay. It clanged hard against his diamond-like shell, would have crushed anything less unyielding. Instead it closed around him and rapidly retracted. By the time it reeled him in, Sanders was nowhere to be seen and Thompson and Callaghan were waiting to haul him through the airlock.

"Go! Go! GO!" someone yelled as Dunjen faded. The order blended with the one still bouncing around in every cell of his body. "Go!" *Just Go!* "Go!" *Just Go...NOW!*

An Alliance Archives Adventure

Katrion Alexander could see no stars.

Well, not from the command deck of the Groom Experimental Complex, anyway. Between the filter of the protective shielding, and the harsh electric glare lighting the compartment, anything that would have been visible to her unaided eye was pretty much occluded. She was surrounded by 270 degrees of pure, inky black. That's why she liked being in space so much. Lately, it matched her mood, more times than not.

Like tonight for instance; brand-new to this post, she'd barely been on the station two hours when the officer of the watch tapped her to cover a shift for someone named Simmons, who was laid up in sickbay. She hadn't even requisitioned her kit from stores yet.

What a complete SNAFU. Everything was off kilter. Schedule delays, launch sequences misaligned, posts vacant…With typical military efficiency, everyone's signals had been crossed. Kat had a recall out for the deck crew mistakenly given liberty, but she didn't hold out much hope they'd surface. Just as well. She could use the solitude, and one command console was pretty much the same as any other when you were in the space corps. They were fond of consistency. Besides, her MO was computer infiltration specialist, there wasn't a system in the corps she couldn't run, take apart, or break into.

She was familiarizing herself with this particular setup when a change in the outside ambiance drew her attention away.

"Oh, mercy," she let out on an appreciative breath as the ship she'd just cleared for departure came into view directly overhead. The *Rommel*, a Chamberlain-class attack vessel, blended into the texture of space, her running lights the only glimmer against the darkness, barely illuminating the dull matte finish of the hull in microbursts. The flashes were all but absorbed by the engineered tincture of the black paint, combined with the almost cellular hatch markings engraved on the ablative hull plating. The ultimate in space camo for ships. Space corps systems registered the vessel—they knew what to look for—but, as of yet, no one else's could. Shielded against every form of observation short of up-close visual sight, the vessel was a stealth marvel, quite the prize of any fleet.

Ping. Ping.

She didn't even twitch as the comm system alert tone sounded through the chamber. It wasn't like she hadn't expected it. Let Stanton stew. She'd encountered the commander of the *Alexi* before. He should be grateful his ship was getting out of here any time this solar week, given the mess she'd had to sort through when she came on shift.

As the *Rommel* deployed, Kat's gut flared with the burn of pre-battle tension. She should be on that command deck, not this one! Instead, she was stuck here while others...her *unit* went to war. And, from now on, she always would be.

The resentment was still raw. Psych-tested out of the combat infantry after their last mission, for reasons military command wouldn't explain. They'd given her two options: punch a keypad, or push a broom. Rebelliously, she'd nearly grabbed for the broom. Let them waste four-plus years of intensive military training right along with her multi-million-dollar transport fee.

Only, her honor stood in the way of such retaliation. Innocent people would suffer who-knew-what atrocities from not only the Legion, but at the hands of pirates and corporations and the faceless, as-yet-undiscovered dangers lurking in space.

Katrion swallowed her bitterness and grudgingly accepted her unsought role of station support staff. She would diligently work every shift she could pull to bring her closer to the day she earned her ticket home. Heck, she hadn't even unpacked her duffle yet, and she was clocked in on the roster. She'd still have to stick around until her tour was over, but at least she'd have a ride out of here when she was done.

The alert tone sounded once again, somehow seeming more insistent. Again Kat ignored it. Unless an emergency signal came through, Control was not obligated to respond to hails from vessels waiting in the queue.

There was no indication this was an emergency.

Hands splayed over the keypad set below flush into the hip-high console, she entered the final release sequence and sent the *Rommel* off ahead of schedule with a silent salute. Katrion watched as it drifted the prescribed distance before engaging its drive system. She couldn't see, from this distance, the residual moisture cloud bubbling in the ship's wake, but her sensors registered the tell-tale vapors as the *Rommel* initiated its electrogravitic drive envelope.

Eyes burning, she had to smother resentment anew. Among the vessel's complement was her unit, the 142nd infantry, or Daire's Devils. Being apart from them felt like a betrayal. Whether on her part, theirs, or the bureaucracy's, it was hard to say exactly, but it didn't sit well. This was worse than ringing out of training. Even more humiliating: at least that would have been her admitting she couldn't hack it, which would have been bearable. No one would have blamed her for knowing her limitations. But this...to have her superiors determine there was something flawed in her. To be labeled, out of all those in her unit, as unacceptable. And to not even know why...

Her fingers clawed the console housing, thankfully in no danger of triggering the recessed keypads. With a deep breath and hard discipline, she forced her bitterness back into its crater and mentally rolled a rock over it. She then turned her focus back on the Void.

With the *Rommel* clear, she began to process the next vessel. This time she opened the channel as the alert tone persisted.

"You incompetent fool! Can't you even follow a deployment schedule?"

Kat's lips tightened into a thin, hard line and her hands fisted reflexively. Bad enough being grounded, but dealing with the notorious Commander Tac Stanton's undisguised contempt was more than she should have to stomach right now. He was such a slug; she would never understand how he'd risen to command level.

"A glitch in the deployment systems required minor adjustments to get things back on track, Commander," she responded across the open channel in her own carefully neutral tone.

"Glitch?! Station Commander Trask will—"

Katrion cut him off. "The *Alexi's* next in the queue; is your vessel ready to deploy?"

"Yes!" The single word was hard and tight. Kat's eyes narrowed. Stanton was way too worked up over a simple delay, even for him.

"Commencing pre-deployment scans, now...position your craft for launch," she instructed him as she reviewed the datafeed for any anomalies. The scans registered a small mass out near Calisto just cresting the horizon. She initiated second-tier scans but they did not reveal any recognizable mechanics or transmissions. Density analysis suggested low mineral content and no ferrous deposits. Just a rock... roughly the size—if not the shape—of a good-sized yacht. As it was outside of the scheduled flight path, she made a note of her observations and beamed a copy of the report to the *Alexi's* flight crew, along with their release codes.

"You are clear to deploy."

She did not linger to watch this vessel. Turning back to her monitors she started on the next flight plan. She didn't get far. The console in front of her registered an unauthorized communications burst tight-beamed to the station. It ended nearly before it could register; definitely before she could intercept it through one of the perimeter sensors.

Probably Stanton griping to Trask because she'd made him wait.

Great. She'd been on-station only a few hours and she already had her first complaint added to her docket.

Kat shrugged off her annoyance. She might not be happy with the turn her career had made, but she had duties to fulfill, and too much honor not to care. Turning back toward the transparent shielding that allowed her direct visual of her domain, Kat scanned the pure-black oblivion. Toward her distant left, in the direction the *Alexi* had launched, she saw a ghostly glimmer, like the after-image of a camera flash, and nothing else. Had the *Alexi* had enough time to engage its drive and rocket out of direct visual range? Kat didn't think so, unless it had had an upgrade recently. It was an older vessel with fusion impulse engines. Still, it was out of sight. Kat sequenced a full-system scan, engaging all the remote sensors linked to her console. She needed to be sure, because something didn't feel right. Reviewing the feed as it processed, she felt every muscle tighten like the steady ripple of a python's coils. Sending a secure quick-burst query to the *Alexi's* comm, she waited for the security-coded confirmation.

The deck comm remained silent.

Combat training kicked in. Adrenaline tightened her muscles and sharp-focused her thoughts in an instant. A growl rumbled in her throat. Her left hand reflexively itched for her gauss rifle, which was currently locked away in a weapons locker aboard the *Rommel.* Instead she hit the print button on her console and the report scrolled out on a thin slice of durable acrylisheet. The hardcopy confirmed her suspicions. There was no sign that the *Alexi* had initiated their drive system. It couldn't have moved beyond visual range on conventional thrusters. It should still definitely be within hailing range.

"Control to Commander Trask," she sent out a hail to the station commander. Precious minutes passed with no response. She needed his clearance to initiate High Alert status. "Control to Commander Trask, please come in, sir," she repeated as she keyed in an urgency code linked to the message.

Still no response. Now her internal alarms went into overdrive. When Trask was on station, there was no time that was completely his own. Everything was superseded in moments of crisis. Station Commanders were *always* on line; their personal comms were bone-jacked directly into their jaw, just behind the ear, same as ships' captains or elite military squads. Her hand went without thought to the site of her now-deactivated, subdermal comm. She missed the buzzing sensation of someone's words transmitting along her jaw. Sometimes she thought she felt the faint vibration that said the comm was still live, but that was wistful thinking.

Setting the hail on auto-replay, Kat made a risky choice. Uncertain of the commander's status and faced with a high probability of potential threat she snapped into action without command authorization. Flipping back the cap over the alert toggle, she notched it to the next level, setting off a klaxon throughout the security zones of the station. No need to panic the civvies...yet.

Not three minutes after the alarm sounded the station's first defense, a wing of Mustang scout vessels jetted from their hangers like canned air from a hull breach.

"Control to Wing Command, do you copy?"

"Mustang Sally readin' you loud and clear, Control, where we headin'?"

Neither the flatness of the transmission nor the seriousness of the situation took the color out of the pilot's irrepressible Texas twang. *Finally, a friendly voice.* Kat allowed herself the briefest of smiles and responded, "Spread your wing out in a vector scan of quadrant 0689Alpha looking for unaccounted for debris, followed by a deep-space scan from that location targeting the vessel *Alexi*, ident-code ND-061.

Presume hostiles are in the area. Should you make contact with the *Alexi*, secure absolute confirmation of the ship's status. Over."

"Gotcha, Sally off." As they headed for the coordinates she beamed to them, Kat initiated high-alert procedure.

Her fingers flew over the keypad. First, she punched in the locator sequence keyed to Commander Trask. A schematic of the station appeared on the display before her. The design spiraled like a corkscrew looped around a central maintenance tube, with pairs of directional thrusters running along the outer edges of the coils. The Command, or C-deck, was in the tail, angled out into space to allow Control an un-obstructed view of the docking area, the shipyard, and most approach vectors, with auxiliary C-decks at key points along the complex.

Commander Trask's designation did not register on any coil.

Nervous tension fizzed the length of her. There was no way Trask had left the station; from just the short time she'd spent in his presence as she handed over her orders, she could tell he was too hardcore, too dedicated. She sent a priority-coded message to the head of station security, with a secondary request to search for the commander once they'd secured the station against outside threat.

Extremely uneasy, Kat took the perimeter sensors off standby and set them to full sector scan. One keystroke brought up all monitors with a split-screen display allowing her view of the total perimeter of the Groom Experimental Complex while she monitored the constant datafeed. She then initiated the security fields around all station defense hubs and essential operations. The personnel manning those stations ran through their own checklist. Orders were transmitted activating all security squads, off-duty and on.

Behind her, the hiss of the command deck hatch sent another thread of tension down Katrion's spine, mingled with a trickle of relief. *Soon this will all be someone else's headache,* she thought, as she input the final sequence in the protocol, sending out the ancillary black-box beacon. From now until it was deactivated, the beacon would receive low-frequency data pulses mirroring those fed to the station's black-box unit from the external sensors, double-documenting the incident to aid Military Intelligence's Tactical Unit should things go decidedly...not well.

The distinctive sound of the commander's footsteps crossed the deck, incinerating any relief Kat had felt. He stopped just behind her and to her right. Her throat muscles rippled reflexively beneath her collar, but her expression remained impassive as she glanced down at the console, where the schematic of the station was still displayed.

What the heck is going on? There should be a blip representing Trask that coincided with the primary C-deck.

There wasn't. Yet, in the reflection off the dome, she could see him watching her, a hard glimmer in his eye. His censure was like a faint, bitter tang wafting from every pore.

"Corporal Alexander, stand down!"

Kat stepped back from the console and turned to face him.

"*What*...do you think you're doing?" demanded Trask, both his tone and expression lethal.

Kat kept her expression schooled and her eyes empty as she replied.

"The *Alexi's* gone, sir. She launched, presumably moved beyond visual, and disappeared. Control observed spatial anomaly, ran prescribed scans." Katrion reached for the acrylisheet printout and held it out to him for confirmation. "Scans register no residual vapor trail, indicating the drive unit was never engaged, yet the *Alexi* does not appear on any of our systems. The vessel was unresponsive to query."

Trask glanced at the report and then back up. "That's it?" His eyes crackling with disbelief on the surface, but she caught a glimmer of something darker roiling just beneath. "You called High Alert...without authorization...for *that*!"

"I initiated a priority alert hail, Commander. There was no response, despite repeat transmissions. I was unable to summon the *Alexi*...or yourself. Sir, station security protocol requires..."

He slashed the air with the blade of his hand. "Enough! You called High Alert, *without* authorization, because you *missed* a bit of drive vapor?! You anticipated an attack scenario because I didn't respond to a *hail*?" His eyes flashed and he looked furious enough to send her out to scrub the hull without an MMU. It took an extreme effort for Kat not to flinch. "Did you see an external threat? Was there an explosion?" She shook her head, little more than a sharp twitch. "Was there identifiable debris?"

She set her jaw and met his gaze head-on. "As yet unconfirmed, sir, pending the report of the Mustang wing deployed." Commander Trask drew in a sharp breath. His jaw twitched and his eyes went very cold. Behind the heavy thud of her heart, she was certain she heard a death rattle...the final moments of her already ailing career ingloriously fading away.

As they stared each other down, the emergency deck crew popped through the hatch.

"Sakmyster," Commander Trask called out to one of the new arrivals. "Kill that klaxon. Initiate stand-down, and order that bloody wing back to station." The commander kept his tone very controlled as he summarily relieved her of her post. "Deck crew, dismissed."

A chorus of "Yessirs" peppered the air as the crew, with the exception of Sakmyster, filed out the hatch.

What the hell? Kat remained at attention as the crew left the C-deck. She kept her eyes forward and slightly out of focus to elude Sak's sympathetic gaze. They'd actually gone through Basic together, which only made this sting all the more. She had a hard time keeping silent when she heard the clack of the keys as Sak stepped the station down to alert status. As he keyed in the final sequence he turned to Trask for further instruction.

"Dismissed."

Sakmyster looked puzzled, but did not question the order. Kat caught her own breath coming out in short, sharp huffs as he left. She forced herself to a more natural rhythm, though her instincts screamed *this is wrong!*

With exaggerated care Trask laid the report on the console before him. He looked from it to her.

"What were you doing on duty tonight, Alexander?"

She wondered the same thing herself, but it was not her place to question protocol with the officer of the watch when summoned to duty. "Simmons is down in sickbay, sir. I was instructed to cover his shift."

Trask looked ready to savage both the hapless Simmons and herself. "And was this cleared with me?"

She kept her expression neutral, though her nerves were bug-crawling beneath the surface of her skin. Something bothered her... about his voice...about the situation. She just couldn't place it, though. "I couldn't say, sir. The order came from Lt. Commander Connor."

The commander's jaw went visibly tight and his hands barely resisted clenching. She was truly in his crosshairs now, though she could not imagine why. According to protocol, calling High Alert had been justified, given the circumstances, and as for being on the C-deck at all; she'd followed orders.

Kat remained silent and at attention, her eyes trained straight ahead. Even so, she noted Trask's gaze flickered ever so slightly to the console displaying the data from the outer quadrants. She watched without watching as his fingers moved over the keypad. He called up the log of her shift.

Trask left the console, coming to stand in front of her, close. "You are suspended from duty pending a full investigation. You are to report to your quarters until summoned. Acknowledged?"

Katrion wanted to protest, but she'd already crossed too many lines. She wasn't worried. There was no doubt an investigation would absolve her. But something was very wrong here. She found herself wishing her unit was still around to back her up.

"I said, acknowledged?" Trask's tone was one short step from erupting.

"Sir, yessir!"

"Dis*missed!*"

With a sharp salute and steps of military precision, Kat executed an about face and left the command deck.

*   *   *

Kat hadn't consciously disobeyed orders. She fully intended to return to her quarters, as Commander Trask instructed. However, her feet stopped at the nearest auxiliary C-deck. Thanks to the stand-down, the consoles were unmanned and the stations on standby. Her combat instincts twitched at the sight. This was the wrong call. Every minute of training she ever had demanded she take action.

Following the impulse, Kat visited the nearest security cache. She returned to the aux C-deck armed with a variable velocity shotgun, a supply of non-lethal riot rounds, and a high-powered taser with plenty of cartridges. Once again she thought longingly of her gauss rifle. Station-board armaments were a joke to someone used to the best the military had to offer.

Kat slipped through the hatch, secured it behind her, and headed straight for the console. With her weapons readily at hand and the hatch secured against entry, she sat down at the keyboard. Tapping into the security protocols, she accessed the monitoring system. Within moments she had real-time close-ups of Trask and the main console fed to her own display, as well as a wide-angle view of the primary C-deck.

The commander's fingers moved over the keys nearly as fast as her own. He accessed duty rosters and security details first; then requests for production specs and technical schematics began scrolling across the display. Kat's gut feeling of wrongness increased.

Trask was after the *Rommel!*

Kat sent up a prayer of thanks that she'd deployed the ship early. That vessel…in the hands of the wrong party…not good. And the specs and the research data, almost as bad.

He wouldn't succeed. She would see to that.

Deftly applying her technical training, Kat intercepted Trask's requests, dispersing them harmlessly in the ether, and tied up his console with error messages and processing loops. It wouldn't stop him, but it bought her some time.

The only chance she had of removing the data from his reach was to initiate Full Alert. At an experimental weapons complex like Groom, that protocol triggered an automatic wipe of the research databases. An annoyance for the scientists, but everything was backed up to the black box, lost to the bad guys, but not anyone else. Much better than having their research fall into the hand of pirates… or worse, rivals. Even they would agree.

Unfortunately, Full Alert was not as simple as flipping a manual toggle.

With the right codes and clearances, it would take a matter of minutes. She didn't have them. But maybe that wasn't important. Instead of a true Full Alert, she could trigger the protocol that wiped the servers and dumped the data to the black box. If she couldn't pull that off, she wasn't worthy of her designation as a computer infiltration specialist.

The keys rattled like hail on tarmac as she navigated the system, careful not to trigger any of the system alerts. With Trask, the head man in charge, turning sides, she had to assume he'd recruited others among the station personnel. One by one she located the necessary codes, identified the protocols, slipped through backdoor channels, the entire time keeping an eye on the monitor for any sudden activity from Trask. It was slow going, though, and every second she took increased the likelihood of someone noticing her activities.

Almost there, she thought. *Come on! Almost there.*

She glanced up, keeping track of Trask, only to have her gaze collide with his. There was no way he could see her because he'd have to first know where she was to pull off the same trick. He certainly gave the cam the evil eye, though.

Then again, maybe he had figured it out. As she turned back to her algorithms someone tried to open the hatch behind her. When the key sequence didn't work, she heard a thud, and then another, but the engineers designed this compartment to be defensible during high-security situations. Unless the person in the corridor had an override, they weren't getting in here until she released the lockdown.

"Shit!" she muttered, as she gave up being sneaky and plundered the system for the final code needed. "They couldn't wait five friggin' minutes before they found me, could they!" Her fingers were a blur as she raced to initiate the dump. In a matter of seconds the data would be out of reach of those attempting to steal it.

And her console went dead.

"Shit! No!" Her fist came down hard enough to dent the console housing. She had no way to tell if she'd been successful. No way to tell if they'd shut her down before she accomplished her objective, and they had her cornered.

Somehow, she suspected they had something with a little more kick than a riot gun and a taser. Not for the first time, she wondered why she hadn't opted for the broom...

She took a moment and prepped her pitiful collection of armaments. First, calibrating the taser to its highest setting, she then loaded the cartridges and slid the weapon in the cargo pocket on her left leg. Next, she loaded the rifle and secured additional rounds in the right-hand pocket. She then moved to the hatch. An intercom next to the door corresponded to a speaker on the exterior wall of the compartment. Set just above it, a micro-display revealed the commander and two others just beyond the hatch.

"What do you want, Trask?" Kat purposely neglected to address him as sir; he'd lost the privilege of her having to say it. She released the intercom button and took up the rifle, standing at the ready.

"You've caused me a lot of trouble, Alexander."

Well gee, how am I supposed to respond to that? Um...good! Of course, she didn't bother to say that out loud. She just tightened her grip on her weapon.

A soft *pop* sounded her only warning. She scrambled back, bringing the riot gun to bear as the hatch opened. Two unfamiliar crewmen stood in the hatchway, with Trask just behind. Before they took a step, she fired, once, twice. High-velocity suppression rounds slammed each man right between the eyes, knocking one of them right back into Trask. The other flew past him. A satisfying thud marked the man's head impacting with the far bulkhead.

Well. At least she didn't have to worry about one of them getting up very soon.

She reloaded quickly and had the barrel trained on Trask before he even finished climbing to his feet. His cohort remained sprawled on the deck, still conscious, but with his head weaving a bit. For the moment, a non-threat. Trask was another issue. He moved through the hatch and approached her with sure, unwavering steps. Kat let him have it with both barrels. He took one suppression round to the temple, the other square in the throat.

She heard a sickening crunch.

"You have got to be kidding me!" Kat swore as Trask barely rocked back with the impacts. He just kept on coming.

There was no time to reload. Barely time to drop the weapon. She didn't even have time to grab for the taser. As the commander reached her, Kat pivoted on the ball of her right foot and brought her left leg up in a roundhouse kick aimed at his head.

"Nice try, you stupid bitch," Trask growled, his tone eerily flat, almost as if it came across a comm. His hand intercepted her foot in a crushing grip. It was like slamming into a titanium hull. He shoved her hard off balance. The moment she landed on the deck her face exploded with pain that rivaled that of her foot. Already she felt her eye swelling.

Her training kicked in, though and she'd barely impacted before she rolled away, bouncing to her feet, ready to do battle. *What the hell were they feeding station commanders these days, anyway?* she thought irreverently.

The humor was a bad sign. The black spots dancing before her eyes were another.

Hello, Kittie.

Oh…goodie, the party wouldn't be complete without hearing things as well. Except…the voice was familiar, and so was the sensation of it buzzing along her jaw and up into her ear. Could it be…Only one person greeted her that way. Someday she'd hurt him for it…but probably not today.

Scotch? she subvocalized, hardly daring to believe. Could it really be her former comrade-at-arms, the wise ass of the 142nd, or was she losing it worse than she thought? There was no answer.

Trask took a swing at her head. She jerked back just enough that he only clipped her jaw.

"Shit!" Kat couldn't hold back the expletive. The spots before her eyes intensified shading the entire deck in varying degrees of grey.

Shake it off, soldier. A different voice came through her comm. It sounded suspiciously like her former unit commander, Master Sergeant Kevin Daire.

What the hell's going on, Sarge? she risked subvocalizing again as she dodged the next strike, ducking low and aiming a side kick at Trask's knee that should have taken him down. She connected, but it was like kicking a wall. A solid wall. Another odd crunch followed the impact, but the man stayed steady. So steady, in fact, he lashed out at her with the leg she hadn't aimed at. He dumped her back to the deck once again.

That quick, Trask pinned her, his hands reaching for her throat.

Get your head back into the fight; your biosensor readings are all over the place, Daire growled, ignoring her question. *We're nearly there.*

Kat groaned. If her head was any more in this fight it would be splattered all over the deck. It was all she could do to resist Trask's grip at her throat. Seeking to disable him before it was too late she slammed her fist into his groin.

Nothing. Absolutely nothing. It was like the guy had no pain receptors.

The world went a uniform grey, now, and rapidly grew darker. She wasn't about to give up, though. Perhaps physically she didn't have the mass, leverage, or force to break his grip…but there were other means less easily dismissed.

Snaking her hand down her left thigh, she drew the taser from her pocket and hit the trigger point-blank into Trask's chest. She heard a muffled *pop* and a crackling sound, followed by the stench of burning ozone and synthetics as the leads impacted, setting the barbs a half an inch deep into the commander's flesh, right through the uniform. His grip spasmed and his body jerked.

Awww! Friggin' Hell! she subvocalized. Microseconds later the charge reached Kat and she too began to dance.

Her world went black.

✳   ✳   ✳

Sprawled out on the command deck of the Groom Experimental Complex, Katrion Alexander finally saw stars. She didn't mind so much at the moment; it meant she couldn't possibly stare at the smoking mass less than a yard away from her. Through the mental haze, she tried not to wonder why the air didn't reek of scorched flesh. She didn't know how long she'd been out, but her muscles still twitched here and there.

Hey, Sarge, she croaked aloud into her comm. *If I break a shuttle they take it out of my pay packet, yeah?*

Silence hummed across the comm a moment, then in a cautious tone Daire answered, *Um...yeah...*

How much you reckon they'll dock me for breaking a commander?

Scotch laughed, and so did Daire, producing an interesting jangle along her jaw.

Daire answered first. *I think we can let this one pass, Alexander. Just don't make a habit of it.*

Kittie...for this one, they'll give you a medal! Scotch chimed in.

Oh goody...more fruit salad to clutter my chest...I'd settle for reinstatement to the Devils. Katrion held her breath. It was only post-battle banter, but her comment was more than fervent.

You were never off the rosters, Corporal, but let's hold that for debriefing. We have a situation to wrap up.

Yes, sir! Relief would have floored her, if she weren't already down. Taking a few deep breaths to settle her emotions and compartmentalize the aches, she hauled herself to her feet and turned her focus back to getting the Devils on board.

What's your location?

Dockside, one klick out and closing. Scotch responded.

Kat did some quick logistical calculations. Automatically she visualized the station's layout from her earlier scan for Trask: The primary C-deck was in the tail. The auxiliary C-deck she was in fell about mid-station. R&D was in the head, toward the planet.

Do you have access to the station schematics?

It's been on screen for the last hour, Scotch answered. *I could draw you a picture, if I had a crayon.*

I'm heading for the primary C-deck, Kat reported. *You can infiltrate the complex via the maintenance tube, tail-end of the station, just past the first coil; comm me when you're in position and I'll key the outer access hatch for your entry.*

Roger, Daire responded. *Now get moving, soldier.*

"Ah, crap!" Kat cursed, as her diminished vision caused her to misjudge the command hatch, clipping it with her shoulder as she exited the C-deck. "As if I didn't have enough bruises."

Ignoring the pain, and the occasional random spasms, she double-timed it back to the primary C-deck.

*　　*　　*

"What took you so long?" Kat grumbled, allowing annoyance to color her tone, rather than the relief she really felt. Damn if it wasn't great to be back with her unit. Even if she and Scotch were headed to clean up a corpse she'd rather not think too closely about.

"After we disabled the *Alexi*, it took us a while to turn around and get back in range."

She stopped dead and turned to face Scotch. "The *Alexi*?!"

"Yeah, seems Stanton preferred the pay grade for pirate captain, more than what he received as a space corps commander."

Kat laughed, but after the initial shock, she didn't pay too much attention to what Scotch was saying. They were almost at the auxiliary C-deck, and while this wasn't her first kill, it had unsettled her more than any other.

"That's why you were here, according to Sarge." Scotch continued. "MI knew something was up, and needed someone on the inside that wouldn't be suspected. 'Course no one expected the shit to hit the fan this soon. You saved our asses by launching us early; else the ambush would have happened the other way around."

As what he said sank in, Kat had to fight down some justifiable rage. Some warning would have been nice. Still, it wasn't Scotch's fault. She'd take it up with Sarge, though, without a doubt. But first...time to clean up her mess.

At the hatch, she hung back, letting her teammate precede her into the compartment. Her breathing sounded erratic and the edges of her vision hazed. She had to steel herself to enter.

"Come on, Kat," Scotch said from the hatch, his hand reaching out to gently grip her shoulder. "Trust me, you need to see this."

Then the understanding moment of connection ended at Scotch's very next breath.

"Besides, how many times have you dreamed of zapping an idiot officer?

Kat growled and smacked his arm, pushing past him onto the auxiliary command deck. She didn't want to do this, but orders were orders. She'd just as soon get it done quickly.

Scotch laughed and came to stand beside her as she stared down at what remained of Trask. Neither one of them spoke for a long, taut moment.

"What the HELL?!" Kat finally exploded.

"Damn, woman, is that all you can ever say?"

With not one nerve left to get on, Kat grabbed Scotch by the collar and yanked him down. "What. Is. That?"

"Don't know what those that came up with them call it, but we've been calling them composites." Scotch knelt down alongside the... body. Kat joined him. He continued, "They're pretty damn good, you have to admit...too good. Near as the engineers can figure, the frame is a carbon fiber/organic matrix composite. Strong as all get-out. Hard to detect, unless you know what to look for. We don't yet...this being only the second one we've encountered.

"You can't see them, but this muddy fluid leaking out...that's full of nanites...thanks to you, fried nanites." He caught her eye and grinned a wicked grin. Kat had to smile back, as shaky as she was.

"These little buggers are packed under the synthskin. They're linked to an operator located somewhere nearby...in this case, likely the real Trask, seeing as there was no difference in voice to give this guy away..." Kat thought of the unidentified mass she's registered out by Calisto when all of this started; if whoever was behind this could make plastic look like a man, maybe they could make a ship look like a rock. Anyway, she pulled her attention back to Scotch, who'd continued talking.

"The operator works the nanites by remote, some kind of surface mapping interface. As far as we can tell, what this guy "saw" the operator saw, and any reactions the composite showed were transmitted real-time through the interface and instantaneously mimicked by the nanites so…"

She must have looked as if she didn't give a damn about the particulars, because he stopped explaining the tech. Kat just shook her head, feeling more and more like she'd slipped dimensions or something, because this wasn't any kind of reality she understood.

"Anyway," Scotch looked over at her, "betcha the FCC never anticipated this."

Kat looked at him sidewise as he stood up beside her.

"FCC?" She didn't have any energy to puzzle out where he was going with this.

"The Federal Communications Commission…"

"I know who they are, Scotch," she growled. "I just don't know what your point is."

He grinned like the irrepressible imp that he was, on or off the battlefield, and nudged the semi-melted husk on the ground with the toe of his boot. "Why, they have strict regulations against pirate copies."

Kat just might have to change her mind about hurting him today.

On Zinn Mensch

A finely wrought tale of deep-space terror interwoven with the routine business of salvage and recovery that engages the protagonists for much of the story. Counterbalancing the mundane with the mysterious, a feeling of impending doom prevails as a mechanical mantra repeatedly injects itself into the narrative, their implication becoming startlingly clear as Kitch tries to resolve the meaning of German words scrawled above a mass of dead crewmen. Their fate becomes too soon terrifyingly clear in an exciting conclusion.

—Bud Sparhawk,
author of the *Shardie Universe* series

ZINN MENSCH

The corridors of the Eisenwald Outpost echoed a slow, ponderous tread. The steps sounded irregular. Something between a limp and a shuffle.

Thud. Screech. Thud. Screech.

It stopped from time to time and the sound of tinkering could be heard. The *pop* of a maintenance hatch opening. The sizzle of a microtorch. The *thunk* of the hatch being replaced. Then the footsteps continued on. *Thud. Screech. Thud. Screech.* An ozone tang followed in their wake, blending with a somewhat organic-rich atmosphere.

There were no other signs of life.

"Alert. Alert. Approaching vessel. Alert. Alert." The automated announcement started off neutral, a mere statement of fact. It calmly repeated itself several times. The treader continued down the corridor, not responding in any noticeable manner.

"Alert. Alert. Approaching vessel. Alert. Alert!" Distressed vocal tones were added, accompanied by the discordant *whoop* of the station's klaxon. Still the announcement seemed to be ignored, despite its increased frequency. The hail was programmed to continue, escalating in intensity, until someone entered the acknowledgement code and the engagement protocol followed.

Another hatch popped, more ozone scented the air. The alert kicked it up yet another notch.

There were no other signs of life. *Thud. Screech. Thud. Screech.*

✳   ✳   ✳

"Captain, the outpost's auto-response has been triggered, but docking personnel have not returned our hail."

Captain Andredi turned away from the navigational display she consulted and looked toward the crewman manning the comm. They were a bit off course, if three light-years could be called a bit. Some serious restocking was going to be needed if they were to get back to their scheduled route and this was the only station within range. Eisenwald was an older outpost, but it *should* be compliant with their digital-beam communication systems. Of course, that was theoretical; there was always the possibility that the facility was so obsolete that they were never upgraded to DBC. They wouldn't be the only outpost still operating with radio-broadcast communications.

"Switch to RBC, Lieutenant Bodine."

"Already attempted, Captain." Bodine responded, pivoting in his chair to meet her gaze. "No response on any channel."

Andredi activated the internal comm system. "Bridge to Lieutenant Kitch, respond."

Kitch replied almost instantly. "Captain?"

"Kitch, prep the waldos. It looks like we might need to initiate a manual docking," Andredi instructed him. "As soon as we anchor down I want you to use the umbilical to run full biometric scans of the station, including test samples of the Eisenwald's atmosphere. No one breaks the airlock seal until all risk of contaminants is ruled out.

"Acknowledged."

The comm light dimmed as Kitch cut the connection.

Captain Andredi liked that. No questions, no grumbling. Kitch knew how to take an order. As a general-purpose technician, he had been a part of her crew for as long as she had commanded the Shipely-class frigate *Mortimer*. She wouldn't trade him for any number of technical specialists, even if they were handed to her budget-free. There was no counting the number of times Kitch had been instrumental in saving all their asses.

"Bodine, maintain communication efforts; I'm going to see what I can pull up on Eisenwald."

✻   ✻   ✻

The waldos were getting old. So was the *Mortimer*. Kitch would be glad when they could give the Old Man a complete overhaul, before something serious went wrong. Until then it was up to him to keep things running smoothly.

They had another hour at least before they were close enough to dock manually. Kitch deployed his toolkit. Inch by inch he examined the hardware, inspecting the seal on each gasket, tightening the connectors, and testing every circuit. Except for a bit of corrosion on the umbilical electrodes all was in order. Removing the component, he went to the store room for a spare. The last thing they needed was a false reading during the environmental analysis.

As he put everything back together, the hatch *thunked* open behind him.

"You run out of duct tape yet?"

One corner of Kitch's mouth edged up halfway to a smile and he gave a little shake of his head. "I figure I still have about half a crate left, if you were plannin' to requisition some more."

"Duly noted," Andredi answered as she moved to the computer console. "So, are we good to go?"

"Yes, Captain." Kitch ran his hand over the waldo he worked on, making sure the casing was in place and secure. Taking the unit up in both arms, he manhandled it into its cradle. Once it was properly in place it took him just a moment to lock down the o-ring and reattach the electrical feeds to the master control box. Satisfied everything was in order he sealed the maintenance panel and turned to his captain. "We within docking range?"

"Nearly," she said, and looked toward the airlock. "We don't have much time if we're to get back on schedule; better suit up, just in case, we really need those supplies. I had Ensign Singh bring up a floater."

Kitch nodded an acknowledgement and moved past her to the equipment lockers. He hated putting the suit on. Thanks to the long bank of LED lights across the chest, meant to increase visibility in low-light situations, he felt like something out of a bad sci fi. Still, he wasn't here to look pretty, and any little edge that helped him stay alive, well, that was okay with him.

Captain Andredi was still waiting when he returned in his restrictor suit, faceplate dangling from the strap held loose in his right hand. His other hand rested atop the lightweight portable scanner built into the hip of his suit. He moved to where she stood by the engineering console.

"What's it look like, Captain?"

She didn't jump, but her motions were super-slow as she cocked her head up in his direction, her eyes still pretty much on the data she'd called up on the display. "The Eisenwald Vorposten...or Eisenwald

Outpost; originally a German-sponsored international waystation, a shift in trade routes rendered its strategic location no longer prime." She paused to tap a few keys, calling up a schematic of the outpost. "Once manned by twenty-five international astronautic personnel, it's now run by a skeleton crew of only ten, mostly German, rotated out on a two-year cycle."

Kitch let out a long breath on that one. Duty on an outpost was harsh enough, out on the edge of nowhere; he couldn't imagine pulling a stint on one twice as long as standard. The only reason for it was cost-cutting; it got mighty expensive retrieving personnel. It was a wonder the Germans hadn't scuttled the outpost all together. Then again, most likely they would, once it paid for itself. "Damn penny-pinchers," he swore, mostly under his breath.

"Yeah, well, let's hope they didn't skimp on the stock-up. According to Command, a new crew should have arrived a week ago, so the supplies would have been topped off as well." She reached out and rapped the monitor, bringing his attention back where it should be. "Here's the bridge; here's the sickbay; and here's the storage bay." Her eyebrow arched as she finally looked at him. Finally noticed the pistol strapped to his thigh over the suit. She didn't comment as she handed him a slip of acrylisheet. "Here's your shopping list. I've included some of the Germans' operational codes Command had in the database. They're dated, but they might still be active. Once we're docked and systems analysis gives the all-clear, I'm sending you over. Give this to their quartermaster, get the goods, and get your butt back here. We're losing time."

"Yes, Captain."

*   *   *

"Alert! Alert! Approaching Vessel! ALERT! ALERT!"

What the hell?! Kitch's grip tightened on his pistol as he exited the airlock, stepping into the corridor of *Eisenwald* proper. Singh moved close behind him, tense enough to set Kitch's teeth on edge. The ensign hefted a rifle loaded with composite rounds at the ready. At their backs, the empty floater followed like a particularly persistent beggar. Kitch began to wonder if Singh's having a rifle was such a good idea. Hell, he *really* began to wonder if they actually needed the supplies.

Unfortunately, the answer was yes.

"ALERT! ALERT!..." Before the auto-response could finish its shriek, Kitch reached over to the docking console and keyed in the acknowledgement codes the captain had armed him with until one of them worked. Once they silenced the alert they continued their infiltration of the station.

The scans hadn't detected any contaminants, but there were no bio signs either. The portable scanner built into his restrictor suit concurred with those on the Old Man. Were they all malfunctioning or not? Either way, things did not bode well for the ten people that supposedly manned the outpost.

"Quick, let's head to…"

Thud. Screech. Thud. Screech.

Singh's hand came down on Kitch's shoulder, the fingers digging in more than just a bit. Kitch had to jerk to the side as the ensign's rifle swung around to the direction the sounds came from. Yeah, he was really rethinking the rifle.

"Captain?" he spoke into the suit's short-burst comm system, activating it.

There was a short hum, and then a click before Andredi's voice came over the microspeaker by Kitch's ear. "What's the situation, Lieutenant?"

"We have movement, but still no bio signs. Any idea what we should expect here?"

"I'll dig through the files some more and find out," she answered, her voice both puzzled and concerned. "For now, head the other way, until I can learn more. Work over to the storage bay and start loading up that floater. Keep in contact with Bodine until I get back with you."

"Aye, ma'am," Kitch answered, his jaw clenched and his grip tightening on the pistol. He and Singh slipped down the darkened corridor.

✳　　✳　　✳

Zinn Mensch…Zinn Mensch…Zinn Mensch…

The words kept repeating in a steady beat. They whispered across receptors. Unstoppable. The unit designated Mark2 tried to ignore them, to process no more than its assigned tasks. There was a loose circuit in compartment C242, behind hatch plate 2-94X; after that there was a malfunctioning environmental sensor in Storage Bay Alpha, zone ZD67. The outpost always required maintenance of one sort or another. That was Mark2's purpose. The words didn't matter. The words couldn't see they were wrong.

Zinn Mensch…Zinn Mensch…Zinn Mensch…

Unnoticed, a subroutine deep within Mark2 answered the whispers, *Nicht Herzlos!* Metal ground against metal as the unit headed first for compartment C242 and then on to Storage Bay Alpha.

Thud. Screech. Thud. Screech. Thud Screech.

✳   ✳   ✳

The only sounds Kitch could hear were his heartbeat thundering in his head and Singh behind him, gagging as he fought not to foul the inside of his suit. Kitch struggled, simultaneously trying to block out the sight before him and take it in. Something bothered him about what he saw. Well, something beyond what a sane person would expect.

"Lieutenant Kitch...Ensign Singh....report!" The deep voice of Lieutenant Bodine came over the comm, breaking the thrall the two of them seemed to be locked in. A hail from Captain Andredi directly followed. "Come off it, Kitch! Talk to us!"

Kitch looked around the storage bay. Strewn in the spaces between the supplies were the bodies of the station personnel. All accounted for, if he wasn't mistaken. He could see some trace of defensive wounds along those arms and hands visible to him, but for the most part the only trauma was a gaping wound in the center of each chest. And then he knew what was wrong.

The deck plates were clean.

"There's not enough blood. There should be more blood," he muttered into the comm. Other than what marked the bodies, he could see no blood at all. This wasn't where they'd died. So how'd they get there?

"What?! Repeat, Lieutenant!"

The world went monochrome as Kitch's heartbeat climbed to a crescendo. Somewhere far, far away, someone tugged frantically at his shoulder, hard enough to spin him around. And suddenly his perspective snapped back into focus.

Thud. Screech. Thud. Screech. Thud. Screech.

The first thing to catch Kitch's attention was the wall. From deck to overhead all he could see was rust-colored words: *Nicht Herzlos! Nicht Herzlos! Nicht Herzlos!* Over and over again until there was barely enough bulkhead visible to make out the letters. Kitch found something familiar about the words. Something that made him wish he'd paid better attention in high-school German.

He forgot about the wall as something else caught his attention: the vaguely humanoid silhouette blocking the hatchway.

Kitch took a deep, settling breath and brought up his pistol to the ready. He knew giving Singh the rifle was a bad call. "Captain," he murmured into the comm. "We found your skeleton crew."

It was all he had time to say.

Edging his left hand up his chest, he hit the switch activating the LED panel on the front of his suit. His heart stopped. A sight right out of a thousand nightmares met his eyes. Towering at least a foot and a half above his head, the knife-wielding mechanoid unit caught in the glare was enough to send a grown man running. Enough to send Singh running, in fact, toward the other end of the bay.

Bad call.

Before Kitch could react, he heard another *Thud. Screech!* and the rust-colored blade plunged deep within the ensign's chest.

Plenty of blood on the deckplates now.

"Aw, fuck!" Kitch raised his pistol and emptied the clip. Hot metal hit cold as the rounds took the mech from the side. On impact, they fragmented and scattered. Small wonder; composite rounds were meant for flesh, not metal. He replaced the clip anyway, all within seconds. The mechanoid turned its head away from Singh's remains. Its single large optical crystal flared, while the small red sensor above it pulsed. Both locked directly on Kitch as the robot tore the knife from the body at its feet and took a step forward.

And again: *Fuck!*

Not waiting to see what came next, Kitch shoved the nearby floater into the mechanoid's path and sprinted for the door. Behind him he heard an almighty crash, followed quite close by a shudder. He didn't dare look, just kept his eye on that hatch, visualizing his skinny, white ass disappearing through it.

ThudScreech!ThudScreech!ThudScreech!

"Captain! Bodine! Prepare to disengage! NOW!" he roared into his comm, fighting for the breath to do so.

He made it to the hatch. Even made it through. But a hard swipe of a robotic arm sent him flying sideway into the bulkhead.

He groaned as he felt a rib or two crack; didn't want to think about the rest of him. Still, he wasn't about to make things easy for the termi-nator here. Instead of scrambling back, he went with his gut, lunging forward past the mech's legs. In passing, he noticed the state of them: one foot was bright and shiny and whole, the other mangled, as if it went a few rounds with a baseball bat, or a nice, heavy-duty spanner. *Thud-Screech*, indeed.

He didn't know which of the poor souls in the other room did it, but good for them. The thing could still move, and pretty darn fast at that, but it had considerable less stablity than it had had when it came off the assembly line. Taking advantage of the flaw, Kitch rolled to his back once he cleared the thing's legs and gave it a hard shove from behind.

As it tumbled in a roaring crash, Kitch got to his feet with a speed to impress. He made it halfway down the corridor before he heard the sound of its tread again. His ribs protested each stride, but now was not the time to take it easy.

He darted away, ducked through the smallest spaces he could manage, the whole time making his way back toward the airlock. No matter what he did, his pursuer never lagged far behind. Just his luck, a mechanoid equipped with a biosensor.

"Captain, Singh is dead. I'm being chased by a mech that seems to be programmed for murder...what the hell am I dealing with here?!" Kitch spoke into the comm in nearly subvocal tones. "Is it too much to hope you know why it's trying to kill me?"

He could hear the sharp intake of breath on the other end, then the rapid tap of keys. "A few cycles back the outpost technician was fatally injured in an accident," she answered. "According to a note on his personal record, Mark Walther was such a heartless bastard the rest of the crew referred to him as the "Tin Man", but his knowledge and technical skills were indispensable."

"What the hell does that have to do with the crazy-ass robot trying to skewer me?" Kitch cut in as he headed down another corridor, the familiar and hated *ThudScreech* echoing closer behind him.

"They knew he was dying. Rather than do without a technician for nearly two years, they neuropatterned his brain, imprinted it on a clean mechanoid. They hoped to retain his technical skills and intuitive responses."

Again, Kitch swore as what she said sunk in. He'd heard of the process, what techhead hadn't, but the results were erratic. Though neuropatterning supposedly only transferred knowledge, fragments of personality were known to creep in. Sometimes things got ugly when they did.

Things were most definitely ugly.

"How close am I, Captain?"

"Sensors place you two corridors over from the airlock, about twenty-five meters."

He put on a bit more speed, his ribs screaming the more his heart pounded. His footfalls pulsed throughout the station. He didn't care if the mechanoid heard. Like it made any difference how quiet he was. Time to get out of here. Rounding the final corner, his foot slid on a slick spot on the floor. The next moment he went gloriously airborne right up until he slammed into the far wall.

Screech.Thud.

Kitch landed face down on the floor, his head wedged against the bulkhead and the deck. It took a moment for the black spots to disperse. He looked up with just his eyes and saw a smeared puddle of red on the deck in front of him too far away to be his own. He groaned. Looked a little higher until his eyes were nearly up into his head.

The mech came closer.

"Airlock?" Kitch slurred across the comm.

"Two meters, aft...what's happening, Kitch?"

"Can't tawk, hafin' too much fn." It seemed like the thing to say, but the words didn't sound right in his ears. He scuttled back a bit, trying real hard not to move his head. The black spots were back.

Suddenly, something clicked, jarred loose, no doubt, by the knock to the head.

"*Nicht Herzlos,*" he muttered, making every effort not to slur those words. Not heartless, he echoed in his thoughts. It almost seemed the mech jerked, slowed. Kitch swallowed and tried to moisten his mouth. Working his jaw, he formed the words once again. "*Nicht Herzlos!*"

He wasn't wrong. Slowly he climbed to his feet fighting for a bit of focus. Aft, Andredi said. Behind him. Thank God!

The corridor seemed to sway a bit and him right along with it. He ignored the sensation and slowly backed away, never taking his eyes off the detail he's missed earlier...Scratched into the chassis of the mech was a crude, rust-colored heart. Step by step Kitch moved toward the airlock, continually chanting his new mantra.

Nicht Herzlos. Nicht Herzlos. Nicht Herzlos.

For a moment, it actually worked. Then he did something foolish. He stopped chanting.

"Get ready to disengage!" he whispered fast to the captain. "Have Bodine trigger the emergency beacon because this restock is not going to happen."

That brief moment was enough to trigger the mech's homicidal tendencies. That powerful arm reached out. *Thud. Screech.*

Kitch pivoted and threw himself that last measure, ricocheting off the bulkhead, certain that metal claw would close on him with each step.

A primal scream ripped from his throat as he slammed into the hatch, falling through it just as the mechanoid's fingers brushed his suit. A slow hiss of air escaped. Kitch allowed the momentum to carry him around until he faced his attacker, his back braced against his own airlock wall. With as hard a kick as he could manage, he sent the robot flying backward.

He could hear the *Mortimer* disengaging. Could feel the rumble travel through the soles of his ship boots. Gladly, his hand came down on the button that closed the airlock. Time to say good bye.

"*Herzlos Kreuzung,*" *Heartless bastard,* he spat out loud and clear.

His German teacher would have been proud.

ORACLE

Man's jarring foothold
A slowly whirling dervish
Drifts infinitesimally by
Breaking up the symmetry
Of heaven's stunning starscape

Polycarbonate coffins
Jettisoned in a final
Reverent journey
Across the sky
Silhouetted against
A shattered, ash-grey globe
Once marbled blue
As a comet's tail
Like falling tears
Mourns the dead
Of eternity

Mother Earth has not outlived
Her children

Throughout human history, the entertainers have always been the weirdos, the freaks, the strangers, the people you don't entirely trust, but the people you can't stay away from. "Normal" people are captivated by them, even as they're repelled by them. In "Travellin' Show," humanity's expansion into space hasn't really changed that. Where once the Rom travelled on paths and roads to bring entertainment to each new town, now they travel through space from station to station to not only provide shows and tricks, but also goods and mail. In addition to being a fun look at the future of the so-called "gypsies," this story also nicely shows the different sides of envying what you don't have. And if you want to continue to get those shows, you'd be well not to mistreat them...

—Keith R.A. DeCandido,
author of *Dragon Precinct,*
Unicorn Precinct, and *Goblin Precinct*

TRAVELLIN' SHOW

Gypsies, tramps and thieves...it was the title of an ancient song from the twentieth century that echoed with my voice, my life—for all that the singer was a woman, and planet-bound. She and I shared the same nose, and perhaps a dark, unfathomable gaze, but not much else, other than the soul of that song. I don't even know her name, though we had fragments of old dig-vids of her singing the words in deep, whisky-rich tones.

I hated her for seeing so clearly. For making me see so clearly.

For many Ages of Man, the human race had longed for the stars. I had them and didn't much care for it. Me, I wanted dirt beneath my feet miles deep, moving in a slow, massive spin I couldn't hope to feel were I as still as dead. I wanted to look up and see the stars twinkle and find nothing but satisfaction in the fact that I could see them through the filter of a planet's sky. I wanted roots, just once in my life, if only for a moment.

I believed someday I would. Someday...if I had to live up to every rotten thing they said about us. The kindest folk said we were all glitz, glam, and sham; everyone else...well, you get the idea.

You see, the frontier of space was much more dangerous than any similar state of existence planetside. People were desperate, harsh, and took what they could get in the way of easing the darkness all around them. They got to believing everyone else would gladly do them worse, so do it first.

That's why there are rules that every Caravan holds to and ruthlessly enforces. Cheat us, and we're gone; harm us, and we're gone for good; kill one of our own, and don't ever sleep again.

The dark is deep and cold. We—the Rom—are a touch of golden warmth in the black, a laugh when the universe is crying, passion where most bodies are worn down to indifference. We are welcome everywhere...once night falls and the stage lights are lit, the carnie booths are pitched, and everyone young and decent is tucked away in bunks. We bring the things that can't be had, the little pleasures, moments of forgetfulness, news from home ironically delivered by those who have never had one, unless you count the caravan ships.

No matter how they looked down on us, there wasn't a man jack in space who would risk being stricken from our travel circuit by mistreating us.

Or so we believed.

* * *

"Paolo, come on...it's time to dock." Terlinda startled me as her voice crackled from the wall comm. My sister sounded annoyed.

I said nothing and finished shaving, rebelliously scraping an antique straight razor across my scalp with slow care, revealing smooth, bare skin that was every inch a lie. On the Kalderaš Caravan there wasn't a patch of skin on any of us above the age of three that wasn't tattooed with vibrant, nanite-embedded ink. Some claimed it was because in space we couldn't paint our caravans as our ancestors did, so we patterned our skin instead.

Maybe that was true, but more importantly the tattoos were both warning and defense, though none but our own were aware of the latter. As far as the universe was concerned it was just one more difference between us and them. An easy way to tell who not to trust...or piss off, but other than that, just elaborate skin art.

Little did they know.

The markings of the Rom did more than earn us those labels of glitz, glam, and sham...at a silent mental command the nanites in the ink projected sensory holograms, creating the illusion of hair, clothes, and even ready-changing features by means of hard-light holo-projections intricate enough to fool even complex electronic recording devices. Mostly we used it to enhance our performances, but it came in equally handy when we had a need to vanish without a trace, or appear as something other than what we are.

The universe knew us by our ink. This is why—when not among the *gadje*...outsiders—my silent protest was to appear unmarked by any color that wasn't flesh, and to retain the growth of hair most of my people had chemically switched off as a practicality of traveling in space. Yes, it meant I had to shave before docking with other vessels or outposts for a show, but I still held the hope that my life would be different someday, and even just that fringe of hair that was not illusion made me feel it might be attainable.

Little did *I* know.

"Paolo! Now!" This time Terlinda snapped at me from the cabin hatch, sending my hand and the razor it held sluicing sideways in a shallow cut across my scalp.

"Ah!" I hissed with the pain, however brief; I felt a sharp tingle across my damaged skin as diligent nanites rushed to repair their roof. Glaring back at her, I took the time to clean the blade and carefully put it away before rinsing the blood and shaving foam from my head. In moments, the only clue I'd bled myself was the fading metallic tang on the air.

"What is the point of all of this?" she asked, her hand gesturing at my illusion of normalcy, annoyance and exasperation coloring her words. "It isn't like you will ever fit among them, no matter what you look like. All you do is waste our time. And cost us double docking fees for holding up station traffic."

I didn't bother to argue anymore. It was an old battle of strike and counterstrike etched into the temporal memory of the ship a thousand-fold. In silence, I moved past her, lowering my head to kiss her brow—which annoyed her further, as I'd had a growth spurt that left me six inches to the advantage of her own five-feet. While she sputtered, I strode down the corridor toward the docking portal and my assigned task. We were not at risk of fines, despite Terlinda's claims; not this time and never again since the first time, before I'd learned to feel the changes in the drive that indicated power-down in preparation for docking. Since becoming attuned to those subtle variations in the engines' sounds I have never, ever been late to my post.

Terlinda growled behind me, her breath huffing ever so slightly as she hurried to catch up. "Are you so ashamed of what we are that you want to be like them? Are you so eager to be *gadje*?" She spat the word, a bitter insult when applied to one of our own.

What she said stopped me, but it was what I heard beneath the words that had me turn back to her. Her surface scorn mingled with a deeper hurt that she tried to hide, bringing glimpses to the surface. I met her eyes, so like my own, deep and dark, if rather more deceptively doe-like. I closed my own against the pain she let me see there. It nearly gutted me to be the cause of it. She was like my own mother, for ours had long ago joined the stars as we never could this side of life. How to explain to her and not hurt her more?

"Camlo,"—lovely one—"there is nothing about shame in this...of any of you or myself." I struggled for the words to explain what I had yet to make clear to anyone in my clan. "Have you never dreamed to stand upon a planet? To feel its unmoving mass beneath your feet? To see the grass and birds and a proper sunrise? To breathe the crisp, clean flavor of natural air and not feel the constant threat of vacuum weighing down on you?"

For just a moment in my life I wanted to know what it felt like not to wander. Had my sister never felt the same?

Before she could answer me, the rumble of the engines shifted to a subtle drone warning me I'd no more time. I left Terlinda with confusion in her eyes as I spun around and hurried to my post before I proved her right about the fines.

*　　*　　*

The Midway Outpost was exactly that: midway between Earth and the furthest colony. It orbits a planet called Xerxes where there are a few scientific installations and one military complex, but not much else, according to the spatial-net. I have never been there before—the planet or the outpost. It takes a long time to tramp around the universe. The last time the Kalderaš Caravan had docked here was sixteen years ago; I had not even been born.

With a swiftness gained by much repetition, we unloaded our wares and trappings from the ship and shuttled everything we would need to set up our traveling show to an emptied assembly bay at the center of the outpost.

Whether founded or unfounded, the reputation of our kind preceeded us. We were watched over closely as we went about our business. Some of us too closely. Each time Terlinda left the Caravan the eyes of the male outpost personnel followed her. I did not like the looks on their faces. Though I was only fifteen and my sister nearing twenty, I knew as her brother it was my place to protect her. What was more, I loved her as I loved none other, and God help anyone who offered her insult or harm.

When she next came down the ramp I walked beside her wearing the appearance of a man taller and more muscled than I could ever hope to be. The tattoos on the seeming—different from those on my actual body—were bold and agressive, all stark black lines and bright blues and reds, like the warnings given off by the skin of a poisonous toad. I didn't need any help from the nanites to darken my expression as I made sure to catch the eye of each of those men staring. Some of them looked amused and went back to what they were doing, others sneered and kept on looking, some rare few were clearly embarrassed and nodded respectfully in our direction before turning away; none of them challenged my silent warning.

And still, for the balance of the offload I kept that image of power and strength. The effort wore on me as I had to remember my perceived physical boundaries, as opposed to the actual ones.

"You are an ass," Terlinda murmured under her breath at me.

"Love you too," I grumbled back while maintaining my looming presence and ducking under a hatchway that I would have otherwise walked beneath with no problem. The others of the clan politely took no notice of my ruse, though for one who knew how to tell they were clearly amused.

Finally, with the pack-out complete, we set about transforming the lackluster bay into a cross between a gypsy carnival and a homeworld bazaar. Lights and bobbles and fabrics in bright, vibrant colors were swiftly deployed and arranged. Right at the entry hatch the other boys and I set up the three-sided square of stalls. The moment we finished one the older women filled it up with luxury goods while we moved onto the next. The stalls were simple frames of aluminum 'bamboo' draped with colorful silk.

In addition to ambiance, they served to block the view and path of those who had not paid to enter the carnival. Beyond this screen Father and my uncles were raising two larger, more private tents, off to either side of the bay—one for business such as the sending and receiving of personal messages, discreetly purchasing certain goods, or treating ills the crew could not or would not bring to the Medbay; the other was for entertainments for which the crew must pay an extra fee to view, such as the fancy dancing and the curiosity acts. Beyond all of that, the rest of the space was for feasting and public dancing. The younger women were in charge there and had already created of the bare, serviceable bay an exotic gathering area that bore little resemblance to its earlier state.

Wiping sweat from my holographic chin—in truth, my damp brow—I watched as my sister and cousins set up the fireboxes, our version of the traditional firepits that would have been found at a true carnival.

Already the scent of spices and meat were on the air and they hadn't even started cooking. My mouth watered. At a table beside Terlinda, other women of the clan set out specialty foods that would soon go on to the encased grill as regulations forbid open flames in the oxygen-rich, canned atmosphere of the outpost.

Terlinda laughed as she stoked the coals and started loading prepared kabobs in the transition area to be moved on to the grill. She made a face at me when she caught me staring. I didn't mind because her eyes were filled with love; it was good to see her without the scowl I usually managed to put on her face. Turning away I bent to clean up the last of the tools we had used to set up the bazaar. As I did, I noticed one of the watchers from earlier nearby. His gaze hooded...one corner of his mouth barely upturned. I did not care for what I saw. The man watched the women preparing the food.

"Can I help you?" I asked, stepping between him and them.

He smirked. "Naw, just working up an appetite."

My jaw tightened at the many ways that could be taken. "If you don't mind, we aren't quite ready for business yet. Thank you."

"So, tell me," the man said, his expression growing sly and a touch hungrier. "Which tent do we go to for a little time with one of the girls?"

It took effort to keep my tone neutral. I may not have succeeded. "None of them. Romany women don't sell their virtue."

The crewman looked confused, and then angry. I was fortunate that I still wore my more intimidating, if illusionary, seeming from earlier or perhaps things would have gone differently. As it was, he lifted his chin and just barely his lip in the ghost of a sneer, his arms crossing over his chest. In response, I sent a subtle command to the nanites beneath my skin to flex my holographic muscles. I held the man's gaze. I saw evil in the soul staring back at me.

Things could have gotten ugly if the station's head of security had not come through the hatch as we stared one another down. The watcher's gaze flickered to the newcomer; mine stayed steady on the man.

"Everything okay, Crewman Tran?"

"Yes, sir," Tran answered as his arms dropped to his side and he turned to salute his superior. It was then that I noticed the security patch on his uniform and cursed beneath my breath. "Just about to inspect this gypsy's load, make sure nothing that belongs to the station *accidentally* got mixed up with it."

I must have growled at the offense because both the crewman and his boss looked at me intently.

"Paolo," Father's voice cracked sharply from behind me. "Let security look, then get those tools back to the Caravan and put away."

With a subtle understanding, the head of security gave a little wave of his hand, a polite smile on his face. "No, that won't be necessary. I'm sure you all have plenty to do to ready things for tonight. We won't hold you."

Startled, I looked up and met his eye. His smile deepened into one with more warmth. I suddenly got the impression I didn't fool him. He nodded toward the hatch and stepped to the side. As I walked away, slightly trembling in reaction, I spared a glance for my sister; she looked safe and happy, surrounded by our family as they finished the final preparations for the carnival. With that sight firm in my mind, I was content to turn and go.

As I moved down the corridor I heard the officer speaking behind me: "Tran, your new orders have come in. You're being rotated planetside; report to the XO for your papers and a shuttle requisition."

I resisted the urge to turn and smirk back at that asshole, who would now miss out on all the carnival did have to offer.

It was petty, but my only satisfaction.

*   *   *

By the time I stowed the tools and endured the latest lecture from my father, who had followed me back to the Caravan, it was time to change. The carnival had been running several hours and shortly the special performances would begin. I once more appeared as myself, brightly colored and intricately marked, swirls and ancient markings clear upon my skin, with a starburst at the center of my forehead that subtly sparkled as the nanites beneath the skin released tiny charges of light like controlled static, only without the shocking sensation. My garb, while suitably flamboyant in cut, was subtle in color. I wore a long open vest of raw amber silk belted over a crisp, white shirt with billowing sleeves and a front that opened in a deep vee to my navel. My pants were supple black leather that just barely gleamed in the subdued light of the Caravan. They were close-fitting, but soft as kid, and no impediment to movement; no small consideration, as I was a tumbler tonight. Finished with my preparations, I went to join the rest of the special performers, who were gathering at the exit ramp.

It disturbed me not to see my sister. She loved the life we led, the performing, the glamour, the thrill. In all my given memory, I couldn't recall a time when she hadn't been the first to the ramp, in her jewel-tone scarves and bangles, flowing skirts and soft, curl-toed slippers. My eyes scanned the group again. All there, but for Terlinda.

"Father..." I called. There must have been some warning in my voice.

He turned from where he talked with Uncle Tomias, the two of them reviewing the entertainment planned for the night, as they always did. Father's brow gathered in concern, the pattern there wrinkled with the expression. "Paolo?"

"I don't see Terlinda."

I could not read his expression, which disturbed me, but his tone remained calm as he said, "Go check her cabin, please." I hurried to do as he bid.

She was not there. But her costume was, waiting on a peg beside her door, ready for the night's performance. I snatched one bangled scarf and hurried back to where my family waited. I did not even have to speak.

As if I even could.

✳   ✳   ✳

My father ordered me to stay behind. He knew. He knew better than I did what would happen if he let me free. If we discovered the worst.

I tried to obey. I told myself that I should be there when she returned, as surely she would. My Terlinda should not come back to an empty ship with whatever grief she may have suffered.

No. I should not think such thoughts. And yet my heart knew no innocent thing had kept Terlinda from all she loved in life. Guilt burned like a brand inside me. I paced and tore at my clothes, battered my mind for any clue hiding there. My thoughts kept coming back to Tran and the look in his eye. The sickness in his soul.

There was no staying put.

Throwing off my costume I pulled on an outfit of all black cotton, close and tight as a second skin, nothing to impede me, whatever I must do. From a locker beneath my bunk I drew a matching set of antique throwing knives I'd inherited from my grandfather, and he from his. They were the only things I had that resembled weapons. I'd been well-taught in their use.

I normally only used them when I performed one of the curiosity acts.

Without a second thought I belted them around my waist. An order to the nanites both hid them from view and cloaked my features in a nondescript face made up of pieces melded from the crew, creating an appearance vaguely familiar but known to none. Armed and armored against resistance I circumvented the lock on the hatch and went out into the station, seeking out the only one who might help me.

Even armed with the directions to his personal cabin, it took some time to find the head of security. More than it had taken to find his name—Stan Wilkes—which I carefully pilfered along with the rest of my information from the station system using hacking skills learned at my granddad's side.

Wilkes did not seem surprised to see me.

"I expected you sooner, Paolo," he said, as I slid through the hatch to his cabin.

I went still, the holo image fluxing around me in my confusion. Then the man blinked and I could clearly see the flutter of lenses flick across his eye. I dropped the seeming.

"I wouldn't be a very good head of security if I didn't have the latest tech, would I?"

He started to rise. I locked my jaw and braced myself for attack, but he sat back down, placing his hands in full view palm down upon his desk. "It's okay. I'm not against you. Your father has been to see me," he explained. "My men are searching now, your people with them; I'm only here to review the security feed, or I would be searching right along with..."

I cut him off. "It was Tran."

Wilkes sighed and lowered his head in acknowledgement. When he looked up I wanted to snarl at what I saw. "It was him!" I stalked forward, my fists clenched and my expression as twisted as my gut. My sister was in the hands of a beast, I had no doubt, and as clear as I knew that, I knew just from looking at him that the man before me was going to say there was nothing he could do.

I blinked and stopped dead. Without seeming to move at all, Wilkes had drawn a riot gun on me. I cursed and stood there trembling, waiting for the door behind me to open and security forces to hurry in. Instead, Wilkes placed the non-lethal weapon on the desk and slowly rose to his feet.

"I suspect you are right, but I can't prove it, and Tran left the outpost less than twenty standard minutes after I sent you back to your ship. The feed *seems* to support that he left alone."

My knees buckled at his words. I would have fallen without the edge of the desk.

That had been over four hours ago. That was when I understood Wilkes's expression: his men weren't on a search and rescue. They were on a search and *recover.*

Something inside me wanted to howl. To scream and cry and curl into a ball. That something was frozen in ice, locked deep down at the angry core of me. I locked gazes with Wilkes and waited for him to say what I knew was to come.

His voice sounded just above a whisper. "I can't go after him based on the feed, even though I suspect it's been altered...any more than I could go after you for stealing a shuttle, *if the feed said it wasn't you.*"

I straightened, then nodded, before turning and walking out the door.

By the time I hit the corridor, I wore another face.

✳   ✳   ✳

Hijacking a shuttle was easier than it should have been. But I guess I shouldn't have been surprised; after all, the head of security was unofficially supportive of my efforts. Still, it felt like a cheat. Not that I dwelled on that then, not with my sister's well-being dependent on my success. Or so I told myself.

There wasn't anyone among the Rom above the age of eight that didn't know how to pilot a shuttle. Personally, I could fly anything, upto and including the Caravan itself. A shuttle was nothing. Now, figuring out Tran's flight path...that took a little more finesse. Not the one he'd logged with flight control, but the one the tracer in his craft automatically recorded. Most people didn't even know those existed.

I'm not most people.

Even so, an ordinary hack wouldn't have gotten me the data. That was why I'd lifted Wilkes's security code earlier, when I figured out where to find him. I suspect even then I'd had his unofficial support.

I'd just left the stratosphere when the tracker on my shuttle pinged the one Tran had taken to the surface. It appeared by the mapping display that he had set down in a secluded clearing about ten miles from the complex he had been assigned to. I tried not to think of why.

It never occurred to me I was, in part, about to achieve my dream. I was too focused to really notice. Or wonder. Too tormented to care.

The more I descended the harder it was to breathe. The more my heart pounded. The harder it was to think. I dropped my engines as low as I could without stalling and glided the craft in, landing about a quarter mile from Tran's location, out of sight of the shuttle.

The hatch on my vessel cycled open and I barely felt I had the strength to climb to my feet. The pull of full gravity was like granite ballast filling me up. The air burned my lungs as I screamed in rage. I had not considered the effects of planetfall on a body that had never before left space.

I forced myself to my feet and somehow made it to the open hatch. If my body were not well-honed by the rigors of performance I could not have managed even that.

I did not so much climb to the surface as tumble down the stairs. The natural light nearly blinded me. When I manage to gain my feet, slow step by slow step, I dragged myself in the direction of the other shuttle. The hatch was open when I got there. I just stood and stared, scarcely believing how both simple and hard this journey had been. In truth, I dreaded what I would find. Dreaded more what I might not. What if she wasn't here? What if I had made the wrong choice and Terlinda suffered for it?

I gritted my teeth and climbed the steps to the shuttle hatch. I was no more than halfway when a sound came to my ears. Snoring. Faint snoring, broken up by a snuffle and occasionally a murmur.

Yes, it took me that long to climb.

When finally I reached the top I slumped against the hatch, not caring if my quarry should see me. It took forever for my eyes to adjust again to darkness.

Inside, deep at the angry core of me, I died.

On the floor of the shuttle lay Tran fast asleep and naked.

Beside him...my Terlinda, her eyes vacant and filmed, the damage to her bare body half-knitted by the nanites before they too began to die. The colors of the ink beneath her skin were fading without the bots' inner brilliance. Tears streamed down my face, but I did not feel them. My chest heaved and my eyes glazed; I did not even realize as my right hand fell to the hilt of one of my throwing knives.

Tran twitched, and snorted, and some benumbed portion of my brain railed at the wrongness of that. Muscles and reflexes trained by countless performances and an even greater number of practices fought against the weight of gravity to do as they had been taught.

*   *   *

The Caravans hold to a code: Cheat us, and we're gone; harm us, and we're gone for good; kill one of our own, and don't ever sleep again.

We would never return to Midway Outpost.

I would never again set foot on dirt.

We left in the night. It was simple, even on a fortified outpost, as long as you had the skill to bypass the systems keeping you in dock. I did, but I wasn't in any shape to. Hell, I didn't even know how I'd gotten us back. That didn't quite matter, though, as we seemed to have retained a certain unofficial support.

Someone else stepped up and unlocked the gate.

In the finest tradition of gypsies throughout history, we faded away among the stars like a memory to protect one of our own.

That would be me. Paolo.

I killed a man, a *gadje*, a vicious dog who behaved worse by far than anything people said of the Rom. I don't even know his first name. Frankly, I don't care. What I know is that he brutalized my sister and she died at his hand.

Tran should have remembered not to sleep.

SELF REFLECTION

I watch myself
stride confidently by
splendid with youthful vigor
graceful, beautiful, miraculous
a tribute to the wonder,
the horror, the folly
of modern science.

As if what society needs
is another excuse
for divisiveness.

With a whole new spin
on self-loathing,
I call him monkey-me
as he runs the maze of humanity
to the scientists' bell.

We may share
the same genetic code
but he is two percent less me,
and two inches shorter...
before my age bent me.

I call him monkey-me
and rue the day
I offered up my cells,
desperately grasping
at the hope for immortality.

An Alliance Archives Adventure

Welcome to debriefing hell.

Kat thought it would just be herself and the members of the rescue team hashing over the details for Sarge, and perhaps the XO of their unit, 142nd Infantry.

Apparently, she was wrong.

From those involved, only she, Scotch, and Sergeant Major Daire were present. They stood before the resident top brass of Military Command. It felt more like an interrogation than a debriefing.

"Corporal Alexander, please relate your account of the events that took place on the Groom facility."

Kat took one measured step forward from where she stood at parade rest beside her commanding officer and Scotch. Stopping ramrod straight, she saluted. At a gesture from the board she resumed parade rest. "Yes, sir. At 2200 I disembarked from the shuttle transport for reassignment to the Groom Experimental Complex. I delivered my orders to Station Commander Trask and was assigned quarters. At 2345 I was called to duty by Lt. Commander Connor."

"You were assigned duty less than two hours on station?" The question came from a stern-faced captain on the end, his stylus tapping a steady tattoo on the datascreen set into the table in front of him.

"Yes, sir. The normal shift crew had mistakenly been given leave, and the crewman I replaced had reported to sick bay."

"Continue."

Kat recounted how she had found things in disarray, with the shift understaffed and deployment schedules misaligned. The one woman on the board, a major, frowned as Kat admitted to deploying the *Rommel* out of sequence, despite the fact that her actions were all that had kept the flagship out of the pirates' hands.

Kat felt her jaw tighten. What did they want? It wasn't as if they'd disclosed the facts to her before using her to infiltrate the station. The inquisition continued with her accounting how the *Alexi* had gone missing and the station commander had been un-responsive to her priority hails. She detailed her actions, from the unsanctioned High Alert to deploying the auxiliary black box. When she reached the point of her encounter with what she'd presumed was Commander Trask, many members of the board shifted forward, their eye bright with interest bright.

"What first betrayed the fact that the individual you faced was not the commander?"

"When I called up the schematic of the station and ran a scan, his presence on the station did not register. When he arrived on the command deck, the scan was still active, yet there was no mark of his presence on the display, indicating he was missing his identchip."

"You did not consider this might have been a system malfunction similar to the disruption in the duty assignments or the deployment schedules?"

"That was my first assessment, sir. However, his actions over the course of the encounter raised several doubts in my mind."

"And how did you respond to these doubts?"

What is this shit? For going on two hours now they'd been debriefed. Her foot throbbed in a steady beat—her face kept time with it until she wanted to scream at the board for being heartless, suspicious bastards—and her patience had disappeared an hour and a half ago. As the questioning went on, and the ache of her injuries ramped up, she was less interested in answering than she was in getting out.

"I sought confirmation of my suspicions, checking the system for file access and using the auxiliary command deck to initiate remote observation of Commander Trask."

"So," Colonel Corbin, the ranking officer on the board, said, the censure overt in his voice. "You opted to investigate the command-ing officer, rather than report your suspicions, is that correct?"

Kat fought the impulse to snarl, keeping her own tone neutral through extreme effort. "A scan of the computer systems seemed to substantiate my concerns; my remote observation of Trask further supported my assessment that he attempted to steal the schematics for the *Rommel.* With no way to determine who among the crew might be involved in the piracy I judged it expedient to safeguard the system data before taking any further action."

More than one member of the review board frowned as her neutrality slipped at mention of Trask's name, as well as at the notable absence of his rank. The rest of the expressions betrayed nothing at her admission of independent initiative and the use of her government-funded training as a computer specialist for the unsanctioned observation of a superior. She was certain that they disapproved. Why she couldn't say. Hadn't she accomplished what they'd intended?

Some glimmer of her thoughts must have slipped past her guard because every brow before her drew down in a scowl.

A familiar vibration went through Kat's jaw. "Lose the attitude, Alexander," Sarge murmured over his bonejack in a tone as sharp and cold as ice-coated razorblades.

Kat drew herself up to attention despite the fact they'd been given leave to stand at rest. Without a word, the others followed suit. They remained that way for another half hour as the board continued to grill her; the questions shifting more to what she could tell them of the function and performance of the composite, than the actual sequence of events that had exposed and subsequently destroyed the imposter.

By the time the colonel issued his curt "Dismissed," Kat's fingers itched for her gauss rifle.

*　　*　　*

"With all due respect, Sarge," Kat said in a tight voice, her eyes locked on the back of her commanding officer's head, "what the hell was that about?"

He didn't answer. He didn't stop or even turn. He didn't tear her a new one like she deserved, actually. For that she counted herself lucky. Stretching her stride despite the agony of her foot, she followed him down the hall and back toward the docking zone and the systems check he'd ordered earlier. Beside her, Scotch easily kept pace, a gleefully amused look on his face as he glanced from her to Sarge, clearly waiting for something to give. Before Kat could catch up they were hailed by the crewman on duty.

The man wore a determined expression, but not for long. "Sir…"

The look Sarge gave him cut the private off, the man's throat bobbing as he swallowed whatever he'd been about to say.

"We're here to check out a systems malfunction on our troop transport," Sarge said. "Keep your men out of our way so we can get the job done and get down to the business of some R&R."

The poor crewman seemed startled as he jerked an automatic salute. The only thing about him with any starch left was his ship suit. Newbie.

Sarge didn't hang around for anything more before he turned sharply and continued on to the berth where they'd tethered. Scotch and Kat were no more than a step behind him. Kat felt microtremors course down her back. Stress. Fatigue. She'd already been on edge *before* spending hours under the lights. What she needed now was rest, but barring that, some action would do. Something told her to get ready for the latter. Tivo, the unit tech, or Campbell, their pilot, always took care of vetting the shuttle after any mission. On rare occasion, she'd even done it herself, but never the sergeant major.

As they neared the shuttle, Kat automatically scanned the docking bay, making a mental note of the cameras and other security measures. She didn't expect trouble, but it never hurt to know what safeguards were in place. They were all pretty basic, but she did note something odd: an alarm sounded, polluting the air with a high-pitched squeal...and no one seemed to pay any attention. In fact, she noticed a clear absence of any hanger personnel in the immediate vicinity, though she could see crewmen at work across the bay. Impressive, that. She didn't know what the alarm was, but she wished she'd had it ninety minutes ago; it could clearly empty a room.

"How come they haven't done anything about that?" she wondered aloud, looking around to see where the screech was coming from. "What is it, anyway?"

Scotch laughed and Sarge shot her a predatory grin; neither one said a word, though, as they did a visual scan of the bay. The laughter cut off as if it'd never been and the familiar gleam of a combat operative entered Scotch's gaze.

"All clear, Sarge."

The sergeant major punched a code into the hatch key pad.

With a curse Kat locked her hands over her ears, the sudden movement throwing her off balance. Instant nausea gripped her.

"What the *fuck*!"

Similar cries echoed from across the cavernous bay as the hatch swung open. The unmuffled sound coming from inside was an assault on her senses. Kat swayed as it shot her equilibrium to hell. Only Scotch's arm bracing her kept her from landing on the deck. Sarge disappeared inside and the sound cut off abruptly. Was this the malfunction Tivo recorded?

"Inside," Sarge called from the belly of the craft. "Now."

Kat found herself back on the bench she'd vacated only hours before. Her ears still buzzed and all her aches ramped up even worse. She groaned as Sarge handed Scotch the field medkit. Within seconds he had her stripped of both her left boot and sock, and had extracted a pressure bandage from one of the pack's external pouches. None too gently he slapped an analgesic, transdermal patch on her ankle before snapping the seal on the bandage to activate the chemical coolant that would further reduce the swelling in her foot. He then encased her damaged foot and loosened her boot sufficiently to slip over it. Lastly, he rubbed a bit of anti-inflammatory cream on the swelling around her eye and along her jaw.

She clenched her teeth and fought not to scream. When the pain dulled after a moment it registered that Sarge was talking.

"You ever pull a fool stunt like that again and I'll have you out of my unit so fast the ink won't have time to dry before you're gone."

"Yes, Sarge." Her error wasn't in being injured, but in not disclosing the fact that she was; in combat that could get a teammate killed, or blow an op. She should have known better. She *did* know better. She'd just let recent events get her head twisted around. Scotch patted her good leg approvingly before pushing to his feet and stowing the medkit back in its place.

Sarge gave a sharp nod and turned to a storage locker. As he swung the hatch open, Kat gasped and found herself beside him before she'd realized she'd moved. Though she'd never personally set eyes on the unit, she knew what it was: an auxiliary black box. The Groom's ABB, according to the etching on the pure black unit.

Thank you, Sakmyster! she sent the thought winging in the direction of the GEC and the former comrade who had trusted her judgment enough to flaunt pseudo-Trask's orders. The rescue team must have intercepted it when they'd come to get her.

A shit-eating grin spread across her face as she looked up and met the eyes of her commander and her team mate. "We've got him!"

With eager hands she reached for the unit only to have Sarge step in her way.

"*That* was them not trusting you."

Kat blinked. Gave her head a shake. Opened her mouth to ask what the heck he was going on about. Then it registered. He was answering her earlier question and her jaw clenched shut.

"*That* was them trying to determine if you had a grudge...or a conflict of interest...."

She remained silent, breathing deep and getting her temper in hand.

"Well, soldier," he said, "do you?"

A few more deep breaths. *Really* deep. She focused hard on not buckling beneath Sarge's continued stare. "I guess that depends, sir."

"On?"

"If they are on our side or the pirates'."

He gave a slow nod and stepped aside.

With care she drew the battered microsatellite—or microsat—from the locker. "Did we do that?" she asked, running her hand over burn scoring and a hefty dent down the left side.

"They take that kind of stuff out of our budget when we don't play nice," Scotch said from the back of the transport. "Must have been our pirate, though how he knew it was there and why he didn't just haul it in and dump it somewhere else, I couldn't tell ya."

Kat grunted and continued to examine the unit. It was important to make sure she didn't wipe the core trying to access the information they were after. The external access was all but obliterated. She would have to crack the case. "Hey, Scotch. Grab my kit, will you?"

The tools landed on the bench beside her. Carefully she turned the unit over to access the bottom. The tech team that had designed this particular ABB model allowed for methods of quick and dirty access that would not endanger the internal circuits. Taking out her microtorch she cut away the base along designated markings that were her safety zone. With the final burn, she switched off the torch and set it aside to lift the battered housing away. As she suspected, the primary ports were useless, but there were several more inside for cases just such as this. Again, she wondered what had done such damage; even as far back as the late 1990s black boxes were known for being near indestructible and the technology had only improved. This unit was top of the line, evidenced by the fact that the receivers were still operational despite the abuse to the shell. And yet someone had clearly tried to turn it to ash.

Powering up her tablet computer—a specialist's unit, with more bells and whistles than a hero's parade—Kat networked the systems and did a hard burn of the data. Her field computer was made for such things, and yet the transfer took forever. There was an impressive amount of data on that ABB.

"Almost done?" Sarge looked on edge. "We have only so long before they wonder what we're doing in here."

"Sorry, Sarge; there's a lot more here than I expected."

Scotch sprawled across the opposite benches. "We could always muss up Kittie's clothes a bit and let them think what they want."

If she weren't crazy-busy Kat would have made him pay for that one. Of course, she cheered herself with the thought that there was always later.

Finally, the dump was done. Not soon enough, though; from the front of the transport the comm squawked.

She stole a moment anyway to scan the data, searching for Trask's last coordinates before powering down. The comm squawked again and Sarge cursed, giving Kat a stern look. Quicker than spit she disconnected her machine. He took it from her and stowed it in the locker he'd taken the microsat out of earlier. She watched him a moment, then turned her attention to the gutted ABB in front of her. She had no clue what to do with it. As she was trying to figure that out, a hand came into her field of view. It gripped a timed charge. Armed.

"Take it," Sarge said. "Slip it among the circuits and weld the housing back together. We'll launch it from the rocket shaft. If they ever find any of it, they won't recognize it from any other bit of debris."

Kat did as ordered. When she was done, Scotch slapped a separator charge on one end for propulsion and jettisoned the evidence.

The comm squawked again and Sarge moved to respond.

"Sergeant Major Daire; go ahead."

There was a pause, then a crackle. "Sergeant Major, the deck crew reports rocket fire from your vessel; explain."

Everyone in the shuttle tensed even further at the sound of Colonel Corbin's voice.

"Sorry, sir," Sarge said, his tone calm and completely reasonable. "My tech noticed some computer anomalies at docking. My specialist was attempting to correct the matter when a system glitch fired off the launch tube."

"A technician will be down immediately to check it out."

"Thank you, sir. That will not be necessary." Sarge didn't even flinch. "The issue has been resolved. My specialist is finishing her report now, complete with diagnostics."

Kat swore she could hear the officer's teeth grinding in frustration, but if so, his voice didn't betray it. "Very well. Have a copy sent to my office."

"Yes, sir. You'll have it in five minutes."

The comm went dead.

"Well?" Sarge turned to Kat expectantly. "That gives you four minutes to fake something convincing; start with that incident docking with the *McKay* a month ago, it's close enough."

Kat moved to the shuttle's computer banks. Her fingers pelted the keys like a driving rain, already halfway to the *McKay* file. She tweaked here, copied there, pulled diagnostics from the last overhaul and doctored the digital time stamp; with seconds to spare Kat had a brand-new report with nary an electronic footprint out of place. Behind her, Scotch let out a long whistle. Sarge just turned and headed for the back of the transport. "Send it," he called over his shoulder as he stowed the gear and secured the locker, rekeying his code so that all was as it had been.

"Sarge," Kat called to him.

He stopped and looked over his shoulder, but didn't say a thing.

"We *did* get him."

Sarge responded with one of his patented nods before he looked away, inspecting the interior of the shuttle to make sure nothing had been overlooked that might betray them. When he finished, he waited by the open hatch for the two of them to join him. Just beyond his shoulder Kat could see several dock personnel had moved strategically closer to their berth. She started to tongue her bonejack off standby, preparing to use the subdermal comm to warn Sarge. Before she could do so she caught the seemingly random movement of his hand.

There was nothing random about it; he'd just ordered her down using one of their field combat gestures. Yeah, something was up, but as long as Sarge was already aware, she would stand down and wait for his cue.

Sarge issued the next order aloud. "Sergeant Daniels, the team's timing was a bit off on the last op; schedule a live-fire exercise for 0700."

"Yes, sir," Scotch said and headed off across the docking bay to inform the unit and log the exercise with official channels.

Kat experienced a surge of adrenaline that flushed the fatigue from her system. Sarge's words said one thing, his hands another. They were going wheels-up in the morning, to use one of Scotch's favorite antique phrases. Alpha squad was being deployed, not the entire unit. And at 0400, not 0700.

Curious. She had to wonder why Sarge was distrustful of the crew...and the command staff.

She took a step forward and winced, forgetting to be careful with her wrapped ankle. She held her breath and caught his eye, just waiting for him to tell her she was grounded. They stood with their gazes locked for a long, silent moment before Sarge gave a subtle nod. "Go rest up, Alexander. You have an exercise to run in the morning."

Kat's breath escaped on a grin. "Yes, sir!" Her salute made him growl, but it was balanced by the understanding in his gaze. He turned and headed off, leaving her to make her way to her bunk with some dignity.

* * *

"Quit dawdling, Kittie, and get your tail in here."

"Oh stow it, Rotgut." Kat snarled at Scotch as she slipped past him and moved into the belly of the shuttle. Everyone else was there already, except Sarge and Campbell. Joining her squad, she passed the load compartment, which was crammed with gear, including what looked to be a full complement of pulse cannons. Someone had been busy. Without a word, she settled into her spot on the bench and in short order reassembled her gauss rifle, checking and rechecking each connection before running a quick systems diagnostic. She hated breaking it down to begin with (a soldier wanted a gun if cornered, not a club) but carrying the weapon through the corridors would have drawn attention.

Everything was in working order.

She sat back, gripping the rifle, telling herself to relax and rest up. Of course, the more time that passed waiting for Sarge to come through the hatch, the more Kat got a bad feeling. She gave up on resting. Instead she gave her gear a thorough inspection, making sure everything was accounted for and stowed within reach. The whole time she tried to shrug off her fear, with marginal success.

The others sat back, reasonably relaxed and bullshitting, but she sat ramrod straight on her bench, gauss across her knees and her eyes locked on the back of the shuttle, hardly aware that her rifle tapped against the bulkhead.

"Stow your weapon, Alexander," Sarge said when he finally came through the hatch. Campbell entered the shuttle behind him as Kat complied. The pilot locked down the hatch and the airlock before moving to join Sarge at the front of the shuttle. Their expressions were hard and focused as they settled in at the drive console and flew through the start-up sequence. The comm squawked and Sarge shot a look and a gesture back toward the waiting team. All eyes were focused on him and none missed the message. Quiet. ID-Dark.

Kat let out a sharp breath, which earned her a hard scowl. She lowered her head in acknowledgement and worked to regulate her breathing even as she pressed her tongue against the roof of her mouth. Theirs was a special ops unit. Official channels would deny it, but they could deactivate their identchips. Those in the back did so, as ordered.

"Shuttle 62-Delta; identify yourself, pilot."

"Corporal Anthony Campbell speaking."

"Identchip scan confirmed. One passenger registered; identify."

"Sergeant Major Kevin Daire present and reporting." Sarge's voice was cool, with just a normal shade of impatience.

"Acknowledged and confirmed. Are you prepared for launch, Corporal Campbell?"

"That is an affirmative, Control. The shuttle *Teufel* is ready for launch."

Launch command made no comment on the given name of their craft, merely continuing with protocol: "Please confirm the purpose and duration of your flight."

Sarge placed a hand on Campbell's shoulder, silencing him.

"Sergeant Major Daire speaking; Corporal Campbell and I are embarking on a test flight to confirm systems are fully operational prior to scheduled live-fire exercise. Flight duration; 2.5 standard hours."

"Thank you, Sergeant Major, you are cleared for launch."

Kat and the rest of the squad strapped in before the docking collar released and the tether disengaged. Until the thrusters took them out of range of the *Rommel,* their drive engines would remain off-line, leaving them without gravity. It was going to be a while. The squad settled in for the wait. Handhelds came out, conversations continued, eyes closed, and peace—or at least quiet—reigned; until Sarge cleared his throat, that is. Everything but the shuttle stopped as the he turned his chair about to face his men.

"We have a situation."

The last eyes opened and the men and women of 142nd infantry—or Daire's Devils, as they were known—sat straight at attention.

"The details of our assignment," and here his gaze settled on Kat as he gave a brief nod of concession before continuing, "have not previously been disclosed to you.

"There is a reason we were assigned to the *Rommel*: It is suspected that the ranks in this quadrant have been infiltrated at all levels and key personnel have been subverted or replaced by composites. Apparently, they have targeted the vessel. Several attempts have already been made, including the recent events at the Groom facility."

Kat gritted her teeth, certain she was on the receiving end of covert glances from the entire squad.

Sarge then went on as if he hadn't stopped. "We, gentlemen, are Military Command's countermeasure. As such, we report directly to General Drovak and no other. Needless to say, this is a covert assignment; the *Rommel* command staff has not been informed. Our standing orders are first, to observe the crew, reporting on potentially seditious acts. Beta squad has drawn this duty. Our second objective: to actively pursue and halt pirate activity in this quadrant. That is where you come in....Thanks to Corporal Alexander, we have a fresh lead on one of the subversives. As a result, this is a fact-finding/intercept mission. The intel we secure could be the break we need to neutralize this particular threat."

With that he unbuckled his harness and floated up to the nearest tether bar. He hauled himself hand over hand to the other end of the transport. At the storage locker he used the leverage of his handhold to muscle his legs down to where he could slide his feet into the bootdocks. Kat watched as Sarge released the lock. He opened the compartment and withdrew her kit. Slinging the strap securely over his shoulder, he disengaged from the docks and hauled himself back toward the drive console.

"You ready for some satisfaction, Alexander?"

She accepted her kit when he stopped in front of her, but she didn't really need it. There was no doubt they were returning to the GEC, or the surrounding sectors, anyway. The data was there on her computer but Kat had already memorized the last known coordinates of Trask's vessel. She rattled them off from memory, and even the frequency at which he'd been transmitting.

"Impressive," Sarge replied in a dead-flat tone. Clearly, he was anything but impressed. "Now power that thing up to verify, and then determine what other useful data we've retrieved." He returned to the con without waiting for a response.

Yeah, so showing off wasn't the best idea. Kat deployed the tablet computer and sat back with it firmly in her grip. Start-up flashed by before she could blink. Opening the microsat data file, Kat quick-scanned what she'd downloaded.

"Oh shit!"

Heads turned at her outburst.

"Report, Corporal."

"Coordinates confirmed, sir." Even to her own ears, her voice sounded stunned as she rattled off the information she'd provided earlier. *I did it,* she thought. *I friggin' did it! Trask and his goons weren't quick enough!* A crow of laughter escaped her.

"And?" Sarge's voice sounded edged with impatience.

"Sarge," she managed in a normal voice, looking up to meet his stern gaze. "We are in possession of the collective data from the research facility....All of it." An understandable thread of real satisfaction crept in to her tone by the time she was done. Before her last encounter with Trask, she had attempted to initiate a Full Alert, which would have dumped the station's research databases in compressed files to the secure black box while wiping the primary servers, thus removing the prize from the reach of the pirates. Trask's people had crashed the system before she could tell whether she'd succeeded. Well, here was proof they'd failed to thwart her.

"Good to know, Alexander." Sarge's tone was still less than patient. "How about seeing if there's any intel on there of immediate use?"

She cringed and turned her gaze back to the file. "There are a number of other drive signatures recorded, sir. It's a long shot, but they might be useful in identifying and tracking the pirates." She didn't hold out much hope for that, but a soldier learned to use any tool that came to hand.

"Safe perimeter reached," Campbell cut in. "Setting course and engaging drive."

✳   ✳   ✳

It wasn't as if they expected anything to still be there. No, they were heading to the coordinates to pick up the trail of Trask's vessel.

Originally she'd taken it for an asteroid—as the pirates had intended—back when she'd still been on the command deck of the Groom facility. The ABB hadn't been fooled; it had picked up traces of the drive signature, the unique particle trail left by the ship's engines. They should be able to use that to track him. Of course, they had a ways to go, with not very much in between. That didn't dissuade Kat from linking the signal from the external cameras so it ran the feed on her screen. She'd always hated not seeing where she was going, whether it was a dirt road in a car, or across the galaxy in a shuttle.

There wasn't anything to see for the longest time. Under drive all the cameras caught was the bright blue glow of rapidly passing space punctuated by random pulses caused by the proximity of something of sufficient mass to minutely affect the electrogravitic drive envelope. There wasn't a whole heck of a lot out there to worry about, and if they did come across something, there were proximity alerts in place to give them plenty of warning. Kat settled back and let the light patterns mesmerize her. She wasn't asleep, but it was the next best thing to it; her muscles took advantage of the distraction, relaxing until she actually slouched against the bulkhead, eyes still fixed on her computer. She was barely aware of hearing the engines modulate for deceleration as they came out of drive—until the light patterns deepened and strobed wildly.

"Watch out!"

An alert on the drive console went off moments after her shout.

"Campbell, evasive maneuvers!" Sarge snapped out the order as he helped man the controls. "Clear trajectory, two degrees port."

They barely missed the burnt-out hulk. Eyes still riveted, Kat hit record on her system, catching every frame as the external cameras tracked the wreckage they'd nearly plowed into. There would have been no coming back from that. It wasn't huge, but according to the data scrolling across the bottom of her screen, it was dense. The images were beyond disturbing.

It drifted there like a recently fissured geode. The exterior was nothing but a rock; the exposed interior was a compact craft smaller than one of the escape pods, the standard kind that had earned the epitaph "The Can" for good reason. What Kat saw on her screen was barely bigger than a sleeptank. The cameras panned some more as the ship passed the obstacle.

Kat gasped and her grip on her computer white-knuckled. From over her shoulder she heard a chorus of "Damn!"s and not a few gulps before Sarge's voice cut through it all.

"Enough!" he barked. "Break it up."

She bit back a more vehement "Damn" of her own. She knew what they were looking at, and she felt cheated. "I was wrong; someone else got him."

"Alexander...disconnect that system link."

Crap.

"Sorry, sir."

Her breath came short and shallow as she broke the connection, unable to look away from the final image recorded: two thirds of an environmental suit still strapped into a conchair.

"Shake it off, soldier, and close that file," Sarge's voice echoed faint as he floated overhead.

"I was wrong..." she murmured again, her finger jabbing the power down button.

"Maybe...we'll have to see," Sarge said. He then turned toward the rest of the squad. "Scotch, Brockmann...suit up for retrieval. I want anything you can find that may tell us something, including the remains, stat.

"Stow your gear and snap to, Alexander. We have a refit to execute." Kat looked back to the rear of the transport; Scotch and Brockmann were climbing into top-end versions of the standard MMU, streamlined and built for combat or recon. Tethered at their feet she spied a neat package of standard retrieval gear, right down to a cryo-bodybag that was similar in principle to the coolant bandage strapped around her damaged ankle. She glanced at the rest of the squad as they maneuvered expertly in freefall, hauling gear from the load compartment, deploying combat armament, and fitting out the shuttle with pulse canons and thermal rockets not usually found on a transport. Tivo already had the cover off the two-stage weapons port, on the starward side—shuttles might not have anything more than basic rockets, but in the Alliance, any vessel could be retrofitted to meet combat needs. Kat watched as the tech slid in a cannon auto-mount, jacked it into the system, and replaced the tension cap, maintaining the shuttle's environmental integrity. There was a brief jolt and a mechanical *whir* as the external seal retracted on reconnect.

"The starward cannons are online and ready, Sarge," Tivo said. Dalton, the unit's deceptively feminine weapons specialist, reported similarly for port and aft cannons.

"Campbell, activate weapons control," Sarge said. "We may not see trouble, but all of you will damn well expect it, am I understood?"

"Yessir!" the squad responded collectively as they completed the refit.

Kat was still harnessed in, tablet in hand. "Sarge, put me on the retrieval squad."

He glanced down and gave her a hard stare. She couldn't blame him; she was the newest member of the unit and though she'd had the same training everyone else did, she didn't have all her clearances yet. "You are not yet rated for zero-g combat."

"All due respect, sir," Kat said, "they aren't rated for invasive data retrieval." She held up her computer. "It's the only way we have a chance of retrieving anything more than physical intel."

Sarge didn't look convinced. "Sure this isn't personal." It was one of those not-questions.

She went for bald-faced honesty. "Does it matter, sir? Because I could lie..."

That drew a quirk of his upper lip, if not an actual smile. Just then Scotch drifted up from behind. "It's good, Sarge, let her come...we could use a mule to haul the gear."

Kat restrained herself from giving her teammate a sour look...or a non-regulation salute; his comment might have been flippant, but his expression remained solid, steady, and serious. Both she and Scotch waited in patient silence for Sarge's ruling. Okay, not so patient, at least for Kat, but she was sure she *appeared* to be patient at least, and that was the important bit.

"Double-time it, Alexander," Sarge said by way of approval, "before our drive-wake propels the derelict out of range. We don't have fuel to waste coming about."

He hadn't closed his mouth on the last word before Kat had her harness disengaged, her rifle retrieved, and propelled herself toward the equipment lockers and her EVA suit, tablet still in hand and her gauss drifting behind her from its strap. She lost a few moments temporarily securing both, but still, she suspected she broke several suit-up records. Maybe she imagined it, or maybe Sarge really chuckled behind her; hard to say, as she already lowered her helmet over her head. Taking her microtorch out of her kit, she attached it to the utility mount on the back of her left gauntlet, then withdrew her tablet once more, slipping its safety tether over her right wrist and ratcheting it tight before activating the auditory command function on the unit. She could operate it in gauntlets, but why borrow the headache? Finished. She activated her bonejack and, with a press of her tongue against her upper jaw, switched it to squad frequency before positioning herself by the airlock.

"Ready for deployment, sir."

Sarge was already back in the drive compartment; only Scotch and Brockmann stood there watching her, 20mm recoilless rifles slung over their shoulders and amusement clear in their expressions despite the obstruction of their helmets. She could almost read their thoughts: *Newbie.*

So be it, she just didn't want Sarge changing his mind. Brockmann propelled herself past them to the airlock, her movements deft and efficient despite the zero-g atmosphere. Scotch stopped in front of Kat and held out a tether. She reflexively accepted it, not even thinking what it was hooked to.

Looking down, she sighed.

"I wasn't joking about the gear, Kittie." Scotch's words buzzed along her jaw. In his other hand he held a pulse pistol. "Stow your weapon. Sarge is right; you aren't cleared for zero-g combat." He handed her the pistol, which she slid into an external thigh pocket. "This is personal protection only, should it come down to an encounter, do not initiate engagement; duck and cover or haul ass back to the transport with what we came for. Brockmann and I will take care of the offensive while you secure the intel." Then he grinned. "You do realize this is all academic, right? Not like there's anything out there for anyone to hide behind."

That took the sting out of the rest of what he'd said.

Their assignment was covert, which meant if it came down to it the higher ups would claim no knowledge of it, rather than raise the suspicions of the subversives. End result: if things went bad, Alpha Squad had all likely written off their careers already. Of course, just in case they weren't hung out to dry over this, violating regs in a conflict situation could ground her, or even ensure Kat never rated for zero-g combat. Not much of a future in special ops after that.

Yeah, with that as perspective, she was fine playing mule.

"Get your asses out there and get this done," Sarge snapped over their squad frequency, "before some overeager command crew over at Groom mistakes us for more pirates."

*   *   *

This was by no means her first EVA. Nerves twitched anyway as Kat hauled the recovery kit. Not the easiest thing; it kind of resembled one of those shower kits…with all the individual, zipped compartments that unroll flat so you can access everything or bundle it up compact for storage…only monster-sized. Bulky as sin and a pain in the ass to maneuver (clearly the designers did not consider the dimensions of the various airlocks it would have to go through), but better than losing a hundred thousand dollars worth of tools to the vacuum of space.

When she finally managed to get out of the shuttle she had her first eyes-on view of the rock-ship. The rest of the retrieval team was already halfway there, putting the shattered mass into perspective: Compared to the vessel she'd just left, it was like a toy. The inside had to have had just barely enough room for Trask to move around, with some storage for necessities. She could not conceive that it was ever meant for manned space travel.

Her suspicions were confirmed as Scotch and Brockmann reached the derelict ahead of her. "Damn!" Scotch's response was drawn out and stunned. "Sarge," he called out over the band, "this man was *not* here willingly."

Kat came up behind him and grudgingly had to concur. It pissed her off, leaving her conflicted in her hatred. Whether the remains strapped to the conchair were Trask or not had yet to be confirmed, but whoever it was, he was a victim, not a collaborator. A closer look inside the pod revealed two things: the body was restrained, not secured, and the vessel had been welded shut.

"Get to work on that system, Kittie," Scotch said as Brockmann grabbed the retrieval gear from Kat and scrambled over the jagged lip. The woman lost no time in transferring the remains to the cryobag and scouring the inside of the compartment for anything that would aid them in their pursuit. Kat didn't know what disturbed her more: the ruthlessness of the pirates, or the detached manner in which her squad mate went about her task.

It's not easy sweating in space. Kat managed, though.

"Come on!" Scotch snarled, drawing her out of her thoughts. "You have a job to do, so do it. I'm not too comfortable with our asses hanging out here."

There was no convenient jack-in port this time. Not because the pirates were being tricky, but because of their ruthlessness. Her search for the primary systems didn't turn up much. Literally. No navigation system. No drive computer. Nothing but life support and communications. This was no ship; it was a coffin. The operational catch phrase here: Drop 'em and leave 'em. Katrion's stomach turned violently. Even if the real Trask was a willing participant, he didn't deserve this end. No one did. Which kind of robbed her of her focus: It was easier to get a handle on things with a face to hate. Trask had been a known quantity; now the enemy was unidentified, which gave them the edge. That really pissed her off.

She forced her mind off of that and back to the task at hand. This was going to be trickier than anticipated. Without any kind of port for infiltration it would take too long to manually hack in; her O_2 would deplete well before she finished, assuming external forces didn't interfere long before then. She powered up the microtorch she'd attached to her gauntlet, physically extracted what computer systems there were, and slid them into her kit. Crawling out from where she'd completed the extraction, Kat bumped into the conchair. She flinched and turned, in her mind still seeing the partial remains; reality inter-jected, though. At eye level, she could now see the bottom edge of the conchair arm. Someone had shredded the foam padding. Not clawed or torn, but picked little bits out quite purposefully. Katrion thought she could make out a name: Gorman...? Corlain? It was hard to be sure; after all, the letters were anything but uniform. Powering up her microtorch once more she sliced through the padding where it was unblemished and ran the laser along the bottom until she could pull the strip away and stow it in her kit with the computer cores. There wasn't much left, which meant it was time to go. She turned to push off.

"Hey, Scotch..." The rest of her words drifted into space as the section of galaxy past his shoulder came into view. "Ah, hell! Company on your six."

Scotch cursed and Kat faintly heard him mutter about vipers in the nest. That was when it clicked that someone on the inside had to have given them away. Was it someone from the *Rommel*? Or one of their own men? Kat mirrored Scotch's curse. But now was not the time to dwell on betrayal; there were pirates to kill.

The rest of the retrieval squad carefully fired their jets for a cotrolled turn, both of them bringing to bear recoilless rifles, though what good they thought the weapons would be against an attacking frigate, Kat couldn't imagine. Of course, how pathetic did that make her when she looked down to spy her pulse pistol in her grip? Remembering her orders, she shoved it back into the pocket she'd drawn it from and secured her gear. With a blast of her thrusters she aimed for the *Teufel's* airlock before Sarge's command to retreat came over the band.

*   *   *

Sound doesn't travel in space. No atmosphere, nothing for it to bounce off of. It was a false cliché, though, that no one could hear you scream. There's plenty enough atmosphere in a helmet, and lots of enclosed surfaces that made the sound seem to go on forever. When one of the team bought it, Kat's head nearly exploded with the sound traveling along her bonejack. She didn't have time to spin around before the side of the *Teufel* briefly lit up with the colors of hell until it looked like it was made of flame. The blast came from behind her; the pirates took out the derelict. Kat knew this because the explosion was enough to send her tumbling. End over end, catching brief glimpses of the fierce, quickly exhausted blaze as unused air tanks in the derelict were ruptured in the blast. Silhouetted by the flames was the large, limp form of one of her squad mates.

It was like being hit with a board. Kat told herself it was Brockmann, after all, the cryobag still floated nearby, but the fear that she was wrong damn near crippled her. She fired her jets to counteract her uncontrolled spin. Forgetting such things as orders and intel and pirate ships with pulse cannons, she went flying toward the wreckage.

"Back to that shuttle, soldier!" The voice was familiar, if not the tone. "Now!"

She didn't sob. She wouldn't sob. Soldiers didn't, you know. (Yeah. Another lie.)

"Where you at, you sonofabitch?" A western twang crept into her voice as she snipped at Scotch. Her temper had always carried echoes of her PawPaw, though this time it was heavy with relief.

"On your 4 o'clock, get your tail to the shuttle; we have to get out of here."

"Brock…"

"Get going," Scotch said. "I've got her, and the sorry piece of shit we came out here for."

Katrion wanted to argue, only her training—and her relief—kicked in.

It took one jet to spin her, and both to send her on her way. The left jet gave a little sputter and an early warning light blinked on in the rim of her visor. Her powerpack was running low. Shouldn't be an issue; she was less than twenty yards from the airlock. Of course, by the time she faced the shuttle it was too late. The attacking vessel spewed pirates with heavier armaments than anything she had. Several broke off in an attempt to deprive her and Scotch of their burdens, and likely their lives; the others took potshots at the *Teufel*, pinning the rest of Alpha Squad on board. The unmarked frigate came around firing warning shots that shook the shuttle. Their flight path was about to bring them in close, like they planned to grapple on to the hull. The *Teufel* just managed to keep them at bay using the thermal rockets. Katrion waited for the shuttle's engines to fire up in a strategic retreat that would take the rest of the squad away from the risk of capture. That would signal the end for the retrieval squad and the mission objective, but she couldn't believe Sarge would sacrifice the squad for just two men.

Daire's Devils weren't that easily intimidated, though: with a *whoosh* and a light cloud of venting atmosphere, the airlock opened. All she could see were Tivo, Dalton, and Kramer, the three best shots in the unit, in positions of cover around the open iris. Each of them had a short-order 50-cal. in their hands and a secondary weapon slung over their shoulders. They were methodically picking off any pirate within range. One of the unfriendlies closed in on Kat's position, despite the fire team's covering fire. There were too many for her team to hit them all.

Kat was on her own. She deployed her pulse pistol and fired. Nothing happened and the pirate drew closer, his weapon trained on her head. Her breath quickened and acid burned her throat. Not like this, damnit!

From the direction of the *Teufel*, Kat spied a flash of weapons' fire as Dalton noticed her predicament. The pirate's body jerked with the impact, the round traveling straight through the environmental suit and out the other side. Blood and atmosphere formed a cloud around the slowly twisting remains.

Better you, than me. Kat shuddered and returned the malfunctioning pistol to her pocket.

With the rest of the pirates occupied, Kat glanced toward Scotch. As her eyes settled on her teammate she wanted to call out, to warn him; a pirate closed in on him from behind. Kat could activate her comm against combat procedure, but even that wouldn't be in time.

No way in hell! With a grit of her teeth and barely a glance at her powerpack warning light, Kat fired her jets full thrust. Her pulse pistol was useless, but her gaze locked on the microtorch still affixed to her gauntlet. She had one chance. The enemy's attention was completely fixed on his target. He had no clue his buddies hadn't dealt with her. Minute adjustments of her body-posture shifted her trajectory until she aimed straight at the pirate's head. She powered up the 'torch and gladly burned the last of her reserves.

Impact. A jolt and a *pop*, a brief swirling cloud as the pirate's suit vented atmosphere, and more of that screaming—this time from Kat—as the momentum sent her tumbling against the inertia of her victim's body, her arm locked in place, the gauntlet scorched and her wrist throbbing.

She screamed again as the wrist bent back against her weight as much as the gauntlet allowed, saved only from a break by the suit's rigid structure and the fact that the torch tip finally cut itself free. She must have accidentally reactivated the comm because Scotch's voice rippled along her jaw, soothing after an initial curse of his own. "Damn, Kittie..." His arm locked around her waist and drew her down as he gave a burst of his jets to halt her spin. "Remind me to steer clear once you are rated for zero-g!" Relief sounded in his voice, as well as a new level of respect.

She shared the relief, but the rest of her emotions jumbled in a confusing hodgepodge too uncomfortable to consider. All she managed was a groan as she tried to use her own jets to back away. They sputtered and she noted the warning light had transitioned to red. She was tapped and trapped. Looking anywhere but at him, she noticed the rest of the Devils had come out to play, even now forcing the pirates back.

"Come on, Kittie, time to go home," Scotch murmured, tucking her tighter against him as he went full thrusters toward the *Teufel*.

"Wait!" She fought against him, though what she thought that would accomplish with her powerpack spent, she didn't know. "Brockmann...and the..."

Before she could protest further, one of their squad zipped past and headed back with the remains of their comrade, and their objective. She damn well hoped they'd garnered something of use. Even if this did put them one solid step closer to pinning the bastards down, it was scarcely worth the loss of a teammate. Inside, Kat seethed, more than ever wanting to get a bit of her own back against the pirates.

Now was not the time, though. A scan of the zone showed that everyone else had already fallen back to the shuttle. Kat gave up and settled in for the ride; Scotch was only looking out for her. That's what teammates did.

They were nearly there when a warning came across the comm. "To your 3 o'clock, stat!" Scotch dodged to the left, sending them spinning. The fire team must have missed one. The heat of the laser blast they'd barely evaded bubbled the surface of Kat's visor while her curses blistered the inside. Apparently the pirates were still in the game. Her stomach spun as Scotch corrected and slammed them past the airlock iris, right into the internal hatch. "Go! Go! Go!" he barked as the airlock closed, practically on the tips of their boots.

As the chamber filled with atmosphere, they shed their helmets, but remained suited. They propelled themselves through the hatch and to the open bench by the drive compartment. Kat and Scotch settled side by side.

"Strap in!" Sarge bellowed. "Dalton, take the con and get those cannons firing."

The *Teufel* shuddered and warning alarms went off. From the sound of it, the pirates were firing chaff rounds off their hull. More useless intimidation. The pirates wanted something, or the *Teufel* would already be a cloud of vented gas and debris. The shuttle's pulse cannons whined and popped. More detonations just off their battered hull.

The game of tag grew old.

"Campbell, ready the thermal rockets; Dalton, charge the pulse cannons and hold fire. Engage on my mark. Target their engines." Sarge issued the orders in a sharp, clipped tone. "I have the con." He brought the shuttle in hard and fast despite the continued fire from the pirate vessel. Kat could visualize his maneuvers, remembering the last position of the enemy ship. He brought the *Teufel* arcing along the pirates' starward side and pulled ahead, giving Campbell and Dalton a clear firing solution from all ports.

"Game over," Sarge growled. "All weapons, fire!"

They were too close. As the frigate exploded, it shook the *Teufel* hard enough that those in back would have fallen to the deck if they hadn't been strapped in. Alerts went off as they took some collateral damage. *Gotcha!* Kat thought. The rest of the squad cheered as Campbell took over the helm and aimed them for the *Rommel's* coordinates.

"Better get some rest, Kittie-Kat," Scotch murmured, pressing his hand to her cheek. She rested her head on his shoulder. Kat wasn't sure which startled her more, the fact that he'd touched her, or that she'd instinctively leaned against him afterward. She started to jerk upright in protest when he said, "We still have live-fire exercises once we get back."

"You mean...we're not for the brig once we dock?"

Scotch chuckled. "Shh. Don't even think it; Sarge has us covered. There's a surprise training op registered by those who cut our orders. It'll have come down channels by now."

Kat swallowed hard and looked up to meet his eye. "And Brockmann? What do we tell them about her?"

His eyes went solemn. "The truth. A pirate ambush. She'll not be the first soldier to fall during training. Now settle in and get some rest already. He's not gonna take it easy on any of us after this. There's too much at stake."

Despite everything that had just passed, she had no doubt Scotch was right. Dutifully, she attempted to shut off her thoughts and let herself relax. Still, the tension bubbled up and out of her like a Tourette's outburst. "I wanted Trask!"

Scotch grunted and pressed his cheek against her head. She ignored the hint and went on.

"Now I have no clue who to kill, damnit!"

He chuckled and reached up, gently rubbing her ear and against the pressure point behind it. The returning tension drained out of her and the world started to dim.

"Better the devil you know..." was the last thing she heard him murmur in agreement before she drifted off.

On By Any Means

What does it truly mean to be human? Danielle Ackley-McPhail explores a question we usually answer only with trite observations about love and friendship and mortality. But she takes us well beyond the standard responses with a tale of the occasional costs of survival.

—Jack McDevitt,
author of *Firebird*

"We declare our right on this earth...to be a human being, to be respected as a human being, to be given the rights of a human being in this society, on this earth, in this day, which we intend to bring into existence *by any means necessary.*"

—*Malcolm X*

His mind was still his own. Very little else was.

Jean-Paul Marot was having a very bad day.

"Okay, now manipulate the upper right limb for me." The cold, clinical voice belonged to First Technician Nigel Burton, his own personal demon. "Focus...concentrate on the particular servo you wish to activate. Visualize the limb lifting, contracting, extending. Flex each digit."

If Jean-Paul had still had teeth, he would have ground them. He bent his will to making the arm complete the actions requested not because he wished to comply, but to get the man to shut up and go away. Something sizzled and sparked; he jerked in reaction and somewhere metal clanged against metal as his foot flexed, contrary to his intentions.

His cool composure no longer evident, Burton cursed. "Will you focus! I would like to get out of here some time this cycle!"

Not willing to answer aloud, to hear the grating sound of his new voice, Jean-Paul pictured the arm going through the requested sequence, both heard and sensed the gentle *whir* of the servos, the soft hiss of the rods extending and contracting through the thin, amorphous alloy sheath that mimicked the Palmar carpal ligament. This time the limb performed as intended. And he had to admit, the movement was smooth, the mechanical sounds nearly nonexistent to even augmented hearing. He was, apparently, a well-oiled machine.

And he hated it.

"Excellent; well, that's in order," Burton murmured more to himself, than anyone else. "Tomorrow, the optics and I'm done."

Done? Then what? Jean-Paul was about to question the man, but he did not get the chance. A click sounded from somewhere behind his metal chassis and as the noise faded he sensed the internal leads connected to his motor functions retracting. With each coiling millimeter of encased wire he anticipated the pending disconnect. *No! Damnit, no!* But the cry was silent, his vocal processors already powered down.

Jean-Paul was left suspended in darkness, deprived of all senses but his thoughts.

✳   ✳   ✳

"Now, please note the advancements in this prototype..."
The voice came up out of nowhere, like the blast of a foghorn point blank to the ear. Jean-Paul would have flinched, but apparently whatever process had restored his hearing had not progressed far enough to allow him control of any mobility functions. He couldn't even scream, though that had not stopped his thoughts from doing so in the long hours of darkness. The urge to pant, to flood his body with oxygen in preparation for fight or flight, was strong. Too bad he was no longer capable. He had quickly learned that unacted-upon autonomous responses flooded the brain with chemical components, producing a somewhat-less-than-comfortable effect when he had no way of dispersing them.

Apparently, Burton had not yet been back to engage his optics, but maybe Jean-Paul could regain some mobility. Calling to mind the exercises of the day before, he focused on the leads slowly uncoiling, willed them a bit more speed; visualized the connectors engaging. Of course, that part of him didn't seem to work that way. There was no noticeable effect as the voice he'd awaken to droned on. "...constructed of an amorphous alloy which we process and cast on site..."

He couldn't help but listen as the voice catalogued his new body's attributes; phrases such as high-yield strength, high corrosion- and wear-resistance, and superior elastic limits were bandied about. The buzz words "minimal costs" and "long-term serviceability" followed.

Despair fed the chemical mix swirling about Jean-Paul's brain.

Long-term servitude was more like it. That was the first reality he had learned on reawakening to the irrevocably altered life he now possessed. The sole survivor of a catastrophic failure in the orbital mines where he was employed, he had been given two options: die a horrible, lingering death for which his parents would inherit a hefty debt, or authorize the transfer of his brain to the developmental exoskeleton that now housed him, which would then provide him the opportunity to work off his medical care and the cost of said interment, thus sparing his parents the burden. Some choice...

When the Corporate voice reached the part in his spiel about profit-and-loss calculations and the potential for a secured and dependable work force, Jean-Paul once again had the urge to grind his non-existent teeth.

"Now, Jean-Paul," the voice addressed him for the first time as his internal leads finally completed reengagement. "If you will demonstrate for our guests…" This time he felt the urge to forcefully grind *the voice's* teeth together as it ordered Jean-Paul to jump through proverbial hoops for the investors, but even as the thought occurred to him, some chemical flooded his preservation mixture and all he could do was comply.

Whoever said slavery was abolished had no dealings with the Corporation.

* * *

Weeks went by, then months; all blended together as Jean-Paul adapted to his new life.

It wasn't really too different from the old one, if a bit more isolated. Once he had functionality back, and learned to manipulate the cybernetic exoskeleton and correctly interpret the augmented sensory data, they filtered him back into the mining crews.

There he was…a hulk among strangers. All the miners from his shift had had the good fortune to not leave the accident site in any semblance of life. Each had gone peacefully to their graves, so to speak, while he'd ended up in R&D. This new batch of rockhounds didn't even know he'd once had a face just like theirs. To them he was mindless mech, nothing but metal muscle. He accepted his pick and his drill and was inserted, usually alone, into the dig sites where the robotic extractors couldn't go. He didn't mind; this way he didn't have to face the others talking around him as if he wasn't there.

The nice thing about having a super-strong exoskeleton and precious little cellular matter—pretty much all that was left of the original him was his brain—Jean-Paul could work long hours as if they were nothing, and process more rock than any full crew. Still, he had to eat, after a fashion.

Just about the time his power packs were running down, a hail came over his internal comm.

"Hey, ultraman, time to check the fluids and top off the tank."

"Acknowledged," Jean-Paul responded. Gathering up both his tools and the bulging sack of ore he'd extracted, he hiked out of the pit and over the short distance to the landing platform. As the shuttle touched down, he mentally heaved a sigh. His solitude had been comfortable. Caught up in the manual labor, he'd almost forgotten the change in his fate; well...as long as he didn't look too closely at his limbs...or the mounds of ore that would have taken weeks or the intervention of heavy equipment to extract. He couldn't ignore the fact that he *was* heavy equipment now. Believe it or not, he missed the bone-weary ache of shifts past.

The loading ramp lowered and Jean-Paul joined the rest of the crew on the shuttle. Silence enveloped the personnel compartment as he dumped his gear and stowed his haul. When he turned around he spied a whole spectrum of expressions on the other miners' faces. Awe, resentment, fear, curiosity...even envy. They ran the gambit, but not one of the men voiced what was on their minds. With another mental sigh, Jean-Paul moved to the alcove at the rear of the compartment, a recent addition tailored to his new physique. They traveled back to the station in silence.

There was nothing comfortable about it.

✻   ✻   ✻

Burton was nowhere in sight as Jean-Paul entered the R&D lab. Maybe things were looking up.

"Hello," a soft, even friendly voice spoke from behind him. He turned a bit abruptly, scrambling with his gyros to regain his center. Just visible beyond the edge of the door a female technician appeared to be cataloging supplies. She was cute and young and completely beyond him in all ways that mattered. Jean-Paul just stared, appreciating the sway of her silky brown ponytail, and trying to keep his mind off the theoretical sway of her hips. He couldn't manage anything else.

"I said, hello," she repeated with a gentle grin as she turned to look over her shoulder with eyes blue enough to be compared to the sky if there had been one.

"W-where's Burton?" He could have throttled himself. Like he cared where the prick was. The man had never once directed a personal comment at Jean-Paul, never bothered to hide his loathing.

She just looked at him, kind of like his mother would have if she'd caught him acting so socially inept. "Sorry...hello." he finally manage, cringing inside at the flat, harsh tones. They hadn't wasted any resources on cosmetic applications when they'd tooled him together.

"First Tech Burton is on sick leave; I'm covering his shift, Mr. Marot," she answered his original question with a pleasant, open expression on her face, as if all were completely normal with this encounter. "My name is Chloe Kendall, lowly lab tech."

Jean-Paul could not speak. The chemical response that would have tightened his chest, had he still had one, overwhelmed him. This was the first respect anyone had shown him since he'd half waken up on the operating table and been forced to choose his own Hell. Slowly, carefully, he focused on his arms, his hands. Worked the servos, careful flexing in an effort to rebalance his mix. "Nice to meet you, Tech Kendall."

"Chloe will do, unless you object...or Kendall, if that's more comfortable for you." She continued without waiting for a response. "So, time for dinner, is it? Just a few more minutes, I need to inspect your seals and gaskets first..."

Her comment sounded so relaxed, so natural; it left him feeling as if his gyros were still spinning out of his control. He sat where she indicated and prepared himself for the uncomfortable process. The back of what constituted his head retracted with a whisper. Kind of silly, but he felt naked. Couldn't be barer than he was now, without becoming a smear on some microscope slide. It didn't seem to faze Kendall, though.

When Burton had seen to this, Jean-Paul hadn't bothered to ask any questions. The man never would have answered; that would have required him to acknowledge that the cybernetic unit he serviced contained a human being. But Kendall...maybe she wouldn't mind a question or two...

"What...what is the preservation mixture?"

Kendall remained silent, but he could hear her bustling behind him. On his part, at least, the silence was strained. Was she unresponsive because her task required total concentration? Or because he's overstepped himself? Worse, was it because she wasn't overly eager to be the one to educate him in the means by which his survival was maintained? His thoughts wanted to scream again, this time at a different type of darkness.

Finally, he could sense the braincase sliding closed. His hope retreated into its own shell along with it.

"Okay, ready to start?" Kendall's demeanor *seemed* to acknowledge Jean-Paul's humanity, but she still didn't answer his question. He nodded and vowed to maintain his silence. She crossed in front of him and took something that resembled an oversized, dual-compartment IV bag from the ambient temperature suspension unit. A lightly tinged, clear fluid filled one compartment, the other was empty.

The bag, holding something between four or five pints of fluid, went on a secure pole mount next to the bench where he sat. Kendall reached beneath his chin for the dual-connector umbilical. That he understood. The one connector fed the replacement fluid to the compartment housing his brain; the other drained the used fluid into the empty side of the bag for ready disposal. The process wasn't perfect. Some mixing of the new with the old occurred, but nothing of much concern given the amount of contaminants regularly floating around in an unaltered human's system. Yeah, the process he understood, but the mix itself... that was a mystery.

He watched as she flipped the release. This part of the process unsettled him. The changing of the fluid was the only truly physical sensation he felt anymore. Not the most comfortable realization. Any other feeling transmitted to his brain through digital sensors distributed at key points of his exoskeleton...more like a cat's whiskers than traditional nerve endings.

"Well, to simplify, it's basically nutrient-infused plasma."

Jean-Paul actually jerked as Kendall's comment drew him out of his thoughts. He had given up on her answering him.

"*Whoa*, watch it..." She braced a hand against his shoulder, gently pressing him back into place. "You're not quite done yet, and I don't feel like cleaning that goop up."

Kendell grinned, softening the quip. He wished he were still capable of grinning back. This was the first time he had the desire to smile since he'd waken up; seemed such a waste to not be able to follow through. "Thank you," he answered, instead. "Plasma...from blood?"

"Yes, exactly. They even have to use the real stuff," she went on. "The synth variety is fine for supplementing a blood supply, but the brain can't be sustained on it alone. There's some necessary element they can't replicate.

"Whole blood would work, too," she added, a thoughtful expression on her face, "but Medical gets dibs on that."

He didn't want to think about someone else's blood cradling... feeding his brain. Bad enough his body wasn't his own. Plasma was sanitized, he could deal with that; a steady diet of someone else's blood...that was a nightmare.

They fell silent as the process completed. Jean-Paul could feel the difference the new mixture made. His brain hungered for it, his thoughts raced with renewed energy. He was ready to take on the world. And yet, as the final drops trailed out of the bag, and he watched Kendall go about detaching the umbilical, dread already started to sour the mix. If things went as they did when Burton was on duty this was where she switched him off.

"Don't. Please..." The words came out toneless, but every ounce of desperation bouncing around his brain powered them. For once, his new body responded seamlessly as he stood.

Kendall hesitated, her hand just above the remote shutdown.

"Corporate will notice the excess power consumption, someone will investigate."

"No, I won't move... I just want to listen, the drain will be minimal," Jean-Paul promised, praying fervently the woman would have mercy to go along with the compassion she'd already shown him. He could not overlook the potential in such a rare opportunity. Burton loathed him, took pleasure in throwing the cut-off switch; knew that deep within the metal alloy housing Jean-Paul's mind screamed every conscious moment until they switched him back on.

"Listen to what?" Kendall asked.

"Anything...everything," Jean-Paul answered. His hearing was sensitive enough that conversations several floors down were just barely audible to him, despite the station's sound-dampening measures. It didn't matter what those who were talking said. As evidence he wasn't alone and disconnected, the indistinct murmurs were priceless. "Just don't leave me locked inside my head. You have no idea..."

Or maybe she did. He saw a look of deep understanding in her eyes. Instead of initiating shutdown, Kendall crossed to the work bench across the room.

"What's a little drain?" her voice held kindness, with an edge of regret, as she turned the knob on a portable sound system one of the other techs had left behind. "Sit back down, and tell me when you can hear this." She edged the knob up until Jean-Paul lifted a servo-powered hand. It was below audible levels for conventional hearing, but to him, it was literally music to his ears.

"Thank you."

✷   ✷   ✷

Jean-Paul didn't see Chloe Kendall again. But each time he returned for his weekly change-out and encountered Burton, he cherished her memory anew. For the knowledge she had given him, of course, but even more so for what she had done for him; the woman had restored his sense of his own humanity. Now, when Burton's hand reached for the cut-off switch, Jean-Paul merely retreated into the memory of his encounter with Kendall. In his head, he even made new ones as he and Chloe danced to music only he could hear, or simply sat and talked like one human being to another. The urge to scream still remained, but not so much that he couldn't resist it.

Mostly, though, Jean-Paul spent his time out in the mines, earning off his debt faster than anyone in Corporate would admit. He no longer worked completely alone—there weren't nearly enough sites inaccessible to heavy machinery to make that practical. And thanks to Kendall, he no longer accepted the role of metal muscle. Upon occasion, he was even known to talk.

Upon occasion, the other miners even answered.

"Hey, Franklin," he called out to the foreman in the middle of his current shift.

Across the tunnel one man raised his head from where he bagged the raw ore that had been dumped out of the robotic extractor. They'd already emptied the Chomp's hopper twice, and similar bundles were stacked everywhere, awaiting offload to the shuttle. They crowded the mine, but Corporate like to minimize pick-ups. Miners just had to deal. "What's up, JP?"

"I'm hearing something odd...a vibration in the rock wall...or something off in the Chomp...I can't tell, which. It's too low-frequency for me to place." Around him the other men shifted uncomfortably, casting glances over their shoulders, looking around at the markers on the wall to see how far they were from the mine entrance. There hadn't been any trouble in this shaft. All that meant to the miners, though, was that they were overdue. Several of the others gave Jean-Paul dark looks. Word had gotten out about him and how he'd gotten his shiny suit. Miners were a superstitious lot, time and technological advancement certainly hadn't changed that. Not for the first time, Jean-Paul wondered if his survival of the last incident had been luck, or a curse.

Franklin, however, merely gave a nod in thanks. "Hey, Antonetti, check the readings; I want scans of the mine tunnel out to fifty meters on all axis." He turned toward the extractor, affectionately called the Chomp, and caught the eye of the mine tech monitoring its progress. "Power the beast down, Otto, give me a diagnostic while we're waiting for the scans.

"Everyone else, settle in for your fifteen," Franklin ordered the crew.

The men mostly hunkered down against the nearest bundle of ore, their eyes closing as they pulled rations from their pocket and methodically chewed, half sleeping through the meal as if they weren't sure which one they needed more. Jean-Paul simply walked from one end of the tunnel to the other, still trying to pinpoint the anomaly that had set all this in motion. It was no use, though. His hearing may have been augmented, but a human brain still processed the data. He'd lost the sound sometime about when everything shut down, unfortunately that still didn't help pinpoint the culprit.

"Everything looks clear, boss," Antonetti reported to the foreman. A similar response came from Otto. Jean-Paul was glad to hear nothing showed up. Of course, he didn't relax any. Just because trouble didn't register, didn't mean it wasn't there.

*   *   *

Fifty meters, apparently, hadn't been enough.

Five meters past that point the faint creak at the threshold of Jean-Paul's hearing culminated in a pop. The rumble of protesting rock followed. Beneath their feet, the mine debris began to dance; dust filled the air.

"Back! Everybody get back!" Franklin barked the order, waving his crew toward the distant mine entrance behind them.

Jean-Paul's sensors detected noxious compounds seeping into the air supply heavy enough to make him glad he no longer had a sense of smell. Fortunately, his system filtered such things out. Around him, the other men hadn't quite realized, though their breath came a little more labored, punctuating the mine's rumbles with sharp coughs.

With the exception of the emergency packs, they abandoned the mining equipment in place as they all turned and fled, as any good mine rat had the sense to do. Only Jean-Paul couldn't keep up. His exoskeleton wasn't designed for running or rapid movements. Shuffling along at the rear as best he could, he watched in horror as the tunnel ahead began to rain down dust. First fine puffs. Then steady streams. The coughing intensified.

Sound was peculiar below ground, surrounded by rock and heavy minerals. Contained, with plenty of angular surfaces to distort and echo. So hard to tell which way it came from.

"Stop." But Jean-Paul wasn't designed to yell, either. No one heard, or if they did, no one paid attention. They did enough yelling of their own, though, as the rock beneath them rumbled a bit more. Dust came down in a sheet on their heads, followed closely by the roar of the collapsing tunnel.

Not again. The front edge of the fleeing group disappeared beneath a cascade of ore. Antonetti and five others vanished from sight. The second tier scrambled back, encountering the odd boulder from above, but escaping alive, if less intact. Four men were left, not counting Jean-Paul, Franklin and Otto among them. They scrambled back toward him, groaning and hissing as the unstable tunnel above them threatened further collapse.

"Back to the Chomp, now," he ordered, though it was not his place. No one argued at his taking charge; Franklin could barely stand and his eyes were glazed. There were signs that he had taken a blow to the head. The others were equally hampered by panic and shock. Jean-Paul lifted the foreman as carefully as he could and moved back down the tunnel to the rock extractor. "Quick, we have to get the hopper emptied before the rest of the tunnel goes."

The men complied despite clear injuries that had to have made the effort excruciating, Jean-Paul set Franklin down where he would be sheltered by the extractor and then added his metal muscle to the task at hand.

There was barely room for the men inside the cleared compartment. None at all for Jean-Paul. If there were any chance he could dig his way out, he would have, but disturbing the cave-in would likely bring the rest of the tunnel down. Instead, he huddled in the lee of the larger machine and prayed the mountain was done falling on them.

Though his current life wasn't thrilling, he found he wanted to keep it nonetheless.

*   *   *

It took six days for most of the men to die. Injury…deprivation…despair. Each took their toll as faces grew gaunt beneath their veil of rock dust. The water gave out on day four, as only one emergency pack made it back to the hopper. By day five, the power pack on the comm lost its charge, cutting them off from any contact with the rescue crews. The despair grew plenty thick then.

As each man lost his life, Jean-Paul bundled the bodies in the ore sacks and slid them in the space beneath the extractor. Finally, at day seven only he and Franklin were left. They now had plenty of room for both of them in the hopper.

"Do you hear them yet, JP?"

"Hard to tell through all the rock, sir," Jean-Paul answered his foreman. "But I believe so." For once he didn't mind that his vocal processors were incapable of inflection.

Made it easier to lie.

"Good…good…" Franklin's words slurred. "So thirsty…"

He wondered how long the man would last. Without touching Franklin, it was obvious he burned with fever. Jean-Paul had problems himself. His power pack levels crept into the red zone, with perhaps two days left if he restricted his movement. As for his preservation mixture, it grew increasingly thick, making it harder to think and, if he wasn't mistaken, he'd begun to crave plasma.

As Franklin fell into unconsciousness, Jean-Paul found himself toying with the connectors of his umbilical. Flashes of his conversation with Kendall drifted through his mind, particularly one comment she'd made: *Whole blood would work too…*

Without intending to, he began to keen. His mind recoiled violently at the thoughts that rose unbidden. If he'd still had a stomach he would have heaved. Despite his need to conserve, he got up and left the hopper. Was it desperation, or could he hear a faint scratching on the far side of the rubble pile? He prayed as he had not done since before his new life. Again a faint sound; and the barest bit of hope rekindled.

Turning to take the news to Franklin, Jean-Paul suddenly found himself tumbling sideway. The only way to describe it was a dizzy spell. He fought to focus. The exoskeleton was a bitch to steer when his mind was loopy. He managed to keep himself off the ground, but fairly staggered back to the hopper.

"Hey, Franklin…" he started, but darkness flooded his optics and he found himself on his knees, gripping the raised hatch of the hopper to stop himself from sliding all the way down. What could only be described as a ravenous hunger took over...A new chemical flooded his brain, something foreign and insistent. Artificial. It kind of reminded him of the investors' demonstration, where his violent impulses had been suppressed, what seemed like ages ago. The craving reared up once more, crippling him. This impulse was clear: Survive.

His soul screamed, even as his hand reached up and withdrew the umbilical. He watched as it extended, completely independent of his own desire; moaned as the feed half of the connector slid into Franklin's carotid artery, the drain half merely dangled.

This couldn't be happening...he didn't want to live this bad! Of course, he should have known the Corporation would protect their investment by any means necessary, though he doubted they would have anticipated this.

Letting go of the hatch, Jean-Paul allowed himself to slump to the ground, desperately wishing the connector would fall out. But no, the greedy little bloodsucker hung on. He could do nothing but watch as the deep red fluid flowed toward him, and the murky, yellowed preservation mixture drained down the side of Franklin's neck. Somehow the man never woke up, though a part of Jean-Paul noticed even yet the shallow rise and fall of his chest.

More and more he saw himself as the monster they had made him. A parasite preserving his own pathetic life.

He wanted to be sick.

He wanted to die.

He wanted to deny how absolutely invigorated he felt now that the process was done. If he'd thought fresh plasma was rich, what he experienced now was like euphoria. Reaching out, he tugged on the umbilical. A crimson trail ran down the front of his chassis from the connector, residual he'd never noticed before when it was just plasma. The spray of lifeblood spurting from across the compartment quickly obscured it. He tore his gaze away from the evidence of his horror, looking instead toward Franklin.

Revulsion and guilt sent their chemical cocktail swirling through his stolen blood. Jean-Paul yanked over the emergency pack and frantically tried to administer a pressure bandage before his savior bled out. His "hands" were too clumsy, the skin too slick. He could hear more than feel as fragile cartilage gave way beneath his efforts. Falling back against the compartment wall, Jean-Paul's tortured moan came out in one long, continuous tone. He couldn't manage anything more.

His spirit wanted to retreat into the darkness he'd previously loathed, to hide from this reality. But that wasn't possible, and he just sat there, optics trained on Franklin, with only one thing to be grateful for: the man would never meet the same ill fate that had brought Jean-Paul to this pass.

Now fully alert, sensory input he'd been too fogged to process before assaulted his brain. First, he noticed the sound of shifting rubble, then the faint cries of the crews. They weren't close...perhaps ten, twenty meters from breaking through, from the sound of it. If it wouldn't have placed them in danger, he would have brought the rest of the tunnel crashing down on the evidence of what he'd done, himself included. Only that was not an option, even if whatever chemical Corporate had programmed into him would let him carry out the act, he would not be responsible for taking even more lives.

Oh God, he prayed. *Please don't let Kendall be among the rescue crew.* He couldn't stand if she were to see him like this. Bad enough his sense of his own humanity lay shattered on the mine floor; he couldn't bear to see the same loathing reflected in her eyes.

He still didn't scream...but he couldn't help but cry.

On In The Dying Light

Among a small ship crew, everyone is familiar, and at times, aggravating. Even civilian ships borrow military discipline to create a structure and culture that works. But introduce an outside agent of some kind, and the dynamics can shift drastically. There are tensions between people, internal struggles, both piled on top of the tedium, and sometimes drama of running the mission. Of course, not all demons can be readily recognized or resolved. For "In The Dying Light," Danielle Ackley-McPhail paints a small, sparse but emotive environment where things turn interesting, bad, then worse. Both gripping and chilling...

—Michael Z. Williamson,
author of the *Freehold Universe* series

"In the Dying Light" by Danielle Ackley-McPhail was one of my favorite stories [...] An *Alien* style horror tale, it is about the dangers of the strange uncharted regions of space. Ackley-McPhail builds tension well, and by the end you may find yourself gripped in the cold sweats of fear.

—John Ottinger III,
Grasping for the Wind Reviews

Danielle Ackley-McPhail's "In the Dying Light," packed into the story a wallop of suspense and excitement, not just at the gunfights and violence, but weaving a strong story through the action.

—Luke's Reviews

[In the Dying Light] called to mind a combination of the movie *Alien* and Jack Nicholson in *The Shining*. Without going into it any more, I'll just say that I really liked the story, and that Danielle definitely can write MilSF with the best of them.

—Douglas Cobb, Boomtron Reviews

An Alliance Archives Adventure

EARTH ORBIT: 42.05.18 – 0715HRS

On the command deck of the Stellar Clipper *McKay*, First Officer Ushimi Yakata ran the final checklist before third shift ended:

DUTY LOG: 42.05.18 – 0715HRS, YAKATA, U.
REACTOR STATUS – NOMINAL;
O2 LEVELS – OPTIMAL;
POWER – FIVE PERCENT OVER-CONSUMPTION.

She frowned at the last item as she printed out a hard copy of the entry. *We're going to have to watch our calculations,* she thought. *We haven't even left orbit and already the systems are running hot.*

It was that damn shuttle Corporate had them balancing on the *McKay*'s nose. They were hauling the spacer's equivalent of a luxury yacht over twelve light years to Demeter just so some CEO could tour his colonial facilities in style...There were so many more important payloads they could have taken with them. Of course, it was the "pay" part that decided things in the end; the rates for transporting luxury items to the Tau Ceti system were ten times that of necessary goods.

Behind her a clunk and a soft *whoosh* announced the arrival of her replacement. A whiff of licorice drifted from close by her ear. She'd stopped counting the times she'd told Karl Dunn not to crowd her. A prime example of why they had a history and no future. She'd had doubts about signing him for this cruise. They had been close once, very close. But not anymore. And with only a nine-man crew, she had no hope of avoiding him.

Her lips pressed in a tight, thin line, Yakata dropped her hand to the toggle by her hip and shifted the command chair back along its track, away from the control panel.

"Hey! Watch it!"

She brought the chair around, her grey eyes leveled at Karl dead on as he rubbed his abdomen where the chair smacked into him. Only his grip on the nearby tether bar kept him bobbing in place.

"Excuse me," she said, her tone cool and formal. "I didn't realize you were so close."

The flat, persistent tone of the proximity warning sounded through the cabin, interrupting any response Karl would have made. They both forgot their personal conflict, their attention riveted on the sensors.

Toggling the command chair back into place, Yakata automatically scanned the ship's attitude and power consumption on the screens flanking the main monitor. At the same time, she called up the isometric collision display. The flashing alert icon vanished from the screen in front of her. In its place appeared a wire-frame sphere with a representation of the *McKay* in the center. Something closed on the ship from behind, moving at a fraction of a meter per second. They had about thirty minutes until it came into range over their drive section.

"Dunn, reach over and activate the aft camera," Yakata ordered as her fingers danced in and out of the button depressions on the control panel. At her command, the main display switched from short-range to long-range scanning. She had to be sure whatever approached was not the forward edge of a meteor storm or something else their ablative hull plating could not handle.

Her scans told her nothing more. She called to Karl, "Crewman, do we have visual?"

Silence.

"Crewman..." Her short, sharp tone telegraphed impatience. "Do...we... have...visual?"

She whipped around, spearing him with a glare. He remained oblivious, his feet tucked into the boot docks and his gaze riveted on the image on the external monitoring station.

What the hell? Yakata had never seen him like this. He looked stunned...horrified. What could be out there?

Remembering the fate of her father's freighter, the *Tyler*, she felt a shiver of dread. Not another wreck...

She couldn't tell; Karl's body blocked the screen. Impatiently, she released the restraint keeping her in the command chair and drifted out. Once she cleared the panel, she rotated and pulled herself toward Karl.

"Step aside, crewman," she barked. His intent gaze snapped to her. Emotions rippled violently across his face. His deep brown eyes darkened to nearly black with them. It unsettled her, but Yakata didn't back off. Dunn's moods were nothing new to her. He had always been too on edge, his emotions close to the surface; like he picked up on random vibes in the air that no one else could feel. In their time together, she had never been able to tell what a given situation would trigger. Now she told herself she didn't really care. She kept her expression impassive and her gaze sharp. "Move it... now."

The muscles along Karl's jaw twitched and his eyes fell out of focus. He closed them and gave his head a little shake. She could see the tension drain away. When he opened his eyes again, they reflected faint confusion. Without a word, he gave the standard heel jerk to free his feet from the workstation's dock and drifted off to the side.

She gave him a measured look before redirecting her attention to the screen. The camera completed deployment, the high-power, ten-optical zoom fully engaged. What a stunning view. Distant stars glittered like metallic flecks on a field of raw black silk and muted colors added an unexpected depth to the starscape. Pretty sights didn't interest her, though. She scanned for her objective with an intensity that mirrored Karl's earlier stance.

The projectile headed toward them wasn't some random bit of space debris; it was clearly manufactured. The shape appeared something like a squat pillar or obelisk, and appeared about the size of her head. It was too far away to make out much more, though the camera hinted at intricate detail.

Rogue thoughts of her father swarmed her mind once more. In his last letter to her, he mentioned a similar find. She'd lost him long before the letter ever reached her. Neither her father, nor the object had been retrieved. Burned into her memory, as clear as yesterday, was the image of his shattered helmet floating in the vacuum of space. She still had that helmet.

She banished the thought. Turning back to Karl, Yakata caught his eye and held it. "Assume your post. I'm heading up to the rendezvous station to retrieve the object."

He remained silent a moment. His jaw ticked and his gaze flickered from the aft display to her face.

" 'Ta..." he began, but she cut him off.

"Excuse me, crewman, how did you address me?"

"Ma'am," he ground out through clenched teeth, frustration snapping in his eyes. "Respectfully, I'm not sure that you should... something feels really wrong about this."

"I have to do this."

The knowing look he gave her disconcerted Yakata. If anyone understood, he did. She didn't like that familiarity or the self-betraying warmth she felt at his concern. "I said get to your post. Start the pre-hyperdrive checklist," she ordered. "The captain wants to jump by 0800."

She pulled her communications hood up over her close-cropped ebony hair and triggered the overhead hatch. With the grace of frequent practice, she hauled herself up through the shaft. Propelling herself past the T-junction that branched off toward the cargo bay, she opened the second hatch into the rendezvous station. She closed it behind her before drifting toward the aft window. Yakata pressed the activation button on the left side of her comm hood. "Command deck..."

A sharp chirp sounded before Karl responded, his voice slightly staticy. "Go ahead, ma'am."

"I need an update on the incoming object."

There was a pause. While she waited, Yakata peered out into space, as if she had any chance of pinpointing the object without the aid of the cameras. It drew closer, but not that close.

Another chirp brought her out of her distraction.

"Ma'am?"

"Go ahead, crewman."

"The object is ten minutes out and closing."

"Acknowledged," she responded, and cut the connection.

Ten minutes. Barely enough time to deploy the arm. She snapped her boots into the dock and engaged the control panel. Powering up the arm, she then hit the sequence instructing it to retrieve the grappling attachment. While the mechanism prepared, she triggered the cargo bay doors. A strident warning klaxon sounded as a large segment of the ship opened to space. The arm rose from its cradle in slow, precise movements. Her teeth gritted and her muscles tensed as she watched. It had to move faster or she would miss the interception point.

With her free hand, she depressed the activator on her comm hood once more.

"Command deck…"

"Go ahead, ma'am."

"Feed me the trajectory of the object."

On the panel in front of her, a micro-display came to life. The information played across it. This was going to be close. She deployed the grappling net to intersect the flight path and held her breath. The object crested the drive section in a gentle arc, and seemed to flare as it came into contact with the sun's rays, bathing the ship and arm in a startling green glow. It faded in the shadow of the arm. Yakata leaned into the console. It appeared her prize might overshoot the net. Reaching for the joystick in front of her, she extended the assembly as high as it would go over the drive section.

Her breath hitched. It still looked at risk of skimming past. *This is ridiculous. It's space debris. There's no reason I should be so upset.* She tried shifting the joystick even further, but the arm had reached fully extention.

Her father's face drifted unbidden across her thoughts. It felt like she failed him…again. She clenched her teeth and forced the thought away. Furious blinking cleared her vision, but she could hardly believe what she saw: the object changed trajectory. The alteration was slight; barely perceptible except for the drive section being there as a point of reference. Still, Yakata had to wonder if she had really seen it. This was impossible. The thing could not have changed its trajectory. Short of mechanical means or an outside intervention, an object moving in space would continue along the same path until it encountered another force. And yet, as the artifact plowed into the grappling net, she forgot all about the laws of physics. The net closed, locking the object into place.

"Yeah!" she cried out, the sound loud and unbridled in the seclusion of the rendezvous station. Only the boot docks kept her from bouncing around the compartment. "Oh, yeah!"

A burst of unexpected static crackled from her comm hood. She felt the blood drain from her face as she went still.

"Hey! Knock it off!" Karl's amused voice came over the connection she'd forgotten to close. "You want to rupture my ear drum?"

"My apologies, crewman," she responded with a degree of dignity she did not currently feel. "The object has been retrieved. I'm locking down and securing the salvage."

She cut the connection.

Shoving embarrassment aside, Yakata input the sequence that returned the arm to its cradle. Another rapid set of keystrokes, and the cargo bay doors closed. She grew impatient with the drawn-out procedure. Recklessness in vacuum, however, could get a spacer killed.

Once everything was locked down, she retreated to the antechamber to climb into her protective constrictor suit. She waited for the green light from the automatic systems check before securing her helmet and engaging the O_2 tanks. Prepped for EVA, Yakata cycled through the airlock into the cargo bay.

She grabbed an empty storage container and hauled both it and herself down the length of the armature. Once there, she anchored the container to the deck and pulled herself up the handholds along the wall until she drew even with the grappling attachment. She hit the release and worked the fingers open.

Her hands twitched over the surface of the artifact and she had to resist the urge to draw off her suit's skin-tight gloves. The object demanded to be caressed.

In shape, it resembled a short, squat obelisk. It tapered slightly from top to bottom and had three columns of unfamiliar symbols running up and down each side. It was metal...apparently old metal, given the deep, dull sheen. The color had a greenish tinge, like ancient bronze. Only this was no metal she recognized. It seemed smooth, almost soft, other than the etching. Otherwise, there were no seams or depressions.

It took extreme effort to lower the thing into the bin. Now was not the time to examine it. She had less than ten minutes to get herself secured for hyperdrive. Unhitching the container, she hefted it to her shoulder and propelled herself toward the airlock. In the antechamber, she slid her burden into a storage locker by the cargo bay hatch and keyed it to her personal code. It would be safe until she could take it down to the lab.

DUTY LOG: 42.05.18 – 1100HRS, KINNEY, CAPTAIN J.

    REACTOR STATUS – NOMINAL;

    O2 LEVELS – 98 PERCENT;

    POWER – TEN PERCENT OVER-CONSUMPTION

    NOTE: SCHEDULE DIAGNOSTICS OF SHIP'S SYSTEMS UPON ARRIVAL AT DEMETER, *MCKAY* EXHIBITING SYSTEMS-WIDE REDUCTION IN EFFICIENCY DESPITE RECENT OVERHAUL. POWER FLUCTUATIONS SHIP-

WIDE, STABILIZED. MALFUNCTION OF ATMOSPHERIC FILTERS IN COMPARTMENTS 8A THROUGH C, CORRECTED. ELECTRICAL FIRES BETWEEN BULKHEADS 10 AND 11, SECTION 5, CONTAINED; DAMAGE MINIMAL.

CARGO BAY ANTECHAMBER: 42.05.18 – 1100HRS

Yakata struggled for hours to get some rest. She just couldn't do it, though. The artifact haunted her thoughts. She would almost say it called to her, but that was as nuts as thinking it had changed its trajectory. She tossed and fussed until Jones and Pittman, the crewmembers trying to sleep in the billets flanking hers, begged her to give up.

That was why she again climbed down into the cargo bay antechamber. Captain Kinney, in position on the command deck, had given her a considering look, but didn't question her. She'd already briefed him about the events that occurred at the end of her shift.

All thought of anything but the artifact fled her mind as she pushed open the last hatch and continued down the ladder, which in orbit had been the floor. She hated the way hyperdrive and the artificial gravity it created turned reality perpendicular to orbital conditions. Kneeling down, she punched her code with rapid jabs and hauled open the storage locker at her feet.

Any thought of spatial geometry evaporated.

Yakata half expected the artifact to be a dream. But there it was, nestled in its bin. She tried to draw it out of the locker.

It wouldn't budge. In the weightlessness of the orbiting ship, the artifact had been nothing to move. Now that they were under drive there was artificial gravity again. Not earth-norm, but enough that they could walk on the deck. If the obelisk was this heavy in three-quarters grav, she didn't want to consider what it would be like under normal conditions. It had to be denser than gold.

No! Yakata straddled the opening, flexed her knees, and inch by inch pulled the container up, until sweat ran into her eyes and her muscles screamed. She was not waiting forty-eight hours until they were in orbit.

PERSONAL LOG ENTRY: 42.05.18 – 1230HRS, DUNN, K.

WE RETRIEVED SOMETHING TODAY. 'TA...EXCUSE ME...FIRST OFFICER USHIMI HASN'T TOLD ME WHAT IT IS. DON'T THINK SHE EVEN KNOWS. WHILE I WAS ON SHIFT, SHE TOOK IT TO THE STORAGE BAY CAPTAIN HAD TEMPORARILY CONVERTED INTO A LAB. SHE

TALKED O'NEAL, THE METALLURGIST WE'RE SHEPHERDING TO DEMETER, INTO HELPING HER TRY TO FIGURE OUT WHAT IT IS.

SHE GOES ON SHIFT IN SEVEN HOURS, BUT THEY'RE STILL HOLED UP IN THAT LAB. SHE'S GOING TO BE A REAL BITCH ON DECK TONIGHT IF SHE DOESN'T GET SOME SLEEP, BUT SHE'S OBSESSING ON THAT BIT OF DEBRIS.

OF COURSE, I CAN'T STOP THINKING ABOUT IT EITHER. IT'S GOTTEN UNDER MY SKIN. IT SHOULDN'T BE ON THIS SHIP! IT HAS ME SO FREAKED, AND I CAN'T EVEN TELL WHY. THE FIRST HALF-HOUR OF MY SHIFT IS A LOST MEMORY. ALL I KNOW IS THAT IT FEELS LIKE WE ARE IN FOR A MAJOR SHITSTORM.

TEMPORARY SCIENCE LAB: 42.05.18 – 1230HRS

"What in the world made Corporate think it was worth the 100-million-dollar ticket to haul you up here?" Yakata growled through clenched teeth. Even as she said it, her hindbrain winced.

Bastian O'Neal, world-renowned metallurgist, lowered his instruments to the work surface and gave her a long, silent look. The dignified expression on his ebony face didn't change, but his hazel eyes were disapproving. He didn't answer. He looked away and took up the artifact in both latex-covered hands, repositioning it for another documenting photograph.

She'd strained to haul her prize down here; he seemed to toss it about as if it were cotton candy. Part of that was due to his clearly prosthetic left arm; but part had to be because of his own innate strength. Someone who didn't know better could be excused for thinking he mined metals, rather than studying them.

The metallurgist set aside his digital camera and picked up the item once more. He turned it in his hands until he'd looked at every side, his finger lingered over the engraving. She wanted to snatch it from his grasp. Uncontrollably, a muscle in her forehead twitched, as did her fingers. How dare he manhandle her salvage like that, hefting it with an ease that she couldn't? She tensed and fought not to scowl at him. What was wrong with her?

Yakata tried to shake it off. This was O'Neal's field. She'd come to him for help and he was kind enough to give it. She should be grateful and respectful, at the very least. It wasn't like her to behave this way.

She took a deep breath and forced herself to calm, to offer an apologetic smile and be pleasant.

Finally, O'Neal set the artifact down. Yakata expected to relax. Instead, she tensed even more; ready, in fact, to hurry forward and grab the obelisk away. But then O'Neal spoke, distracting her.

"I can't identify it."

"What do you mean you can't identify it?!"

"The tests were unable to determine the age or composition of the material."

Her resolve to be polite evaporated. "What did Corporate do... send you up here as a tax write-off?"

Seething with frustration, Yakata grabbed for her artifact.

O'Neal stepped in her way.

"If you're done insulting me?

"There's one more test I can run, but I need some equipment from the storage bay. My imaging spectrometer is our last option on-ship."

She glared at him and had to force her negativity down. It was harder to do. Without a word, Yakata moved to the terminal set into the chamber wall, her feet straddling the boot docks.

The muscles in her shoulders bunched and tightened as she keyed in the commands calling up the ship's manifest. He watched her. Surely plotting to take her salvage for himself.

Whoa! Where did that paranoia come from? She forced it away.

Finally, she located his equipment and requested immediate retrieval. Closing out the screen, she whirled to face him. For a moment, everything held a greenish tinge like the one she'd noted when the object crested the drive section. The sense of looming increased with the glow. It faded so quickly, though, that she had to wonder if it were her vision causing the effect. That would explain the flickers out of the corner of her eye. Yakata clenched her eyes shut and popped her neck. It sounded like several rounds of gunfire.

"Sorry, O'Neal, can't imagine why I'm so edgy. Jones will bring your spectrometer down in short order. Why don't you head to the mess for some coffee...I'll comm you when the equipment gets here."

"That's okay. If I'm here when it arrives I can hook it into the ship's systems quicker. This has already taken longer..."

"O'Neal," Yakata cut him off, her tone sharp and brittle, even to her own ears. "Go get some coffee. I'll have the spectrometer rigged up when you get here."

For a moment, she thought he would refuse. Her suspicions flared brighter and she had to consciously force her fists not to clench. She didn't trust him here; didn't want him here, unless he was in the middle of a test. Even then she had issues.

Her gaze again locked with his. She read concern in his eyes. But did something else lurk beneath that? Something sly? Calculating? Damnit! She couldn't tell! It took more effort to mimic something of a reasonable tone. "I have to be here to sign off on the retrieval. If you don't want any coffee, could you at least get me some? I'm dying here."

TEMPORARY SCIENCE LAB: 42.05.18 – 1245HRS

Yakata vibrated with impatience as O'Neal finished calibrating the spectrometer. She wanted to snatch his hands away from the knobs and buttons and yell at him to get on with it. It wasn't just an overwhelming need to know. That she could have handled. No, it was more like whatever lurked behind her drew closer, just out of sight, just out of hearing range. Always there, always watching... Some part of her equated it with the artifact. She had to know what it was now, but the technology would do them no good if it weren't set up properly. She understood that.

Then why was she ready to scream when he slipped a common bit of steel in the spherical sample chamber and fired up the machine?

She couldn't restrain herself any more. "Come on, already!"

"Do you want accurate results, or do you just want me to go through the motions?" O'Neal's voice came out a low, controlled rumble, contrasting sharply with her outburst. "If you don't care if the results are accurate, you're wasting my time and I'm out of here."

His response made Yakata want to scream even more, but he was right. What was wrong with her? Her impatience did not serve either one of them well and she couldn't afford to have him abandon the test. She could probably figure out the machine, but the data it spit out would be indecipherable to her. Taking a deep breath, she forced herself to calm.

"Sorry."

It took a lot of effort not to fidget as O'Neal watched her closely for a moment. The concern had returned, along with a thread of irritation. He clearly wanted this to be done as much as she did, even if their reasons were different. Without a word, he turned back to the spectrometer.

"Okay, we're ready."

Yakata's pulse sped up. She reached for the artifact, only to flinch back as a mild static arced between it and her fingertips. It seemed to cling to her hand like the persistent suction of vacuum through a hull breach. Like something tried to suck her out the tiniest hole, only the hard surface of reality kept her from going through. Before she could say something, the pull abruptly released and a surge of rage and frustration swelled over her. She shook it off. Looked up in a daze. O'Neal had lifted her prize away and slid it into the chamber in place of the metal bar. He made no comment and Yakata saw no sparks when he touched it. Had the phenomenon been her imagination? She couldn't resist creeping forward to glance at the operator's display as the spectrometer charged up to pulse full-spectrum light at the object from four points within the sphere.

The hum of the machine seemed to come up through the deck plates until she expected her entire body to vibrate with it. A flaring light intensified abruptly until it engulfed the machine and the room. The power surged and the deck plates vibrated more violently beneath Yakata's feet. Both she and O'Neal flinched in that instance of brilliance before they were engulfed by utter darkness. The only sound was a sharp gasp. She couldn't tell which of them it came from. She could no longer hear the spectrometer or any of the ship's normal background mechanical noises. Other than their nervous breathing, silence dominated the pitch black.

Yakata struggled not to panic. Where was the hum of the hyperdrive? The click of relays opening and closing? The sizzling snap of the comms? Sounds every spacer took for granted; their unrealized security blanket in everlasting night. Yakata shuddered.

The darkness seemed to last forever; in truth it was less than twenty seconds before systems re-engaged with a whir. Not even long enough for them to fall out of drive.

Right on the heels of everything powering up, all comms within hearing distance gave a strident chirp.

"...eport...All crew, report!"

She reached for the comm on the console and toggled the activator to respond to Captain Kinney.

"Yakata here. O'Neal and I are in the Science Lab."

"What the hell was that?"

Yakata didn't have an answer. She couldn't have gotten one in, anyway, as a stream of responses came over the comm. All crew were accounted for.

"Everyone to stations, run full diagnostics. Let's figure out what the deal is before it happens again," Captain Kinney ordered before closing the comm line.

Turning to O'Neal, Yakata noted the confusion on his face as he looked at the read-out from the spectrometer.

"What? Something go wrong?"

O'Neal turned toward her, his head shaking. "The test completed before everything shut down, but this doesn't make sense."

She walked over and read the printout:

Processing Error 021:

Spectral Anomaly – Negative Scan

"*Kuso shite shinezo!*" Yakata hissed through clenched teeth.

O'Neal looked at her odd. "I don't know what you just said, but it sounded painful."

Yakata flushed. Among spacers cursing was one thing, profanity was a part of their make-up. But in front of others she generally conducted herself more circumspectly. She was just grateful the man did not speak Japanese.

"I apologize for my rudeness. But, damn!" She slammed her hand down on the casing of the machine. "All of that and it's unidentifiable!"

"Not just unidentifiable...it's like nothing's there. The machine didn't even register the walls of the chamber." His expression grew considering. "It's as if the artifact absorbed the light. But to do so this completely...it's impossible for none to have gotten past it."

"Malfunction?"

"Not one I've ever seen, but there's one way to find out."

Captain Kinney had ordered everyone to their stations. But she had to know. She could always double-time it to the command deck.

O'Neal opened the chamber and reached for the artifact. He hissed sharply, as if in pain. His body arched and shuddered. The look of terror in his eyes sent panic through Yakata. It must be the prosthetic. She remembered the static that had clung to her hand when she'd touched the artifact earlier.

Yakata yanked an equipment bag toward her and rapidly rifled through it. Tucked in the bottom she found a set of insulated gauntlets.

She donned them and braced herself against the workstation. With all her weight behind the effort, she hauled on the obelisk until it left his grasp. It came away with the sound of metal scraping metal. Yakata landed in a heap across the compartment, the obelisk heavy on her chest. O'Neal collapsed across the table, greenish static arcing and popping along the length of his arm. He shook his head and groaned. After a moment, he leveled a glare toward Yakata.

Perhaps it was the sparks, or perhaps just the light, but as he stared at her in silence, it seemed his eyes reflected the green hue. He slowly stood and stalked across the room to where she lay. When he reached out his hand, her eyes went wide, expecting pain.

She searched his face for some clue as the man remained silent. His eyes darkened and she couldn't read the swirl of emotions dancing through them. She shivered. He closed his eyes with a sigh. When he opened them all she saw was impatience in their green depth. Green? But....

"The gauntlets..."

She yanked them off and held them up, never taking her eyes from him. He donned the gear and lifted the artifact from her chest. She gasped as breath flooded back into her lungs to full capacity. Damn, that thing was heavy, she swore to herself.

O'Neal turned his back to her. He deposited the obelisk on a metal tray on the table and reinserted the control element he'd used to test the machine initially.

The second reading of the steel bar was identical to the first.

Without a word, Yakata returned the artifact to its storage locker. Using her body as a shield, she keyed the lock with her personal code.

She turned and found O'Neal staring at her. Yakata carefully slipped past him and hurried from the compartment, trying to ignore the faint odor of scorched latex lingering in her nostrils.

PERSONAL LOG ENTRY: 42.05.18 – 1250HRS, DUNN, K.

McKay's systems just flatlined. Everything's back up, but talk about freaking out. What the hell is going on?

Haven't felt like this since I was four and Da took me to the reptile house at the Bronx Zoo. I zoomed all over that place. Couldn't stay still...until I came to the king cobra. Something had pissed it off. It mantled and swayed three feet high in the

AIR, RIGHT UP CLOSE TO THE GLASS. IT KEPT UP A HISS, LOW AND MEN-
ACING. DON'T KNOW HOW LONG I STOOD THERE WATCHING ITS TONGUE
FLICKER IN AND OUT ABOVE ME, BUT I COULDN'T MOVE. NOT EVEN
WHEN IT STRUCK. LIGHTNING-FAST IT SLAMMED INTO THE GLASS. TO
THIS DAY, I SWEAR ITS FANGS LEFT LONG GROOVES IN THE SURFACE,
DRIPPING WITH VENOM.

I STILL REMEMBER THE STENCH OF TERROR. RIGHT NOW IT'S STRONG IN
MY NOSE...A HUNDRED TIMES STRONGER THAN IT WAS WHEN I WAS
FOUR. AND I HAVE THAT FEELING AGAIN...LIKE DEATH IS HOVERING
ABOVE MY HEAD AND I'M NOT SURE IF THE GLASS IS GOING TO HOLD.

DAMN...CAPTAIN JUST CALLED DUTY STATIONS.

COMMAND DECK: 42.05.18 – 1310HRS

Yakata hauled herself through the command deck hatch from the
McKay's main shaft into a tangible silence. The shaft ran the length of
the ship and was fitted out with a ladder that doubled as a track for the
slow-moving utility lift. The track could either be climbed or used for
crewmen to pull themselves along, depending on the ship's attitude. She
had scaled it at record speed, but apparently she hadn't been quick
enough.

"First Officer Ushimi...the comm system may have been affected by
the anomaly. My order to report to duty stations doesn't seem to have
reached all compartments." The captain's words were even and void of
tension. His gaze was not. The look he gave her was harder than the artifact she'd left in the lab. "With this sudden glitch, I'm concerned that
diagnostics might not show up all malfunctions. I'll need you to conduct
an on-site inspection of every comm station and hood on the *McKay*."

Yakata flinched on the inside. "Yes, sir. Right away, sir."

Captain Kinney was known for his swift and fitting discipline.
Actually, she'd gotten off easy; she should have been the first on the
deck, not counting those who were already there.

There was a sound beneath her feet. She stepped aside to clear the
hatch. An acrid aroma preceded Dunn as he clambered to his post.

"Ah, very good." The captain's smile was not very pleasant, though
his tone seemed to be. "Crewman Dunn will assist you."

DRIVE SECTION SERVICE MODULE: 42.05.18 – 1700HRS

This was it. The final comm station on her half of the list. Yakata
sighed as she pulled out the checklist and ran the last test. Carefully, she

removed the housing then used her Fenix utility light and a telescoping mirror to visually inspect the wiring. After that she tested the connections. Finally, she closed the unit and toggled the activator.

"Dunn..."

"Go ahead..."

"Drive section comm inspection complete, how are you coming with the Engineering unit?"

"System's green to go." Dunn's voice remained even but Yakata detected an edge to it. It was barely perceptible, but his breath came out in quick, shallow huffs. She waited for him to report something catastrophic, but he remained silent.

"Okay, that's all of them. Wait for me at the main shaft." Yakata cut the link and toggled the activator again. "Command deck..."

"Go ahead." The captain's voice came through the relay sharp and precise. Yakata winced. He would remain on deck until she relieved him. That was part of what drove home the lesson. Her failure to follow orders affected everyone, right up to the captain, whom she respected more than anyone alive. Nothing, short of a fatality, would have made her feel worse about her lapse in protocol.

"On-site inspection of the communications system complete," Yakata responded, keeping her voice neutral.

"Acknowledged. I'll be waiting to hear your report."

"Yes, sir." Yakata groaned as she cut the link.

With haste, she secured her maintenance kit on her hip, slid the flashlight into its belt loop, and left the compartment. The sensors flanking the door registered her exit. The drive room went dark and the dim, stand-by lights of the causeway brightened. After nearly a decade of service, she generally took the lighting system for granted. Today she newly appreciated the comfort it represented. Even without the recent system's failure, Yakata was uneasy. Her nerves vibrated beneath the surface of her skin and her eyes ached from trying to penetrate the dark spaces around her. She'd yet to spy anything staring back. Her skin crawled though as she imagined a thousand pairs of eyes creeping forward into the now-darkened room behind her. Clenching her teeth, she cocked her head from side to side until the vertebrae ceased to pop. To her left, she thought she heard the faintest sound from somewhere near the pressurized tanks. Probably a loose valve. She made note of the section where she suspected the leak, and set off for the main shaft.

Dunn was not at the rendezvous.

Toggling the activator on her comm hood, the barest edge of anger sharpened her tone. "Crewman Dunn, report..."

Silence.

"Dunn, what is your location?"

Still no response.

What in the world was going on? Their personal comm hoods were the first to be tested. Both had operated fine. She went to the comm screen in the main shaft wall. With a couple of jabs, she input the protocol that instructed the system to display the current location of all crewmembers.

She glanced down the list of names and locations: Captain Kinney and Crewman Suarez—Command deck; Crewmen Jones and Chapman—Environmental Control Compartment; Specialist O'Neal — Temporary Science Lab; Crewmen Pittman, Jenks, and Gunter—Mess hall; and Crewman Dunn...

Port lateral airlock! Yakata powered down the display and set off back the way she came at a hard clip.

Bad enough they'd both drawn discipline duty, reporting back late would be impossible for the captain to gloss over this time. She tried her comm hood again, activating it with such force she could feel the surrounding fabric pull. "Crewman Dunn...respond..."

Nothing. She put on a little more speed through the shaft. A tight sensation took root in her gut. She tried again, "Come on, Dunn, talk to me. What's going on?"

No answer. The airlocks came into sight. Even in the dim light of the corridor, she could see a dark smear on the floor.

"Dunn! Damnit, Karl! Answer me!"

Yakata closed the last few meters. Dropping to one knee, she touched a finger to the slick spot. It came away bright red, the sweet, metallic tang unmistakable.

What happened? And where was Dunn? Sensors indicated the port airlock, but both chambers were dark. There should be lights. Lighting was automatic. She stepped to the side of the hatch portal and reached for her flashlight. The high-powered beam cut through the black pit beyond the glass.

Yakata gasped. For a second she could do nothing but stand there and stare at the horror revealed by the light: an EVA suit sprawled against the far wall, blood a solid curtain across the faceplate of the helmet.

A burst of static reminded her that the comm hood was still active, on stand-by. The sound snapped her out of the shock.

"Command deck..." She was surprised how low and calm her voice remained. The rest of her trembled. "Command deck, acknowledge...."

The only response was another burst of static.

She moved to the comm unit in the corridor wall and tried again. Again static hissed and crackled through the corridor, echoing through her comm hood. She moved back to the airlock door.

The beam of light glimmered on the helmet like sunlight through rubies. She could make out nothing beyond the faceplate. Swallowing hard, she swept the airlock with light as far as she could from side to side. Nothing. Not even more smears. No movement. Still, something did this. Yakata was acutely aware of the blind spots to either side of the hatch.

She punched in the sequence to open the airlock. The keypad didn't respond. She tightened her grip on the flashlight. It was awkward manipulating the manual release one-handed, but, with determination, she managed it. The hatch opened smoothly. Out wafted the heavy, copper-penny scent of blood and something else, something bitter and sharp. The lights still didn't engage.

"Dunn, can you respond?"

She peered into the room, her head just past the collar as she flashed the light into the corner to the right of the door. Nothing.

As she brought her light around to the other side, the comm hood gave a more energetic hiss. She flinched back at the unexpected sound. A blur of motion from the left caught her eye. Metal slammed against metal. From the shadows, hoarse breathing punched up into a roar. She now recognized the acrid odor in the air. She'd smelt it on the command deck, when Dunn came up the hatch.

There wasn't time to call out to him. There was only time to move. An industrial-grade spanner crashed into the airlock door just millimeters away her head. Again, the weapon rose. She couldn't continue to evade; not in this restricted space. She brought the utility light up to block the spanner's descent and allowed her body to fall back upon the deck. The move cost her the light, which went spinning away, but her bones were intact.

She stared up into Dunn's face. He was barely recognizable. His eyes were wide and wild, a long, bloody scratch marred his face, and sweat stood out in hard beads on his forehead. The rest of him was coated in blood. He did not seem to recognize her. She watched as a tremor ran through his body. No matter what had passed between them, she didn't want to hurt him, not even to get away. She would, but she didn't want to. She prayed he came out of it.

"Dunn...Karl, what happened to you?"

She held her breath. For a moment, his pupils expanded. Recognition floated just beneath the surface. Then her comm hood hissed. His echoed in response. She had most of a second to watch him retreat behind the terror.

"Oh shit!" Yakata braced herself. This was going to hurt. Her only hope lay in the leverage of her position and her greater lower-body strength. The spanner came down full force. She dodged her torso as best she could, but took a glancing blow to her shoulder. Her left side went numb on impact. She wrapped herself around the spanner with her good arm and drew her legs up sharp. Snarling, she planted both feet in Dunn's gut and shoved for all she was worth.

The weapon remained in her possession, though it was close. Dunn went flying. Yakata winced as he crashed into the lockers, landing awkwardly on the sprawled EVA suit. She bit her lip at the fresh smear of blood across the dented metal. Bit harder against the impulse to go help him. Instead, she rolled to her feet and slammed the airlock hatch. Using the spanner, she wedged the door closed as best she could. Praying it would hold, she headed for the main shaft at a hard clip. Within the first five strides, the pain in her left arm triggered a grey haze across her vision. Gasping, she stopped running immediately.

Yakata blinked furiously, forcing herself to take slow, deep breaths, until the haze went away. Behind her she could hear banging, enraged and violent.

Gritting her teeth against the pain, she loosened her web belt and slipped the wrist of her damaged arm into the gap between belt and pants, angled across her stomach. She hissed with the pain and the sounds from the airlock increased in intensity.

She forced thoughts of Dunn out of her mind and tightened the belt against her wrist, immobilizing the damaged arm as best she could. Once again, she set off, this time at a gentler, swinging lope. Her gut clenched. As she left the cacophony of the drive section behind, the faint sound of a warning klaxon could be heard elsewhere on the ship.

Yakata toggled her comm activator again. "Command deck... Come in, Captain Kinney." Not even a hiss sounded in her ear. "Deck officer, respond."

No answer; and her comm went dead, completely dead.

Abandoning her gentle pace, Yakata ran full out for the transport. The lift was slow, but one-handed, she would be even slower hauling herself up the ladder to the command deck. Her eyes locked on the lift mooring as it came into sight. The knots in her shoulders eased the slightest increment. The platform was there. She added another burst of speed.

Her steps faltered as she drew close. Something was not right. The lift wasn't seated properly in the track. It hovered about six inches off the mooring. She stopped where she was and tried to peer beneath it.

How had she missed the thin, crimson rivulets snaking across the deck? The fine, meandering tributaries flowing from the crushed body of Crewman Mory Chapman? Yakata fought the urge to be sick.

Was Dunn responsible? Was this why he wasn't at the rendezvous? Why he didn't answer her hails? Why his suit had been covered in blood? Her throat spasmed and she had to swallow hard as she moved closer to examine the mechanism.

The body was tangled in the power couplings, bits of it pulped by the gears. Even if she could get the lift into motion, it would shred what was left of him. Only his face was untouched.

His expression would haunt her.

A sound echoed up the corridor. Cursing, Yakata re-tightened her belt against her injured arm and climbed onto the lift. Her added force caused the platform to drop another inch. There was a sickening crack as something organic gave. She clenched her teeth and closed her eyes, emptied her mind of everything, and started up the lift. Before it had gone more than a few meters she slumped to her knees.

CENTRAL SHAFT, UPPER UTILITY LIFT MOORING: 42.05.18 – 2100HRS

The lift locked into its upper mooring. Before her was the command deck hatch. She should get up. She had to report. The captain was waiting for them. Them. Not just her. Reality came rushing back. Yakata yanked herself to her feet with her good arm and gripped the ladder-track for balance. The hatch was open and the deck lights were at standby dim.

Every nerve in her body pricked. The command deck was un-manned. It was never unmanned. Leaning into the ladder, Yakata braced herself. She released her grip with her good hand and reached down into her maintenance kit. Near the bottom, she found the telescoping mirror she'd used earlier. Taking the reflective end carefully between her teeth, she angled the head and drew out the handle as far as it would go. She then edged the tool around the hatch. There were no bodies on the deck, and there were none walking around, either. Not that she could see, anyway.

The lights flared higher as she pulled herself through the hatch. She squinted against the sudden brilliance. It took a moment for her eyes to adjust. Closing the hatch, she keyed the lock with her personal code. Dunn wouldn't corner her again. Her shoulder throbbed in agreement. With a grimace, she settled into the command chair. The display in front of her was completely lit up. Alerts flashed over nearly every inch of the ship, a confusing dance of flood, fire, and vacuum. Sometimes all three at once in the same compartment. How much of it was real?

Clearing the screen, she prayed nothing would go critical before she could get this sorted out. She ran diagnostics, keying in commands one-handed. Half of the alerts disappeared. Next, she toggled the comm on the console. Nothing. Not even static. She had to try, though.

"Yakata to all crew, report." She set the hail to repeat and went back to diagnostics. It was halfway through and there were no major malfunctions yet. A host of minor ones, but those they could survive. Of course, that assumed the diagnostics system wasn't fried as well.

She then input the command to identify the locations of all on board, just as she had when she looked for Dunn. It took longer this time. The computer spit out multiple conflicting responses. There was no way to tell which one was accurate.

While she waited for diagnostics to complete, Yakata moved to the emergency kit. She selected an analgesic patch. After tearing it open with her teeth, she palmed it and slipped it past the collar of her coverall. It was cool, instantly soothing her battered shoulder, taking the edge off her pain. That taken care of, she settled back into the command chair.

Diagnostics was at ninety-five percent. Another alert went off as the logarithm completed. Yakata's eyes moved from the diagnostics display to the main console. It was the proximity warning. It shouldn't have gone off when they were under hyperdrive. She stood and went to the external monitoring station. Nothing appeared on the fore view. Yakata activated the aft cameras. Her finger trembled as she depressed the button. Her vision greyed out one moment, only to telescope into sharp focus the next. Something drifted by the lens out by the drive section, caught in the electromagnetic pocket of e'space surrounding the ship. Several somethings, in fact. Yakata swallowed against the acidic tang climbing her throat. Visions of her father's helmet overwhelmed her, eclipsing the images she didn't want to see. She distanced herself through extreme willpower and zoomed in on the debris.

"...all crew, report."

"Shit!" Yakata yelled as her own voice suddenly called out through both her comm hood and every speaker on the deck. Communications was back. She killed the auto repeat and sent out a fresh hail.

"Command deck to Captain Kinney..."

Her voice trailed off as she tweaked the settings on the monitor. The objects had come into focus. Her eyes slammed closed. But even with them tightly shut she could still see the empty gaze of Captain Kinney staring at her from the vacuum of space.

PERSONAL LOG ENTRY: 42.05.18 – 2230HRS, DUNN, K.

FUCK YOU! I DON'T KNOW WHAT YOU ARE, BUT I KNOW WHAT YOU'RE DOING NOW, SO FUCK YOU! YOU MADE ME HURT HER. I WOULD NEVER HURT HER. SHE IS THE ONLY ONE WHO CARES. WHO STILL MEANS SOMETHING TO ME...

I KNOW YOU CAN ACCESS WHAT I'M WRITING HERE, BECAUSE YOU KNEW HOW TO MESS WITH MY HEAD. WELL ACCESS THIS: YOU WILL NEVER GET ME TO HURT HER AGAIN. YOU WILL NEVER TOUCH HER AGAIN. I WILL DESTROY YOU!

DUTY LOG: 42.05.19 – 1230HRS, YAKATA, U.

REACTOR STATUS – INDETERMINATE;

O2 LEVELS – FLUCTUATING;

POWER – DATA UNAVAILABLE.

NOTE: SC MCKAY OPERATING UNDER EMERGENCY CONDITIONS. SHIP-WIDE MALFUNCTIONS WORSEN. MEMBER OR MEMBERS OF THE CREW UNSTABLE. CAPTAIN KINNEY; DECEASED, MEANS UNKNOWN, BODY EXPELLED FROM SHIP BY UNIDENTIFIED PERSONNEL. AT LEAST THREE OTH-

ERS LIKEWISE EXPELLED, POSITIVE ID CANNOT BE MADE. CREWMAN CHAPMAN; DECEASED, ACCIDENTAL OR BY DESIGN. CREWMAN DUNN; UNSTABLE, VIOLENT, TEMPORARILY RESTRAINED IN PORT LATERAL AIRLOCK. REMAINDER OF THE CREW; STATUS UNKNOWN. FIRST OFFICER USHIMI YAKATA ASSUMING COMMAND.

Out of habit, Yakata printed a hard copy of the duty log. Events must always be documented. Not that she expected anyone would ever read this account. As she tore the sheet from the printer, her eyes drifted across the page. She cursed and jerked her hand away. The page drifted to the deck, bold, black letters stared up at her:

THEY'RE ALL DEAD. YOU'RE ALL DEAD. DIE ALREADY, BITCH.

There was the faintest of sounds behind her. She whirled. O'Neal came through the hatch across the command deck, the one leading to the cargo bay and rendezvous station.

She took in the metallurgist's appearance: his coverall was torn, and dark stains across his chest glistened wetly. There was no sign he was the party injured. At his side, his prosthetic arm slowly flexed, as if the motion were unconscious. Yakata met O'Neal's gaze. She did not recognize the man staring back at her. His eyes were cold and hard, alien and bereft of humanity. His expression was neutral; as if she wouldn't notice something else lurked beneath.

There was so much wrong with this picture, Yakata thought fleetingly.

"You plan to do what you're told?" he asked in a slow drawl, nodding toward the slip of acrylisheet on the floor.

His tone sounded as flat as his expression. Yakata's eyes flickered to the printout.

"I don't take orders from a piece of paper," she growled. "And I sure as hell don't take orders from you."

"We all have to answer to someone."

"Yeah, well the only person I answered to is drifting out by the engines," Yakata spat back at him. "Who do you answer to?" She moved to the side as she spoke, edging toward the hatch.

"You'll meet soon enough." The neutrality was gone. Pure evil crept through O'Neal's voice. He followed her movements like a raptor tracked prey.

Forget that, Yakata told herself. With the line of her body to block the action, she lowered her right hand back into her maintenance kit. Very carefully, she eased out her utility knife, her hand through the wrist strap and the hilt solid in her palm. She depressed the release button on the pommel and the blade silently deployed.

Yakata's muscles rippled beneath her skin. She braced herself, poised to react to whatever move O'Neal made. Her only real option was evasion. If he got a hold of her with that prosthetic, he would crush her before she could even flinch.

As the metallurgist advanced, a tremor went straight through Yakata's body. It took her a moment to realize it wasn't internal. She sucked in a sharp breath. Her gaze flickered away from O'Neal to the main display. Alert icons flashed, one by one. The system was losing power. Within moments they would no longer have enough to sustain hyperdrive. There was a boot dock just behind her and a tether up and to her right. She was going to need one of them shortly.

It would have to be the boot dock; she had too few functioning hands to grab a tether and use the knife. She edged herself closer. Let him think she was afraid of him; that she futilely distanced herself.

She was ready when the bottom dropped out of the universe. The ship shuddered as the electrogravitic drive envelope disintegrated. Simultaneously, she leaned back and jammed her heel into the dock. She was barely secure when there was a pop and a flash as intense as a hundred strobes going off right there in the room. Yakata squeezed her eyes shut just in time. From the heaving sounds, O'Neal had been caught unaware. She opened her eyes as reality uprighted itself in an orbital orientation. O'Neal floated in an uncontrolled sprawl on the far side of the command console. Around him floated globes of acrid vomit. As he bumped them, they burst into a dozen smaller globes, minus what clung to him. Feebly, his hand reached for the edge of the console.

Yakata grinned. In this state, he was no threat at all.

He groaned, and she laughed. She couldn't help it.

She went somber quickly, though, as hatred sharpened his gaze. Smelt it as the stench of malevolence overpowered the odor of bile. He looked ready to launch at her. Yakata tightened her grip on the utility knife. Let him try. He was a ground-pounder. Space was her element, and this was her ship.

There was a clunk and the manual release on the command deck hatch spun toward open. Yakata froze. Once she'd keyed the lock, even the manual release required her personal code to open the hatch.

Only one person onboard had the slightest chance of figuring it out. Dunn.

Confusion dulled the evil glint in O'Neal's eye. She watched fury flood his expression as the hatch swung out. The open portal remained empty.

Yakata didn't relax. Now she had to be on her guard on two fronts, and her ex was no rookie in space. He must have been the one to disable the drive system. He certainly had the knowledge.

"Don't just stand there, 'Ta!"

Dunn peered around the edge of the hatch as he snapped at her. The scratch across his face was crusted over. His expression danced between violence and panic. She shifted her grip on the utility knife and turned her body so that her good arm could strike at either O'Neal or Dunn.

From the far side of the command console, O'Neal let out a serpentine hiss. She resisted the urge to turn to stare at him. Dunn was the more potent threat at the moment.

She watched the muscles of his face clench and twitch in response to the sound O'Neal made. Dunn's breath quickened. The massive spanner he'd used earlier came into view. She braced herself, ready to yank her heel out of the dock the second she knew which direction to propel herself. But his attention wasn't on her. Dunn's eyes were locked with O'Neal's. Her gaze flickered from one to the other. Between them, they blocked the only ways out.

"Will you move it before he figures out how to get both of us!"

Yakata jumped, startled as Dunn spoke in rapid Japanese. She'd forgotten he knew her language. It wasn't something they'd used often. They both knew that O'Neal didn't share their knowledge. The entire crew was required to familiarize themselves with his profile before he came on board. She was surprised Dunn had enough of a grip on himself to use that knowledge.

"What...and I'm supposed to trust you over him?" She slashed back in the same tongue. "He's not the one who tried to cave in my head!"

"Just move it, 'Ta!" Dunn continued in Japanese. Sweat gleamed on his forehead and his eyes were wild.

Before she could dodge aside, he lunged. His free hand latched onto her belt. She snarled as he jerked her loose from the dock. Yakata gasped with pain, her damaged arm wrenched about by his handling. Her head spun at the sharp, sudden movement. Dunn angled her toward the hatch with practiced ease. At the same time, the hand gripping the spanner swung out, aimed at O'Neal's head.

There was a solid *thunk*: the sound of metal against flesh. Silence followed. Threat floated thick on the canned air. Yakata shifted her head to look back at O'Neal. His green eyes glowed with malice. She cursed and lost the thought as her quick glance took in his unbloodied head and Dunn's spanner caught by the metallurgist's flesh hand. Some oddly detached part of her brain wondered why he hadn't just grabbed it with the prosthetic.

Her answer was a strangled gasp from Dunn. With no visible effort, O'Neal's cybernetic limb crushed Dunn's wrist, the one holding the spanner.

The sight refocused Yakata's rage in an instant. She tried to wrench away from Karl's grip, throwing herself back as far as his tethering hold allowed, to lash at his attacker with her utility knife. The tip sliced through O'Neal's shirt, barely scratching his shoulder. He didn't even flinch.

Her curses cut off abruptly as Dunn shook her hard.

"Go! Now!" Karl snapped. Pain glimmered in his eyes, brilliant and jagged. Beneath that, he wordlessly pleaded with her. She stopped struggling, her brow drawn down in confusion.

Executing an effortless turn, she used the tip of her toe to propel herself off the overhead toward the hatch. She torpedoed through the opening, dropped the utility knife to hang by its strap, and caught the hatch collar with her good hand. Behind her there was a sick grinding sound.

She pivoted, catching sight of Dunn on his knees, his captured arm bent impossibly high behind his back. She growled and started to draw herself back onto the command deck. She couldn't leave him to this.

"No! I said go! One of us has to get away...head for the Cans, now!" Despite his obvious pain, he continued speaking in Japanese. Yakata hissed in objection, but she dipped her head in a brief, sharp nod before pivoting around to zip down the main shaft. Behind her, she heard a loud snap and the sick sound of laughter drifted through the hatch. She had to fight the impulse to turn around and tear O'Neal to shreds.

"Yes...do run, little rabbit...I'll be along as soon as I'm done here. Shouldn't take long."

Yakata's blood thickened and her heart froze. O'Neal had just spoken to her in flawless, textbook Japanese.

An agonized scream came from the command deck. It rose sharply before an abrupt end.

* * *

Her good arm burned nearly as bad as her injured one. She ignored it and grabbed another rung of the ladder-track, slingshotting herself down the shaft. The echo of Dunn's final scream followed her. It filled her head until she heard nothing else. She tried to force the memory into the fading recesses where it could not touch her.

It resisted.

The flickers of movement were back. The flashes of light behind her, just to the side of her vision. Halfway down the shaft it got to her. Growling deep in her throat, she turned to confront the phantoms that stalked her. A practiced flick of her wrist sent the utility knife back up into her grip and a moment's pressure deployed the blade. Her momentum sent her colliding with the substructure. The impact to her damaged arm sent true sparks across her vision, followed by a grey haze. She blinked it away and cursed.

The shaft behind her was empty. There was nothing there, and nowhere anyone might hide. She retracted the knife and let it drift at the end of its strap. With a little more care, she turned and continued to haul herself along, both arms throbbing as she went.

Her comm hood gave a sudden burst of static. Yakata jumped. Another growl filled her throat to pulse against her jaw. She nearly snatched the comm hood off to shred the delicate wiring.

"What the hell are you doing?!"

The unexpected outburst stayed her hand. Dunn. How...? Her gaze snapped to the command deck many stories above her head. She couldn't see him. He must be watching her on the monitors.

"I told you...to get out of here! Get to the Cans...now!" Dunn's voice was thin, strained.

"What happened to O'Neal?"

"Don't know...I passed out. He's not here." Sounds of movement filtered through the comm; rustling, a sharply drawn breath. What might have been a sob.

"Dunn? Dunn!" Yakata's suspicions disintegrated beneath a fresh wave of concern.

"Don't yell, 'Ta." Karl's voice was low and weak. "You're making it hard to think.

"He left me for dead, which means he's after you."

"I don't understand what's going on here," she whispered.

"It's that damn artifact," he snapped back, but his voice quickly faded, slurring and losing focus. "None of this started until we salvaged that thing. It's screwing with our minds. It's screwing with the ship. Somehow it's infiltrated the system...and..." Static disrupted him in sharp bursts. "...anything electronic...nly use manual overr...only. Not malfunc...deliberate."

"The artifact! I have to get the artifact!"

"No!...amnit! Get the hell off this ship. Now!"

Immediately, uncertainty sank firm fingers into her thoughts. She had more reason to doubt Dunn than to trust him. And O'Neal had already proven their attempt at speaking covertly had failed.

"Move!"

No. Perhaps O'Neal left him for dead...or not. Dunn had attacked her once already. She couldn't help but wonder if this was a trap.

She would get her artifact, and then she was getting off this ship. It was foolhardy to continue to the airlocks, though. That's where they expected her to go. Besides, the Cans—as the escape pods were called by any spacer with experience—had precious little reserve, and almost no maneuverability. The distress signal was a joke. She wasn't ditching this ship just to suffocate slowly in space.

Like a swimmer doing laps, Yakata flipped end over end and hauled herself the way she'd come. The pods weren't the only option. There was that payload attached to the forward coupling, the inter-orbital shuttlecraft meant to transport Corporate bigwigs to their facilities surrounding Demeter. Even if O'Neal knew about it, he wouldn't expect her to try and escape that way. Transports were shipped dry, no fuel, no external tanks, and just enough juice to power the maneuvering thrusters and internals. Right now the shuttle was a big, floating box. But—most important for her—that big, floating box contained enough air to support seven adult males for fourteen days, without cracking the reserve tanks. That...and a state-of-the-art distress beacon.

All she had to do was reach it. Yakata renewed her efforts, keeping her eye on the reflectors as she went. No one threatened to come through the hatches ahead of her. As she neared the hatch leading to the Temporary Science Lab, she again glanced both ways down the shaft.

Wherever O'Neal had gone, he wasn't stalking her.

Yakata opened the hatch and dove inside. She thanked God that the drive had not reengaged. The only blessing in this whole thing: weightlessness certainly made it easy to get around. Not to mention the obelisk would have been a dead weight if the ship were still under gravity.

Lights flared as Yakata slipped into the compartment where the artifact was stored. Immediately she noticed the door to the locker hung open, and nothing remained inside.

"No!" Yakata hissed with rage. She looked around, her gaze darting frantically, as if the obelisk might be sitting right in front of her. But it was useless. It was gone. She slammed the locker door and whirled, her anger taking over. The spectrometer still sat affixed to the table. It mocked her. She'd known O'Neal was out to screw her over. Her good hand snapped out, denting the housing of his costly machine. She let it fly again. It felt good. She took aim once more, until a reflection in the battered metal caught her eye.

O'Neal! She dove away from his raised fists, certain that any moment she would feel the crushing blow from his prosthetic. None fell. She twisted in midair, fighting to control her motions, to palm her knife and deploy the blade.

As she came to rest against the far bulkhead, Yakata felt a ripple of laughter seize her throat.

"What the hell?" she murmured aloud. The room was empty. No O'Neal hovered, ready to pummel her to pulp. Yet...

Yakata gripped her knife tighter and propelled herself toward the spectrometer. Had she truly lost it? Or was this proof of the sinister force Dunn claimed now possessed the ship? She tapped the dented surface with the tip of her utility knife. Tapped it right over the reflection of O'Neal. The micro image flinched back. Yakata giggled. It sounded jagged.

That was it then: she'd gone over the edge. She giggled again and chased the figmentary O'Neal around the spectrometer with rapid taps of her utility knife. She laughed full out and tasted salt drip over the rim of her lip onto her tongue. A sob slipped out next. The knife drifted down to its strap and she rested a gentle hand against the reflection.

"I'm sorry...I'm so sorry..."

She brought her face right up near the metal, noticing the terror on that tiny man's face. He wasn't looking at her, though; his gaze stared off into the room. It took her a moment to realize there were now two O'Neals trapped in the metal. Perhaps it was an accumulative thing: the longer she stared the more the image would multiply. Her next giggle bordered on a wail.

That was when the *ching* of flexing metal reached her ears. Her eyes went wide. She leaned against the machine. Clarity seeped back into her own reflection. The memory of the last time she and O'Neal had been in this room came to her. He'd taken the artifact out of the spectrometer and gone into painful convulsions. Her gaze snapped to the tiny O'Neal with the hazel eyes, somehow trapped within his own machine while something went around in his body. He gave the slightest nod. "I am sorry," she whispered as she snaked her hand around the housing.

With a mighty heave, she flung the machine at the O'Neal creeping up behind her, the one with something alien peering out of stormy green eyes.

Power couplings snapped. Metal collided with metal in a satisfying crunch. The creature's roar deafened her.

As she rocketed past, aiming for the hatch, she spared half a glance for her would-be attacker. The spectrometer drifted away from him. Massive bruises shadowed O'Neal's already dark shoulder. The prosthetic attached to it was crumpled, but the fingers flexed, if somewhat haltingly.

Her aim was off. She'd meant to cave in his head.

There was an odd gleam in O'Neal's eye as he locked gazes with her. She jerked her eyes away and maneuvered out of arm's reach.

She was nearly clear when he lurched up. His flesh hand shot out and grabbed her ankle. Screaming with rage, she flicked her wrist and palmed the dangling utility knife, the blade still deployed. She lashed out. The edge bit deep into the back of his hand.

She jerked the knife free and kicked out with her unfettered foot at O'Neal's still firm and bloodied grip on her ankle. He laughed up at her. The trapped O'Neal pounded furiously from the far side of his reflection; the evil one raised his battered prosthetic and caressed her calf with deceptive gentleness.

Frantic, Yakata tried to yank her foot free. She succeeded only in drawing him closer. Again the prosthetic stroked her leg, this time higher.

"Shh...it'll be okay..." he mocked.

Her vision went dark and flat. Nothing had depth or shading. Nothing was as crisply clear as his grip on her leg. Nothing mattered more than freeing herself from that hold. Without a second thought, she brought her knife around again and impaled O'Neal's hand...

...straight through to her ankle. More blood filled the room.

"Augh!"

O'Neal laughed over her scream as he tugged his hand away from the blade, bisecting his own flesh. The damage did nothing to hinder his movements. But for her, the motion sent shafts of breath-stopping pain shooting from her foot to the top of her head. The knife remained lodged in the muscle just above the ankle.

"Bad girl...you were supposed to head for the Cans."

Yakata whimpered. Clenching her teeth, she yanked out the blade, sending pearls of blood spinning through the bay. The strap went back over her wrist. The hilt locked in her grip. Again armed, she kicked off toward the hatch.

From just inside the room, O'Neal's laughter stole her breath. She waited for him to haul her back. She could already feel his fingers locked around her. Not again! She sent herself rocketing forward with reckless force. Her body careened off the interior walls. She slammed against the hatch collar with her bad shoulder. The injured foot snagged on the door. Agony nearly crippled her as her vision clouded and a buzz filled her ears.

It wasn't enough to drown out O'Neal as he called after her. "Run, little rabbit, run...it's so much fun to catch you."

✳   ✳   ✳

Despite O'Neal's taunt, there were no sounds of pursuit. She was under no illusion it would remain that way. Tumbling into the main shaft, Yakata planted her good foot against the track and shoved off, bulleting toward the nose of the ship. She cursed at the lights. Some sections activated as she passed, others went out, plunging her into darkness. She ignored it. After all her years on this ship, a little darkness wasn't going to screw her up.

As she neared the command deck there was a faint green ambient glow, like that given off by digital displays in the dark. It was impossible to make out if anyone was there. O'Neal was somewhere behind her, but what happened to Dunn? Intense sorrow gripped her heart as she remembered the last time she saw him. Yakata forced it away. He was either dead, or a danger to her.

Cautiously, she eased past the command hatch, keeping to the far side of the shaft. It was slow going, but she made it to the staging bay two levels up without incident. A glance behind her revealed no obvious motion, but her nerves vibrated with tension.

She turned back to the open hatch of the staging bay. The mechanism to seal the two-meter wide opening could close in less than thirty seconds. She released the knife and reached into her pouch for a spanner, wedging it into the grating where the retractable hatch was housed. It wouldn't hold long, but should another...malfunction occur, the obstruction would give her a little extra time to get clear.

Reaching just past the opening, she felt around for a tether bar to haul herself through. Something brushed against her hand in the darkness. She jerked back and palmed the knife, bracing herself for an attack. A whisper of sound taunted her ears. Her grip on the knife tightened even more, but nothing else came at her out of the dark. Yakata breathed out a growl.

Fine, she thought. *I'll do it the hard way.*

She flung herself through the hatch, rocketing past the opening and deep into the bay, her body angled to intersect with the lift track. Instead, she collided with something soft and yielding. It was impossible not to scream as arms came around to encircle her.

No! She would not be caught so easily! Yakata brought up her knife and thrust brutally into the one blocking her way.

"'Ta..." The whisper was faint, and right by her ear. Yakata moaned and her knife hand jerked back. Warm globules bounced against her skin as the blade did more damage coming out than going in. The pinpoints of warmth sent her trembling.

No! Oh, God, no! Please no! Yakata's thoughts were frantic. She released the knife as if it were a contagion. Her now-empty hand scrambled around in her maintenance pouch as the knife bobbed on its strap. *Where was it? Where, damnit?* She forgot all about escape as she searched for her spare light among the jumbled tools. As her hand wrapped around it, and she depressed the button, a sudden clang from the direction of the hatch startled her. She fumbled the light. It made eerie arcs as it spun in the darkened bay, revealing small slices of her surroundings. Her gasp echoed through the compartment as the rotating beam briefly illuminated a blood-coated hand. Yakata lunged for the maintenance light. Before she could bring the beam around, there was a deep, rumbling chuckle behind her. She whirled and the main lights flared to life in the bay. She flinched and squinted against the sudden brilliance.

"My...and haven't you been busy?" O'Neal rested against the lift track, his arms crossed over his chest as he watched her. She noticed his gaze sweep the chamber. He frowned faintly as he looked right, but he made no move toward her or the room.

The last thing she should do was take her eye off him. The impulse, however, was irresistible. Yakata pivoted until she could see the whole of the bay.

The blood rushed from her head. She barely heard O'Neal's malicious laughter. Around her floated three bodies. Her unaccounted-for crewmen...She immediately recognized the one to the right as Dunn, much bloodier, but still clearly him. The closest to her, however, was John Pittman. From his gut streamed a trail of ruby-red bubbles.

She was overcome by the urge to fling the utility knife from her, only that would have cut her probability of survival down even lower. It was an effort to tug her eyes away, to get past the horror. She told herself he was already dead. Beyond Pittman floated Anita Suarez, her expression softer, more feminine in death than it had ever been in life. Old spacer that she was, she looked like a frightened child now. A frightened child frozen in intense and unbearable pain.

Yakata refused to look more closely at Dunn.

She cursed and turned on O'Neal once more, her knife in her hand, though she didn't remember flicking it up. O'Neal continued to laugh.

"'Ta...no...."

Again, the bodiless whisper by her ear. No...from her comm hood! Only Dunn ever call her 'Ta. She glanced sideways, trying to catch the subtle motion breathing alone would have caused. It was so hard to tell at this angle.

"Damn it, 'Ta, come...get this thing..." The strained whisper was no product of her imagination. He 'drifted' ever so slightly; just enough to reveal the outline of a line-gun hidden in the curve of his body. Behind him she could see the half-open storage locker the tool had come from.

Without another thought, she braced both legs against the wall. Pain rippled from her ankle, but she needed equal force to keep herself headed straight as she launched forward. O'Neal arrowed toward Dunn, as well, but Yakata was closer.

Grasping the gun and using her momentum to pivot the rest of her mass, she braced the improvised weapon against her body and jerked the release.

There was a *whoosh* and a *thud*. O'Neal went rocketing across the bay toward the opposite wall. His head slammed into the hull and then the only motion was his body recoiling from the impact.

Numbness set in. *Could that be it? Was it that simple?* she thought as she drifted where she was, the gun still gripped in her hand. Beside her, Dunn moaned and it barely reached where her psyche had retreated.

The steady tug on the rope, though...that went right to her nerve centers.

"Oh, shit!" She let go of the line-gun and wrapped her good hand in Dunn's vest.

"N-no...you have to survive," he murmured, batting away her hand. "Can't do that hauling my ass behind you."

"Bullshit!" she growled. "You made it this far, I'm not leaving you here to die."

"I'm...I'm d-dead, either way."

She ignored his failing whisper, and pushed off, sending them past the bodies. Her mind shut down as she did so, focused on one goal: freedom. Nothing existed but the nose dock of the *McKay* and the payload it led to.

And suddenly, they were there.

She let go of Dunn's vest to work the manual release. The hatch clanged open and she reached for Dunn once more. He gripped her hand back. His trembled violently. She turned to look at him, to gauge how much distress he was in.

"No!" she shouted, as she spied O'Neal past Dunn's shoulder, raising the retracted line-gun. But it was too late. She felt the impact as the hook embedded itself in Karl's back. "No...no..." she sobbed. Not Dunn. Not when she... "No...I l-love you! No!"

Tears streamed down her face as she watched the awareness faded from his eyes. *No.* But this protest was silent, weak. *Does it matter now,* she wondered, *if I get away?* But the tug of the line decided her. She roared with rage and yanked back. O'Neal and whatever rode him would not have Dunn.

She brought up her utility knife and severed the line. Grabbing Karl's vest, she tugged him through the forward airlock. He bobbed behind her as she cycled the hatch. Yakata was numb as she took them through the yacht access. She gave him a gentle nudge to send him drifting deeper into the cabin as her hand danced automatically through the manual release sequence for the docking ring.

As they separated from the *McKay*, she could swear she heard the ghost of laughter.

She dropped into the command chair of the luxury yacht, barely noticing the sensual caress of fine doeskin leather. Her only concern was powering up the systems. Lighting and atmospherics engaged, followed by the exterior cameras.

The numbness faded as she realized how near Demeter they were. There was hope of rescue. A solid chance for survival. Her hand hovered over the distress beacon, but drew back, leaving the unit inactivated. Why bother? Dunn was gone.

"No...you must survive."

Yakata shivered as Dunn's earlier words whispered through her thoughts. Clenching her eyes shut against the heartache, she brought her hand back and slammed it down on the distress beacon button.

Rescue would come now. And she would have to go on. Alone.

As that realization hit her, she watched the *McKay* fire its engines. She deftly manipulated the contoured joystick controlling the external camera, panning it in the ship's wake.

What is he up to now? she wondered, unable to turn away. The *McKay* angled further to the left and the display in front of her blazed fiercely, blinding her a moment. The system adjusted the filters until the brilliant sun was no more than a distant, glowing disk marred only by a rapidly diminishing black speck.

"Enjoying the show, Ms. Ushimi?"

Yakata jerked as O'Neal's voice came over the yacht's speakers. She cursed herself for forgetting to disengage the remote sensors connecting the two ships.

"Why?" she hissed.

"Where's the terror," he purred, "if there's no one left to know exactly how fucked you all are?

"Oh yeah, and thanks for the ride."

As his words faded, the yacht's lights flickered out, plunging Yakata into darkness. She fumbled with the control panel, frantically trying to reengage them, to no avail. Her only illumination was the display in front of her.

She couldn't hold back a whimper. She was no longer comfortable with the dark. O'Neal's disembodied laugh wrapped around her just before he closed the link. She was so shocked it took a moment for her to realize the *McKay's* hyperdrive had engaged.

Horrified, she watched the ship's graceful arc; the shimmer of its electrogravitic drive envelope mesmerized her. Yakata held her breath. She could still see the glittering trail streaming behind the transport, but knew it had, in fact, already plunged into the sun. Eight minutes later, the sunlight contracted, the glowing ball getting smaller and smaller.

O'Neal's voice echoed in her head. An old memory from when he had still been himself and the spectrometer had fed them an impossible reading on the obelisk: *It's as if the artifact absorbed the light.*

She shuddered and watched as the star died, its fire eaten up by an ancient evil no larger than her head.

Yakata found herself in complete darkness with her dead.

Dunn. The spaced crew. In her panicked mind, she pictured each of them in a mask of her father's face.

Her breath came in rapid huffs and her body shook until she had to grip the console to remain in the chair.

How long before we all die? she thought, staring in the direction of Demeter, an entire planet suddenly and inexplicably plunged into bitter-cold darkness.

The comm hood crackled and Yakata's heart seized.

"Yummy," O'Neal's voice whispered malevolently in her ear. "Want to come get us? We'll do dessert..."

Yakata screamed.

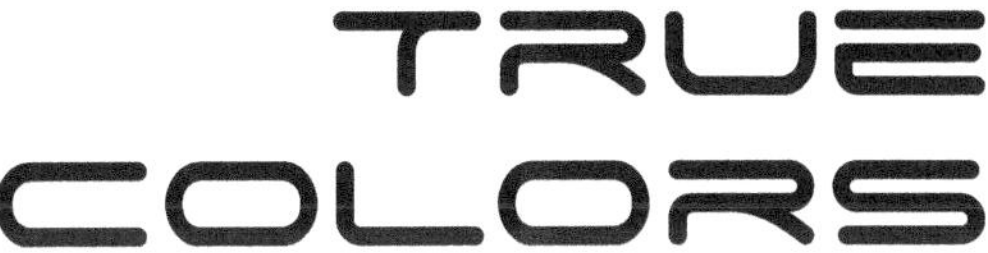

An Alliance Archives Adventure

There was no stately procession to the airlock. No pomp and ceremony as the hatch opened. Brockmann's body wasn't set adrift in the vastness of space to echo the dignity of an ancient warrior's burial at sea.

No.

She was taken away in a body bag the moment the *Teufel* docked. By the time the 142nd Infantry—or Daire's Devils—mustered in the barracks common room for debriefing, a corpsman presented Sarge with a two-inch, compressed-carbon cube and a bag of effects. That was all that was left of Corporal Suzanne Brockmann, Special Forces, one more offense credited against the pirates that had invaded the sector.

Corporal Katrion Alexander felt her hands flex, accompanied by a familiar itch in her fingers. That could have been her reduced to a geometric shape. Almost was...*twice.*

She must have moved without realizing it. Beside her Sergeant Jackson "Scotch" Daniels cleared his throat and stepped between her and her pile of gear. Well, more accurately, between her and her gauss rifle.

"Down, Kittie, down," he murmured, his hazel eyes capturing her gaze. "Ain't no pirates here."

Kat growled. She did that a lot lately.

There was no time to comment. She and the rest of the unit snapped to attention as Sergeant Major Kevin Daire accepted the remains from the corpsman and ignored the bag of effects. Turning his back on the man, Sarge cradled the cube in his left hand and drew his combat knife with his right. He then bowed his head; the unit gathered round and followed suit. Not a word was spoken aloud as each of them bid farewell to their fallen comrade. Nor as, one by one, each of them stepped forward and, with their blades, scratched a line into the smooth, shiny surface of her compressed remains. Each of them maintained silence as they fell back to form a loose circle around their leader once their part was complete. Sarge looked up and met their gazes. Without looking away from them, he raised his knife and etched his own line, bisecting those left by the unit. Each line segment on the cube was a solemn oath that the pirates would be brought down.

The vow was made.

Only then did Scotch step forward to secure Brockmann's personal effects from the still-waiting corpsman. Whatever was in that small, compact bag would be shared out among the unit according to need. The rest would be held in reserve or given where it would best serve. Unlike Kat, Brockmann had no family to send material belongings back to, even if the military were willing to foot the bill.

The corpsman turned to leave.

"Wait." Sarge motioned for Kat and Scotch to step forward. She suppressed a flinch and came to attention in front of him. "Alexander, Daniels...accompany Corpsman Kane back to med-bay to be cleared for return to duty."

Shit. It was only to be expected, though; Kat had been banged up from her previous encounter with the pirates, and both of them had been with Brockmann when their squad had come under fire a second time. She ran a hand over her dark, regulation-length bristle of hair and accepted the inevitable as she followed Scotch and Kane to the lift.

Sarge turned to the rest of the unit. "Command has called a general inspection for 1700 hours; use this time to get your billets in order." Not waiting for acknowledgement, he tightened his fist around Brockmann's cube and about-faced. In silence, he returned to his chamber to secure their fallen.

*　　*　　*

Forty minutes in med-bay got Kat a noxious cream to bring down the swelling around her blackened left eye and a shot in her wrenched ankle that hurt ten times worse than the original injury for all of thirty seconds, after which she felt nothing. The damage was still there—a lingering reminder of her first encounter with the enemy—but the pressure bandage would take care of that. She also received authorization to return to duty.

Poor Scotch. He was still in there arguing as Kat left med-bay to head back to the barracks. As a first-hand witness to Brockmann's termination, Command wanted Scotch to submit to a psych evaluation before reinstating him to active status. The last thing she heard clearly was him suggesting they submit to a self-administered rectal probe.

Kat chuckled. She wasn't hanging around to see which near-immovable force triumphed. In fact, she hightailed it out of there before someone stopped to wonder how her brainpan was after finding half of Trask—former commander and alleged pirate—floating in space. After all, they might decide she was too happy about it.

Toggling on her bonejack, Kat couldn't resist a parting jab. *Come on, Scotch, ten minutes on the couch and the shrink will have you visualizing cute little kittens and white sandy beaches, it'll be fun!*

Scotch tossed an off-color suggestion her way. *Talk about torture. I'm allergic to cats and the only beaches in this sector come with an atmosphere that would dissolve the flesh off human bones in thirty seconds. I'll have to pass, the torment would be too much to take…I might crack, and then where would we be? Now get the hell out of my head so I can deal with these quacks!*

Kat laughed, winking one dark brown eye at him as she switched the comm off and made her escape.

She hadn't known that, about the beaches, but then she wasn't exactly a beach bunny, was she? As she entered the lift she forced away the naughty thoughts of Scotch lounging on the sand somewhere with his blond buzz cut bleached white by the sun, instead turning her attention to the data they'd retrieved from the Groom microsat. Not only had they gained documentation of the pirates' attempted pillaging of the research facility, but Kat and her squad had intercepted the intended loot: the full research and development files on the *Rommel*, the state-of-the-art flagship of the fleet. They had it, but the pirates wanted it. Bad.

Sarge had the encrypted files secured in a lock box in his quarters, but he'd had Kat burn a backup as well. They'd hidden it on the *Teufel*, along with the rest of the stuff they'd retrieved from the pirate derelict on the mission that had gotten Brockmann killed. The black box data was the easy part; the computer cores Kat had extracted from the vessel, those were going to take some finesse. Right now, everything they had gathered was secreted away in a shielded compartment located near the *Teufel's* engine reactor where a scan, visual or otherwise, would not be able to detect their presence. Only Sarge, Scotch, and their unit commander, General Drovak, knew the intel was there waiting to be disseminated.

Kat didn't even want to think about trying to crack the code. Fortunately, that wasn't her job. All Sarge had to do was turn the material over to the general or one of his agents as soon as possible. The whole situation had her nervous, though. With rumors that the crew assigned to the *Rommel* may have been compromised, Kat couldn't be sure who they could trust outside of their own unit.

She shut down that thought and focused on getting back to the barracks. Kat looked up as the decks ticked by. Almost there. The lights fluxed, and the car slowed. For a moment, she thought she was screwed; there wasn't much time left to get her billet in order before the inspection. She half-expected a jerk and the *thunk* of the lift coming to an abrupt halt in the tube, but the lift continued to descend. With a hiss, the doors opened on the common room she had left less than an hour earlier. If not for the neat stacks of gear she would have thought the unit had left without them.

She sniffed. Something had made it past the air scrubbers. The remnants were faint, an acrid bite deep in her throat. It was an effort to keep her breathing regulated as she walked across the chamber. Her impulse was to hold her breath. Her body's was to breathe faster. Neither would do. It was an effort to draw shallow until she reached her gear. She outright had to force her fingers to flex and loosen enough to pick up her gauss as she paused by her own pile of equipment. She grabbed her breather as well and jerked it over her eyes, nose, and mouth until the thick gasket settled snug against her skin.

Kat should have felt silly, but she didn't. Paranoid came to mind... but she continued to wear the mask, hoping the filters were enough to combat whatever was on the air. She also held her rifle at the ready.

That alone made her feel better.

"Hey, Sarge...." she called out, the words only slightly muffled. Her breath came a little faster, and she forced it back. All the billets were closed, except one. Kat angled left and headed toward the compartment on the end with deck-eating strides. "Yo, anyone there...?" she called out.

Silence.

Kat drew closer, swaying a bit as her breath picked up again, as if she couldn't get enough oxygen. Lightheaded she braced herself against the open hatch. The air coming through her breather still held a hint of that acrid odor. She swayed again and her head dropped forward of its own accord.

For a split second, she saw an out-flung wrist, mottled clear around with bruising, caught between the hatch and the frame. The pattern of the discoloration disturbed Kat but her thoughts couldn't focus on why. She leaned forward to push the door panel into its retraction slot to reveal the unit's weapons specialist, Corporal Christine Dalton, which was kind of odd in itself, as this wasn't her billet. The details drifted out of focus, though, as Kat's brain slowly fogged over. She leaned forward to check for a pulse. As she did so, something snagged her mask, tugging it askew. A faint hissing sounded as the gasket seal parted from her skin and the earlier odor intensified. After that, all Kat saw was a swirl of darkening colors drawing her down into the black.

✳   ✳   ✳

"Time to change your name, you pain in the ass," a familiar voice grumbled over her, "before you use up all nine lives. Come on, Kittie...*atten*-hut!"

Kat grumbled and shoved at the hands lifting her semi-vertical.

"Yeah, you go ahead and fight, g'on, give me what-for," he went on. "Just do it with your damn eyes open."

She cracked said eyes just enough to recognize the familiar walls of med-bay and Scotch's hard, pale features leaning over her. At his back a med-tech and a corpsman tried to get around Scotch's bulk to separate them. Her eyes opened yet further, and she waved the men off. Scotch's grip loosened until most of her body once again came in contact with the bed, but he didn't let go. Kat could almost swear she heard a relieved sigh as his eyes closed on whatever expression they held. She didn't speak until the others had moved outside of the curtains that had been drawn to give her a measure of privacy from the other cots.

"What happened?"

Scotch looked up and met her gaze, his eyes dark. The muscles in his jaw tightened. When he spoke, it was low and through his teeth. "I was hoping you could tell me. We've been infiltrated. Someone introduced a sleeping agent into the barracks wing...a time-release gas grenade hidden in the central duct. The atmospheric sensors were disabled. Someone set up an induction fan to force the fumes into every compartment in the wing." His grip tightened on her shoulders once more until she grunted at the pain and tried to pry his hands away. He didn't seem to notice as he went on.

"He's gone. Sarge is gone."

Kat gasped and stopped fighting against Scotch's hold. If not for his hands on her she would have curled in a ball. Grief and rage and confusion darted around inside her like a rat trapped in a cage. Sarge couldn't be gone, not in such a senseless way. He was in charge of her unit, sure, but he was also a friend...no, family. Actually, after what they'd been through, closer than family, which said a lot. Damn, if only her thoughts would stop swimming.

"They took him," Scotch went on, his tone lethal and low as he bent his head close to hers. "They took him, and we have to get him back."

His words arrowed past the faint buzzing still in her ears. Her head whipped up and this time Kat snarled.

If Scotch hadn't leaned in, he would have been safe.

But he did.

Instead of continuing to resist his grip, Kat used it to her advantage. She drew back and slammed her forehead into his frontal lobe. He didn't see it coming. Of course, she wasn't so pissed that she didn't pull back a bit at the end. No sense in knocking out the only person she was absolutely certain hadn't sold out to the pirates.

"Aw! Fuck!" Scotch swore. "Go'damnit!"

"You bastard," she snapped back at him. "You had me thinking he was dead!"

Med-bay personnel came streaming through the curtain before she and Scotch could truly get into it. They were smart this time; they'd sent in men with some muscle. Not that they needed it. Scotch was more than ready to get out of striking range.

"Sergeant, you have to leave now."

"Oh save it, we both are," Kat cut in as she swung her legs off of the bed. The hand not bracing her came up and brushed the sore spot forming on her forehead. She fought off a trace of dizziness and ignored the technicians' protests. The men fell silent, though, as she marched through med-bay, her backside bare in a classic hospital gown that hadn't changed one wit throughout time. Her lips twitched in a faint smile as she heard the "damn" breathed behind her in what sounded like Scotch's voice. Not that she cared who else saw—being in the military quickly stripped away any sense of body-consciousness—but Kat snagged a second gown from a nearby pile, shrugging into it like a robe.

On her way out, she noted only nine members of the 142nd were still in med-bay, other than Scotch and herself. "Where are the rest?" she called back over her shoulder.

"Those that have recovered were relocated to the crew quarters for now." Scotch had to raise his voice to be heard. Kat smirked as he caught up with her halfway to the lift. He had her neatly folded uniform under one arm.

"I could have you up on charges for striking a superior officer."

"Ranking, maybe..." she drawled, with hints of her PawPaw's voice seeping into her tone. Scotch pouted in response and rubbed at the bruise darkening his forehead.

"Anyway," Kat went on, "we don't have time for that bullshit. Sarge is out there somewhere waiting on us."

The pout vanished.

They headed to the barracks in silence. Once they were in the lift, Kat watched closely as the levels changed. Again, several decks before the barracks the lights fluxed, and the car slowed. Her eyes narrowed. Reaching out, she depressed the button to stop the lift, and then sent it back two levels. Once it got there she sent it to their original floor once more.

What? Scotch asked over the secure squad band, watching her closely.

She said nothing, but waited. Again, the unit fluxed precisely at the point it had before. Kat resisted the impulse to dart her gaze about the close compartment as she finally responded in the same manner. *The lift did that earlier, too. And now it's done it twice again. As my PawPaw likes to say: once is chance, twice is coincidence...three times is enemy action. Someone wanted to know when company was coming.*

Scotch grunted and nodded in agreement as the lift stopped at their level.

When the doors hissed open, Kat found herself greeted by security personnel with riot guns poised to fire. She tensed and stopped absolutely still. What she wouldn't give for her gauss...or at least some fatigues.

"Scotch?"

He stepped forward, and the guards slung their weapons and fell back to parade rest. Apparently, *he* had clearance. With a nod at the men, Scotch moved past them into the chamber. Glancing warily at the grinning security detail, Kat followed; as she passed their position, she was glad she'd thought to cover her back. She already felt naked enough without her weapon.

"You could have warned me," she hissed once they were well away from the guards.

Scotch merely put on a suffering look and ran his free hand over his forehead once more.

"Prick," she murmured and broke away, heading for the compartment she shared with four other members of the unit.

The first thing she noticed was her tablet computer sitting neatly on her footlocker when it should have still been locked inside. She swore and went right for it. Suddenly, Scotch was there, intercepting her before she could lay a hand on the case.

"I taught you better than that, Corporal," he growled.

She froze instantly, not used to Scotch really pulling rank. He was right, though; her lack of caution was both sloppy and foolish. Good way to get people killed. Good way to end up cubed.

"Sorry."

"Get dressed," Scotch ordered, holding out her uniform, and abruptly he left the billet. As soon as the hatch closed she stripped off the double set of gowns and drew the military-issue tee shirt and black fatigues on over her skivvies. She'd sheathed her combat dagger on her hip and had just slid a ship boot carefully over her pressure bandage when Scotch returned. He carried a cluster of odd items: latex gloves, a pouch of talc, what looked like an industrial hand wipe, and a thick, chunky flashlight. Perched on his head was a set of high-tech protective goggles. She'd forgotten Scotch had some demolitions training. She'd never seen him actually put it into practice, as it wasn't his primary MOS. He clearly knew his thing, though. Kat watched in fascination as he set the items down in a neat, orderly row, pulled on the gloves, and drew the goggles down over his eyes. He motioned for her to back away.

First, he picked up the powder and sprinkled it over the tablet. The stuff revealed nothing but the unblemished surface of the casing. "Kill the lights," he ordered, in that non-Scotch tone. Kat complied. When she turned, he had the squat light in his hands and was clicking it through a number of settings, the light altering with each one. Black light. Normal light. Ultraviolet. Supernova, and a few she didn't even have a made-up name for. It was almost ritualistic, only fast. *Click.* Trail the light over the tablet computer in the ceremonial pattern. Trail the beam along the thin gap between the bottom of the unit and the top of the locker. *Click.* Repeat. "Lights," he ordered.

"Sir, yes sir!"

"No signs of a trip wire or other trigger," he murmured as he ignored her wiseass attitude and gently ran his hands over the computer in a final check. Clearly confident the unit wasn't rigged to blow, Scotch motioned her forward. Kat moved closer and watched as he turned it on.

Upon seeing the screen image, Kat cursed loud enough that one of the guards opened the hatch and peered in.

"Sergeant?" Tension ran through the man's tone as his gaze went from her to Scotch, who had subtly shifted until the guard didn't have a line of sight on the tablet.

"Sorry," Kat answered for him. "Bumped my foot...." Tugging up on her uniform leg she bared the bandage on her left ankle. The guard just stared at her, a long look down to her ankle and up again, less like he doubted her, more like he remembered the earlier view. She allowed steel to infiltrate her gaze. "Thanks, we're good."

Scotch didn't need to give her a look for her to know he was annoyed with her. "Thank you, soldier. You can return to your post." It wasn't like the guy could argue; Scotch outranked him too. Kat resisted the urge to peer through the hatch to confirm the guard had moved back across the room.

"Low profile, Alexander," Scotch muttered beneath his breath. "Try to remember we *like* not being noticed right now."

She nodded but said nothing as he turned back to the tablet.

And bit back a curse of his own.

Someone left her log-in window open. Typed in the user id field were the words: BRING EVERYTHING. Vague enough, but Kat knew exactly what was being demanded. The bad guys wanted the data, not just the specs on the *Rommel*—which they presumably now had once they cracked Sarge's encrypted copy—but the computer cores as well. There must be data there the pirates didn't want them to access.

The message wasn't all, though. Stuck to the keyboard frame, as if she'd left a note for herself, were a set of navigation coordinates. There was something else visible on the screen, but the log-in window was in the way. Kat hesitated before reaching out to the touchpad, looking to Scotch for permission.

"Well it's not like they're going to sabotage the thing when they want something from us." Still, before stepping out of her way he tore open the hand wipe and sanitized the keypad and any other part of the computer she might touch. He then pulled off the protective gloves over the soiled hand wipe and dumped it all in the waste basket by the door.

Kat stepped forward and leaned down to the touchpad. As she typed her code the log-in window closed, and an incoming message alert was visible. Her nerves tingling, Kat clicked it open to reveal an image file of Sarge, unconscious on a beach somewhere, looking like nothing so much as a relaxing tourist. Or he would have, if not for the BDUs and the hint of a bound wrist just visible where his arms crossed behind his head. She rattled a few keys trying to get as much data as possible, but whoever had sent this had some tech savvy because the electronic footprints had been erased.

"What the hell?" Kat whipped around until she could see Scotch's face. "How long were we out?"

"You've been out for six hours; we estimate Sarge has been missing for a little longer than that."

"Six!" Well, that explained the shake-up call in med-bay. Scotch never had been very patient.

Scotch nodded, concern and exhaustion shading his expression. "You got the lightest dose. Those billeted furthest from the main vent came out of it first. Those closest are mostly still down. One or two went under hard.

He looked grim. "I was the only one not hit." Of course, he'd been in med-bay...arguing. "When you entered the barracks the lingering gas triggered the atmospheric sensors in the lift, which hadn't been tampered with. That alerted Environmental."

Something wasn't right about this.

Okay...something *beyond* the obvious wasn't right about this.

Kat's chest muscles tightened as she processed what Scotch said. She looked back at the photograph, and her nerves jangled uncomfortably as the potential threat became clearer: What if the *Rommel's* ranks weren't the only ones compromised?

Making sure he watched, Kat moved her fingers over the keyboard. In part, she searched her system for malware the pirates may have left behind, but she also used the motions to disguise a few hand signals. Every unit had their own code, a secret way to communicate in the field. She flashed the sign for 'infiltrator' and then briefly glanced up to catch the sergeant's eye. Scotch's grimace deepened. Kat made another slight gesture signifying 'fake' and nodded at the image still on her screen. At that one Scotch looked confused.

"Figures," Kat muttered aloud. "We're stuck here breathing in canned air, and Sarge lands on the perfect beach somewhere, working on his tan."

It was obvious the moment her meaning came clear to Scotch. He himself had pointed out to her there were no perfect beaches in this sector, and certainly not within a six-hour transit window. Scotch's left hand moved; ran through his hair, scratching his ear along the way. The message masked: Play along.

"Someone's gonna pay."

Kat nodded, then pointed at the coordinates; "Any idea where that is?"

Scotch's expression was grim. "Not a clue."

They didn't even know if the pirates actually had Sarge, or if this engineered image was completely bogus. Kat swore heatedly as she stripped the note from the housing and shut the system down. "There's not much chance these navs will take us to him."

"Nope. Seriously unlikely."

Kat smiled anyway. It was a nasty smile. She could tell just by the feel of it.

"But I bet we can get someone there to lead the way."

Scotch nodded. His eyes looked hard, but his expression was so neutral it was scary. Kat shivered. He reached out and brushed her jaw. Odd for him to do, but she got the message and activated her bonejack.

"Go on, you," he said to her. "Now you're decent, head back to med-bay and check on the rest of the unit. Make sure everyone reports to the new crew quarters, Deck Gamma-18," he instructed her aloud. But over the bonejack he continued, *It's 0430 hours right now, we deploy no later than 0530. Get those coordinates to Campbell so he can plot a course, then prep the unit for deployment; anyone asks we still have a scheduled live-fire exercise.*

"What about you?" she asked by the same means, then vocalized for the benefit of the guards and anyone else listening; "Yes, Sergeant."

Her jaw buzzed as Scotch continued over the 'jack, *I was cleared for entry in here so I could inspect the barracks for any other...surprises and disable them. I best get to that, and see what else I can't learn about our 'friends' at the same time.*

He grinned as she left and Kat was reminded of her earlier smile.

*   *   *

Where's Dalton? | *We lost Campbell.*

Kat and Scotch both spoke over the squad band at the same time. Kat barely felt the ripple along her jaw she was so worked up. She said nothing and waited for Scotch to go on.

What?! His tone clearly indicated he wanted to have heard her wrong.

Kat repeated herself. *We lost Campbell.*

Silence. *I'll be right there.*

Five minutes later Scotch stalked into the common room of the crew quarters. He headed right for her. Even in the midst of battle, she'd never seen a more intense expression on his face.

Kat's teeth ground and she swallowed hard, feeling the ripple of tense muscles all the way to her feet. As he approached, she reached into her pocket and pulled out the contents. By the time he was in front of her, her fingers uncurled to reveal the all-too-familiar sight of a compressed carbon cube: Campbell's physical remains.

"Soldier, report."

Kat complied, her voice kept flat and neutral only by rigid control. "According to the report registered by the medtech on duty, at 0400 hours Corporal Anthony Campbell succumbed to complications triggered by a delayed reaction to the foreign substance inhaled into his system."

By the time she finished reporting her voice acquired a hard edge, and Scotch had gone from white, to deep red, to white again, the expression on his face both uncharacteristic and disturbing. Kat was sure it must be similar to her own.

"Where. Is. Dalton?" Scotch's voice vibrated with cold, quiet rage.

Kat's breath caught. What had he found in his search? His fingers flickered in the sign she'd used earlier. 'Infiltrator'.

Kat's grip tightened on the cube, and her temper stirred. Betrayal was never easy to take, but when it was someone you'd fought life-and-death beside...It was hard for Kat to keep her expression blank. "Corporal Dalton is unaccounted for."

There was only one place Dalton would head: the *Teufel*. They had to assume she had Sarge, which meant, other than the actual encryption code, she had everything she needed in one tidy package, if she managed to launch before they caught up to her. The *Teufel* wouldn't be easy for Dalton to manage alone—*God help them, let her be alone*—but it wasn't impossible either.

If that happened, Sarge was as good as cubed.

Apparently, Scotch was of a similar mind.

He nodded at Campbell's remains.

"Keep that safe for now, Kittie," he said. "Sarge'll need it in a while."

Turning to the assembled unit, his stance and expression warned each and every one of them that disloyalty would be met with extreme prejudice. If there were any other traitors among them, they had to be pissing themselves on the inside.

Kat immediately nixed that thought. If she started doubting the rest of her teammates, the unit was doomed. Cohesion would be lost and with it their edge. The key was to be alert, not suspicious. She blanked her mind of any misgiving and focused on Scotch.

"I will not take the place of a damn fine commander when there is anything I can do to put him back in it," he said. "So grab your weapons and follow me, or get the hell out of my way."

Kat, gauss rifle in hand, followed in lockstep with him as he went out the hatch heading for the docking bay.

*   *   *

They didn't storm the shuttle.

It would have felt good, but it also would have backed Dalton into a corner. Not that that wasn't where they wanted her...they just didn't want her aware she was in it. Instead, they stopped one level above and gathered in a huddle.

"Diaz, Connor, Danzer, Kopeky...you're going EVA. I need you to institute a security lockdown of the docking collar and disable the release mechanism. You make our ship a permanent part of the *Rommel* if you have to, understood?"

"Acknowledged," they answered, their tones low and intent, their responses in near-perfect synch.

Scotch gave them a sharp nod and sent them on their way. Silently the men moved off to do his bidding. He then turned to the rest of the unit, quickly splitting them into four-man squads, each with their own coordinated task.

"Kat, you're with me," he said as he headed back to the lift. "Leave your weapon here."

"Yes, Corp...*what?!*"

He pivoted and gave her a hard look. "Leave. The weapon. Here. Or do you want Dalton to know we're on to her?"

Kat's grip tightened on her rifle. Her teeth clenched and her neck popped at just the thought of going in not loaded for bear. But he was right. It wasn't Kat's only weapon; it was just her most obvious.

"You're a pain in my ass," she ground out. Thrusting the weapon into the hands of a teammate, she accepted his pistol in return, shoving it the waistband of her pants as she stalked after Scotch. "So, let's hear the plan."

"We go in like we're following their instructions, then we keep her talking so the others can do their jobs. If we have a chance to take her down, we do."

There was no one in sight as they exited the lift and made their way across the docking bay, not even the watch. Kat kept alert, her eyes roving across the area searching for movement. As they drew closer it was clear the *Teufel* was there, but still in lock-down.

Kat cast a questioning, sideways glance toward Scotch as he entered his security code. She remained silent, though, and ready to follow his lead. It wasn't worth setting him off. He was pissed and clearly ready for a fight. She could see it in the glimmer that darkened his hazel eyes to hardened bronze. That was the only thing that gave any hint to his current disposition. Didn't matter, though.... Any adversary close enough to tell was already shit out of luck.

The two of them boarded the shuttle as if this were a standard pre-mission inspection. Scotch went in first. Ducking through the airlock portion of the vessel, Kat nearly ran up his ass. She could feel the tension pulsing off of him. "Hey, what gives?" she asked as she stepped around him and into the crew compartment of the shuttle. She thought she heard a sound from the cargo bay. She started to move in that direction when Scotch snapped out a sharp "no!" His hand came down on her arm. He drew her back, but suddenly the pull eased, though his grip did not. Kat glanced over her shoulder at him. The edge of her lip curled instantly, and she scowled. Her hand brushed the cube in her pocket. It looked more likely that poor Dalton wasn't unaccounted for after all. Disturbing to realize that the medbay staff had been infiltrated.

Very deliberately Kat reached up and lifted Scotch's hand from her so she could pivot full around. The entire time she was careful to move very slowly.

"Welcome back from the dead, *Campbell*," she spoke in tones of silken steel to the man standing behind and to the left of Scotch. "What happened? Did Hell throw you out for giving the Devils a bad name?"

Scotch's eyes narrowed. Message received. Not that he could do much with it. Turned out he had a pistol to his head. If Campbell hadn't been a dead man before, he certainly was now.

"You know, Alexander, that mouth of yours is about the only smart thing about you." Campbell responded. "You have two choices," the traitor told her, "Secure Sergeant Daniels, or I'll take him out."

Like the latter wasn't going to happen at some point anyway.

Kat looked down at the zip restraints Campbell held out but she didn't move to take them.

Scotch snarled and made as if to turn.

...Until the gun slammed upside his head. At the same time, Campbell used his free hand to jerk Scotch off balance. "Don't even try it, Daniels...I need her; you're just insurance.

"Just to be clear: you play nice, Alexander, and Scotch here doesn't bleed," Campbell went on. Kat suspected there was an unspoken 'yet' in there somewhere. "We want the data, all of it, and the encryption codes. Now get him zipped before I make it a non-issue."

Snatching the zip-ties, she started to circle around the two of them. Campbell's gun clicked as he thumbed the hammer back.

"Like I didn't get the same training you did...do it from there. Just reach your arms around him, and make it good and secure."

Kat's mind scrambled to identify her options. Her only weapons were her combat knife and the borrowed pistol, but drawing either would be too visible. Campbell would have time to fire before she even got either unsheathed. Her hand-to-hand training wasn't much good at the moment either given that Scotch stood between her and the enemy. She had to hope an opportunity would come clear. Or at least that they could stall Campbell long enough for the Devils to close in...which meant she had no choice but to comply.

It was like hugging a statue. Even with Scotch cooperating—albeit unwillingly—Kat had to press herself obscenely close before she could secure his wrists behind him. While she did that something hard shoved into her gut. She let her eyes drift up slow, as if she was trying not to focus on this forced intimacy, and met Scotch's eye. He kept his gaze hooded and every muscle clearly taut, but he remained absolutely still.

Except for his hips. He deliberately shifted them forward, his eyes never leaving hers. She gasped. A second ago she would have thought it was impossible for the two of them to get any closer—short of stripping off their clothes and making a concerted effort to occupy the same space—but just that subtle press was enough for Kat to realize that wasn't his anatomy poking her, it was the hilt of a combat knife. Then, not so subtly, Scotch deliberately teetered, as if off balance, like when Campbell had jerked him back earlier.

Kat kept her eyes on Scotch, catching the minute shift of his gaze toward the traitor. She drew a deep breath and let her eyes drift closed, then slowly brought them open again, in silent acknowledgement.

Resting her left hand on Scotch's chest as she drew her right back around to his side, Kat allowed a look of calculated vulnerability to flit across her features. Seemingly in response, Scotch dropped his chin, as if in defeat, but more importantly taking his head out of alignment with the barrel of Campbell's gun.

It was risky, but it wasn't like they had a lot of options. And still, for a fraction of a moment, she hesitated as visions of Scotch with the top of his head blown off short-circuited her nerves. And then his jaw flexed, sending static-like tingles along her bonejack, but no words. He didn't need them, she understood completely.

Then there was no time to wonder. A crash came from the cargo bay, as if something heavy fell to the deck. Kat couldn't have arranged a better distraction if she'd tried. For just a second, Campbell's attention veered. Not knowing if either of them would see the outside of the shuttle ever again, Kat shoved Scotch into him with her left hand even as she drew the combat knife with the other. Bodies tumbled to the deck. The gun fired once. A scream ricocheted through the shuttle as Kat came down hard on top of the others. Something soft gave beneath her knee. Someone screamed again.

Kat couldn't worry about any of that now. She'd already lunged, her left hand locked on Campbell's gun, shoving it down and away before he could fire again. Her right hand brought the combat knife to bear, letting momentum carry the blade down through Campbell's eye and into his brain. The body spasmed, jerking and thudding against the deck until everyone and everything was coated with the traitor's blood.

Scrambling back into a crouch, with the knife still in hand, Kat yelled and lunged again as someone came at her from the shadows of the cargo bay. A solid kick from that direction numbed her wrist and hand.

"Stand down, Alexander," the approaching figure ordered, stumbling from the cargo bay into the crew compartment.

Kat swore, and her legs buckled as the adrenaline ran out.

"Well, I'll be damned," Scotch said, as she landed atop him. Over the squad band Kat heard him give the Devils the order to abort.

Sarge stood over them, swaying slightly. The right side of his face was a mass of bruises, and someone had wrapped his left arm in a field dressing from wrist to elbow. His hands were bound in front of him, though Kat suspected they hadn't started out that way. There was fresh blood on the gauze and what looked like a smudge of bootblack on his sleeve. There were pronounced lines around his mouth, and his eyes were glazed with pain. Beneath that Kat recognized the deep, sharp pinch of recent betrayal.

He toed Campbell's body. "Thanks for taking out the trash."

On *Last Man Standing*

A great movie was once released with the tagline, "In space, no one can hear you scream." This story gets around that by having subvocal communication, but it still has echoes of Ridley Scott's classic, only it's not an alien that menaces a company ship, but something just as deadly. Luckily, ships have engineers. I think what I loved best about this story was that, if it wasn't for the guys who do science, everyone would die.

—Keith R.A. DeCandido,
author of *Dragon Precinct,*
Unicorn Precinct, and *Goblin Precinct*

LAST MAN STANDING

We are ready to try our fortunes *To the last man.*

—*William Shakespeare,*
King Henry IV. Part II. ACT IV Scene 2.

The *Caliphus* landed on the moon MineCorps had designated A-RCK-01 amid a cloud of fine, rust-colored particles. Dust was everywhere, invasive. If not for the high-grade ion field protecting the surface of the ship and its various venting and intake systems they would already be in trouble. From an impartial view point, it was a spectacular effect: an aura of red dust limning the ship from ten inches past the buffer. The crew, however, was ill at ease, left to imagine the total encapsulation they could only view in swirling fragments on the monitors.

Tom Henry was beyond concerned. As the mission engineer, he, more than anyone else, was aware that the ionic drive was not designed to combat such a constant assault. The particles made him uneasy. For lack of a better word, he thought of the matter as dust, but it didn't move right; it appeared slick, almost greased as it slid along the ion field like it was trying to get through. He held back a shudder. This was bad. Their orders were to set up dirtside and stockpile ore until the star-freighter *O'Connor* arrived. Not only was that not currently possible, but every instinct he had screamed at him to lift off immediately, and the contract be damned.

"Your assessment, Mr. Henry?" Captain Jared Troy asked, rising from the chair and coming to stand at his shoulder.

Tom ran a series of computations before responding. The data scrolling across the monitor reinforced his concerns. "The dust storm extends beyond the range of our hull sensors, I can't pinpoint when it will end. We're okay for now, but we have twenty to twenty-five standard hours before the system is overwhelmed if it maintains this density."

Captain Troy straightened and turned toward the rest of the crew. "You heard the man, suit up and get out there, you rock hounds. This has become a hit-and-run extraction."

"Sir," Tom interrupted. "I don't know what this storm will do to their suits, or the equipment." The moon was large, with three-quarters Earth-standard gravity and an oxygen-rich atmosphere, but the chemical composition of the air was not friendly to humans.

Troy's mouth twisted in annoyance. His eyes narrowed and he leaned back over the console. "Planetary evaluation ruled out a corrosive atmosphere and did not register anything over a level-one bacterium, correct?"

"Yes, sir."

"So, the worse we should be facing is some dirt, yes?"

Tom looked away, his expression tight. He focused on the monitor and by sheer will forced his voice neutral. "It would seem so, Captain."

But he didn't believe it.

Troy moved across the deck to the hatch. "Donovan," he called into the crew compartment. The foreman, climbing into her EVA suit, looked up, her expression closed as she continued to slide on and seal her gauntlet. "Sir?"

"Here's where that mech unit of yours proves its worth. Get it out there pounding rock...and double the crew while you're at it, we can't risk the Chomps so get the extra men running sack relay," he ordered. "I want a constant stream of ore feeding in to the cargo bay at all times."

Kate Donavan nodded sharply in acknowledgement as she tugged her helmet into place over her short bristle of dark brown hair, Kate's jaw worked as she toggled her comm active: "Anything else, sir?"

"Check-in is half standard. We don't know how much time we have so monitor your systems closely. Any sign of malfunction is to be reported immediately."

Two thirds of the mining crew scrambled to comply, the other four remained huddled around the monitors, makeshift markers changing hands as they made book on everything from the time the ion shield would fail to how much ore would end up in the hold before it did.

Tom Henry kept his eyes locked on his station monitor; already sections of shield sensors showed signs of strain. He continued to watch, his lips moving silently in prayer.

✳   ✳   ✳

Kate Donovan regularly worked side by side with her crew. In part this was to make sure no one slacked or took unnecessary risk to secure a bonus, but it was also so she could watch Jean-Paul Marot's back. She had to, no one else would. Not even Jean-Paul Marot. The titanium-plated ass had a death wish.

No one else aboard knew their new mining mech was actually a cybernetic prototype. To them he was just another bit of hardware. Only Kate knew and by contract she couldn't reveal to anyone there was a human soul beneath the chassis. It had been a hard contract to win and though she had wondered at the reason for the odd clause when she'd triumphantly signed the deal, she also hadn't realized how hard it would be to keep silent. Jean-Paul did his best to act the part of inhuman mech, but in a hundred little ways he betrayed his humanity, even if she was the only one to realize it. She had lost count of the thoughtful ways he'd helped her out on shift, both with tricky tasks and unforeseen mishaps. He'd even saved her ass a time or three.

She followed close behind as he passed through the waiting decontamination unit and headed down the ramp to the planet's surface, pickaxe in his right robotic hand, massive jack hammer held casually in the other. Red dust swirled disturbingly around him the moment he was past the ionic shield, adhering to the flexible Kevlar-fabric laminate that sheathed his frame. He unconsciously swiped his optics clear across his arm as no mechanical being would have and headed for rock.

Hey, JP, Kate subvocalized across her comm on his private band, *not too far. There's plenty of surface ore close to the ship. Start with the port-side outcrop there while I organize Troy's bucket brigade.* He didn't acknowledge her command verbally, but set to breaking up the easy-access payload that had placed this moon at the top of MineCorp's A-list. She toggled the comm to the crew frequency and started barking instructions to the rest of the shift workers. In short order, sacks of dust-covered iron ore were being ferried into the hold.

*   *   *

Everyone earned out their bonus that day. They were beat. Everything was red with dust—right down to the men. Between the mech and the extra men, the ship's holds were full before second shift was halfway through and the crew even managed to set up the steel storage hoppers on the surface and started filling them. Once those were full they would be shuttled to the *O'Connor* on its arrival. For now, the entire crew called it quits for the day. As the final hold hatch closed, Tom keyed the sequence locking the ship off from the decon unit. When it was secure he remotely extended the vent shaft until it pushed through the ion shield. A clever one-way valve on the end of the shaft kept the moon's atmosphere from contaminating the ship.

Okay, Donovan, he commed the foreman. *You and you're 'hounds are cleared for decon.* He felt his tension ease a bit as the monitor displayed the men and women piling back into the ship with their gear. The mech unit was the last aboard. Once it cleared the walkway Tom spoke over the crew frequency: *Please stand clear of the closing door, decontamination commencing.*

Directed jets of air dislodged particles of foreign matter from the crew while fans in the duct system sucked the contaminants down the flexible vent shaft and ejected it past the ion shields before retracting back into place. Then, though all of the crew had been through the process before, Tom issued the standard warning for the next stage of decontamination: *Please close your eyes in preparation for low-grade irradiation.* As the final stage completed, Tom Henry ran a scan on the chamber before sounding the all-clear and initiating the release sequence.

Several of the returning crew, including Donovan, were in the process of loosening the seals on their environment suits as they waited for the hatch lock to disengage when a low curse transmitted across the crew frequency. One of the men had dropped his pick. He seemed to sway as he bent to retrieve it, then crumpled to the floor.

Shit! Donovan's startled voice came over the comm. *Do not release your seals!* she ordered the rest of her crew as she moved toward the miner. Tom immediately keyed the interrupt, setting off the automatic alert, and reversing the release. It looked like John Palmer, but it was hard to tell. He wasn't out cold, but he remained flat on the deck as Donovan conducted an eyes-on inspection.

Tom's earlier unease returned as he watched the monitor. There was no sound feed currently active in the chamber, but it was clear from her expression that the foreman reprimanded the crewman. Tom switched on the intercom and the internal recorders. "Donovan, report."

She looked up, her navy blue eyes darkened by the displeasure clearly visible through her faceplate. "Mr. Henry, please send a medtech to the decon quarantine unit, Crewman Palmer apparently sustained a suit breach in the field. Injury appears minimal, but shows signs of dust contamination." Her words propelled Tom's tension to another level all together. Bad enough the potential of some foreign contagion, worse, in Tom's opinion, that Kate Donovan was at risk. He sent the order to medbay and continued to monitor the decon unit.

"Aw come on, boss, it's barely even a scratch!" Palmer interrupted. One hard look from Donovan and he cut off his protest.

"Not a word, Palmer," she growled as she helped the man up. "Safety protocol exists for a reason. You will observe it from here on out or it will be my boot kicking you out the door. Am I understood?"

Tom watched as she turned and scanned the room. Her face tensed, concern overshadowed by anger as she clearly noted those that had breached the seals on their protective suits. With a nod toward quarantine she spoke to her crew in a controlled voice. "Okay, Palmer, Simms, Chou, Colman...pick a bunk and get your butts inside. The rest of you, remain suited." She then turned to face the monitor.

"Mr. Henry, please reinitialize decon procedure," she requested, closing the door behind her as she entered the quarantine cell next to Palmer's.

❋   ❋   ❋

Jean-Paul watched as his single link to humanity closed herself in what potentially could be her coffin. That shouldn't matter, but even after the repeat decon completed he remained facing her cell.

Miners were a superstitious lot; if they ever learned of his past, those standing around him would as likely as not shove him off the ship; out with the bad penny, and all that. If anything happened to Donovan they wouldn't have to. He'd tried to keep distant, but in the silence of his mind he considered her a friend. A dangerous thing, in his experience...for the friend. All too often, people in his proximity ended up dead. One accident after the other had left him the last man standing. The first had landed him in this mobile metal suit. The second landed him in hell as the suit forced him to take another's life to preserve his own...and he could do nothing but comply. That chemical command was the first thing he'd forced the Corporation to deactivate, when he'd sued them to become a free agent, but the damage had been done. In his own mind, it had cost him the last of his humanity. That was one of the reasons he'd become a roamer, taking only short-term contracts before moving on to another crew. Less time for his shitty luck to kick in, less opportunity for people he liked to pay for it.

This time the strategy had failed him. He suspected it was because Donovan reminded him very much of Chloe Kendall, the last friend he'd allowed himself since he realized what kind of monster the Corporation had created in him. His hand unconsciously tightened on the haft of the pickaxe until the sensors in the "fingertips" registered a deformation in the metal.

Go on, JP, Donovan cut into his thoughts. *It's just a precaution. We'll be out of here before the* O'Connor *hits orbit.*

For the first time in almost a year, Jean-Paul spoke, if only over his private frequency: *Quarantine is seventy-two hours, the* O'Connor *arrives in forty-eight.*

So I suck at math! Get out of here, we'll be fine! She waved him away with the gauntlet she'd just removed. *And don't forget to run a systems scan as soon as you hit your bay, I want a full report, even if I am on forced down time.*

Jean-Paul brought his pick hand up in salute, before slowly turning and leaving the now-empty decontamination unit, passing the harried medtech on his way through the main service corridor that ran the length of the ship. JP silently moved through the crew compartment toward his own bay only to have his preservation mixture flood in chemical-response to the ever-present betting markers transferring from hand to hand.

It took him a lot of effort to resist tightening his grip with the anger and further damaging the equipment.

✳　　　✳　　　✳

Kate heard the chatter over the crew frequency long before she received word from anyone on the command staff.

The *O'Connor* was delayed by a meteor outburst. The trail was far-reaching and heavy with particles, obstructing the entire distance between the star-freighter and the *Caliphus*. Their flight crew were waiting for the shower to pass before continuing on to A-RCK-01, where the star-freighter would take up a geosynchronous orbit above the mining site until its massive cargo holds were full.

It could take many standard days for the route to clear. This delay could cost them every bonus written into the contract. Not to mention the hefty penalties that would be levied against them if they fell behind schedule. Tom Henry had warned her in a private message that Captain Troy had ordered the crews back on shift in between dust storms. The captain hadn't the decency to inform her himself. She was glad they were still making some progress, but with her trapped in here things were running less than smooth.

Rising from her bunk, Kate moved to her computer access, first checking for any messages from Tom or reports from her assistant foreman before checking on Palmer's status. He'd been put through the full spectrum of diagnostic testing, but all results were negative for any identifiable contagion or foreign antibody. The miner mostly slept, complaining about feeling weak and tired. The medtech suspected the onset of anemia and was treating Palmer accordingly, but protocol demanded the four of them remain in quarantine the full seventy-two hours. Time was nearly up.

"Hey, Mac, you have a timer set out there or something?" she called out over the open intercom as she settled back on her bunk. "It's not like one of us is going to up and keel over in the last ten minutes."

She saw the medtech look up from his most recent batch of tests and cock his head. "Let me see if I remember the phrase properly...'safety protocol exists for a reason...'"

"Yeah, yeah, talk to my ass, why don't you?" she groused back. Every person on the ship had overheard her comments to Palmer. She was the first to agree, but the only thing she showed symptoms of was boredom and frustration. Outside this ship was a site they'd contracted to mine and in her head a clock counted down to their deadline. Her eyes never left the monitor.

Finally, Mac Taylor punched a few keys on his system and pushed back from his chair. Moments later, the lights on the monitoring sensors lining her walls blinked out. Kate was up and waiting at the door to her cell before the hermetic seal parted. As she pushed through into the decon unit proper, the doors to either side of her swung open as well. She turned and scanned her crewmen; Simms, Chou, and Colman looked a little twitchy, much as she herself felt, but otherwise hale. Palmer...he looked like something bit into him hard. Pale and tense, with an odd blue cast to the whites of his eyes. A sideways glance at Mac, who didn't seem fazed, was only marginally reassuring.

"We cleared for duty, then?" she asked.

"Except for your buddy Palmer here, yeah. Need to build up his iron levels a bit before you send him out on shift again."

Kate nodded and turned to her crewman. "You got lucky, John. You go get fixed up, and while you're on medical leave, you be sure to read your procedures manual, am I understood?"

With a disgruntled look at drawing quarter pay, Palmer nodded and followed Mac from the chamber. Kate turned back to the others.

"Well? What are you waiting for? You've just had a three-day vacation...get to work!" The three of them groaned as they preceded her out of the decontamination unit. It was damn good to move further than eight full steps in a row; it was even better to walk out under her own power, with the freedom of the ship and beyond still open to her. Kate headed for the crew compartment to catch up on the status of the operation. There was only so much she could run by wire.

"Hey," she called out as she entered the chamber from the main shaft. "I see an awful lot of loafing going on here."

Her comment was met by laughs and groans and shouts of "Look who's talking!" All of it was good-natured. It was like breathing uncanned air after the isolation of quarantine. She swept a sharp glance around the room, her eye gleaming. "So, who took the book on me?" More groans, followed by dirty socks and empty meal packs lobbed at Tom Henry, whose cheeks were amusingly flushed at being caught out. Strange, he usually stayed out of the betting. Glancing at Tom, Kate allowed the warmth she felt to show in her eyes as she indulged in a faint smile, her first in three days. "You, sir, can afford to buy me a steak, then." More laughter and the subtle air of tension in the compartment dissipated. Tom looked stunned, though pleased, and slowly nodded, but she'd already moved past, going to check on Jean-Paul.

"It's not there," a voice called from behind her.

"What?" Kate turned and spied Captain Troy standing in the command deck hatchway.

"It's not there," the captain repeated. "I sent it out with the shift. Your crew was falling behind."

Kate ate her response to that criticism, merely nodding in acknowledgement as she pivoted and headed for her equipment locker, all the while expecting Troy to summon her back. She didn't like him or the risks he took with her people, but she was a contractor on this job and he was the boss. That meant she had to play nice; which also meant she stayed as far from his proximity as she could manage. She breathed a little easier with each step she took away from him.

Then she heard the sound of boots behind her, and the clang of another locker opening nearby. She looked over into Troy's reproving gaze and actually had wistful thoughts of quarantine.

✳   ✳   ✳

Hey, JP, coming at your back, with company. the subvocal voice coming over his comm, combined with the familiar address triggered a complex chemical response the moment Jean-Paul heard it. Annoyance, chased by relief, pleasure, and warmth; it was hard to focus under the bombardment. He carefully put down the equipment he was using and pivoted around.

It was a mistake on several levels. First, what machine would halt its given task randomly? Second, why should it matter to him that Kate Donovan was well and out of quarantine? Machines did not have friends. JP had to endlessly remind himself of that. He had a practical reason for being glad to see her, though. In her absence, Captain Troy had been running Jean-Paul nonstop like a piece of heavy equipment still under warranty. The chassis could take it, but JP's brain was getting loopy, making it hard to manage the servos and gyros that controlled his mobility and balance; more than once he caught himself swaying. No small concern when you were a 400-pound metal behemoth surrounded by frail men of flesh. What was more concerning, he'd started getting a few low-level alerts from his exoskeleton's monitoring system.

Kate came up to him and looked him over before turning to scan the mounds of ore waiting for the rest of the crew to catch up on stowing. Without a word, she walked over to the storage bins and peered inside.

JP, how long have you been out here? she asked across his private frequency.

He remained silent. It wasn't like she really needed an answer to know he'd been out here too long, and talking to her was a bad habit to get into.

You pig-headed ass! she hissed, before turning to Captain Troy. "Thank you, sir, for your diligence on my behalf during the quarantine period." She kept her tone carefully neutral. "Things appear nicely ahead of schedule here. If your inspection is complete, I need to run some *mandatory* maintenance on the JPM unit. We can't have it breaking down, not with the nearest repair facility light-years away."

Jean-Paul had the urge to laugh without the means to do so. Troy's face turned neared puce in color, but there was no way he could argue.

As if there were no question, Kate turned and headed back toward the *Caliphus*. With extreme care, JP followed.

❋   ❋   ❋

"What the hell!" Kate's hands clenched and unclenched reflexively as she stared at the diagnostic report spit out by JP's charging and maintenance station. There were half a dozen warnings. Nothing serious, but definitely concerning and detrimental. Best to start with the simplest issue first. "You've got a problem with your ground wire." Moving to the indicated section, she detached the protective Kevlar skin and opened the access panel so she could eyeball the situation. "Hmmm...must have been a defective batch, looks like some of the copper coating is worn away. The steel core is starting to oxidize." Taking a can of compressed air, she blew away the corrosion to get a better look at the situation. Then she noticed another spot on a nearby o-ring. In fact, anything that wasn't titanium seemed to have sprouted rust. There wasn't much, and it wasn't bad, but it was disturbing. Better to replace it all now before the situation got worse. A trip to the spare parts locker uncovered sufficient replacements. She was even able to swap out most of the corroded bits with titanium, rather than the older steel alloy.

"Okay, pal, I'm going to have to power you down for maintenance." A sound came from JP, short, sharp, and cut off, but she didn't need to hear it to know he was very unhappy with this part. "Don't worry, it shouldn't take long." Maybe it was her imagination, but the silence that met her reassurance seemed thick with displeasure. Couldn't be helped, though; she couldn't do this kind of repair with his system active. With care, she reached in and disconnected the ground wire first. As she extracted it, the intercom squawked an alert.

"Aw, *sh*-it!" Kate swore as the sound startled her, causing her to jerk back. A sharp pain went through her arm as some internal part of the cybernetic unit gouged her hand. This was the very reason she'd deactivated her comm. Fool that she was, she hadn't thought to kill the intercom as well. Her breath hissed out as she gritted her teeth against the pain.

"Donovan, report!"

A few more curses ensued before she managed to extract herself from JP's inner workings. Heading for the intercom, she slapped the toggle active with her uninjured hand as blood dripped from the other.

She quickly wrapped it in a clean rag from a pile she had nearby.

"What?" Her tone was less than civil and there was a long pause on the other end.

"You're needed in medbay immediately."

How convenient; thanks to them, she had a need to be there. "Give me ten minutes."

"But..." the tech protested. Kate heard the slightest thread of panic in the word. There were some frenzied sounds in the background. Probably some rock hound got a little juiced up. Well, they would have to wait.

"I said ten minutes. It's the best you're getting." She released the toggle and returned to JP, quickly, but carefully replacing the ground wire. She would have taken the book on that one. Finished in Guinness record time, she closed the access panel and powered his system back up.

JP made a sound that was almost a gasp as his sensors and motor functions were restored.

"Sorry," Kate said in a rush. "I'm not done yet, emergency. Didn't want to leave you in limbo. Be back as quick as I can." Not waiting for an answer—it wasn't like he'd talk to her anyway—she flew from the compartment and down the corridor leading to medbay. *It's probably nothing,* she told herself, but as she neared the medics' domain there was an ungodly shriek, followed by several crashes. Cursing and thuds continued to pour down the corridor.

"Aw, crap!" Maybe not quite nothing.... She picked up her pace until she full-out ran, grabbing the edge of the open hatch and slingshotting herself into the compartment. Her breath caught in her throat and she stopped short at the sight of Palmer. At first glance he looked like someone had put a dusty shipsuit on one of those terracotta warriors from ancient China and then brought it to life. But when she saw his face it was less serene, than taut and hard like granite, etched in agony. He could barely stand straight as he tore at the med supply cabinet, frantically trying to get it open, as Mac and the other tech fought to restrain him. Each time he moved a cloud of dust particles swirled in the air around him.

"John!" Kate yelled.

Palmer's thrashing efforts stilled as he turned to look at her, his gaze a curious mix of hatred and terror and pleading. "Make it stop," he groaned. Now that he wasn't flailing around she could see that his body trembled and his teeth had cut through his lip. The blood marking his face was more brown than red, barely visible against the dust permeating his skin. "Please," he begged. Before anyone could move Palmer tensed, his back arching as a high, thin gasp fought its way from his throat. His eyes rolled into his head as he crumpled to the floor.

Kate looked up and met Mac's panicked gaze. "What the *hell* was he doing dirtside without a protective suit?" she asked.

Mac gave a twitching shake of his head, and then another, but managed nothing more. Next to him, looking like she'd been on the losing end of a prize fight, Medtech Eva Sanchez wore a haunted expression as she brushed a bit of dust and blood from her cheek. "He hasn't been outside. He hasn't left medbay."

A tremor shook through Kate Donovan as she looked down at her fallen man. He was as red as the crew that just came off shift, and way too still. Her breath coming just a little quicker, she knelt beside him and started to feel for a pulse. Eva's hand darted out and smacked hers away.

Kate gave her a cutting look. "Like it isn't already too late for that." She reached out again, placing the tip of two fingers against Palmer's throat. It took a lot of effort to leave them there long enough to be sure he was gone, before drawing them back. When she did she couldn't help rubbing at the slick, oily sensation of the dust on her skin as she tongued her comm active to the captain's private frequency.

"Troy," she hailed, "we have a problem."

✳   ✳   ✳

Having drawn monitoring duty, Tom Henry was alone on the command deck when the captain hurried through the hatch, clearly a man with a purpose. Clad in a full environmental suit, Troy had a large rucksack over each arm and another on his back. They were jammed full of supplies, with meal packs and other necessities sticking out the top of each of them.

Tom swiveled in his chair and waited expectantly. He could feel the puzzled expression creep across his face.

"Seal off the command deck, Mr. Henry, and prepare to lift off."

Without realizing it, Tom came to his feet. "Sir, there's a double shift crew still dirtside!"

The look on Troy's face burned along Tom's nerves like dry ice on bare skin. "Want to join them?"

"I don't know what's going on, but you are not stranding those men." Tom squared his shoulders and braced himself.

There was a mad glimmer in the captain's eye and there was something off about their color.

In two strides, Jared Troy stood at his side. Before Tom could react, the captain grabbed him by the shipsuit and raised a cutting torch to within an inch of his head. Troy's finger was on the switch. Tom tensed and prayed the frantic working of his jaw would be construed as a nervous response to the situation. He triggered the comm frequency assigned to Donovan and subvocally sent one word across the link: *Help!* Something must have betrayed him, though. Jerking him sharply off balance, the captain shoved him toward the hatch. With the torch still to his head, Tom dare not resist.

"On second thought, I'll cover takeoff myself."

The captain thrust Tom from the compartment with enough force to send him sprawling. Before he could gain his feet, the hatch closed and he heard the locking mechanism slide into place. Tom tried the manual override, but Troy had used his executive code to lock down in siege mode. Already the ship rumbled and groaned as her flight system powered up. There was no way to stop it now. While the designers had factored in the potential for mutiny, none of them had ever considered a scenario where it was the captain hijacking the ship.

A quick roll of his tongue across his lower jaw triggered every frequency aboard ship. "Code Red! All crew return to ship, secure for liftoff! Move it, people, *now!*" It didn't matter that Troy heard right along with everyone else; the crew had to be warned.

An incoming message across Donovan's frequency: *What the hell's going on, Tom?*

"You tell me! Troy's gone rogue, he's holed up on the command deck...he's initiating immediate launch, without everyone on board."

Silence, thick and heavy.

Palmer's dead.

"What?!"

He's dead...cause unknown.

It was like hitting a wall. That peculiar feeling a person gets when their grip on consciousness or reality slips, like everything is detached, muffled, safely distant; the mind lying to itself. "Oh, shit!" The words were hollow, like they came from the far end of a tunnel, even though the voice was his. Worry for Kate was the only thing crisp and clear to him.

Shake it off, Tom. We have to get those men back on board before it's too late.

There it was: something to focus on. "Yeah, I'm heading for the external hatch."

But it took him too long to get there. As he ran, the *Caliphus* rumbled and shook. At some point ahead of him, a man screamed as the engines engaged, forcing the hatch to close automatically. Tom reached his target moments too late. The first thing he saw was a wide crimson streak running the length of the wall panel that served as the mass-deployment ramp. At the base of that wall a crewman lay in a crumpled heap and a growing pool of blood. Two others stood close by, frozen in horror at what had just happened.

Cursing, Tom scrambled for a supply locker near the panel, pawing through it until he came up with an extra-long plastic zip tie. He moved to the injured man and looped the strip around the stump where the foot had been severed, yanking it tight until the blood ceased to pump across the floor. Staring in stunned silence at the bloody streak, Tom got the impression the crewman had made a leap for the ramp once it had already begun to close and could not clear his foot in time. It also occurred to Tom that there were only three miners in the compartment, leaving five men unaccounted for.

"Anyone else make it back on board?" he asked, praying the others had just ignored procedure and left the decontamination unit. But the two men standing shook their heads, guilt shadowing their eyes.

Jared Troy had a lot to answer for. Tom prayed those stranded had been far enough from the blast zone when the engines fired. Their environmental suits contained hydration packs capable of sustaining them for up to a week with strict rationing. They also contained a nutrient solution that would hold them at least as long. Assuming they'd been clear of the liftoff, there was the chance of rescue.

"Okay," Tom said, setting those thoughts aside for now. "We have a situation. You two are to remain suited until cleared by medical. Everything else will be explained when we're safe in orbit. Now help me get your friend strapped into one of those quarantine bunks, then secure yourself for launch." It was difficult to stand, let alone move against the forces of liftoff, but they all managed to strap in.

Donovan, he sent over the foreman's private frequency. *We only got three. One of them needs treatment for a traumatic amputation.*

She cursed quite impressively. *Better than none,* she replied. *Troy can't leave orbit as long as that meteor cloud is in the way...that will give us some time to salvage this situation. Meet me in medbay once the ship reaches apogee. We need to plan.*

✳   ✳   ✳

"The unmitigated bastard!" Kate seethed as she paced medbay waiting for the last of the crew to arrive. With her were the four off-shift miners, the two medtechs, and Hal, the third member of the flight crew, in charge of navigation. JP crouched out of the way in the med-chem shower, the only space large enough for him.

Her head whipped around as Tom Henry entered medbay, followed by the rest of the miners on board, the injured man supported in a chair carry between his suited crew mates. The medtechs scrambled to assist, but Kate's attention riveted on Tom. She glanced at the intercom by the hatch before speaking. The activation light remained dark.

"He's diverted all systems control to the command deck and cut us off from the interstellar comm. Can you get us in?"

Tom's brow furrowed as it took him a moment to process what she'd said. As he did, his gaze ran over her, lingering on her bandaged hand, while barely meeting her eye. She saw relief flicker across his expression as he nodded his head. "Yeah, it will take some time, but Troy doesn't know enough to keep me out all together."

"Good, get on it," she said. "We have to warn the *O'Connor* not to dock with the *Caliphus,* not until we know there's no danger."

Tom had just turned toward the systems substation in the corner when Mac called out from across the room, his words muffled slightly by the mask covering his mouth and nose.

"Donovan! We have trouble!"

Kate, with Tom right behind her, hurried across the bay where the medtechs were working on the injured miner. They'd just started cutting him from his suit, all except the injured leg. Kate grabbed a mask and slipped it on before she rested her hand on Mac's shoulder, leaning around him for a look. She hadn't been able to tell who the injured man was when they'd first brought him in, still suited and slumped over. She saw now that it was Bobby Fletcher, the new man on the crew. *Just a kid, really,* she thought, and she ached for him as she glanced at his mangled ankle. Something struck her as she took in the color of the drying blood, echoing a memory she couldn't place.

And then he looked at her.

His eyes flickered open and he looked right at her. Pain filled his gaze and the whites of his eyes had a decidedly blue cast to them. Kate's breath caught as he shut them again and a rust-tinged tear escaped, leaving a trail in the faint dust she hadn't realized coated his tan skin. Then the memory clicked: just like Palmer, only much faster. His body began to twitch with increasing violence. Seeing that, Mac and Eva scrambled, forcing Kate back as they grabbed the edge of the gurney and shoved it into a quarantine cell similar to the ones down in decon. They then slammed the hatch shut and triggered the lock. From there they moved to their diagnostic stations. Not bothering to sit, their fingers flew over the keys as they darted around the room from system to system.

In Bobby's cell, a nozzle in the wall released a cloud of gas. The man went still, with only his chest rising and falling gently as the power lights flickered on indicating the cell's monitoring sensors had been activated. They did nothing else to care for his wound or make him comfortable.

"What are you doing?" Kate demanded. "You can't just leave him like that!"

She heard the rest of her crew get to their feet and come to stand behind her, grumbling ever louder as the medtechs went about what they were doing without responding. Stalking forward, Kate was about to yank Mac around when Tom intercepted her, laying his hand on her arm. He said nothing, but there was a sad, almost frightened look on his face. She glared at him and pulled away. "Why are you stopping me? It is their duty to take care of that man!" Kate was furious. She didn't know Eva for nothing, but Mac...she'd gotten to know him, to like him. It made no sense that he would ignore Bobby's suffering. "Why?"

Mac spoke over his shoulder, his voice tight and strained, his eyes never leaving his monitor. "There's no more to be done..."

"No more to be done?!"

Eva's head snapped around, her expression livid. "He's already dead, Donovan, all but the dying, just like Palmer, and so are the rest of us if you don't get off our backs and let us try and figure this out. We need to know what's going on in there now, before it's too late.

"Now everyone out of here! Why don't you do something useful, like figure out how to regain control of the fucking ship!"

Tom's arm slid around Kate, and Mac's voice murmured over her private frequency. *He's in no pain, Kate, we made sure he's in no pain.* She recalled the gas that had filled the chamber and nodded, though the medtech couldn't see the motion with his attention still completely on the monitor. Whirling away from Tom—and the sudden, uncharacteristic urge to curl into the protective shelter of his arms—Kate motioned for her people to follow as she left medbay.

JP already waited in the corridor. Not caring if the others would see it as odd, she touched his arm briefly, knowing the sensors there acted much the same as nerve endings. He wouldn't admit to needing the comforting touch, but she did. Jean-Paul was her friend, and though he wasn't in danger of infection the same way the rest of them were, she realized at that moment that he was just as much at risk: stranded and alone, should anything happen to the rest of them, left waiting to die a much slower death.

"Come on," she spoke aloud to those following. On impulse, she reached back, this time taking Tom's hand in hers, pulling him along. "We need a plan."

*   *   *

So far Tom had regained read-only access to the system via a generic service code, but that was all. And it was all he was likely to get, unless he cracked the captain's command code because Troy had registered a charge of mutiny against each of the crew members with command access, automatically locking them out of the system. None of them had anticipated that. They were currently holed up in one of the storage compartments because everything else was blocked to them.

Tom continued to stare at the monitor, wishing he could accomplish more, particularly as Kate stood with her hand on his shoulder watching everything he did. Sadly, the truth remained; he wasn't a professional hacker. He knew some tricks, but that had only gotten them this far.

"Can you get us a read on what Troy's up to, at least?" Kate asked, pulling Tom from his thoughts. "Maybe slave this monitor to his so we can tell what he's up to?"

"Not...quite...not without him realizing it, but something close." It was brilliant, actually. And he hadn't thought of it. Tom shook his hands loose and rolled his head from side to side, desperately trying to relieve the tension in his neck.

"Okay, here we go..." He punched in the codes for remote diagnostic viewing starting from the time he went on shift to now and there it was, a complete list of the commands Troy had entered since taking over the command deck. As the list scrolled, Tom felt the bile rise from his stomach and creep into his throat. *Kate...* he sent over her private frequency. *Kate...*

What?

He pointed at the screen. *He's preparing to vent the ship.*

Kate sat down hard on a crate beside him. *He's nuts! He'd go right along with us, wouldn't he?*

Tom shook his head, running his finger along several very canny commands the captain had entered. *He's already isolated and sealed the command deck. The only ones sucking vacuum will be us.*

Environmental suits...

Tom shook his head and nodded toward the far end of the storage compartment, where Hal and the miners were looking for any consumables among the stored supplies. *He's locked us out of the crew compartment. The only suits we have are already in use.*

A nearby stack of crates went crashing to the deck as Kate shoved herself to her feet and vented a bit of anger with a well-placed fist. She kicked a few more for good measure.

"You done?" he asked out loud.

"It's been a bad day, okay?" she growled through clenched teeth.

He had to smile at her. "Don't worry, it's not over yet." Tom patted the crate for her to sit back down. Apparently, she was curious enough to comply.

Now, pay attention here, he told her, going private once more. *We're locked out of the command systems, but it never occurred to Troy to restrict maintenance.* He shot her a smile that had to be just a bit smug as he typed in several commands. *To vent the ship requires the coordination of several interconnected programs, each one responsible for a different stage of the process. This is to prevent accidental venting. It also means that if one of the programs fails to complete its part, none of them can do their job...*—with a flourish, he hit the final key—*I've just started the next system on a self-diagnostic, and scheduled each of the others to begin their own scan, offset by ninety minutes each.*

Done preening? Her words weren't precisely encouraging, but her expression was both relieved and impressed. Tom smiled back at her a bit sheepishly, before he took a chance, leaning closer and murmuring just loud enough for her to hear: "What can I say? Engineers don't often get to show off for the pretty ladies." He watched her flush, but she didn't take the bait...yet.

"How much time did you just buy us?"

"These systems are pretty complex...likely about eighteen hours. Enough time for us to come up with a mechanical workaround."

Kate smiled and for a brief moment all Tom's tension fell away. "My hero," she murmured.

Dare I risk that I'm reading her wrong? Tom reached out to brush a finger lightly across her lips. Kate watched him do it but didn't protest. He was about to lower his mouth to hers when she jerked back and grabbed his hand, holding it up to the light. "Shit..." She whirled away and disappeared out the hatch before Tom even knew what was happening. Puzzled, he looked down at his hand only to notice a faint smudge of red dust on his finger.

"Shit..." Tom slammed his fist into a nearby stack of crates.

It was clearly still a bad day...

...And it wasn't over yet.

*   *   *

Kate sat on a gurney in medbay staring at the faint tremors running through her hand. Nerves, that was all...so far, anyway. She imagined if she stared hard enough she could see her pores exuding dust. The machinery in the background beeped a bit more vigorously.

"Stop getting yourself all worked up."

The hand Kate had been watching fisted. "Then tell me what we're facing here, Mac. And what you can do about it..."

"Well, you're infected. I suspect we all are, but I can't say to what degree without testing the others. Let's get them down here and see where things stand, then I can brief everyone."

"But..."

"It's in the air, Donovan. We're not talking *if*, we're talking how far along. Getting everyone together isn't going to make a bit of difference."

Kate nodded, but her hand fisted tighter. She accessed the crew frequency and ordered everyone to medbay, then sat back and waited. It wasn't long; Tom was the first through the door. She couldn't meet his eye but was aware, comforted even, as he perched beside her on the gurney, not touching, but close. JP was the last; he moved to the space directly behind her gurney and crouched into his version of sitting. At her back, where no one could see, she briefly felt his robotic hand reach out and lightly touch her shoulder, as a friend would.

"Everyone settle in and listen," Kate raised her voice, sounding steadier than she expected she would. "Mac's got something to say."

They all turned to look at the medtech expectantly. Mac leaned over his keyboard and brought up a view from the external sensors, he then turned and looked each of them in the eye. "It's not dust, it's an airborne organism.

"It doesn't meet any of the organic profiles on record so none of the sensors or diagnostics picked it up. Planetary evaluation didn't catch it because their rovers are made of titanium. The organism feeds on ferrous iron, any source…from raw ore to hemoglobin, it doesn't matter, as long as it's oxidized. Initial warning signs are similar to those for anemia. In the final stages, intense internal pain and what appears to be dust exuding from the skin." He turned and tapped a few more keys, replacing the live feed with a medical slide none of them had the background to identify. He tapped another key and the slide split, the two sides disturbingly similar but for color and some variation in the cellular structures. "The one on the right is a healthy blood sample. The left side is an infected one." When Mac turned to face the group, Kate was struck by his somber expression. "Both of these were taken from Fletcher. The first when he was placed in the decon quarantine unit, the second…moments before he died."

There were gasps and curses from the group, and several of the men stood up as if there was something to fight. Kate just went kind of numb. "But, that was just a matter of hours. Palmer took days to even show signs."

She flinched as Mac turned his gaze back to her. There was such sorrow in his eyes. "Eva thought it was a matter of saturation. You breathe it in and there's not much there. Your body can fight it off a while, like you would any airborne infection, until it gets a foothold. If it enters directly through the blood stream it attacks and multiplies too rapidly for the white blood cells to combat it. The larger the wound and the longer it's open, the more contamination there is, the quicker the body succumbs. Other conditions also affect the rate of decline."

Mac's voice caught as he finished the last statement.

When Kate had first arrived, she'd assumed Eva was resting. Now, she wasn't so sure. Coming off of the gurney, she moved in front of him, where he couldn't avoid her. "Mac, where's Eva?"

The medtech flinched but continued with his briefing as if Kate wasn't there. "In extreme cases where the infected party has a chronic or temporary iron deficiency, such as anemia or rapid blood loss, the organism attacks the iron-rich organs of the body."

"Mac?" Kate tried again.

He continued to ignore her, stepping around her and moving to the pharmaceutical cabinet across the room. Unlocking it, he drew out several large bottles and one smaller one, which he set to the side. Pulling empty prescription pouches from a nearby shelf, he divvyed the bottles among them until he had ten identical bags of large oval brown pills. He tossed one to each of the men.

"Iron pills. Take two now and then one pill twice a day until we find a way out of this. The organism is apparently lazy; it continually goes toward the most easily accessed iron first. This should slow things down."

Kate had enough. She got right in his face and barked: "Mac!"

He stopped still. Didn't look up. When he spoke, she could barely hear him. "She's dead, Donovan...just like Palmer...just like Fletcher...and just like Captain Troy..."

"And so are you, unless you start taking these." He handed her the bag of iron pills and the small prescription bottle he'd taken out earlier. She turned it over and read the label, her brow drawing down in confusion. Hormone supplements? Kate looked up and trapped Mac's gaze. And then he spoke, only over her private frequency. *She had her period, Kate...she just...had her period, and now she's dead. She didn't even know.* And then he said aloud, "Take them."

Kate's hand closed reflexively over the prescription bottle. In a woman's normal cycle there was heavy iron loss. Kate shuddered. With a nod, she popped the bottle open and took her first dose dry while he watched.

Satisfied, Mac stepped around her and back into the midst of the group.

"Wait..." she called out, spinning around to face him. "Did you say *Troy* is dead?!"

Mac looked over his shoulder and nodded. "He's what broke this, gave us a comparison we needed to isolate what was going on. That's how we found out it will attack the organs. The captain had a history of anemia. He thought he was safe in his suit, but by then it was too late. Because he was in his suit the medical system automatically tracked his basic biometrics; from nearly start to finish we had a complete profile. Long enough to learn exactly what it does to us…long enough to learn the organism dies very quickly without oxygen…."

"Funny, that," the navigator, Hal, growled out. "So do we!"

If she hadn't been looking in their direction, Kate might have missed the look on Tom Henry's face at Hal's outburst. The look was familiar, just like that little *ah-ha* moment back in the storage compartment. "Tom? Whatcha thinking?"

"I have an idea…" he said. "But first, Mac, how many resuscitation ventilators do you have on board?" Kate thought she saw where he was going with this; ever since the invention of the original Draeger Pulmotor back in 1907, resuscitation ventilators were standard equipment for all mining operations.

A glimmer of hope returned to the medtech's expression as he glanced toward the back of medbay where there was a ward of twelve beds. Each had a ventilator built right into the bulkhead above it. He slowly nodded his head as he answered: "Enough."

"Excellent…is there a master switch capable of activating them all at once?"

Mac nodded, approval clear in the set of his features.

"So," Tom went on, turning back toward the men. "Before the bug got him, Troy initialized a full atmospheric vent on the *Caliphus*…"

Anger kindled in the men's eyes, tightened their jaws. Kate shifted nervously and Tom darted a look in her direction, giving her a bit of a wink.

"Kate and I managed to stall the process, but it's still in place. If we put that process back on track, we can purge the organism from the ship."

"What about us?" one of the miners asked. "Mac said we already got it."

"Well…" and here Tom looked nervous, "we'd have to go down with the ship, so to speak…."

The uproar was deafening. As the miners surged forward Tom stood his ground. Kate moved to his side, as did Mac, but the deciding factor was JP, who rose ominously from his crouch.

"Listen to the man," he commanded everyone in the flat, mechanical voice only Kate had heard until now.

Oh my God! You spoke! she sent over JP's private frequency.

Not now! he shushed her, and sheepishly she had to agree. She was just so stunned. "Go on, Tom," JP prompted out loud.

Tom didn't look nearly surprised enough in Kate's opinion, as he continued outlining his plan. "If Mac puts each of us under beforehand, when the ship vents we will suffocate, no pain, no awareness. We program the ventilators to activate two minutes after the ship has been purged. Ventilators come on, we come back…no more bug."

Silence, then Mac cleared his throat. An uncomfortable sound, an unhappy sound.

"Won't work, Tom…the ventilators aren't the type of thing you can program. There is a master button, but it has to be manually operated."

Tom swore softly beneath his breath, only to surge once more as he leaned forward, that gleam back in his gaze. "I'll wear a suit…push the button myself, then when you come around, Mac can do the same for me…"

Mac already shook his head. "There's no way to ensure all the organism is vented that way. You'd just be resetting the clock, eventually we'd reinfect."

"Damn it," Kate said, gripping Tom's arm in support. "There has to be a way to make this work!"

No one said a word. From one face to the other there was some degree of uncertainty, lost looks, and fear. Someone shifted. Someone else coughed, until someone smacked them.

"I can do it."

Everyone turned to look at JP, only they didn't see him; they saw a machine, something Kate was heartily fed up with. *So sue me,* she told Jean-Paul subvocally, before she deliberately violated her contract. "Crew," Kate spoke into the stunned silence, a serene smile on her face, "I'd like you to meet my friend, Jean-Paul Marot, he's a cyborg."

✳   ✳   ✳

In the end, they'd cancelled all the diagnostics Tom had scheduled except for the one that had been running. That had allowed them time to get everything set. The crew was strapped in, JP was anchored into place, and in ten minutes, the venting process would complete. It was time for him to sedate the crew.

The flashback hit with the force of a comet, leaving Jean-Paul disoriented. He swayed, his consciousness once more doubly trapped: his physical form within a tomb of fallen rock and as a passive observer in his own brain unable to stop the events unfolding against his will. Once more he saw himself reach out, saw the battered and bloody form of his foreman clinging doggedly to life, saw himself slide the end of the umbilical into his friend's neck, stealing Franklin's chance of survival. Saw the blood forever on his own "hand".

For the first time since his encapsulation, Jean-Paul Marot managed a vocal scream. It was pitiful. It came out in a low, constant tone, reminiscent of the ancient time of television and the sound broadcast when a station went off the air.

Not again. Please, God, not again, he thought, the plea held a frantic edge as he felt his mind crumble at the prospect of what he had to do. What if it didn't work? What if some of them...all of them, didn't come back? He was drowning in chemical despair at the risk of being responsible for even more deaths, this time by conscious decision. For God's sake, he'd volunteered! If this did not work, he would well and truly be a murderer. The "scream" increased in volume and intensity until something slapped the side of his brain case.

Tom Henry had extracted himself from his resuscitation ventilator and come up beside him. JP focused on the rage twisting the man's expression. "The longer you take, the more they suffer, the more chance some of them won't survive; either hit the go'damn button or get out of my way.

"But you'll die." His monotone vocals did not convey the anxiety this caused Jean-Paul.

"But *she* won't...not if *I* can help it." Tom's voice was thick with conviction, flavored with disgust at Jean-Paul's hesitation.

And there it was, the real reason JP had volunteered.

"Go back to your bunk, my friend." JP answered. "It's time."

He waited, his titanium hand on the button, as Tom hooked back up.

The last thing Jean-Paul heard as he killed them was Kate's slurred voice over the crew frequency: *You still owe me that steak, Tom Henry.*

SCIFIKU 1

feel, automoton,
reflective betrayal
in polished metal

On To Look Upon the Face of God

What if you woke up to see the vast empty of space all around you, to feel the slight shift of breath that is sure to run out of oxygen, and to hear nothing but your own voice calling a Mayday?

I liked this story a lot. I particularly love that in some ways it reminds me of *Life of Pi*. Nice story with a good emotional punch!

—Brenda Cooper,
co-author of *Building Harlequin's Moon,*
with Larry Niven

TO LOOK UPON THE FACE OF GOD

An Alliance Archives Adventure

Private Cassandra Franklyn opened her eyes to a perfectly formed snowflake suspended in space. Outer space. She blinked furiously, gave her head a sharp shake within the confines of her helmet, then looked again. No, not suspended...formed up on the visor of her EVA suit. It wasn't alone.

Her body shook, but she did not move. The joints of her suit were frozen, the faceplate veined with encroaching lines of frost. Biometrics pinged an adrenalin surge alert. What the hell happened? Where was the ship?

Activating her comm, she attempted to contact her vessel. "Franklyn hailing *Clark*, please respond...over."

Silence.

Flexing the tip of one finger, Cas opened all frequencies on her comm.

"Mayday, Mayday. This is Private First Class Cassandra Franklyn of the Dominion patrol vessel *Clark*, I am adrift and requesting assistance." She tagged the hail with her coordinates and set it to repeat, then activated her retrieval beacon. After a couple repetitions, the tension of her own voice sounding in her ear was too much. She turned off the internal speakers. The system would flash if there was an incoming response.

Cas wasn't holding her breath.

The suit had the equivalent of a black-box recorder. Taking a deep breath, she played back the last...*two hours*. Her chest tightened as she noted the time stamp. Then a ghosted image of the *Clark* appeared before her eyes. She groaned, the sound cutting off as a bright flash played across her see-through display. Then the image jigged like crazy before rotating wildly away from what could only be an explosion. The recorder caught brief flashes of the ship as she'd continued to tumble through space. And then the real thing showed through her display. She must still be tumbling. The remains of the *Clark,* amid a slowly spreading field of debris, drifted a klick away. Tiny flickers of flame erupted as pockets of ignited gas burned through interior seals, venting into space.

Cas squandered a bit of her suit's remaining power to counteract her rotation, stopping when she faced the wreckage, the vapors of a memory drifting to the surface of her mind. She'd been EVA. They were having a problem with the port-side thrusters. Diagnostics couldn't pinpoint the problem, so Captain Reyes sent her out for an eyes-on inspection.

He'd saved her life...for a while, anyway.

From the looks of it, she'd been just on the edge of the blast radius, making her potentially the sole survivor of the catastrophic systems failure. Friends, squad mates, as many as fifteen people likely dead...There was no way of knowing if their shuttle, *Lewis,* had gotten clear, but surely, if it had, Dylan would have found her by now.

She shoved that thought away and edged up the volume slightly on her hail, finding reassurance that it still ran. Then she turned her attention to assessing her situation. The suit took some damage, she could see some scorching on her arms, and there were a couple of warning lights...pale amber only, not flashing red. It was hard to say if any of that corresponded with an injury. Nothing hurt, anyway. She merely hung in the vastness of space, drifting powerless—or near enough.

Her brow lowered and she snarled. *No! Not powerless.* The suit had thrusters; she only needed to redirect enough power to warm them up and perhaps she could close on the wreckage. Something might remain. An escape pod, the shuttle...she couldn't tell from here, but it was possible.

Her fingers moved over the operational toggles built into her glovetips. Slowly, her back began to warm, the leads to the thruster units vibrating as she watched the status display intently. Warm-up was complete and the pack moved into the power-up phase when an intense burn traveled up her back. On her display, the warning light for the thrusters skipped amber and went right to screaming red.

"Shit!" Cas cursed aloud, instinctively trying to arch her back, though it wasn't physically possible. Her fingertip went to the appropriate toggle, but the failsafe shutdown kicked in first, before anything blew. She sighed and her head dropped forward. Damn…

Time to reassess the situation: the suit had oxygen for six hours and a reserve for two hours beyond that. The power charge had a six-hour capacity, under standard use. Two hours of oxygen was already consumed, but the power had gone into conservation mode as soon as biometrics had registered her unconsciousness, thus the deep chill. Her aborted effort at propulsion had burned up perhaps an hour's worth of juice, but if she returned her operating systems to the bare minimum she could stretch out the life of her power module at least as long as the oxygen would last, giving herself that much more time to be discovered. She estimated about seven hours in the near-dormant state she was in now. It was that, or give up. Activate the euthanasia protocol engineered for just such a situation as she found herself in. A little bit of gas in her oxygen mix, and she'd go out quiet and peaceful, knowing it was coming but unable to care.

She could. In theory, anyway…It just wasn't in her to give up, though. She dropped her suit back into conservation mode and started meditation techniques to slow her breathing.

Like she expected it to make a difference… Like there was any chance she would be found at all, let alone in time. But she couldn't just give in to the inevitable. She spent the first few hours talking to God…begging, pleading, cursing, crying…Then she'd shut everything down, silently watching the stars, her field of view slowly growing smaller as ice crystals occluded the heavens. By hour six she had no tears left, no hope; only in a distant, abstract way did she wonder what it would be like to die, suffocating in a form-fitted coffin, slowly encased in ice within her suit.

Cassandra pushed that thought away and sorted through the memories of a lifetime; her childhood, her youth, her brief stab at acting like an adult. Everything she had to live for. Of eating sandwiches with Grampy perched on the end of the pier at Hancock Lake, their feet dangling in the cool water, while bullfrogs sounded off in the rushes, stars and fireflies providing the only light to see by…of competition-level dancing lessons with her mother, which Cas loathed because she had no choice, and trips to the planetarium with her dad, which she loved because she *did*…the blur that was basic training…long weeks of utter exhaustion punctuated by sudden moments of intense yelling as Sergeant Kraemer chewed out the platoon in a deep bass voice…the utter awe inspired by her first up-close-and-personal introduction to the stars...meeting Ensign Dylan Tyler when she was reassigned to *Clark*...Her throat tightened until she gritted her teeth and increased volume on the hail once more.

In that final, gentle hour floating through the heavens, Cas tried not to admit to herself that she was bidding farewell.

The carbon dioxide alert had gone off ten minutes ago, and the power gauge was deep into the red. At peace with her reality, she closed her eyes and continued to breathe deep and slow, refusing to panic as she willed the tension from her body. Her fingertips tingled, as did her lips, and she couldn't feel her toes. Cassandra made her final peace with God and, to the strains of a half-remembered lullaby, let sleep take her.

*   *   *

In The-Time-Before there was the Spiraling, felt, but not seen, a thread throughout all that was, strung with the substance of the universe like a strong silk cord knotted with gems. The heavens sang in celebration of its being, the stars twirled to the rhythm, and the Urdura *kept the measure of the dance by the beating of their hearts, giving voice to the silent song as they skipped along the Spiraling with the unconscious grace of children at play.*

And then there was born to the Urdura *a heart deaf to the music of the universe. Bitter and cold, this blighted soul sought to break the balance it could not join. Discordance sounded its jarring strands. Malice soured the notes. Thus came the Sundering, a time of darkness and despair as many voices of the song were silenced, and the stars fell out of step. The* Urdura *were flung loose, blind to the paths they used to tread, lost in the dark of forever. They cried out for The-Time-Before, souls haunted by the echo of the starsong.*

In The-Time-After they wandered, ever seeking their way home.

Then...one day...a child began to dance, Spiraling away from the elders, who had long since forgotten the steps.

*   *   *

"You are not *Urdura*..."

It was a silent whisper coming from all sides of her oxygen-starved brain. Nonsensical. Absurd. Perplexing...Not what she'd expected of the hereafter. *Urdura? Was I supposed to be? If only someone had told me...*

"You are *not Urdura...*" The words had a sense of pouting, a sullen rebuke flavored with disappointment, colored with confusion and a hint of wonder. After, there was silence, deep and empty, as if the whisperer moved on. Cas struggled with logic that would not parse, her mind grasping for concepts she could comprehend. Panic fluttered through her chest. She'd had enough of alone.

In her muddled reasoning, only one voice could possibly come out of nowhere...

"God? Are you still there?" she whispered hurriedly, the words trembling from lips she could not feel. Something was wrong. Gravity tugged at her limbs...impossible...Cas tried to pivot, to shift enough to spin her body, straining with senses that would not, could not see her surroundings for the shrouding darkness. And then she was falling, colliding with a surface with more give than plasticrete, but less give than foam...or space...much less give than space, where she had been floating.

Where she'd died.

*Umph. Uhhh...*her body recalled the lessons Kraemer had drilled into each muscle, rolling her across the curve of a shoulder, over the bulk of her respiration tanks, and up onto feet more sure than she was. The muscles had learned well. They managed to keep her upright, crouched and poised though growing tingles pelted her nerves like needles of ice rain. Roused abruptly to sensitivity, her shoulder throbbed. *Who knew there would be bruises in the afterlife?*

There was no one to fight, nothing to see, just absolute black, with tiny sparks of light, as if she were about to pass out again, but not quite.

Awareness returned. No. Not hers. The other...

"God?" Cas breathed, awe and wonder and doubt commingling. She began to sense a deep pulse, more felt than heard.

"*We* dance the Spiraling." There was a correction in there somewhere, though Cas could not quite find it in the seeming *non sequitur*. As she fought to focus, her chest heaved while her skin and every nerve ending in it roused. There wasn't enough air. The tiny green sensor light on her helmet rim indicated her respiration tanks were absorbing oxygen from somewhere, storing it as they were designed to, but it wasn't enough to keep pace with her pounding heart. The tanks had been near empty the last she remembered. She needed to slow her breathing. Her mind struggled to implement her meditation techniques, but it was no use. Cas gasped, instinctively drew breath faster as dread returned. The memories of dying were too fresh. Her legs trembled and her head spun. Micro flashes lit her personal darkness, keeping time with her frantic heartbeat. Cas crumpled to the unseen surface beneath her feet.

"You are not *Urdura*..."

The whispered words followed her into unconsciousness.

✳   ✳   ✳

There is a moment of silence, the cosmos poised and waiting. Like music held for a measure. The tension builds. Anticipation hangs on a note not yet heard as a child finds its way through a melody it has not been taught. The music takes on the essence of a lament; the story of a child, lost and alone.

In the Time-To-Come, the Urdura *will speak of the Meandering... the silken thread of the Spiraling tangled and looped, off beat until the universe itself is without rhythm. In that time, planets tremble and skies are aflame; the fires of stars are extinguished and hearts cry out as fear quickens the pulse into a frenzied reel.*

A single soul cries out: Home!

An anxious universe balances on the cusp of fracture...

✳   ✳   ✳

Reality whirled about Cas in a dizzying counterpoint to her spinning head. She lay there, still and silent, every sense open and seeking clues to her surroundings. Beneath her hand, felt through the skin of the servo glove of her EVA suit, there was a steady thump. Familiar, lulling...It was like someone combined a pulse with a dance score reminiscent of her ballroom days. Her own heart strove to match the languid, too-slow beat until she reared up and away from it. The air around her was warm, close, and it carried an organic scent that came through faintly, despite the filters on her respiration tanks. It reminded her of grass. Head still spinning, a giggle rose from nowhere, escaping before Cas realized she should suppress it. Grass...in the middle of space...or was it heaven?

Only why, then, were things so dark?

Something within her yelled at her to focus, and she remembered... light. Her fingers trembled as she reached up to initiate her helmet-mounted LEDs, realizing too late that she should have lowered her radiant shields against the sudden blaze. Her eyes instantly squeezed shut. Slowly, she squinted, waited for her vision to adjust, then opened them a bit more. Trained for survival, she first took a quick glance at her suit's gauges: oxygen, 35%; power 10%.

That couldn't be right. She'd tapped out even her reserve oxygen before her world went black. True, the tanks were self-replenishing, engineered to absorb any oxygen in the surrounding atmosphere, but...she'd been floating in space, there *was* no oxygen. Her temples throbbed as she tried to make sense out of insanity. Cas cursed and instinctively raised her hand to her head, though there was no way she could touch it through the helmet. What was there to figure out? Clearly, she was no longer in the vacuum of space, which meant she had to be within the pressure hull of a ship. Of course, that wouldn't do her a damn bit of good without power to keep her suit from freezing up solid. And yet, as Grampy liked to say, where there is life, there is hope. And wasn't it already a miracle she was alive?

Or was she?

If that wasn't enough to mess with her head....

Shoving the crazy-making thought aside, Cas gazed around her, awed yet again. "My God...," she murmured, her breath coming a bit faster, until she reined it back. Reaching up, she turned off the LEDs, both to conserve her power and to be sure of what she saw.

A long time ago, when she was just a child, her father had shown her a photograph of the Earth. It had been taken of the side in rotation away from the Sun and the cities glittered and blazed like gems against dark velvet. That was the moment she'd set her heart on making it to space. The memory had never left her and neither had the wonder, even years later when such a sight could have been called routine, seen firsthand. It came to her mind now as a poor shadow to her surroundings.

The space she stood in was rounded, convex, like she stood within the planet looking out at that electrified topography from the inside. Cavelike, only smooth and dry, she found herself in a chamber that seemed to be constructed of black glass, semi-translucent, encasing a million muted points of light, pulsing and flashing to the measured rhythm she'd noticed upon waking. Slowly turning, Cas noted that every surface was the same: the walls, ceiling, and floor—though none of them resembled anything she would label such. There were no other features, other than a rough ledge, about two feet deep and one high, edging the walls and a narrow arch leading elsewhere. Cautious steps took her to the closest wall where she dared reach out and run a gloved hand over the surface. For a moment the dancing colors mesmerized her, clearly responsive to her touch. Cas shivered in reaction to what the gloves told her. Micro-sensors in the finger pads mimicked nerve receptors. The surface was not rigid or hard; it had the feel of relaxed muscle. Warm, tensile, alive...

Ridiculous, but then what about this situation wasn't?

With her touch, came a return of the Awareness.

Cas expected something more: A face formed in the lights; a being that challenged her ability to describe; a nightmare, even, from her youngest dreams. There was none of that. Her...rescuer... remained unseen. There was nothing but a change in the pressure, as if the atmosphere increased until it weighed down upon her sufficiently to register on the suit sensors. She felt poked and prodded in no more than an instant, without even a touch she could feel.

Cas tensed, no longer muddled, no longer oxygen-starved. Her instincts reared up and her stance subtly changed. She didn't know what she faced, but she was more than ready to fight, she just hadn't figured out how.

And then the being spoke.

"You are not *Urdura*...you cannot help us." There was finality to that thought. It set Cas's heart racing and clamped tight across her throat. It had the sound of her end echoing behind it.

"How do you know?" Cas asked, her words taut, her tone challenging, aware that her life hung upon them.

"We are *Urdura*," the Awareness answered, as if it should be obvious.

"*How do you know*," Cas repeated before going on, "that I cannot help?"

The universe stilled around her. The Awareness seemed to press down upon her. She fought it, but the pressure increased until she went to her knees beneath the weight. "You will show us."

It was not a question.

Cassandra didn't even have time to ponder how, when, without warning, the contents of her life, her knowledge, everything she had ever seen or done or learned was dredged and sifted. From her knees, she collapsed to the deck beneath the onslaught, her nerves screaming and every neuron of her brain on fire. She relived it all, moving from the here-and-now to the far reaches of her past. Fragments of her life were strewn about until the whole of it made little sense and likely neither did the pieces. *Eating a jelly donut. Blasting a Legion fighter craft from the sky. Dylan. Cleaning the bathroom. Getting dressed down by her CO. Her first kiss. The pain of a stubbed toe, and Grampy kissing it away. The time she froze at a dance competition.*

The *Urdura* slowed at that, then stopped completely at Cas's first time at summer camp, paused long enough for the pressure in her head to ease. She felt a fleeting sense of connection, understanding, for a brief moment it was like they were kindred spirits. And then the Awareness clamped down, dug deeper, with a purpose, drawing out every memory of loss and loneliness, as if looking for something beneath. Cas sobbed uncontrollably at the sudden onslaught, the pain fresh and new and brutal. With the replay of her Grampy's death it was too much. She set her teeth and snarled. Digging in, she focused her will power. Every speck of what she was came up hard and shoved the Awareness away.

"Enough!" she said from a throat both raw and tight. Rage punctuated that single word.

"You cannot help us," came the whispered response, and Cas finally glimpsed what had only teased the edges of her thoughts before. There was something young about the mind brushing her own—young and sad and lonely to a degree Cas had never been. Lost. It was all there before her...wide open, the mind of the *Urdura.*

Cas brushed against that mind as the Awareness had shown her to do, only softly, gently. She closed her eyes and let herself see dizzying sights she could scarce comprehend. Large ebon shapes twirling among the stars, glimmering with the light of their touch; creatures beyond her imagination moving in measured steps across the heavens, so familiar...almost like.... Her mind bent itself toward making sense of foreign feelings and images intertwined, a haunting tune threaded through each memory, half-formed, an almost-song. Interspersed with the wonder were images of other creatures, some like her, some in the truest sense alien, all standing in Cas's place. She dug a little deeper, trying to focus, trying to control the flow of memories, to discover their fate. And when she nearly had the truth, losing some of her gentleness in an effort to finally grasp it, an anger to rival her own reared up and pushed her away.

"You are NOT *Urdura!*"

The atmosphere drained away, the charging light on the edge of Cas's helmet went out, and slowly her feet lifted from the firm surface beneath them. It felt the same as an airlock being depressurized, and with that realization her hands shot out, firmly grabbing the edge of the arch before she could be sucked through.

"No! Stop!" Cas commanded, as she would to a recalcitrant child. "*Now...*"

Her eyes narrowed as the shifting lights beneath the wall's surface caught her gaze, a precise and purposeful pattern, like a little girl practicing steps before the balance bar, over and over the same thing, not yet knowing how to link one to the other. Cas's intuition leapt upon the pattern.

She took a deep breath, and then let it out. "I can help you..."

"You are not..."

"I know! I know," Cas snapped. "I am not *Urdura*...I'm not, but I *can* help you." And she gifted the Awareness with her early memories that had not been delved into: the memories of graceful steps and guided turns; twirls and bows and waltzes with half-remembered partners no more eager than she had been. Gifting even that deep, hidden joy Cas had unexpectedly found in the midst of performing. The joy she would have gloried in if it weren't buried beneath requirement.

For the first time, if only in her thoughts, Cas danced for the love of dancing, the *Urdura* avidly keeping step. It seemed like forever, but eventually they slowed, then stopped, and Cas held another breath, knowing her future would be determined in the next.

The Awareness swelled around her, the pressure returned, and Cas's feet drifted down until they rested on the alien surface.

"You are not *Urdura*."

The breath exploded from her, fogging her visor in the now cool air.

"No...no, I'm not," she responded, beyond weary and not knowing what else to say.

"But you *could be*..."

And with that, Cas knew she would live.

✻   ✻   ✻

In the All-Time, note builds upon new-remembered note until the Harmony is restored. The Wanderer twirls among the stars, returning home, there to share the memories gifted by another upon the Spiraling.

✻   ✻   ✻

Cas came to drifting slowly, the sound of her CO_2 alert buzzing along the length of her, echoing off her skull. Her throat tightened and a single tear slid down her cheek to pool along the edge of her comm hood.

"But I can dance," she murmured in delirium, desperation and determination fighting in each word. Her head seemed to float more than the rest of her.

"Can you then?" an amused voice sounded in her ear: male, relieved, and vaguely familiar, but not the expected tones of the Awareness. "I think I'm gonna make you prove that to me, Cassie."

"You said I could be *Urdura*," Cas cried out, not comprehending the other's words, not even the altering of her name, which she would normally object to.

"God, are you there?" To her own ears, she sounded frightened.

Aboard the shuttle *Lewis,* the pilot gave a confused look to the ensign manning the comm. "What the heck is she talking about?"

"Does it matter? We found her!" The ensign answered, a slight quaver to his voice. "She has to be nearly out of oxygen, I wouldn't expect too much sense right now."

The pilot nodded. "Let's get our lost sheep aboard."

*   *   *

In The-Here-After it is spoken of Cas, the Could-Be...the Was...the Is. She is spoken of in reverence, in joy. The name she is given is Savior and the Urdura *dance her memory of deliverance.*

I've been there. In combat, that is. Of course, my combat was on the ground as an infantryman, not in the air as a combat pilot. But I've had to research aerial combat for some of my military science fiction novels. I think I got it right. For "Ghosts on the Battlefield," Danielle Ackley-McPhail must have done the same research I did. There's a considerable feeling of reality in this story, and that's of greatest import to me in military fiction, SF or otherwise.

—David Sherman,
co-author of the *Starfist* and
DemonTech Series, with Dan Cragg

GHOSTS ON THE BATTLEFIELD

An Alliance Archives Adventure

They were called the Morrigans. Raven. Crow. Corby. Jackdaw. Rook. And their unit leader, Captain Jayne Corvidae, was known as Scarlet Jay. They were AeroCom's battle-honed goddesses of war. They had more campaign ribbons across their collective chests than any other flight in the group, and more demerits on their records than their entire wing combined, mostly for fights started by greenies eager to prove themselves tougher than the dames. Still, fighting's fighting, no matter who starts it.

Or who *finishes* it.

They held that record too, though they didn't consider it something to brag about.

They were the Morrigans. They had more important things to do than crow.

✳   ✳   ✳

Jay popped her head through the common room arch as she hurried by. "Briefing room, ten minutes." A machine-gun series of "Ayes" followed her down the corridor, cutting off sharply as she straight-armed her office door, letting it slam behind her.

"Damn it! I can't believe he's doing it to us again!" She took a swing at the old-fashioned training bag she'd had installed in the corner. If it weren't chain-anchored to the floor it would have slammed into the wall.

"Ten minutes isn't going to be enough, is it?"

Jay spun around and glared at Raven—First Lieutenant Chen Po—who had just slipped in the door. It was an effort to unclench her jaw—and her fists—to respond to her lieutenant. Breathing deep, she squared her shoulders, ran a hand over her spiked bristle of vibrant red hair, and put an arm out to steady the still-swaying bag. When she was as calm as she was likely to be, she spoke.

"We're shepherding another crop of green."

Raven grimaced and closed the door behind her as she moved fully into the room. "Nope...a *week* wouldn't be enough."

Raven was right. They were a combat flight, used to taking the fight to the enemy in atmo or space, but ever since General Calloway took over command of their group two months ago they'd been on baby-sitting duty, responsible for buffing off the rough edges on each batch of fresh pilots assigned to his command. There was only one thing worse than sitting on her thumb or banging heads with airmen that hadn't yet clued to the fact that they weren't winged gods, and that was guilt. Calloway made sure her duty periods were all three rolled into a great big miserable ball. The two of them had a history. Back in flight school she'd made a stupid mistake, cut the wrong corner. It had resulted in the death of the General's son. Calloway didn't much care for her, which she could understand and respect. What she didn't hold with was the fact that he took it out on her pilots as well.

"As of 0600 tomorrow we'll be patrolling the DMZ in two-hour shifts. One Morrigan, one newbie," Jay said as evenly as she could, with a hard-knuckled grip on her temper. Her deep brown eyes narrowed with annoyance as she handed Raven a stack of personnel jackets. "There's one clear problem child in the bunch. He's with me on first patrol. The rest I'll let you sort out."

Raven nodded, sending her short, straight black hair swaying around her face. Then, with a knowing glance, said, "Okay. Take one more swing."

The training bag still rattled its chain as they left the office, expressions neutral, backs straight, and eyes hard-edged.

✳   ✳   ✳

It was 0Dark00 on the planet Demeter. Jay was there to run the preflight on her bird, an AC-360PH—AeroCom-360 PlasmaHawk— straddling a single hybrid aerospike engine. The fighter wasn't the latest or—some would say—the best, but even the most skeptical admitted that Scarlet Jay could work magic behind the stick. She didn't know if it was magic precisely but she knew the old girl the way a cowboy knew his horse, every trick and habit and the fine nuances of each little shimmy. Up in the atmo they were one and they got along just fine, even if the Hawk did have a tendency to argue.

Her checklist done, Jay slid her digital pad in her flight suit pocket and reached up past her jumpseat into the dead space between the jet's skin and its frame. The tinkle of a small bell ringing reached her ears and she smiled faintly as the sound of the biker bell she'd tucked up there faded. It had been a gift from her Granddad when she'd gotten her wings; to keep the gremlins away, he said. Granddad had been both a pilot and a biker and understood such things. He was long gone, but that bell went on every bird she flew. It was like having him at her shoulder, looking out for her, reminding her she had a right to be there. In the tough spots, she'd even dare say she almost heard his voice in her ear.

"Man...whose bad side are you on to get saddled with that?" said a voice from behind her, way too informal, she might even say insubordinate. She turned, and her suspicion was confirmed. It was her greenie. And he was bad-mouthing her fighter. There was no reason to point out that if he were permanently assigned to the squadron, he'd be flying the same thing.

She looked at him over her shoulder as she slid down the rails she'd climbed to the cockpit. What she saw was a golden boy: from his burnished hair, to his light brown eyes, and straight on to his attitude. "Get your preflight done, Pilot Panski. We lift off in thirty."

"Already done," he answered.

He piloted an AC-010 NovaStream; the absolute newest craft in the division. It was a couple rows over up the line. Not exactly line-of-sight from her location, but Panski would have had to have walked by her PlasmaHawk to get to there.

"Really? Must have been awful early. I've been here an hour and I can't say I saw you come in." She spied the outline of a familiar hand-held device in his flight suit pocket.

Technically, the NovaStream was capable of remote preflight. She didn't know whose bright idea that was, but it resulted in enough deaths in the testing phase that the remotes had been banned, and yet every once in a while a newbie tried to get away with using one. But, as she herself had learned long ago, there were some things only eyes-on could tell you and there wasn't a seasoned pilot in the ranks that wouldn't stand hard on those skirting the rules.

As she hit the tarmac, Jay pivoted and took three long strides to where he stood.

"Hand over the preflight remote," she ordered.

With a sullen look buried deep in his eyes, he pulled it from his pocket.

She plucked the non-issue gadget from his hand, her eyes hooded as they locked with his. "Did you happen to notice the bars on my collar, Panski?"

His face went expressionless and he instantly snapped to attention, belatedly saluting.

She continued, "Regulations state on-site, manual preflight is required before going airborne, is that understood, *pilot*?" Her tone and demeanor would have made Granddad proud. She didn't usually stand on ceremony, but she could pull rank with the best of them when it was called for. This was a lesson he definitely needed to learn.

"Ma'am, yes, ma'am." She almost couldn't even see the way his jaw muscles tightened in protest as he responded.

"Now go do your walk-around. And be sure to double-check the navigational array. Maintenance warned that there's been a problem with drift on some of the flights."

While Panski strolled toward his jet, Jay turned and headed for flight control, the contraband remote in hand. Her mind was still on the pilot, though. Even if she hadn't read his jacket she would have known all about him. This guy came not just from a career military family, but from presidential stock. That combination went one of two ways; they either produced a next generation of soldiers that was squeaky clean and by-the-books, or ones that walked around with a sense of entitlement and felt their connections lifted them above military protocol and deportment. She didn't have to guess which side Panski came down on. She only wished she couldn't see so much of her younger self in him.

And it's my job to readjust his perspective, she thought. *Joy.*

"Hey, Deeley." As she entered flight control she tossed the remote to the sergeant behind the desk. "Add that to the contraband lockbox, please." While he took care of that, she pulled out her digital pad and slid it into its port on the mainframe—a safeguard against wireless interception—logging in their flight plan and officially beginning their duty shift. "See you in two hours," she called as she again pocketed her pad and left control.

There were sounds of life rising around the flight line; jets being maintenanced and fueled, pilots coming off patrol, and Panski trying to chat up Raven, who waited with Jay's helmet in hand. He had so picked the wrong Morrigan. He was also done with his PF awful quick.

She ran her hand over her right arm, where the flight suit hid an old scar from her cadet days. For a moment she considered going over and running the check herself, but if they were on the ground much longer they would be late for patrol. And Calloway was just looking for reasons to add another black mark to her jacket. They just didn't have the time. She was going to have to give Panski the benefit of the doubt.

Jay accepted her helmet with a nod and a "Thanks" before turning on Panski. "Get it in gear, pilot." She nodded him toward his bird, then turned back to Raven.

"We're patrolling the east leg of the DMZ. Intelligence indicates some isolated Dominion activity along that stretch, but otherwise it's been quiet." As she briefed her second, she tugged her comm hood, with its integrated earpiece, into place and settled the helmet—emblazoned with a stylized diving scarlet jay—overtop. She tightened the chin strap as she continued, "Run some flight exercises, get the Morrigans and the new pilots used to operating together. Anything comes up, you know the drill."

In response, Raven reached out and knuckled her helmet, the Morrigans' private ritual for luck. "See you back in two, SJ. And don't worry…I'll keep them in line for you." She then stepped back behind the red safety lines and saluted as Scarlet Jay climbed into the cockpit.

One of the ground crew scampered up the rails to lock her harness into place. When he was done and slid back down to the flight line, Jay powered up.

"How you doing today, Hawk?"

"All systems optimal," the flight computer responded; the vocal tones not quite neutral, though by no means mistakable for human.

Jay affectionately rubbed her hand along the control panel then began warm-up procedures, activating her comm, starting the engines, and, as a back-up, running internal diagnostics before signaling flight control they were ready to taxi. As she waited for confirmation, she commed Panski, "Pilot, you have my wing. Once we are informed of our runway you will follow my lead, heading 03-niner, climbing to seven thousand feet, and maintaining patrol altitude. Acknowledge?"

"Acknowledged, Captain," the pilot responded, his voice expressionless over the communications system. "Heading 03-niner, climb to seven thousand feet, and maintain patrol altitude."

Tension crept along her limbs as Jay powered up the rest of her systems in habitual sequence, flipping toggles and pressing buttons until the control panel was fully engaged. Her eyes trailed across the gauges and displays. No warnings flashed, no alarms sounded. She let the rumble of the Hawk's engines soothe her. Found comfort in the sharp scent of aviation fuel and oil that always lingered over the hanger bay before settling her respirator into place. As the engines warmed up, Jay closed her eyes a moment, waiting for Deeley's voice to sound in her earpiece. By the time they were given clearance to taxi out to the runway she had gotten her balance. She reached back with her left hand and tapped Granddad's bell, then toggled her comm.

"You set?"

Silence. What was he doing, napping?

"Panski? Are your systems green to go?"

"Green to go, Captain."

"Okay, roll her out nice and easy. We're slated for runway ten-alpha."

"Ten-alpha, Aye."

Her shoulder muscles tightened, and Jay had to force them to relax again. Something about this guy put her on edge. She didn't trust him with her back...or at it. There was a general feeling of laxness about him. As if he saw nothing wrong with cutting corners. She knew all too well that attitude got pilots killed...and not always the one taking the shortcuts.

Ten years ago she had been a raw cadet. Top of her class in flight school, the most recent in a long line of Ace pilots going back to her many-times-great Granddad...her head had been so far up her ass she'd have smelt dinner coming down if she hadn't been so oblivious. Cadet Justin Calloway had been her wingman. For the final flight exercise before graduation she had been less than thorough in her preflight. At three thousand feet, executing a hard bank-and-roll maneuver, her right rudder locked up, sending her plane crashing into Justin's. She'd been able to eject, suffering no more than a broken arm in the impact. Justin had lost his life in the resulting fireball. The accident had been attributed to mechanical failure and she had been allowed to graduate—with something less than high honors—but she knew the truth. Her friend had died because she'd been sloppy. His father, General Calloway, was just as certain and never let her forget it.

Not that she ever could.

"Scarlet Jay, please proceed to runway ten-alpha," Deeley broke her reverie, reminding her she held up the flight schedule.

"Going wheels up, flight control," Jay spoke across the comm. "See you in two."

"Wind to your wings, lassie," Deeley answered, as she took to the sky.

Jay grinned at the sergeant's informal hail. He was never less than regulation face to face, but over the comm he loosened up once in a while and that felt good, like a pale echo of her Granddad watching over her each time she flew.

And then they were airborne, and that faint shiver of nerves returned as Panski took up position on her wing.

*　　*　　*

Take-off had been uneventful.

Patrol was downright dull. Jay decided it was time to assess Panski's flight capability…not to mention give her nerves a rest, before she climbed right out of her skin. Toggling her comm, for the first time in half an hour, she spoke. "Panski, take lead for a bit."

Rather than simply pull ahead, the pilot executed the type of fancy, rolling dive rarely seen outside of an air show or combat and brought his NovaStream up in a sharp climb before leveling out in front of her. Jay didn't comment, merely noting the way he handled the jet, which grudgingly she had to admit was with a fair amount of skill, and just as much flash.

She watched the jet in front of her closely, noting a tendency to drift right, which Panski periodically corrected for. Hard to say if it was due to a heavy hand on the stick, or a bug in system. She made a mental note to have it checked out. Other than that, she didn't find much to fault in his piloting. He showed promise once his attitude got knocked into shape.

Jay shifted her focus to the dual-monitor set into her control panel. After all, they were out here to patrol. One monitor played a recorded feed from the previous day's fly-over, the other was a real-time image fed to the screen by high-powered surveillance cameras mounted to the exterior of the fighter. Together they allowed those on patrol to note subtle alterations that might signify a move by Dominion forces.

The demilitarized zone was quiet today, not even a rabbit sticking out its pointy teeth. Their flight took them over mile after mile of low scrub and the occasional sapling that hadn't been routed out yet. Other than the patrol road to their right, running along the edge where the border met the DMZ, there were no other defining features. The monotony left her with little to occupy her mind, which, left to its own, dredged up an old bone to worry at: Calloway and his efforts to basically ground her flight. His official position was that new pilots needed skilled veterans to acclimate them to the reality of combat on the line. Jay had it from trusted sources that his not-always-private stance was that women didn't belong in the cockpits of fighter craft. That was her fault, based on that one ill-fated flight, but it colored his opinion of female pilots across the board. Never mind that their physiology made them better suited to pulling high-g's, allowing them to execute maneuvers that caused their male counterparts to black out. Or that their fine motor control gave them the delicate touch modern aircraft demanded. And forget about the fact that their ability to multi-function and their utilization of both lobes of their brain aided their adaptability under high-stress situations. None of that mattered. Not in the shadow of his son's memory.

From that point on, Calloway wasn't just old-school...he was ancient-school.

And there wasn't a thing she or the Morrigans could do about it. Not without damaging their careers. Nothing pissed her off more than having no viable recourse. What was more, she had to remember it wasn't the greenies' fault. It was so easy to let the situation color her responses to Panski and the new pilots in general. Not a good habit to get into.

"Variation in terrain," the computer called a sudden disparity in the camera images to Jay's attention, distracting her from her thoughts. She glanced at the screen. It was difficult to make out what was there; she would have to make another pass.

"Hey...Flash,"—it suited him much better than the unfortunate Panski—"I'm circling back to investigate an anomaly."

A moment of dead air, then he responded, "Acknowledged, Scarlet Jay."

She banked left into a turn that brought her skimming over the terrain they'd just covered, using the digital zoom to capture the landscape below to document her report. The anomaly appeared to be a camouflaged perimeter sensor that had come partially uncovered. The sensors were used to alert of aerial movement over an area. She didn't recognize the design, which pretty much meant it was Dominion. The question was: how many were there besides this one, and had their patrol already been tagged?

With the intel secured, she guided the Hawk back into wing position, only to discover the patrol road was to the wrong side of them. They weren't just drifting slightly; they were half a klick into the DMZ.

"Pilot, we are off course," Jay spoke across the comm. "Correct your heading and return to Allied airspace."

"What the hell are you talking about?" Panski responded. "Heading confirmed as 03-niner...ma'am."

Being informal was one thing, but he clearly forgot he addressed a superior. She let it go. They had bigger issues at the moment. "Radar engaged," the computer announced. She glanced at the screen; there was the faintest ghost on the very edge of her radar, not even strong enough to consider a blip, but also clearly not stationary. *Probably nothing,* she told herself with one eye still on the radar. That uneasy feeling returned.

"Forget about your instruments for a moment," she instructed him. "Calculate your heading by the sun." She glanced down at her chronograph. "It is precisely 0730."

Jay waited, gave him a moment. She could see him taking visual. Across her comm came the sound of rather inventive swearing.

Before she could respond, a more strident warning sounded in her cockpit.

"Radar engaged. Radar engaged. Radar engaged. Radar engaged." Like an antique record album skipping, the flight computer repeated itself, only this was no malfunction. A quick glance down at her radar showed multiple ghosts on the display; so faint she would have discounted them as noise if they weren't advancing so steadily.

She scanned the horizon for confirmation. Whatever was headed their way was too far off to be seen. Her nerves stilled and a warm current of adrenaline flowed through her until each muscle was taut and her mind sharp focused in combat-readiness. They needed to get back to friendly territory.

"Veer off!" she ordered Panski. "We have bogies."

A hard bank left took her back toward their designated airspace. After a moment, though, she realized Panski hadn't followed suit. "Flash, veer off now, we are not authorized to engage in full air-to-air."

"I'm trying, damnit!" Jay could hear a thread of panic in his voice. "I have a systems malfunction." Glancing back, she watched as the NovaStream dipped and bobbed erratically on the currents as if the flight control profile no longer correctly registered the parameters of the aircraft.

This was much more than a simple case of drift.

"Pilot Panski, I take it you blew off the eyes-on preflight?"

There was a long moment of dead air. "Ma'am, yes, ma'am," he answered quietly, as any pilot scared shitless would.

Swearing, she banked again, reversing her trajectory.

No doubt the ghosts on the radar were Dominion aircraft, which pretty much confirmed they'd seeded the DMZ with perimeter sensors. There was no way this was in response to the one she'd spotted; the enemy couldn't have gotten airborne this quickly if that were the case. And with the NovaStream going buggy they couldn't outfly the incoming fighters. She mentally assessed their resources: the Hawk had 20mm Valkyrie internal cannons and starburst missiles mounted beneath each wing, four to a side. The NovaStream didn't have cannons, but it had eight each of heat-seekers and starbursts. Not nearly as much firepower as she would like. Maybe that would last ten minutes in full engagement. Setting her comm to command frequency, Jay called in for air support and was promptly acknowledged by Deeley. She prayed the forces arrived in time. A glance down at her radar showed the ghosts getting closer, the pattern denser. It looked like they had two flights closing in. With an efficiency garnered on the frontlines of more battles than she could count, Jay powered up her weapons systems and focused her thoughts on figuring a way out of this mess.

Her gaze tracked on the thin ribbon of road below and to her left, pretty much the demarcation between the Allied border and the DMZ. It was used by their ground patrols. Right now, none were in sight. Too bad. They were equipped with mobile SAMs and maw deuce 50-caliber machine guns; that would have come in handy as ground support. Well, looks like they were on their own.

"Hey, Flash, I need to know if you have enough control to maneuver..." She waited for him to acknowledge.

"I think so." His voice didn't shake but the words were tight and short.

She grimaced. Not good enough. "You need to confirm. Test her out now before they're on our tail."

She breathed out a silent sigh as he wrestled the NovaStream's nose down and into a left bank, the stick fighting him the whole way. The jet wobbled as it pulled to the right against his guidance, but he was able to correct. He then reversed the maneuver with much more control.

"Okay, here's what I need you to do...see the patrol road?" He made a vague sound she took as assent. "We are going to reverse course and head full throttle back toward base and intercept with our reinforcements. That road is your marker...it stays to your left wing at all times. Understood?"

"Loud and clear, Captain."

She had to respect his fortitude. No matter how he came across before this, under fire, so to speak, he was holding up better than some veteran pilots she'd flown with. In theory, once they were over Allied territory they were safe. Jay wasn't holding her breath on that. The Dominion wasn't known for playing by the rules.

"I've reported our situation. Our job now is to hold our own until our backup arrives. Get your weapons systems armed." As she spoke, she flipped the master switch for her own cannons and armed her missiles.

Panski's muttered "Acknowledged" spoke volumes through gritted teeth. She could hear the strain in his voice. Her own gut was in more knots than a fishing net as she watched over the limping NovaStream. Flashbacks from a decade past sent a shudder through her. Blood pulsed like a drum in her ears, for the moment louder than the engine roaring at her back as she held her breath, her full attention locked on Panski. The NovaStream bucked hard as it sliced through a thermal. Jay gasped and the same sound echoed from the other cockpit. There was a sour taste in the back of her throat.

"Pull up!" Jay called out. "Keep that bird in the air!"

"All respect, ma'am," the pilot snarled, "I'm fuckin' trying!"

Scarlet Jay held her peace after that, sending up Hail Marys and shadowing the craft from two hundred feet above his flying altitude. He got the NovaStream pointed the right direction and both of them put on some speed.

"Hey, Deeley," she hailed flight command once more. "I don't particularly want to be the only girl on the dance floor. You have an ETA for me?"

"Air support is wheels up and on the way, full burn. They should reach you in T-minus-fifteen minutes...but between me and you, Calloway ain't happy, says...."

The sergeant's words cut off abruptly and sounds of a sudden commotion came over the comm, followed by a familiar voice. "Corvidae! No screwups this time."

Scarlet Jay clenched her jaw on what she wanted to say to the old bastard. "Duly noted, sir."

"I mean it!" Calloway snapped. Rage burned through the words whereas he had always been cold and abrupt with her before. "You better bring that pilot back alive with all his bits still where they belong or you're through, acknowledged?"

Hostility came across the line in scorching waves. That was when it occurred to her, somewhat shamefully, that outside of receiving orders, she had never spoken to him, never approached him as Justin's father. For the past two months she'd taken everything he'd heaped upon her but she had never said what needed to be said. And this might be her one and only chance. The comm wasn't exactly private, but it would have to do.

"General Calloway," she said quietly and with absolute sincerity. "I deeply regret the loss of your son, I was careless...stupidly so, and I cannot tell you how sorry I am that I was not the only one to pay for those mistakes." She purged ten years of guilt, but she didn't lie down and offer him her throat. Her tone took on a bit of steel as she continued, "I know that can never be enough, but as my flight record will attest, I am no longer that cadet, I have learned from my mistakes and I *have* paid for them more than you can ever know."

He sputtered in response...likely preparing to yell; she didn't give him a chance.

"All due respect, sir, I have to go so I can concentrate on not making new ones."

She flicked the comm to short-range only and put the General from her thoughts. She likewise switched off the Hawk's verbal address system. Things were about to get hairy. She couldn't afford the distraction.

"Um...Jay..." Panski's voice cut in.

"Go ahead, Flash."

"Either my radar is acting up too, or we have trouble coming in at ten o'clock."

Jay glanced at her radar for confirmation. "Damn! They've circled around to cut us off!" She considered their options: cut deeper into Allied air space and pray they didn't follow, stay on course to the base and try and outrun them, or opt to engage and try and buy some time for backup to arrive. "How's the Nova responding?"

"She's fighting me," he responded. "I can strong-arm the stick, but I can't throttle above 400 knots or she shimmies like crazy."

That left them only one real choice, to face the enemy. "Okay...work it the best you can. Go for evasive maneuvers, and only take the sure shot. Keep your heading toward base as much as possible; I'll run interference and do what I can to take them out."

"Acknowledged." He saluted her from his cockpit and she had to grin as she returned it, then, firewalling the throttle, she took it to the enemy.

It had been months since she'd seen close-in aerial combat. Her chin dropped and her fangs were out as she rushed to engage the lead element. She clawed for altitude as she closed the distance. The ghosts on the radar blossomed into full blips, sending warning lights flashing through the cockpit; her eyes narrowed in response, but she kept her gaze focused on the sky outside her canopy and at her six. Below her, just above the cirrus deck, she could barely make out the needle-like profile of four Dominion Hyperwings, advanced remote drones that had evolved considerably from the old Predator technology.

"Come on, Gomer...bring it," she muttered under her breath, unconsciously falling back on the slang learned at her Granddad's knee.

No doubt these were just the advanced scouts. Somewhere in the atmo were fighters headed this way. They had to take the Hyperwings out before the enemy reinforcements arrived, or she and Panski were done for. Two of them broke off and headed for the NovaStream. The other two came at her from split vectors.

"Flash, deuce bogies headed your way!" Jay had just enough time to call the warning to Panski and then she had no more attention to spare. A hail of lethal artillery came spraying toward her, lit up by a flare of tracer rounds.

She swore with enough heat to blister even her Granddad's ears as she jinked to the right, then dipped her wing to the left and rolled the Hawk, diving for the deck. Working the stick, she pulled up into a steep climb, scissoring across the nearest drone's flight path, trying to come in behind it. Every time she tried to get a bead on one of them, the drones reversed, spoiling her aim.

"Come on, already! I wasn't serious about dancing!"

Scarlet Jay came down in a screaming dive and broke off sharply as she worked the Valkyrie's radar controls, furiously trying to get lock. And then she had it; the drone off her right wing lit up as she came around in a tight turn. Jay depressed the trigger on her cannons and crowed as incendiary ammunition devastated the rear half of the craft.

The Hawk soared through the flack as the debris rained down on the DMZ.

"Boola-Boola!" Jay yelled in triumph, though the comm would not carry the "kill" to command.

From off to her right, strafing fire dimpled her canopy and Jay reflexively ducked in her harness. "Shit!" A quick glance through the canopy showed a bit of smoke trailing from her right wingtip, but she saw no sign of flame.

Before it could fire again, Panski buzzed the attacking drone close enough that the wake from his slipstream sent the craft into a dip, ruining the targeting lock. He then executed a hard bank and roll to evade before arcing away. The drone veered off to follow.

Her teeth bared, Jay yanked the stick in tight and slammed the throttle into full burner, booting the left rudder, sending the Hawk into a 135-degree slicing turn. The damage to her bird pissed her off. She closed on the pursuing drone, flying in close, then let loose with a starburst when she had the enemy craft square in the cone of vulnerability. A scan of the sky and Panski's thumbs up were confirmation he had taken care of his two as well. Her grin felt good and vicious, as she returned the gesture, but their triumph was short-lived.

The cockpit lit up like Christmas as the radar flashed both red and green, alerting her to incoming enemy aircraft closing fast and friendlies just pinging at the edge of the radar. It was a race now, one she was afraid the Dominion pilots were going to win; yet she dare not comm the rescue fighters. Right now they were beyond enemy radar range. If she made any attempt to communicate it could very well be intercepted, robbing her side of the element of surprise.

She didn't know what the Dominion was after, but she was here to see they went home disappointed...if at all. Estimating the approach vector and speed of the enemy craft, she took the fight into the vertical. The Gs were crushing as she whipped into a steep climb, bringing the Hawk to 12,000 feet. She held it a moment, then stomped on the rudder to get the nose turned back down.

The dive took her right through the center of their formation, scattering the squadron of Boru 47-Vs—the Dominion's delta-wing fighters—sending one careening into his wingmate. Panski came in from below, only a little unsteady, and took another out with a starburst missile. The fireball surely lit up the sky. Jay couldn't say, though, she was too busy watching the ground rush toward her. With every muscle straining she fought the stick, leveling the bird a bare two hundred feet off the deck. She laughed with the rush as she climbed back up to engage. With backup approaching they no longer needed to conserve their ammunition. She and Panski harried the Dominion fighters, dipping and diving among them like crows tormenting a hawk.

The old girl took damage, but nothing crippling. In fact, now that the pressure was off, Jay was having way too much fun. One of the Borus veered off, turning tail back to base with one engine trailing a plume of thick, black smoke punctuated by periodic shooting sparks. She'd sent at least one more crashing to the deck with a starburst. There were two left, both of them hard on her tail, and then her luck ran out. A warning klaxon shrieked through her earpiece. At least one of the enemy fighters had lock on her Hawk.

"Crap!"

The Hawk's engine screamed in protest as she rolled hard left and pitched down. As she did, she hit the chaff release on the stick, launching a cloud of debris in her wake to break up the radar lock.

"You aren't good enough to take me down, Demon," she taunted, though there was no way the Dominion pilot could hear her.

As she powered away, her gaze darted down to the radar. Whoever flew to their aid was nearly here. She set her heading for intercept, with just enough wobble and limp to give the enemy pilots the impression she was having difficulty. All the while, she lured them closer to the kill zone. No telling who command had sent on the rescue run but they were fresh and presumably fully loaded. Daring a second glance she made a quick count and whistled long and low as she counted ten Allied jets coming in fast. By now they had to be pinging the enemy radar.

There was no way two lone Dominion pilots would engage such an overwhelming force over Allied territory. Jay anticipated they would cut out and run away.

She was wrong.

"On your six!" Panski called out over the short-range. Jay craned her neck for visual confirmation through the cracked canopy. The remaining jets were closing fast, working furiously to gain target lock.

She must have pissed them off.

Jay dipped and bobbed and spun off for all she was worth to spoil their aim. She took the Hawk low, blending in with the ground reflection, using every trick she knew to pull ahead. Cannon fire and missile impacts chewed up the terrain. The Hawk shook with half a dozen impacts but somehow held together.

And yet, no matter what trick she pulled she couldn't shake them.

"Take it vertical," Panski called out. Going with her gut, she instantly obeyed, yanking back the stick and giving the Hawk full throttle, she shot up into the lightening sky mere seconds before two of Panski's heat-seekers flew up the tailpipes of the Boru fighters.

"Way to go, Flash," she called over the short-range as she brought her craft back down, banking wide and circled above the NovaStream, noting the fresh battle scars dotting the fuselage, taking in the burning debris from enemy aircraft scattered far and wide below. She considered the other pilot, the way he stepped up to the fight; not hotdogging it, but working as a team. A smile tugged at her lips. She had to admit he didn't have all that many rough edges left to buff.

"Hey, let's get that bird back to base and figure out what's wrong with it."

As she set her heading to intersect with the approaching friendlies, she reengaged her long-range comm and hailed flight control. "Scarlet Jay to command," she reported, the words heavy with satisfaction. "The party's over, and we're coming home."

SCIFIKU 2

stare into a star
to find your inner fire
cosmic awareness

On First Line

In "First Line," by Danielle Ackley-McPhail, you'll find the same crackling action and deft pacing that you may have come to know in her other fiction. However, since many reviewers will point to those qualities, I want to take a moment to gesture at something subtler, but no less a hallmark of her writing: its intense engagement with humans in crisis. And, by means of a footnote, understand that—in Danielle's fiction—the "crisis" she depicts is often as unique and quirky as the emotional involvement within and between her characters is intense.

I won't spoil the twists and unusual crises of the protagonist of "First Line" by revealing any plot specifics, but I will guarantee you this: you won't forget this story. With just enough peripheral science to build plausibility, Danielle unfolds a tale of both human and machine tragedy, sacrifice, and dark immortality that will remain with you long after you've read the last word. Strongly recommended!

—Charles E. Gannon,
co-author of *Extremis*,
with Steve White

An Alliance Archives Adventure

Go! Go! GO!" the squad leader barked into the comm.

The order pinged her transceiver, a sharp reminder of many missions past. Quieter than the barest whisper, hard, taut, and intense, it triggered automatic responses in a battle-honed soldier: a flood of adrenaline, combat awareness drilled in by special ops training and countless field missions, a fierce impulse to bring a weapon to bear.

In one instant, she went from drifting through oblivion, to combat-ready.

She was no longer capable of adrenaline rushes, but the rest of her reflexes were still on the mark. It wasn't supposed to work that way. By all rights, there shouldn't be anything left of Lieutenant Sheila "Trey" Tremaine. Well, nothing capable of such a knee-jerk reaction to the issued order.

Now who the hell's cock-up was that?

There were large gaps in her memory, or at least she presumed there were, seeing as the last thing she could recall was dying. She used to be an officer assigned to the 428th Special Ops unit, MOS: demolitions specialist, but when an enemy round took her down, on its way to taking her out, she'd been offered a chance. She remembered that too (before the dying part). The head of the tech division had shown up beside her hospital cot once it was clear she was well on her way to succumbing to her injuries.

Horrible way for a soldier to die, by the way: slowly, in a hospital bed, a burden to the very society you were meant to serve. Feeling worse than useless. It just wasn't right. You either kicked ass and survived to fight another day, or you took a shitload of them down on your way out. That was the way it was supposed to be. For a soldier. Anything else just felt wrong. They'd lost two men saving her should-have-been-dead ass. The only thing worse than waiting to die was staring that guilt in the face the entire time.

"How serious do you take your oath to serve, Lieutenant?" the bureaucrat had solemnly asked.

She'd allowed her gaze to sweep across her broken body before giving him a look as sharp as a knife's edge. Her lip had curled up in a bare approximation of the warning sneer her unit would have recognized before she tore into someone particularly dense. Of course, her clear status of "non-threat" made him oblivious to her reaction at the insult he'd issued. If she'd had any energy left for anything except guilt and dying, she would have shown him how wrong his assessment was.

"Very," she responded, if faintly.

That was when he offered her an approximation of immortality. Okay. Maybe not. But definitely a way to make up for dying the wrong way, and an opportunity to protect her unit in a way she'd never imagined.

"We'd like to neuro-scan your brain," he went on, very matter-of-fact, as if he were discussing the watch schedule, or what was being served in the Mess. "To preserve your expertise and instincts." He went on to explain the great advancements in this process and how they would then be able to imprint the scan-capture onto a neural matrix so that her training and experience would not be lost at her demise, but could be utilized in this time of conflict to ensure others did not fall as she had...*blah, blah, blah.*

Manipulative prick.

"Why wait...till now?" she managed. After all, she'd been there in that cot quite a while.

There was an uncomfortable silence on the egg-head's part. "The process is terminal."

Well. Okay. So was she, apparently. Not that she hadn't figured that out already. Still, she'd been tempted to say no, just for the piss-poor way he handled the proposal. The idea itself intrigued her, though. The way he explained it, if she agreed, her thought processes would be imprinted on the newest generation of packbot to augment the technical data already hard-wired in, with the intent of mating that automated programming with her learned reflexes and evaluative capabilities. She didn't get all the technical bits; after all, her training was in demolitions, not computers. But really, the only thing she needed to understand was that a part of her would live on to fight those that had taken her out.

Ultimately (clearly), she'd agreed. The clincher, in the end: the mech in question had been requisitioned by the 428th. The guy should have mentioned that to begin with. That was her only real enticement. What did she care about revenge? She'd believed in why they were fighting. That and protecting her men mattered to her more than any petty revenge.

"Will they know it's me?" she managed to ask. The answer was no. "Will I know it's me?" Again, no.

"Though urban legends persist to the contrary," the egg-head assured her, "there is no evidence to substantiate the rumors that personality is transferable with this process."

She'd taken his word for it. She'd wanted to believe some part of her would go on, would continue to serve. That didn't mean she wanted to be conscious of it.

Her body had failed just as the final neural pathways were scanned. Trey knew this, because even that the process had captured. Now, she was the next level in advanced warfare. And contrary to all assurances, she was still self-aware.

Trey took stock of her current situation. Besides overall being FUBARed, sensors indicated she was currently being jostled, but the motion spoke more of stealth than open assault. Something close to excitement, leavened by a bit of apprehension went through her. It wasn't supposed to work this way. But what the hell; too late now, right?

There were murmurs going back and forth across her transceiver. Just bits and pieces, mostly sub-vocal sounds rather than words. She understood this, though. Most of the communicating going on between the deployed team was done through gestures and glances. They'd been a team a long time. Who needed words?

Of course, that meant Trey was in the dark. The packbot that housed her was in standby mode. The transceiver was active and ready to receive input, but the cameras that would be her eyes were powered down and she had no access to the subroutines that would power them up. It was like she was tied up and blindfolded.

Not something she was into.

She was used to being in charge, or at least an active participant. The deal she'd made was not quite looking so good at the moment. The waiting, the not knowing, did a number on whatever part of her personality had glommed onto the scan.

Finally the forward motion stopped.

Trey felt a jolt as power flooded her system. Data was keyed in, leaving her disoriented. She was, after all, merely a passenger within the robotic interface, a data source that allowed the CPU to interpret scenarios for the handler based on her collective experience. She was a resource with not one whit of control over anything.

Yeah, maybe her deathbed wasn't such a good place to make life-altering decisions. She may have been a demo specialist, and understood the mechanical workings of the packbot, but from the inside she couldn't follow impulse one of the directives being fed into the unit for the pending incursion. This passive-observer mode definitely had the potential of evolving into her own personal hell. At least as a part of the military she'd had the freedom to act within the structure of command. In combat, she was used to taking charge, even. Trey was not a passive creature.

She felt better once the internal gyros registered a change in the robotic unit's orientation as its handler drew it from his pack and lobbed it into the crumbling shell of a building.

"Boombot deployed, Sarge," Trey's handler subvocalized into his bonejack. "Unit transmission at...85 percent optimal." Nothing sounded like it used to, but from the irreverent terminology, Trey figured Coop was the soldier reassigned her demo duties. She hadn't known him so well, beyond an officer's familiarity with those she led, but he'd always been the one to add some hint of humor to every mission. By her reckoning, wisecracks were one more part of his armor, right along with his ballistic mesh. She found it comforting, herself.

"Damn...we need better than that, soldier," responded whoever had taken over as team leader—Trey couldn't help feeling a bit smug that it had taken two men to replace her...at least, until she recalled her new role was "Boombot," and why.

"Adjust your frequency; no one goes in until that 'bot is transmitting at 95 percent minimum. *I'm* not losing any men to sloppiness."

The implication wasn't lost on Trey. For the briefest instant, she had the overwhelming impulse to go "buggy" on the colossal shit. Let him see how "optimal" he could be when things were out of his control and there was pressure from the higher ups to achieve the mission directives now.

Hell, he was the one nice and cozy at the fall-back position, while here she was completely over the front line. Of course, it was so easy to forget she was only a passenger. Right up until Coop started fiddling with the controller.

Talk about weird. Trey could "feel" as he adjusted the packbot's settings, maneuvering the unit around the crumbled remains of the building, manipulating the camera angles. She heard him murmur about the darkness. It should have served as a warning, but she totally didn't pick up on it. When he triggered the variable-intensity LEDs she would have flinched, if she could have. The sudden light had the intensity of a bomb blast without the fade away. She could visualize her eyes snapping closed. And suddenly, they did. Or at least, there was an abrupt return to total darkness. It was a coincidence, of course, but a welcome one. Well. For her.

Coop swore like a cross between a marine and a twenty-dollar whore.

A flood of data transmitted to the 'bot. Then once again, supernova. Trey reflexively "flinched" and was returned to total darkness. She was in awe as the revelation dawned. Maybe passive observer wasn't her lot after all.

"Military-issue piece of crap! We don't have time for this!"

There was that guilt again. What was relief for her was just a dangerous complication for the squad. But it did demonstrate that perhaps she had some control over her fate. To test the theory, she triggered the circuits that brought the lights up again independent of Coop's efforts, only gradually. Okay, enough experimentation. She had some amount of control. That alone made her just a bit more comfortable in her titanium skin.

Enough.

She didn't want Coop scrapping the mission because 'Boombot' was malfunctioning. She "stepped back," releasing control to the handler.

It was odd not having to go to any effort to do her job. She had finally reached the state seasoned soldiers both dreamed of and dreaded: where a combat zone didn't require active thought to evaluate. Of course, she'd had to die to achieve it.

Always a down side, wasn't there?

Between her knowledge and the packbot's superfast processors, analysis of the building interior was instantaneous. The moment the cameras panned across a zone all the potential hot points were identified and assessed, simultaneously scrolling across the unit's micro-display and the handler's monitor.

All threats on the first floor were old activity, already neutralized. As the last lower-level quadrant scan completed, Trey and the packbot approached the staircase. A sensor extended from the 'bot until it connected with the first riser. Next the unit emitted a supersonic peal, followed by a probe shooting out from the front facing, forcefully punching up against the structure. Again, data analysis was instantaneous. The sonic blast revealed nothing but the standard staircase infrastructure. The impact test confirmed the architecture was sound and not rigged to blow or collapse. With the all-clear given, the handler activated the 'bot's front flipper assembly. Trey found herself fascinated as the flipper extended up and forward until the belted track grabbed the next tread. She found the sensation odd as the servos engaged and the front of the unit raised, following the flippers up the steps. The monitors continually tracked the stability of the structure as the process repeated, until the 'bot rested soundly on the upper level.

There was nothing there or in the rest of the surrounding buildings. Nothing recent, anyway. Plenty of signs of neutralized ordinance, along with one or two that had clearly been triggered, but by the levels of accumulated dust, signs of animal habitation, the weathering...all indications were that the outpost had been abandoned by all parties.

"Echo sector has been cleared for occupation, sir," Coop reported over the comm to his squad leader.

"Our ETA is 0700," was the response. "Have your men set up base operations and then stand down until we arrive."

Trey wanted to protest as the 'bot's systems were again powered down and the unit was returned to Coop's MOLLE pack. She noticed that once the rest of the system was shut off and beyond her reach, her own power source was likewise reduced until she operated under what felt like brown-out conditions. Apparently, Coop put her in her own version of stand-by.

Part of her railed against the restrictions; she was just getting the feel of her new situation, the freedom and capabilities she had never dreamed would be open to her. But then, the squad leader had no clue she was anything more than a complex data dump. Having to admit that made her seethe. Not that she had a right to. She'd signed on for this tour, after all.

As the outside world went away, she perversely wondered if this was how her tablet computer had felt each time she'd shut it down. And had it likewise amused itself in the darkness plotting theoretical rebellion?

* * *

Was it days or weeks or even longer that her existence went on this way? Trey had no clue. Well...she knew the chronological time and date stamp that queued up each time her systems were powered back up, but you know...when you spend an eternity in isolation in between those fraught, tedious moments of recon, the relative time bore no connection with a clock or a calendar. Trey, in short, felt ancient. And kind of like she was suspended in purgatory.

Another crumbling structure stood before her, another potential hotbed of insurgents. It was time to earn herself one step further from hell.

As she went about her duties—she no longer thought of herself separate from Boombot, though her identity of Trey was still very real to her—her processors filtered out the background chatter from the waiting squad. She heard increasingly too much of it. The men were getting too relaxed the longer they went without encountering opposition. It made them sloppy.

Already several had to be patched up by the medic after tripping over the remnants of a misfired hydra mine. The plungers had been obscured by the overgrown ground cover, but that was no excuse for the soldiers' blunder. Trey would have torn them a new one for being that sloppy on her watch. Demerits would have been the least of their problems. Fortunately for them, if not the whole squad, the payload had long ago been triggered. Trapped in the can at detonation when the lid malfunctioned, the mine apparently had geysered, rather than blowing out in a radial pattern; otherwise there would have been nothing but a crater as testament to where it used to be. Of course, as cold as the thought was, perhaps it wasn't a good thing the mine had been spent. If the men had gotten more than a gash or a scrape for their inattention they would have learned their lesson better. Sloppy soldiers often got more than just themselves killed.

Speaking of which, Trey chastised herself for dwelling on the folly of others when she had her own duties to execute.

* * *

Nightmares were the worst part of standby mode. Yeah, even that plague of every soldier hadn't been left behind. Kind of hard to wake up from a recurring hell when you had no body, no icy sweat to wick away, no rapid breath to ramp down to a normal speed, nothing physical to distract you from the images you could never forget, or to remind you they weren't happening in real-time.

Trey wished she had enough control to power herself back up. Of course, it wasn't like she could drop and do push-ups until she tumbled into a deep, dreamless sleep, as she would have done in her other life, so what was the point? Though she could imagine how Coop would freak if he'd caught her trying it.

Trey settled for reviewing the data she'd so far gathered in their recon of the sector. Something about the zone made her uneasy. She caught glimpses in her nightmares, hints of whatever had her "nerves" buzzing, but just as in her flesh-bound dreams, everything was shadowy, more impressions than anything else. Well, except for the blood. And the screams. Shrugging it off, she went back to analyzing the data. Had she been here before? It was so hard to tell. After all, as she already noted, the world was a heck of a lot different through the camera-eye of a 'bot. Whether or not she covered familiar ground, she got a bad feeling the closer they drew to the next sector.

There had to be something in the data and damn if she wouldn't find it. She wasn't about to lead another squad straight into the guns of the enemy.

✻   ✻   ✻

Hours later she finally recognized what she was looking for. It was oDark00 and the squad had been on the move for two hours. They were entering unsecured territory. This was the sector her unit had been heading for that fateful day. The one where good men died retrieving her.

Up until now, Coop had reserved her for establishing the all-clear of structures in zones their side had already pacified, cleaning up any parting gifts left by the insurgents. This time when Coop powered her up she discovered he'd reconfigured her chassis with the explosive ordinance detection kit, increasing her speed and adding more muscle to her manipulator arm. Now she ran point for the squad across uncleared terrain, looking for more aggressive threats along their path. Already, she and Coop had discovered and disabled half a dozen hydras and discreetly marked and redirected the squad's route around countless claymores. Those that came behind them would have more leisure to decommission the munitions. Their squad wouldn't risk it now. To do so would slow them down at best, and give away their position at worst, should even one mine be mishandled.

"Sarge, copy," Coop subvocalized.

"Acknowledged, report," came the response.

Coop kept it short, as even comm signals could be intercepted, if the enemy cracked the frequency. "Cleared to perimeter, sector Tango; squad heading in. Going comm dark."

"Roger."

The rest of the unit would now follow via the cleared corridor.

Trey was so on edge her lip would be twitching, if she'd still had one. She was surprised she wasn't shooting sparks as it was. She felt charged enough for a full fireworks display. Earlier, while exploring the internal pathway of the packbot, she discovered the protocol that would initiate self-destruct should the unit be compromised. If she could figure out how to trigger that at will, it could come in handy. If nothing else, she'd feel better knowing that, at least in a way, she was armed. She set a portion of her...conciousness to the puzzle as she continued rolling along.

Eventually, she came upon a civilian compound. It had been hit hard, as had many she had seen before. Coop ran her up to the first of the buildings with infrared sensors activated. There were some thermal, but nothing larger than the planet's equivalent of a rat.

She saw no traces of munitions rigged to blow, though there were signs of recent habitation. Local wildlife, perhaps, or squatters displaced by the recent conflict. There was nothing to imply occupation by a military force, though. Trey assessed the risk factor of the building at a level three, and fed the cautionary note to her handler. After careful inspection sent up no additional red flags, Coop guided her to the next building. Inspection continued in a similar manner through most the compound, bringing her about to the main structure.

By now Trey twitched like anything, if only on the inside. There was still nothing registering on infrared, but her mics were picking up trace sounds that might be stealth movement...or might just be a branch in the wind. She was running all four cameras, though only data from the primary was feeding to the control monitor. It was odd being able to scan forward and still watch over her own shoulder; not as reassuring as it should be, though. After all, it only served to remind her she was out here solo.

As she entered the final building her instincts started grumbling. Flashbacks of her nightmares sprang to the forefront, demanding she back out of the structure, double-time.

With sheer determination and her virtual jaw set, Trey ignored the impulse and powered through to do her duty.

The lower level was clear. More signs of habitation, less clear as to the source. Her unit had rudimentary olfactory sensors Coop never seemed to activate. Chances were he didn't even know they were there. It was a new feature Trey herself had never seen before this model, only recently discovered. She made an executive decision and brought them on-line. Traces of human sweat. Food. Some particles of ordinance components.

Shit.

There were times she definitely hated being right. Her self-preservation instincts were all but standing on her non-existent head screaming. She ignored them once more, rolling up the stairs and turning down the upper corridor in the direction from which the odors were strongest. Trey could feel an internal tug as her actions diverged from those dictated by Coop and the controller, but this was a case where instinct (the combat kind, rather than the self-preservation kind) demanded a different course of action. Her primary camera had a fiber-optic extension for situations where the bulkier unit would not serve. She extended it now as she approached the first doorway. At the same time, she readied the self-destruct protocol. Just in case.

There was time for her to identify a crude munitions lab and roughly fifteen operatives clothed in thermal-dampening suits positioned around the room before a hand shot out and grabbed the extension.

Crap! She tried to backpedal, but as he drew her within range, his other hand brought up a silenced pistol and fired on the camera assembly, shattering the lens.

Before he could do more damage, she aimed a probe at his leg and zapped him with enough current to fry his brain. Her olfactory sensors overloaded on burnt flesh as her manipulator arm came around to drag the corpse out of her way.

The enemy forces were not idle. She transferred optical to her backup camera and assessed the situation. Weapons had been brought to bear and the soldiers were converging. She couldn't handle them all, and the lab and its contingent were a serious threat to her unit and the offensive. Without a second thought, she initiated the self-destruct protocol, ready to die a warrior's death.

*   *   *

There was yelling and a sudden sizzle of sound as Coop lost visual. He breathed a curse and his hands clutched the controller tighter, though it had gone nonfunctional. He was still receiving data from the 'bot. In fact, impossible as it was, the unit somehow seemed to be moving independently. Before he could settle on a plan of action, an image reappeared on his monitor, the angle skewed as it came from a secondary camera. He watched in stunned silence as more than a dozen Dominion soldiers rushed the Boombot.

"We have hostile contact," he called to his men, who scrambled to defensive positions on all sides. Coop turned his attention back to the monitor. He tried once more to pull the 'bot back, but it was no use; the unit still didn't respond to the controls. He watched with a mixture of awe and frustration as it revved forward, grabbing the foremost enemy's rifle hand in what oddly looked like a judo move, snapping it. The soldier dropped his weapon. The corresponding scream echoed oddly, coming both through the 'bot's comlink and more faintly from the building a half a klick away.

"What the…" he murmured, startling the unit's sniper, who crouched beside him. Coop stared hard at the words that appeared on his monitor.

<<GO BACK TO HELL, DEMONS!!!>>

The words triggered a memory of many a past mission.

It couldn't be. There was no way. But he'd been assigned to this unit a long time, most of that time in this squad. Under the command of Lieutenant Tremaine…His left hand moved away from the 'bot controller to the keyboard, rapidly tapping just four keys…

<<T…R…E…Y>>

On the last stroke there was a pop, and a fireball engulfed the structure under surveillance.

"No!" Coop yelled, silence no longer an issue. On the monitor, in the camera-view window there was nothing but snow as the comlink with the packbot was severed. He gulped at the final entry in the log window:

<<LtST - initiating self-destruct.>>

His fingers flew over the keyboard, frantically trying to call up the final transmission made by the 'bot, which was programmed to back up its system data prior to self-destruct. As he did so he couldn't help wondering, was he imagining things, or had he just lost his lieutenant...for the second time?

*   *   *

"Go! Go! GO!" the squad leader barked into the comm.

The order pinged her transceiver, a sharp reminder of many missions past.

She jerked to awareness with a start, her nerves tighter than a well-set trip line. In one instant she went from drifting through oblivion to combat-ready.

There were large gaps in her memory, or at least she presumed there were, seeing as the last thing she could recall was blowing up a room full of Demons...and preparing to die...again. *So who the hell's cock-up was this?* she thought, as the 'bot was powered up and tossed through a nearby gaping hole that used to hold a window.

"Treybot deployed, Sarge," Coop subvocalized into his bonejack. "She's transmitting at...99.5 percent optimal."

SCIFIKU 3

byte me deep, cruel world,
my complex humanity
in binary trapped

On A Legacy of Stars

Marshall McLuhan once asked me who was my favorite science fiction writer. On most days, I would have answered Isaac Asimov, but on this day I said Olaf Stapledon, because my head was in the cosmos and I was thinking of his *Star Maker*. Would you believe me if I told you there's something of Stapledon in the story now before you, Danielle Ackley-McPhail's "A Legacy of Stars"? Read her liquid lyrics, and tell me they did not lead you into the "heart of a star," if you feel like doing anything more than softly dreaming.

—Paul Levinson,
author of *The Silk Code* and
The Plot to Save Socrates

A LEGACY OF STARS

"I open the door of heaven."

—The Goddess Sesheta,
The Book of Coming Forth By Day

Have you ever gazed into the heart of a star?

I have. You are blind to anything else forever after, no matter if your eyes are yet capable of seeing. The memory dazzles your vision, your mind, leaves you in open-mouthed awe at the wonder of it. No commonplace sight that the universe may offer can hope to compare.

I did not intend to alter my perception so radically. I had no choice in this.

My name is Sesheta.

It was not always, but any other name I may have laid claim to is long lost to me. Some may know, might even tell you if you ask, but otherwise it would not occur to them, blinded as they are, by the lingering light of that star.

In darkness...I shine.

This likewise was not always so.

On the day of my rebirth, I was led to a chamber in the ship no other was allowed to access. Etched into the hatch was a single word: Library. I wondered at that as the simple portal opened. Inside was dark, near complete, but for a pinpoint of light on the far wall. The atmosphere was stale, heavy with the scent of dust, despite the steady rumble of cycled air.

"Go," my keeper ordered. A gentle shove to my back sent me forward fearing to stumble, fearing what might obstruct my path, unknown, unyielding...but there was nothing.

"Go, child. You must. There is no other...."

He was ancient and all to him were 'child,' no matter that I was no untried youth.

I went forward, though I could not bring myself to anything but timid steps. My breath trembled in my chest. I remember this. I can yet feel the slick skin of sweat coating me, clinging my clothes to my body, chilling any bare skin. Nothing came up hard against my shins...nothing sent me tumbling to the deck. The point of light grew closer, if no bigger.

Don't ask me how I knew. Such details simply are since I took up my mantle.

"You must look through," the keeper murmured at my back, distant in both space and my awareness. "Place your eye to the hole."

His voice sounded sad to me, but beneath that hope and dread and uncertainty colored his words. It was an echo of my own heart.

Fearful, but obedient, I advanced until my breasts flattened against riveted steel. The placement of the glass-covered hole forced my head to bow in compliance.

It was the last time I would assume such a position.

I saw everything and nothing. Every color of light flooded my vision and all the knowledge of the universe was at my command, wrote itself into my very being until such a simple thing as a name scarce had room for itself, it was buried so deep. For an instant and forever I heard the music to which all light dances, the singing of stars and the beating of their hearts, felt my sweat-dampened hair ruffled by the solar winds, tasted the bitter cold of space, scented by the aeons.

I saw forever in the heart of that star.

Do you wonder that I was so changed?

Tst! Pay attention!

I rose that day from where I'd crumpled with my clothes, myself, my fears burned away. I turned back to face my keeper. By the glow of my bare skin I became aware of the pictures on the chamber walls, etched glyphs, symbols of another age at once both strange and known to me. They were obsolete, lost in the shadow of all knowledge crowding my thoughts.

I retraced my earlier footsteps, no longer timid, no longer blind, though I still could not say if the sight was that of my eyes. I stopped at the threshold where my former keeper had abased himself. I brushed my fingertips across the crown of his bowed head. The fine strands of his aged hair shimmered a moment and the ancient gasped, his body taut and trembling.

Such is common for those star-touched.

Hair thickened, gleamed with an ebon hue recalled from long-ago years, skin smoothed, and twisted joints straightened until ageless youth rest beneath my hand.

"Rise," I told him who had for so long remain faithful, "and attend me."

We walked across the heavens, opened the doors of transcendence, ushered a great many souls. I can tell by your eyes you would ask me why, if only you dared. I will tell you. Mankind was easily lost among the heavens, without someone to guide the way.

Ages passed unnoticed. Time means little when starsong echoes in your ear.

He is gone now, in case you wonder. They are all gone, but for my remembering.

I am tired, child...and there is no other...place your eye to the hole.

ABOUT THE AUTHOR

Award-winning genre author and editor, DANIELLE ACKLEY-MCPHAIL, has worked both sides of the publishing industry for over eighteen years. Her works include the urban fantasies, *Yesterday's Dreams, Tomorrow's Memories, Today's Promise,* and *The Halfling's Court,* and the writers guide, *The Literary Handyman.* She edits the *Bad-Ass Faeries* anthologies and *Dragon's Lure,* and has contributed to numerous other anthologies.

She is a member of the New Jersey Authors Network and Broad Universe, a writer's organization focusing on promoting the works of women authors in the speculative genres.

Danielle can be found on LiveJournal (damcphail, lit_handyman), Facebook (Danielle Ackley-McPhail), and Twitter (DAckley-McPhail). Learn more at *www.sidhenadaire.com and www.badassfaeries.com.*

ALSO FEATURED

MIKE MCPHAIL's lifelong dream was to join NASA and become a mission specialist. He attended the Academy of Aeronautics in New York, as well as enlisting in the Air National Guard. Among his works are a number of stories, including "Chimera", in the anthology *No Longer Dreams*, based on the *Alliance Archives*™ series and its related Martial Role-Playing Game™; a manual-based, military science-fiction that realistically portrays the consequences of warfare. To learn more about his work, visit www.mcp-concepts.com.

JOHN G. HEMRY (a.k.a. Jack Campbell) is the author of the best-selling *Lost Fleet* and *Lost Fleet: Beyond the Frontier* series under the pen name Jack Campbell. His new novel *Lost Stars: Tarnished Knight* releases in October. Under his own name, he's also the author of the 'JAG in space' series, the latest of which is *Against All Enemies*. His short fiction has appeared in places as varied as the latest *Chicks in Chainmail* anthology (*Turn the Other Chick*) and *Analog* magazine (which published his Nebula Award-nominated story *Small Moments in Time*). John's nonfiction has appeared in *Analog* and *Artemis* magazines as well as BenBella books on *Charmed, Star Wars*, and *Superman*. John is a retired US Navy officer who lives in Maryland with his wife (the incomparable S) and three great kids.

STEVE WHITE is an American science fiction author best known as the co-author of the Starfire-series alongside David Weber. He is married with 3 daughters and currently lives in Charlottesville, Virginia. He also works for a legal publishing company. He previously served as a United States Navy officer and served during the Vietnam War and in the Mediterranean region.

BUD SPARHAWK began writing science fiction in 1975 and, after two sales, stopped writing for thirteen years. Since again taking up the pen, his stories and articles have appeared frequently in *Analog, Asimov's*, and other SF magazines as well as anthologies. Bud has been a three-time finalist in the Nebula's Novella category in 1998, 2002, and 2006. More information may be found at http://sff.net/people/budsparhawk.

Keith R.A. DeCandido is the author of about 50 novels, including a mess of media tie-ins in universes ranging from *Star Trek* to *Supernatural* to *Kung Fu Panda* to *Farscape* to *Leverage* and more, plus he has two novel series that are fantastical police procedurals—*Dragon Precinct* and its sequels (in a fantasy setting) and *SCPD: The Case of the Claw* and its forthcoming sequels (in a superhero setting). He also edits, podcasts, blogs, studies and teaches karate, and much more. Find out less at www.DeCandido.net.

Jody Lynn Nye lists her main career activity as "spoiling cats." She lives northwest of Chicago with one of the above and her husband, author and packager Bill Fawcett. She has written over forty books, including The Ship Who Won with Anne McCaffrey, a humorous anthology about mothers, Don't Forget Your Spacesuit, Dear!, and over a hundred short stories. Her latest books are View From the Imperium (Baen Books), and Myth-Quoted (Ace Books).

Jack McDevitt has been on the final Nebula ballot 11 times, but has never won. *Omega* was named best novel and given the John W. Campbell Memorial Award in 2005. He has received the Phoenix and SESFA awards for lifetime achievement, and twice won the SESFA Award for best novel (*Deepsix* and *Seeker*). He has also won the Locus Award for best first novel (*The Hercules Text*, 1986) and the UPC International Prize for best novella, "Ships in the Night." McDevitt is a former naval officer, an English teacher, a customs officer, and has trained managers for the US Customs Service. He lives in Brunswick, GA, with his wife Maureen.

Michael Z. Williamson writes science fiction, fantasy and military fiction. He was born in the UK, raised there and in Canada before moving to the US. Mike is a 25 year veteran of the US Army and US Air Force with service in Operations Desert Fox and Iraqi Freedom, and his military experience features prominently in his fiction. He has consulted on military matters and disaster preparedness for several TV shows and movies. He lives near Indianapolis with his family, cats, and enough firearms to stage his own revolution. Next Tuesday. Unless he is distracted by fine Scotch.

Pete Prellwitz was bitten by the writing bug at an early age and has never been cured. Starting with an awful (but produced!) Thanksgiving play in 4th grade, Pete's writing skills fortunately have improved over time. He currently has nine novels in print/ebook, as well as short stories in multiple anthologies. His next novel, *Redeeming The Plumb*, is due out in 2013, along with two or three more anthologies. Pete and Bethlynne—his wife of 30 years—live in Jeffersonville, PA with four of their sons and two dogs. To learn more about his works visit: http://ShardsUniverse.net.

BRENDA COOPER has published fiction in *Analog, Asimov's, Nature, Daybreak, Strange Horizons,* and in multiple other magazines and anthologies. She is the author of the Endeavor award winner for 2008: *The Silver Ship and the Sea*, and of the sequels, *Reading the Wind,* and *Wings of Creation*. She co-authored *Building Harlequin's Moon* with Larry Niven. Watch for *Mayan December*, coming soon from Prime Books. By day, Brenda is the City of Kirkland's CIO, and at night and in early morning hours, she's a futurist and writer. See her website at www.brenda-cooper.com.

DAVID SHERMAN is a former United States Marine and the author of eight previously published novels about Marines in Vietnam, where he served as an infantryman and as a member of a Combined Action Platoon. He is an alumnus of the Pennsylvania Academy of the Fine Arts and worked as a sculptor for many years before turning to writing. Along the way he has held a variety of jobs, mostly supervisory and managerial. Today he is a full-time writer.

DR. CHARLES E. GANNON is a Distinguished Professor of English (St. Bonaventure University) and was a Fulbright Senior Specialist in American Literature & Culture from 2004-2009. Dr. Gannon's series include hard-sf interstellar epics (the Fire With Fire series), urban fantasy (the forthcoming Taints), and he also collaborates in several others, including two New York Times Best Selling series: the Starfire military sf series (e.g. "Extremis") and Eric Flint's Ring of Fire series (e.g. "1635: The Papal Stakes"). He has also had many novellas published or forthcoming in various anthologies (Ring of Fire/1632, War World, Man-Kzin Wars, David Weber's Honorverse, etc.) and in Analog SF Magazine. You can visit and learn more about his various SF universes and projects—past, present, and future—at: www.charlesegannon.com.

PAUL LEVINSON, PhD, is Professor of Communication & Media Studies at Fordham University in New York City. His eight nonfiction books, including *The Soft Edge* (1997), *Digital McLuhan* (1999), *Realspace*

(2003), *Cellphone* (2004), and *New New Media* (2009; 2nd edition, 2012) have been the subject of major articles in the *New York Times*, *Wired*, the *Christian Science Monitor*, and have been translated into ten languages. His science fiction novels include *The Silk Code* (1999, winner of the Locus Award for Best First Novel), *Borrowed Tides* (2001), *The Consciousness Plague* (2002), *The Pixel Eye* (2003), and *The Plot To Save Socrates* (2006). His short stories have been nominated for Nebula, Hugo, Edgar, and Sturgeon Awards. Paul Levinson appears on "The O'Reilly Factor" (Fox News), "The CBS Evening News," "NewsHour with Jim Lehrer" (PBS), "Nightline" (ABC), Dylan Ratigan (MSNBC) and numerous national and international TV and radio programs. His 1972 LP, *Twice Upon a Rhyme*, was re-issued on mini-CD by Big Pink Records in 2009, and was re-issued in a vinyl remastered re-pressing by Sound of Salvation/Whiplash Records in December 2010. He reviews the best of television in his InfiniteRegress.tv blog, writes political and media commentary for *Mediaite*, and was listed in *The Chronicle of Higher Education*'s "Top 10 Academic Twitterers" in 2009.

9 781942 990550